# DEFY
# THE

A Novel

# NIGHT

# DEFY THE NIGHT

A Novel

## Heather Munn and Lydia Munn

Kregel
*Publications*

*Defy the Night: A Novel*
© 2014 by Heather Munn and Lydia Munn

Published by Kregel Publications, a division of Kregel, Inc.,
2450 Oak Industrial Dr. NE, Grand Rapids, MI 49505.

ISBN 978-0-8254-4321-3

Printed in the United States of America
14  15  16  17  18  /  5  4  3  2  1

*To Renée, Anne-Marie, Friedel, Charlotte, Laure,
and all the other young women who faced exhaustion, fear, isolation,
and sometimes even death to bring hunted children to safety
during World War II in France*

## Chapter 1

# Barbed Wire and Broken Boots

"I just didn't know war was going to be so *boring*," I said.

Lucy rolled her eyes at me.

"Or so *cold*."

Lucy pushed open the door of the *mairie*, and I flinched as the wind swept in, sharp as razors. *La burle*, that's what they call the wind here—the north wind, the bad one. I should've known when we moved to Tanieux from Paris: *if they've got a name for the wind, watch out.*

We'd stood in line in that wind for two hours—two hours in the bone-cracking cold waiting for our turn in the mayor's office to get our families' ration tickets for February 1941. Waiting for those pigs in the Vichy government to tell us what we couldn't buy.

Well, I shouldn't say pigs. Not that they aren't—they are. But rationing's necessary, Papa says. Rationing's something they even do in England.

Where they're still free.

The ration-ticket line still stretched halfway across the open *place du centre* as we walked gingerly down the steps. There was ice everywhere, hard, flat Tanieux-winter ice, the kind that's been ice so long it's grayish-white and doesn't reflect the sun. I looked at that long line of people, their hands deep in the pockets of their worn coats, scarves wrapped around their faces, heads down, standing and stamping their feet like horses tied up in the cold. You couldn't see the halters they were tied with. But they were real.

I stopped for a moment, looking at them. Behind me the *mairie* doors opened again, and I saw the line shuffle slowly forward. Something in me snapped. "Race you home!" I shouted to Lucy. I could hear the raggedness in my voice, the edge of anger. I didn't really want to race—I just wanted to run.

I just didn't know what else to do with all the anger in my body.

You know what war is? You shut up and tighten your belt and do what you're told. That's war. You stand in line on the *place du centre* like a dumb animal while the *burle* sweeps across it like a wind from the steppes, because you have to. For you and your family to eat. You forget what meat tastes like, and butter, and cream. You eat potatoes and beans and drink water and then you sit down by the radio and listen up for what They've decided to do to you and your friends next.

I thought we were going to fight. Drive Hitler back, kill him maybe. I wasn't ready for the world to go insane, for him to win, for him to *take over my country*. I didn't expect my own people to start *working with him.*

I've got this friend, Benjamin. More my brother's friend, I guess, but he lives with us. His parents paid room and board for him till they went missing in the invasion. He thought they were dead. It was months before we heard where they were—in Marseille, hiding from the government. Because they're Jewish and they're not French citizens, and here in our new insane world, that is not okay.

Because Jews and foreigners—that's whose fault it is we lost the war. That is the official line straight from the mouth of the great

Marshal Pétain and his government in Vichy, from which he governs us: the south of France, the so-called unoccupied zone. And yeah, maybe I take it a little bit personally. Half my friends are Jews, and practically *all* of them are foreigners. I was the new girl from Paris here the year the war started. I made friends with the other new kids. And now my own government was offering to oblige the Nazis by sticking the other new kids behind barbed wire. They were setting up internment camps for it. My parents had told me. They were putting refugees from the civil war in Spain in there because, I suppose, they were Communists. And they were putting foreign Jews in there because . . . oh yes . . . that's who made us lose the war, as if it was *them* that drove into our country with tanks. And they were putting Gypsies in there, because—as far as I can tell—they just didn't like them. They were putting men and women and kids and old people in there, and for nothing they ever did.

And Benjamin hadn't seen his parents in almost two years, because it wasn't safe for them to take a train.

And there was nothing I could do. Nothing but run blindly across the ice-crusted cobblestones, with Lucy behind me.

"Magali! Don't be *stupid!*"

Speaking of foreigners, Lucy is Irish. They are not actually arresting Irish people at this time. That we know of. Lucy doesn't even have to be here—she could live in America with her journalist father. But she lives with her aunt instead, on the top floor above the bookstore.

I was just coming up on their building when the world spun around me—hard. My right foot flew up into thin air, and for a moment all I saw was deep blue sky and the ground coming up to meet me. *Crack.* I could feel the jolt in my teeth.

I opened my eyes. Gray Tanieux ice. Blue winter sky. Lucy's blond hair and freckled face above me, her blue eyes anxious. "Magali? You all right?"

"Ow."

"You didn't hit your head, did you?"

"No. Just my hip. Ow."

Lucy gasped. "Your boot!"

I froze. My boot. My precious, only pair of boots, stitched and re-stitched by Mama. New leather shoes were worth their weight in diamonds, but new boots? There was no such thing. And it hadn't come apart at the seam this time. There was a crack in the leather itself, gaping like a mouth.

"She's going to kill me," I whispered. But the truth was worse than that. *She's going to cry.*

"More importantly," said Lucy, "you can't get any more boots."

"I know," I snapped. Lucy is a fun person most of the time. I swear. I stood up carefully, favoring the boot. There was hard flat pain all through my hip. "I'll fix it."

"You don't even—"

"I said I'll fix it, okay?"

"Uh-huh, Magali. Let me know how that goes."

We glared at each other. A voice behind us broke the spell.

"*Bonjour,* Lucy, Magali." It was Madame Alexandre, the pastor's wife, and her voice was brisk. I snapped up straight. To *attention.* Madame Alexandre, she's a person you listen to.

She stepped up quickly to give us the *bise,* the greeting kiss on both cheeks. I gave her a nervous grin. "How are you girls?" she said. "Do you feel strong enough to brave the cold a little more today? I have a refugee who needs guiding to le Chaux. The Laubracs there will take her in. The priest just sent word."

I *like* Madame Alexandre.

Lucy was saying sorry, she couldn't, she had to help her aunt with the washing. *Because my aunt doesn't know how,* she didn't add. Her aunt teaches at our school. Knows Greek and Latin; needs a maid.

"I can do it," I said quickly. "Madame."

"Ah, that's excellent. Well, I think I should feed her first . . . Are you free after lunch?"

"Yes, Madame," I said. *Free*, I thought. *I love that word.*

THE BELL on the door of the Café du Centre dinged as I opened it, and beautiful warm air hit my face. The place was full of voices and warm smells: fake coffee, fake cocoa, fake barley-flour pastries. I won't kid you—they made my mouth water. I don't even remember what the real stuff tastes like.

"Magali!" Madame Santoro paused, a tray in her hands, her black hair stuck sweaty to her forehead. "You have come to help Rosa and Nina, no?"

"Um . . ." I could hear the clink of glasses, back in the kitchen, and my friends' voices. I imagined plunging my frozen hands deep in warm dishwater. "*Sure.*"

"Thank you, *querida*. So busy on ration day. You are much help."

I slipped into the kitchen, pulled my coat off, and let the steam warm my numb face. Rosa's black eyes brightened when she saw me. Rosa's from Spain and definitely the prettiest of my friends— long black hair and soft, shy dark eyes. I gave her the *bise*, and then the same to Nina. Nina is Jewish, from Austria, and she's probably the least pretty. I don't say that to be mean. She has brown hair that's kind of curly and frizzy, and she either looks you in the eye too long or not at all. She was sitting at the sink on a high stool, her crutches leaning against the wall. I stepped up to the sink with her, but Rosa tossed me a dishtowel.

"Can't I wash? My hands are *freezing*."

"Nina's washing. She needs to sit."

"Just one little minute?"

"Is no problem, I can stand." Nina slid off her stool.

"*Magali.*"

"No, Nina, it's all right, you don't have to stand." It's not like she can't use those crutches. She walked here from Austria on them. But Rosa had those reproachful eyes again. "I'll just warm my hands real quick and then I'll dry." I plunged them in the warm clean water and groaned with pleasure. Nina keeps her dishwater really nice. "Hey Rosa, you free this afternoon?"

"For what?"

"A very important mission from Madame Alexandre."

She looked at me sideways, drying her plate slowly. "With who?"

I dried my hands on my dishtowel. I hated that suspicious look of hers. "With me. And Nina if she's free."

"Free?"

"Yeah. You know. Not busy."

"Oh." Nina's face fell. "Fraülein—I mean, Mademoiselle Pinatel, she need me in bookstore. I—"

"It's all right. I'm taking this lady to le Chaux who speaks German, but I'm sure she understands pointing and following."

"Nina's taught me a little German," said Rosa softly.

"More than a little! You are very good!"

"I make Gustav laugh."

"Oh, you must not take serious Gustav. He laughs always."

I rolled up my dishtowel and flicked it at Rosa. "So? Can you come?"

"Please stop doing that, Magali."

"C'mon. I didn't do it hard."

Rosa frowned and turned away from me. I sighed and picked up a glass. "C'mon, Rosa, please come. I don't want to walk home from le Chaux by myself."

"You should go, Rosa. You can then practice your German. And meet this woman—from where does she come?"

"Poland. She walked here. In sandals."

"She walked from Poland in sandals?" Rosa frowned, but the corners of her mouth were turning up. "*Really,* Magali?"

"Well, no, see, she walked from le Murat in sandals. She got off the train there by mistake. She'd heard of Tanieux—"

"Oh, but this is good!" Nina's eyes shone. "It is good that people are speaking of it." *She* heard about Tanieux when she was practically dying of fever and malnutrition in the Lyon train station. Heard about it from a random stranger on his way to boarding school—*my* school—who decided to buy them tickets here too. His name's Samuel. He's in my class.

"Yeah. So then she walked the rest of the way. Four hours, in the *burle*."

"When?"

"Yesterday." We all shivered.

"I'll go, Magali," said Rosa.

If CHANAH Minkowski had needed to walk from Poland in sandals, she could have. I could see that right away. She was the tallest, strongest woman I'd ever seen, and I know a lot of farmers. She looked like she picked up a pitchfork every day and tossed around bales of hay without breaking a sweat. And then went out to plow. She had shoes now, and Rosa and I had to jog to keep up. My hip hurt and snow was getting into my boot, but I didn't say anything.

Around the crossing at Chabreyres she slowed to a walk and looked around. The hills were white, crisscrossed with thin black lines of fences and their blue shadows, broken by darker patches of woods. Madame Minkowski turned to me and broke the silence, pointing down. "Shoe. Is bad."

She just had to bring that up.

"I'm all right."

"No. Is need, shoe. Not all right." She frowned at me. "I can help. Can . . ." She made some motions with her big gloved hands. "I need . . . *eine Ahle und eine Nadel*. Large."

"You . . . you can sew it up?"

Madame Minkowski nodded.

I turned to Rosa. "What was that German thing?"

Rosa burst out laughing. "In your dreams, Magali! I don't know *that* much German!"

"It's only a couple of words!"

"It's some kind of *tool!*"

"You need goot shoe. You need." Madame Minkowski was looking at me with her big, hungry eyes. It almost scared me. "How old, you?"

"Sixteen. Uh, almost sixteen. I mean, uh, fifteen."

"Say again?"

"*Fünfzehn*," said Rosa.

"Ah." Madame Minkowski nodded, and brightened for a moment. Then her face kind of shut down. "Like . . . *meine Tochter*," she said, not looking at us.

Rosa's eyes widened. "Her daughter," she whispered.

"Where is she?" I said. Before I could think.

If Madame Minkowski's face had shut down before, now it *locked*. She was looking at nothing; at something the wide white landscape was hiding, something terrible we couldn't see. "I don't know," she whispered.

Oh.

There was a long silence.

I could imagine her, the daughter. Strong like Madame Minkowski, but pretty too, with friendly eyes. I could imagine her mother's big arms around her in a crushing hug. Something started to hurt in my throat.

Rosa put her little arm around the woman's big back. A moment later Madame Minkowski had swept us both up, pulled us into this hard, deep, gut-wrenching hug, the two of us crushed in her arms. I hugged back, as hard as I could. Madame, I want to save your daughter, I thought.

But I didn't say anything.

"Goot girls," she said. "You are goot girls." And she let us go, and we went on down the road.

MADAME MINKOWSKI did fix my boot. She got across to Madame Laubrac what she needed, and sat by the fire stitching while the rest of us drank hot *verveine* tea. Tight, neat, strong stitches. You could see right away what kind of a guest *she* was going to be. She gave us each another bone-crushing hug when we said goodbye.

The boot was tight and warm the next day, walking down to school. My classroom used to be a barn, and it's dark and warm inside with the woodstove going, and all the wooden shutters over the windows. I sat there in the dim electric light, listening to the teachers and not hearing what they said, trying to draw Madame Minkowski in the margin of my notebook. That look in her eyes when she said, "I don't know." I couldn't draw her right, of course. I couldn't get her out of my mind.

I sat there drawing her until Monsieur Weiss came with Nina for chemistry class. Nina is in the *sixième* class with the twelve-year-olds usually, because her French is so poor, but for math and chemistry she's with us. She sits in the front row with her head thrust forward on her neck, drinking it in, taking notes like mad. He repeats things in German for her. *I* don't even understand what he says when he's speaking French. She's his favorite student.

My mother loves her too. She eats at our house almost every week.

She's like that, Nina. How could she *not* be the adults' favorite? She was homeless and almost starved to death, so now she thinks getting to go to school, do dishes at the café, and sleep in a bed is the greatest privilege known to man. Or rather, woman.

I don't always like her, to be honest. I thought I was going to, when we met. She'd walked halfway across Europe and sneaked across two different borders in the dark. I thought she'd be . . . well, *cool*.

The first time she ate with us she was so tense. Her smile

stretched too tight. Too nice, too . . . *eager to please.* Like she thought we'd kick her out or something. It made me embarrassed for her. The second time she ate with us, she broke down sobbing in the middle of the meal for no reason I could see.

That night my mother took me aside, after dinner, and told me about the camps.

She told me how they'd taken what used to be refugee camps and strung barbed wire around them, put men with guns in guard towers. She told me how they'd been arresting people for months, on the quiet: *sans-papiers,* people without papers. Refugees, foreigners, people who weren't welcome here. They put them in these camps with straw to sleep on and fed them two pieces of bread a day plus turnip soup. People got sick and died in there, and nobody cared. She told me about the day the Germans had sent France trains loaded with more than six thousand Jews they'd decided to get rid of, and the government refused them, and the train sat unopened for three days in Lyon. When they opened the cars, some of the people inside were dead. The rest got taken to one of those camps.

She told me Nina and her brother almost got taken to one too. When they first got here, the stationmaster—if you can imagine—thought they looked like trouble, and almost got the mayor to call someone up and have their papers checked. They didn't have papers, because they'd burned them so no one would know they were Jewish. They had to lie low for a while after that.

"Nina needs our protection," Mama told me. "It's not foolish for her to be afraid. It's smart. I don't believe *Monsieur le maire* would do anything against her now, or Monsieur Bernard either. I think they've accepted the presence of refugees in Tanieux, like it or not. But I want you to be careful just who you speak to about Nina, Magali. Don't mention to anyone that she's Jewish, or that's she not French. Can you do that?"

"Yes, Mama," I said. But I was thinking, that's all you want? To keep my mouth shut? They're putting people behind barbed wire just for who their parents are, and all you want is for me to be quiet? Do nothing?

I'd heard Madame Alexandre talking with Madame Raissac the day before in church. I'd heard just the one thing Madame Alexandre said, in a low clear voice: *God will judge them.* I remembered that, looking at my mother's serious eyes, and I thought, why? Why does it have to be *God will judge them?* Shouldn't it be *God is judging them,* one of these days now, soon? And I thought, why do we have to shut up? Why? When it seems like God is doing the exact same thing about this stuff that everyone else is doing.

Nothing.

Monsieur Weiss started to wipe the chemical formulas off the board. I came back to myself with a jerk, and looked down at my paper. I hadn't copied anything I was supposed to.

I'd spent the hour drawing tangled strands of barbed wire all over the margins of my paper. Even over Madame Minkowski's face.

When Monsieur Weiss rang the bell for lunch break it was snowing, thick flakes blown almost horizontal by the *burle.* It had already drifted boot-deep against the doors. But I wasn't going to let that stop me. "Hey Lucy, want to meet the train?"

"In this? You joking? It won't come in today. Besides, I have to make lunch." She gave me a *bise.* "See you!" She jogged off into the snow.

Fine. I jogged off myself, ignoring the twinge in my hip, and took a left up the Rue du Verger to the public girls' school. Rosa'd go with me.

"In *this?*"

"Please, Rosa?"

She looked at me, and her soft, pretty face went still. "Lucy wouldn't go with you, would she?" she said quietly.

"That's not why!" I try not to lie. I really do.

Rosa looked away.

*Just come to the station with me, Rosa. You know you want to. If you're mad I didn't ask you first, well I asked you now, didn't I?* "Please?"

Rosa and I used to love meeting the train, back when we were the two new girls together—before Lucy came. Everyone in Tanieux loves our train. It's probably the one thing Monsieur Bernard, the Vichy-loving stationmaster, and I have in common. "I bet you *la Galoche* does make it. She's a *tanieusarde*, a little snow doesn't scare her."

Rosa lifted one shoulder and almost looked at me. I grabbed her hand. "C'mon!"

When we got there you couldn't see very far down the tracks in the swirling snow. Monsieur Bernard stood there with his kepi and his clipboard, ramrod-straight against the gusting wind. But I was right. A long, high whistle came from up the track, and soon there came her smokestack out of the blinding whiteness, cutting through the mist and snow, the flakes melting in her hot-white steam.

"I told you! She's not scared of *this!*"

Rosa laughed. "She's not a *person*, Magali!"

"Sure she is."

We watched her pull in with a long hiss of brakes; watched the men begin to unload crates from the cargo cars. The passenger car doors opened. I clutched Rosa's arm.

A little girl came first, in an old gray coat two sizes too big for her, a blue wool hat jammed over the dirtiest, most matted hair I'd ever seen. Then a little boy with a runny nose and red, infected eyes that made streaks down his filthy face. I stared. A toddler with a scarf wrapped round most of its head climbed down. And then a young woman.

She was clean, in a brown wool coat and hat that fit her; she didn't have the look of a refugee. Except for the gray weariness of her face. And the huge, battered suitcase, and the baby she clutched to her chest with her other arm. The conductor stepped down behind her with two more suitcases and set them down. She didn't even see him. She had dropped her suitcase in the snow and closed her eyes.

Monsieur Bernard stepped up to her. I had seen him do this routine before. "*Bonjour, Madame.*"

Her eyes flew open.

"What is your business in Tanieux?" His voice was challenging.

It was magic. She took one look at him and her spine snapped up straight, and I found myself looking into wide-awake, steely gray eyes in a face that gave no quarter. "Would you direct me to the residence of Monsieur César-Napoléon Alexandre?" she rapped out firmly in perfect French, looking him in the eye like it was *him* who was out of line.

I stared at her.

Monsieur Bernard stepped back a little. "Certainly, Madame."

I was in love.

Rosa pulled at me, but I shook her loose and stepped up. "He's our pastor, Madame. We could walk with you there."

Her eyes flew wide open again. "Oh," she said. "Would you?"

I KEPT an eye on the little girl with the tangled hair and carried the suitcases. Rosa took the boy by the hand and carried the toddler inside her coat. The woman came behind us with the baby and the last suitcase, stumbling with weariness in the ankle-deep snow. I could see we ought to leave her at Pastor Alex's door, whoever she was, and not get in the way. I could see it was no time for a bunch of questions or any other kind of talk. It was time for her and those kids to be given a warm bed. And a bath, hopefully. For the kids.

Still I couldn't help asking, as I showed her in the Alexandres' gate and put the suitcases down. Because I just couldn't work it out. "Madame? Where are these children from?"

"Paquerette. It's Paquerette." I blinked at her. "My name." She shook her head a little, as if gathering her thoughts. "These children are from the internment camp at Gurs."

My heart beat fast. "Madame—"

"Paquerette."

"Will you be here tomorrow?"

She looked around at the driving snow. "Probably," she said.

## Chapter 2

# Joan of Arc

"AND THEY just let her take them?" Julien sounded like he didn't believe a word of it.

"Well, they're here, aren't they?"

"Are you sure you heard her right about where they were from? They don't just let people out of those places."

I ground my teeth. That's boys for you. They think you don't have *ears*, let alone a brain.

"Oh, *oops*. I guess I heard her wrong." I spoke fast, anger pushing inside me like steam. "I thought she said 'the internment camp at Gurs' but I guess she must have said 'Saint-Etienne.'"

"Julien, Magali. Be polite to each other at the breakfast table." Papa's voice was commanding.

"Yes, sir."

"Yes, sir."

"Actually, Magali is right," said Papa. *Unbelievable, eh?* "There are several aid organizations that have succeeded in obtaining releases for children from the internment camps. Pastor Alex and

21

I are in touch with the Protestant one—the CIMADE—and I think this woman you met, Magali, was their representative." He brightened. "Ah—and I haven't yet told you the news from yesterday. The Quakers wish to donate to the Ecole du Vivarais— substantially—with the, ah, unofficial understanding that children in need will be housed in the dorms."

I looked at my father's lit-up face. *Unofficial, huh? You mean 'in need of hiding,' don't you, Papa.* I have to say, my father picked the right school to become principal of, even if it is a tiny brand-new boarding school that has to use old barns for classrooms. *Hiding people. People Vichy was out to get, and wouldn't. You can't have them, pigs. How d'you like that?*

"And they're really releasing kids from camps?" Benjamin leaned forward, his eyes intense. "How do they convince them?"

"Generally by proving that they're sick enough to be seriously at risk. A great deal seems to depend on the camp doctors. And of course they need a parental release as well."

He kind of froze then. Silence fell. He turned to Mama.

My mother used to be short and plump. Before the war. Now she's just short. She has black eyes and curly black hair, just like me—the only thing we have in common. When she's afraid, her eyes get very dark and her face gets pale. She looked like that now; like she was looking at something terrible no one else saw. Almost like Madame Minkowski. Except *her* daughter was right across the table from her.

I looked away.

"It's never done against the parents' will, Maria," Papa said earnestly. "Some parents refuse."

"*Refuse?*" Benjamin's voice cut like a knife. "*Why?*"

My father looked at him uneasily, and then at Mama. Mama looked at Benjamin, steadily, her face still white. As if there was something she was thinking of saying, but wouldn't. As if he should know better than to ask. Papa swallowed. "I don't know," he said.

My mother said nothing. But I swear she looked like she knew.

WE WERE snowed in that morning; the street white and quiet, a half-meter of snow blown against the doors. A blessing and a curse. It meant no school even though it was Saturday—Thursday and Sunday are our days off. It also meant I couldn't go anywhere till a lot of people did a lot of shoveling. Which I couldn't help with, naturally, being a girl. I spent the morning cranking the wringer while Mama washed the whole family's clothes.

Then finally, after lunch, I was free.

I walked between banks of knee-deep, thigh-deep snow, feeling my heart beat fast. I was going to meet her for real now. "It's Paquerette," she had said. "My name." She'd been so tired she was stumbling, and she'd looked Monsieur Bernard in the eye and had frozen him out, to perfection. I had never met anyone like her before. And I didn't even know her. I just knew she wasn't sitting there looking tragic; she was saving kids, as many as she could. Everyone I knew had been in mourning for a year—the funeral of France, of freedom, oh, so sad.

And I'd finally met someone who was still fighting.

I could feel my heart beating in my throat as I knocked on the Alexandres' door.

SHE WAS beautiful, too. I hadn't seen that yesterday. High cheekbones, light gray eyes, a face out of a painting. Perfect hands, wrapped gracefully around her cup of horrible fake coffee. She had the kind of class I'll never have. She still looked exhausted and her hair wasn't combed and she had definitely slept in her dress at some point, but none of it made a difference. If someone took the Mona Lisa and dragged her through the mud, who'd notice the mud?

"Bonjour . . . Mademoiselle Paquerette . . ."

Her half-closed eyes snapped open. "You," she said. I stood there with my mouth open, looking for something to say with it. As awkward as my brother when he's trying to talk to Nathalie Dufour. I realized I was staring, and shut my mouth.

"Just Paquerette. You can call me *tu*, please."

I just stood there, my chest tightening. There was no way.

*Tu* is the familiar way of talking. *Vous* is what you call someone when you're being respectful. And kids, including fifteen-year-olds, are respectful. Adults call you *tu*; you call them *vous*. It's the way it works, it's the way it is, it's the most basic politeness. A kid who calls any adult outside her own family *tu* gets smacked, but good.

"But . . . but Mademoiselle—"

"Paquerette, Magali. I mean it, I'm not Mademoiselle to you or anyone here. I have a job to do. I get children out of camps and bring them safely to where they're going. There's no time in that for *vous*. There's no time for Mademoiselle or who my father is or any of it. Understand?"

I swallowed. Tried to shape the word Paquerette with my lips. "I . . . I can't."

"You'd be surprised at the things you can do." She said it flatly. Like a fact. "If you have to."

"I'm sorry, Mademoiselle." I couldn't help it. I'm French. My mother raised me right. Besides—she was a *hero*. You just don't say "hey, you" to Joan of Arc.

She sighed. "Well. Do your best."

"Mademoiselle?"

She looked at me. "Yes?"

"How come they let you take those kids?"

"We asked."

"But . . . why do you think . . . they said yes?"

She took a sip of her fake coffee. Madame Alexandre came in with my cup of real mint tea and sat down with us. I thanked her. For a moment there was no sound but the crackling of the fire. I glanced at the living room where the kids were. The boy was sitting on the floor, staring straight ahead of him out of his red, sore-looking eyes. I saw what I hadn't seen yesterday: his belly was swollen. It looked very strange with his skinny arms and legs. The girl was sitting beside him, watching us out of the corner of her eye and chewing on her hair. It was clean now, I saw, but still tangled.

"Well," said Mademoiselle Paquerette finally. "My boss's theory is they want to appear humane. Next best thing, you know. To *being* humane." Her gray eyes were like Tanieux ice. "We've had a worker placed in the camp since fall, but it's only recently she's had success at getting children released. We're hoping it lasts, but we've got our fingers crossed. So I'm bringing them as fast as I can."

"Do you always have that many kids? With a baby too?" And three big suitcases. I know a bit about kids, I used to keep my little cousins back in Paris. Three kids under six and a baby, on a train—maybe several trains. All alone. Aunt Nadine wouldn't have done it for a thousand francs.

Mademoiselle Paquerette's head was in her hands, and she was shaking it violently. She came up for air. "*No.*" She took a deep breath. "Never again. Do you hear me? Oh what a trip that was."

"Never again?" said Madame Alexandre.

Mademoiselle Paquerette's face twisted up in a very ironic smile. "Oh, that means 'anytime,' didn't you know?" She turned to me. "I've been trying, so far, to take them all as soon as they're released. Leave no one behind. It just . . . it doesn't seem right."

Madame Alexandre nodded. "Considering the state they're in . . ."

Paquerette cut her eyes over to Madame Alexandre and nodded. "Yes, well." She turned toward the kids. "Elsi? Would you like some tea?"

The little girl eyed us suspiciously. "What's tea?"

"Here. Come and taste it."

She came over, her eyes fixed warily on us. She didn't take them off us as she took the cup Paquerette handed her and put it to her lips. She drank slowly, watching. She put the cup down.

"Is my mama coming?"

Paquerette swallowed and went pale. She turned her whole

body to face the girl. "Elsi, your mama can't come. She wanted to. We all wanted her to. But they won't let her leave the camp. They only let children out. I'm sorry."

The girl just looked at her. Those eyes.

"Your mama wanted you to come here because she loves you. She wanted you to be in a place where there's enough to eat, even if she couldn't come too. Mademoiselle Jeanne will keep asking the camp people to let people like your mama out. I—"

"Will they let them?"

Paquerette looked at her with such a darkness in her eyes I thought she was going to weep. "I don't know," she whispered. "I don't know."

I GOT to show her the way to the *place du centre*, to a little guest-house called *l'Espoir*, where she was taking the baby. She told me on the way what Madame Alexandre had meant by "the state they're in" and why she hadn't wanted to talk about it in front of them.

"They all have lice—every one of them. *And* fleas. I only hope I haven't spread them to the Alexandre family, bringing them in unwashed like I did. You saw them yesterday, how filthy they were. They're not given enough water to wash, not to mention— in this weather—the barracks are barely even heated, and as for hot water . . ." She shook her head, and held the baby closer. "You didn't see them before we put the donated clothes on them, either. They were in rags, Magali. They didn't have underwear. The boy had nothing to put on his feet but broken sandals. In the snow."

I opened my mouth and closed it again.

"You know what they said to us, Magali? When we were trying to place a worker in the other camp, Rivesaltes? They said, 'Oh, if you had your way, these people would live better than most of the French!' Yes, protecting your children from frostbite, what sinful luxury," she said bitterly. She looked at me quickly. "I'm sorry. I need to calm down. I only just met you—"

"It's . . . it's all right. I just wish . . . I could help."

She looked me over, for a moment, and didn't say anything. We were at the guesthouse door.

MADAME SABATIER, who ran the guesthouse, welcomed us in and sent her daughter Madeleine to make us tea. When someone comes to your house you have to give them something, it's the rules. We sat down on the big sofa across from the fireplace; a wide oak coffee-table was in front of us, gleaming in both firelight and slanting winter sun from the south window. Madame Sabatier took the baby from Paquerette and put him down on it, and unwrapped him.

It's not like I knew much about babies. But even I knew they weren't supposed to look like *that*.

His diaper was clean, but he had a rash. Over half his body. It was an angry shade of red, especially on his bottom, where it broke into oozing sores. His little arms and legs were way too skinny for a baby's, and *his* stomach was swollen too. Madame Sabatier turned him over and over gently in her hands, staring. His little eyes screwed up, and he let out a weak wail.

"So you see," said Paquerette.

Madame Sabatier nodded. Her kind, seamed face had set, her mouth turned into a thin line. "And you say this child was in the infirmary?"

Paquerette nodded. "Because the mother is sick."

"And you say there are . . . others like this."

"If my coworker can obtain releases for them. Both my coworkers . . . at the other camp it is almost as bad . . . Madame, there are so many. Far too many for you and your daughter to take in alone. You'll simply need to tell us your maximum."

"Maximum?" said Madame Sabatier. "You just keep bringing them. We'll find a way."

THE BABY'S name was Grigory. They let me feed him formula. He sucked weakly on the bottle. We built the fire up and kept him by it, naked except for a loose diaper, to air out his rash and give Madame Sabatier's salve time to work. Madeleine showed me how to pin the diaper, but she wouldn't let me practice because he went to sleep. Paquerette went upstairs, to a room that the Sabatiers had prepared for her to stay in whenever she wanted, and took a nap.

I went home at six thirty, for supper. It was only when I was halfway there that I remembered I was supposed to help cook. Because Nina was coming over.

I got to the bottom of my stairwell so out of breath I had to walk up it for once. Slowly. I guess that's why they didn't hear me.

"It is only that when I am with her I feel strange." The voice came through the wall from the kitchen. "It is not her fault." A serious, girl's voice, with a German-ish accent. Nina. I froze. *Not whose fault?*

"What do you mean by strange, exactly?" That was Mama. I heard the clang of her opening the stove door, checking the coals. I'd done this with her a hundred times.

"That I am a strange person. That I am not normal."

Silence.

"With the *sixième* class it is not so bad, it is only that they are children. But when I am with her class with Monsieur Weiss . . . they are almost as old as me. But there is nothing, we have nothing to talk about. Do you see? I cannot become again . . . normal."

Yeah. It was me she was talking about.

"Nina, you are normal. Look at me." My mother's voice was warm. "Nina, it's normal, when you've known such things, to find it harder to talk to those who haven't. Magali hasn't, nor most of the other girls. It isn't *your* fault either."

More silence.

There was the sound of feet, in the hallway below. I hung up my coat and took off my boots, noisily. There were no more voices. I opened the door.

"Hi Mama," I called. "Sorry I'm late."

Mama came to the kitchen door. "Nina's helping me, so it's all right." She wasn't smiling. "This time."

*I saw the baby she brought back, Mama . . . its stomach was big— they said that's malnutrition . . . they let me feed it . . .*

Never mind.

I DID tell them, at supper. I just couldn't *not* tell them. I told them about the baby. I told them what the Rivesaltes camp people had said to the CIMADE. I told them about how they had no water for washing, and had fleas. Nina and Mama looked at each other. Papa said it wasn't a fit subject for the table, but he was pleased I had helped, only was I finished with my homework for Monday? Tomorrow was Sunday, remember?

I helped Mama with the dishes, after Nina went home. Had to do my part and all. I opened my mouth to say something about the baby and she informed me that Monsieur Weiss had told Papa he didn't think I was grasping the material in chemistry.

Our school's "progressive." They don't give grades. I thought that was going to be great, but when the teachers see your father everyday, I don't see how it helps.

"I just want to know if you're really trying, Magali. I'm sure it's a difficult subject to understand, but . . ."

"Yeah. It is." *But see, what happened was, I didn't take notes because I was thinking about Madame Minkowski . . . and then I, well, I got the notes from Jean-Luc Rivas. Because it was a good excuse to talk to him. Because he's cute. I know. I know. And I think he wrote down the formula for hydrogen sulfide wrong, because I did memorize it, but when Monsieur Weiss had me write it on the board in the afternoon . . .* "I *am* trying, Mama."

"You know how much we're spending to get you a good education, Magali."

I snapped my mouth shut and turned away from her. She just

*had* to bring that up. I was raised to respect my elders. I only wish my elders had the first notion of all the things I've managed not to say to them.

*Did I ask for your education?*

"I want you to have the chances I didn't have."

I dried a glass, and didn't look at her. That's right: my mother did not have chances. My mother was a farm girl in northern Italy during the Great War and almost her whole family died, and other bad things happened which we do not talk about—in my case because I have no idea what they were—and she didn't get to finish school. That last part is the part she talks about the most. For some reason.

"What am I going to do with chemistry?" I said, trying to keep my voice even.

"Pass your exams," said Mama instantly. "And get into *lycée*."

I kept drying.

"It just seems sometimes as if you don't care, Magali."

*Brilliant, Mama. Got it in one.*

"There's a war on," I said in a low voice. "It seems like there are more important things—"

"You're young, Magali. You're at a crucial point in your life. If you don't prepare yourself for something different now . . ." She lifted a soapy hand with a plate in it. "You'll come to my age and *this* is all you'll know how to do."

I looked at her thin, blue-veined hand. *It's not all you know how to do, Mama. You can sing.*

*Mama, I met this woman. She hasn't given up. She's saving kids' lives. She looked Monsieur Bernard in the eye and he backed down. What do I study to be like that?*

*You tell me that. And then I'll try.*

"Were you going to say something, Magali?"

I bent my head. "I'll study harder, Mama."

I TOLD Lucy all about it in church in between listening to Pastor
Alex talk about Jeremiah. Julien gave me his big-brother frown
for talking during the sermon. No matter that I was talking about
*saving babies' lives.*

I took Lucy down to l'Espoir in the afternoon. Lucy didn't turn
a hair when Mademoiselle Paquerette said to call her *tu*. They call
everyone *tu* where she's from.

"Where's your other friend, Magali? The one I met at the train?"

"Um, the path to her house isn't cleared yet." Strictly this was
true, even if it was a really *short* path. Plus Rosa's Catholic, so she
wasn't there for me to whisper to in church. Lucy looked away. Her
theory is that my problems with Rosa are one hundred percent my
fault, even though Rosa and I were fine before she came along.
"Anyway she hates snow. She's from Spain, her family's only lived
here a couple of years."

"Refugees?"

"Yeah." I tend to forget that. "But they run the café now. And
they speak French and stuff."

"But she does speak Spanish?"

"Yeah."

"Do you have anyone who speaks German?"

"Lots," said Lucy quickly. "There's Benjamin, he lives at Magali's
house—"

"He hates speaking German though. But he speaks Yiddish."

"—and Samuel Rozengard who's in our class, and Nina
and Gustav except they're still working on their French, and
Mademoiselle Pinatel who owns the bookstore speaks German—"

Mademoiselle Paquerette was shaking her head. "It gets better
and better."

"Paquerette?" Lucy said, and it jolted me. "Is that your real
name?"

Paquerette gave her a keen look, and I wished *I* had asked her
that. "No."

"I didn't *think* it was a French name," said Lucy.

"It's not," I blurted. Because it wasn't, okay? In France you name kids after saints, not daisies, and there was definitely no Sainte Paquerette. "Except for cows and stuff." As soon as it was out of my mouth I felt my face turn hot.

Paquerette's eyebrows went way up. "Well," she said. "I like a woman with discretion."

I *never* blush. I swear. "I'm sorry. I didn't mean to call you a cow." I could've slapped myself.

"It's all right. I like cows. I named myself after one, as a matter of fact."

"You *did?*"

"Yes." But the amused look on her face was gone. Just vanished. Like when you're standing on the bridge and a cloud blows over the river. One moment you're watching the sunlight flash on the ripples, and the next you're looking into dark, deep water. She didn't say anything more, and we didn't ask her about the cow.

WHEN SCHOOL let out on Monday I ran straight to l'Espoir. They told me I had missed Paquerette by about a minute, but I knew the way to the train. She turned and smiled when I caught up to her. She didn't have the exhausted lines around her eyes anymore. She told me she was glad she'd gotten snowed in—God had known how much she needed a rest.

I didn't know what to say to her as we approached the station. I didn't know how to say all the feelings that were banging around inside my body. *I love you. I want to be like you. Take me with you, Mademoiselle.* I stopped before we turned the corner, knowing what the station was like—the bustle and the loudness—knowing there'd be no talking there. She stopped too.

"Ma—" I looked at her, at those light gray eyes, and I made myself say it. "Paquerette." She was Joan of Arc, and all I wanted to do was go down on one knee and give her my sword and swear allegiance. But that means obeying. "Paquerette—what can I do? Is there anything I can do, to help you?"

Paquerette's smile broke out like the sun. "Of course, Magali." Her bright eyes looked right into mine, and I stood up straight. "Listen. I am going to take Madame Sabatier up on her offer. I am going to do it because I know that here in Tanieux she will have the support she needs when she needs it, which includes fine young women like you, and both your friends. You help her with all those babies, Magali, and you get your friends to come, too. It will help me tremendously."

"Yes Ma— Yes, Paquerette. I will. I promise."

"Thank you, Magali." She bent to give me the *bise*. This was goodbye. I kissed her, and as I did, the long, high whistle of the train sounded in the distance.

And Paquerette turned, and set her face toward it, and walked away.

Chapter 3

# Do Something

"No, MAGALI. You hold him like this. Upright."

"I *am* holding him upright."

Rosa frowned at me and took Grigory out of my arms. She put him against her shoulder and exactly one second later he quit crying and let out a tiny little burp. She rubbed his back and smiled.

"Only if it's anything like yesterday you're going to have to do that five more times," I warned her. Sure enough, he'd already started squirming again.

Rosa rubbed Grigory's back some more. "Yeah, Tomás did this too when he was a baby. It takes them a while to learn how to burp correctly."

"Isn't life complicated enough, without being born not knowing *how to burp?*"

Rosa laughed. Grigory burped again. His rash was gone, and his arms were starting to have those little baby dimples in them again. It's amazing the difference a week of good feeding can make.

We were coming over to l'Espoir almost every night. It was our job to do the evening feeding, change him, and put him to bed. It was lucky I managed to convince Rosa's mother to let her come, because I wouldn't even have known where to start. I got all pitiful about how I didn't even know how to change a diaper, which was one hundred percent true, and she smiled at Rosa and told me some story about how Rosa had saved her little brother's life one time when he started choking. She said she'd tell her husband that after supper was no time for a young girl to be working in a café anyway.

I met the train twice a day. Paquerette had said she was going back to Gurs for another group, and that most trips took five days to a week; four if she was lucky. I took that for my instructions and met the noon train with Rosa every day, starting on the fourth day, and then the five-thirty train with Lucy—or alone—because Rosa was working in the café. Lucy wouldn't even come see Grigory. She said she was terrible with babies.

It was a full week before Paquerette finally came in, on the five-thirty on Monday, with *four* kids and a baby. Two skinny brown-haired girls maybe eleven or twelve and a girl and boy two or three years younger. They were clean, so I guess she'd found a place along the way where they could bathe. They were all Jews from Germany, and their mother had died of pneumonia in the camp. They'd been released because they were orphans now. They looked absolutely shell-shocked.

Paquerette looked just about on her last legs too. The kids were headed for the new Swiss Aid home, les Chênes, down south of town. I told her I knew the way—my scout troop helped clean it up before it opened—and offered to walk them there. She hesitated for a moment then gave me a look of such relief I felt warm all through. She rummaged in her bag and pressed their papers into my hand. "Don't lose them. Give them all to Monsieur Thiély personally. All right?"

"Yes, Paquerette. I'll make sure."

"Hanne, Lise, this is Magali Losier. You can trust her. She'll show you the way to the home."

It's a good half-hour's walk down to les Chênes. You cross the bridge and go past the boys' school and on down the south road through the hills. I carried the little ones, each in turn, and Hanne and Lise walked quietly beside me, pale and exhausted. Finally Hanne asked what kind of food they had at les Chênes.

"Oh . . . potatoes, cheese, carrots, beans." Grandpa had just sold them potatoes. "Stuff like that."

All of them perked up. "Really?" said Lise.

"Definitely. Uh . . ." *Sooo . . . what's the food like in that internment camp?* "It's a good place," I said. "Monsieur Thiély's really nice. He's Swiss."

"Are there any Nazis here?" asked Lise suddenly.

"No!" I stared at her. "No, none at all."

"See?" said Hanne. "I *told* you."

"There aren't any in this part of France. This is the unoccupied zone."

Lise shook her head. "We saw some one time, at the camp," she said in a low voice.

"Oh." And Gurs was in the unoccupied zone too. I didn't like the sound of that. "Well, they've never been here. We're not important enough for them to take over, my father says, even if they came south."

"That's *good*," said Hanne, with a firm nod.

I left them with one of the counselors, in the kitchen, fixing them a snack. I looked back at les Chênes for a moment, from the road: the broad stone house and the two ancient oak trees in front of it, one on each side, their bare branches muscular and beautiful. *I'm glad they get to live here*, I thought, and then, *I should work here, instead of with the babies.*

But I had promised. I had promised Paquerette.

I WENT to see her at l'Espoir the next day. Mama made me wait until afternoon so she could get her rest. She sent along a packet of *tilleul* flower tea that she'd dried herself, as a present for Paquerette and the Sabatiers. We sat and drank it by the fire. The babies were napping, both of them: Grigory, and Hanne's baby sister Lilli. Paquerette sat with her eyes half-closed in pleasure, her hands around her warm cup, then opened them and asked me what I had learned about babies. *That I'm not too crazy about them.* "Well, they spit up a lot." I'd just plain gotten used to walking around with a white blotch on the shoulder of my sweater.

Madeleine Sabatier laughed. Paquerette smiled. I set my teeth. "And they're very sensitive," I added with dignity. "When I get frustrated with Grigory, like if he's not drinking fast enough, he stops drinking completely."

Paquerette's eyebrows rose. "That is true. You're observant, Magali."

I sat up a little straighter.

Paquerette nodded. "Yes, it's true. You know, this new baby, Lilli . . . We had a *contrôle* on the train between Toulouse and Narbonne. Of course everything was in order, but those children . . . I think they must have been through a great deal. As the police got nearer to us down the line of the train, I could *feel* Lise shaking. And Lilli, I had just fed her and she'd been sleepy and calm—she started screaming." She looked into the fire, biting her lip, and then glanced at Madame Sabatier. "Thank you," she said quietly. "Knowing I can bring these children to you takes a weight off my heart."

PAQUERETTE LEFT again. I waited. I went to l'Espoir and fed Lilli, while Rosa fed Grigory. When the time came I started meeting the train again. I tried to get Murielle and Sylvie, my friends from my scout troop, to meet it with me, but they were busy after school. I was alone again when Paquerette came in with two young boys

and a toddler. She looked like she'd had the worst trip ever, again.
They were meant to go to Madame Alexandre to be placed with a
family. I offered to take them again. She hesitated.
"They don't speak any French. They're from Poland." She
rubbed a hand across her face. "Of course I haven't been able to
communicate with them either . . ."
She let me take them. I had the toddler up on my shoulders and
the smaller boy by the hand and I was walking across the *place du
centre* when it happened. The older boy—six years old—started to
scream. A real scream—pure fear.
The kid on my shoulders started screaming too. The older boy
was shouting something in some foreign language—people were
starting to turn and stare. The kid I had by the hand seemed ready
to bolt. I hung on like death, looking round frantically for someone who spoke . . . spoke . . .
Nina swung out the door of the café on her crutches, and headed
for me. Someone must have gone into the kitchen to get her. She
came right up to us before saying anything. She spoke a few words
in a low, urgent voice. In Yiddish, I guess. The boy shut up and
looked at her. She asked him a question. There were tears on his
face. He pointed at the *mairie* and said something. Nina spoke to
him some more. He nodded. The one I had by the hand nodded
too. I finally let out my breath.
"They thought that you are taking them *there*," said Nina, pointing with her chin at the *mairie*. "They saw the French flags. They
say, they were before arrested in such a place. I have said to them,
they are safe with you. Where do you take them?"
"Just to the pastor's house." I swallowed. "Uh, Nina? Uh . . ." *Are
you free in the afternoons? Around five thirty?*
I asked her about it as we walked back from the parsonage. She
looked at me out of the corner of her eye when I said *meet the train*,
and by the end there was no expression at all on her face. Like it
was frozen.

"And, um, it helps Paquerette so much . . . um . . . Nina?"

She didn't say anything for a good three seconds. Then she spoke in a low voice. "You want that I go to the train station?" Her eyes, when she said *train station*, looked like she was saying *hell*.

"Um . . ."

Nina shook her head, fast little shakes. I could hear her breath starting to come hard.

"Nina, Monsieur Bernard's not going to do anything to you. I've seen at least ten or fifteen groups of refugees get off the train and he hasn't tried to stop a single one." The next moment I remembered a few things I'd seen and realized I should have made that *hasn't tried very hard*. But the kids, and Paquerette, she could help them *so much*. "My mother says he's given up. I bet he even knows you're here, anyway."

At that last sentence her eyes got bigger and darker. She drew back. "Has someone told him? Are you sure?"

"No! I just mean, you've been here for half a year, all I mean is . . ."

She stood there and looked at me, one of her looks that goes on way too long. I scuffed my boots in the old snow.

"I cannot go," she said finally, and turned away.

I went home angry. *Yeah, that's the thing about Nina. That.* Mama says she's right to be scared. Fine. Papa says that courage isn't being without fear, it's doing what has to be done in spite of your fear. *I wouldn't let being a refugee make me like that, when somebody needed my help. Afraid of Monsieur Bernard. As if he was the Gestapo or something.*

I told Rosa about it that night, while Madame Sabatier was bathing Grigory. She just sat there looking troubled. And then she told me Nina was right to be scared. I almost put Lilli down and walked out.

On Wednesday Paquerette left for Gurs again. On Monday I started meeting the train every day to look for her. I went at noon with Rosa, and we stood shivering in the bright, cold air. At five thirty I went by myself, with my hood up against the *burle* that had started to blow. I felt someone come up beside me, and turned. "Hi," said Rosa quietly.

"Your mother let you off?"

"Just for fifteen minutes."

The train came in. Paquerette wasn't on it. We turned back and walked back up the street toward the *place du centre*, and as we passed the Rue du Rosier on our right, Nina came out of it, walking carefully, her crutches clicking on the ice. She looked at me and immediately looked away. She was pale.

"Hi Nina," said Rosa without surprise.

I looked from one to the other. Neither of them met my eye.

NINA WAS there again the day Paquerette came in—Wednesday, a full week after she'd left. Paquerette's eyes were rimmed with red, as if she'd been crying or hadn't slept for two days, I wasn't sure which. She was trailing *seven kids*.

"Paquerette, are you all right?"

She gave me a quick headshake, and turned to count the kids. Two of the youngest—six-year-olds or so—had those swollen bellies. The older ones were looking round the station platform like someone was going to show up and shoot them. One of them had a bandage over his cheek. Paquerette turned around, appearing profoundly relieved that her count had come out right. "The younger ones are for Sylvie," she said in a ragged voice. "Spanish. Rosa, you can take them if you're willing. The oldest three are for les Chênes. They don't speak French and they're in a bad way. I think I'd better take them myself." She took a deep breath and her spine straightened. She looked at me. "You can help."

"We've got Nina," I forced myself to say. "She's . . . back there. What do they speak?"

They spoke Yiddish. We stood in the mouth of Nina's alley and she spoke to them in a low voice in Yiddish, and they started to look a little less like they were about to get shot. *I knew* I was right about bringing her. She spoke, and they nodded. She turned and told us she thought she and I could take them where they were going. Paquerette looked at her like she'd just handed her the world, all fixed. *It was my idea. Mine.*

It was a very long walk, at the pace of Nina and her crutches. At the pace of the boy with the bandage and his scared, angry eyes, and the girl beside him that jumped like a frightened deer when some farm kid whooshed past us on skis, and then doubled over and started dry-sobbing uncontrollably. Nina crouched awkwardly, her bad leg stretched out stiff in the snow, and held her around the shoulders and talked to her. In Yiddish. I stood there not knowing what to do with myself. I carried the seven-year-old on my back most of the way. So at least I did that.

When we rounded the bend and came in sight of les Chênes, I actually prayed. I looked at those two bare oak trees with their roots deep down in the soil, down where the freeze doesn't reach, and this wordless feeling rose up inside me, something like pain and hope. *Oh God, may this place heal them. Please.* I think that's what it would have been. If there'd been words.

"I FELT like I had to take them all. Had to. I couldn't leave them in that state, I couldn't choose between the two families or split them up. And then . . ." Paquerette scrubbed her hands over her face. "Then our train was stopped because of a wreck down the line. We stayed in one place for a full ten hours. All I had was a loaf of bread in my bag, that was all I had to feed us all. And they *fought* over it—physically. They used their fingernails. Did you see Rosario? The next youngest? You can still see the scratches on her arm."

"I'm guessing you didn't eat, then?"

She shook her head. Madame Sabatier pushed another piece of

bread at her. She started to shake her head, but then picked it up and took a bite. Then she took a breath, and put her hands on the table. "But I haven't told you my news yet. Rivesaltes has opened up!"

I blinked at her. "Opened up?" She couldn't mean they'd let everyone go . . .

"They're finally letting us place a worker in the camp, and it's going to be one of my dearest friends. I'm going there to help her get established. That's the other reason I took all these children from Gurs—Jeanne has no more releases pending after those. So I'll be able to spend a little time with M—Marylise—without making anyone wait." She smiled, and I got a suspicion that wasn't her friend's real name.

"How long?"

"I don't know, Magali. It'll depend."

She was gone for almost three whole weeks.

I fed babies and put them to bed. I washed diapers. I sat in my classroom and wondered what Paquerette was doing, and I looked across the aisle at Jean-Luc Rivas and wondered if he'd ever figure out how much more *interesting* I was than pretty little Claudine Faure. At break I stood out on the riverbank beside our barn classroom with Lucy and Murielle and Sylvie, looking at the ice that crusted the Tanne and the dark, cold, swift-flowing water out in the middle. March came, and kept on coming; the ice began to crack and wash downstream. Still no Paquerette.

I helped Mama make supper. I went over and did homework with Lucy. Rosa came over and did homework with me. We spread our books out on the carpet by the fire. Benjamin joined us. He helped Rosa with her geometry and was much nicer about her not understanding what a hypotenuse was than he's ever been with me. One night he walked us down to l'Espoir. But he didn't go in. Babies, you know.

Benjamin got a letter from his parents that some traveler had brought to Pastor Alex, and he walked out the door into the cold and dark after supper, going nowhere, without his hat, and was gone all evening. I don't know that I would have noticed he'd gone out if he hadn't run into me and Rosa as we were walking back late after a tough evening with Lilli, who seemed to have something wrong with her. We saw him up the street from us, walking slowly with his hands in his pockets, and when he turned for a moment his face gleamed in the moonlight as if he was crying. Rosa quickened her pace.

I slowed down. I don't like to mess with Benjamin when he's upset. It can be kind of embarrassing.

"She hasn't been able to breathe right for two months," Benjamin was saying when, having nowhere else to go, I finally reached them. There weren't tears on his face now, but his eyes were red. "There's a doctor who's safe for them, but he hasn't been able to help her."

"I'm so sorry, Benjamin," Rosa said softly.

"Who?" I asked.

"My mother," said Benjamin, and turned away.

"Oh . . . she can't go to the hospital?"

He shook his head angrily. "What do you think? Every time they go anywhere someone might check their papers, they're risking their *lives!*"

"Wow," I said. "I'm sorry." Rosa just looked at him with her big dark eyes.

"And he can't have a job either. They can barely pay their rent and I'd bet anything that place they live in is a rathole. And my father's no closer to getting them a visa out than the day he set foot in Marseille." He took off his glasses and wiped his sleeve across his eyes. He looked away from me, toward Rosa.

There was a moment of silence. I saw Rosa reach out tentatively and put her hand on his arm. I froze, looking at them. Looking at each other in the moonlight.

*No, now. Not really, right? Surely your mother wants you to marry
a nice Jewish girl . . .*

The answering thought sent a chill down my spine. *His mother
might never know.*

I stood shivering, there in the dark.

"You look so cold, Benjamin," said Rosa. "Can we walk you
home?"

We did.

HE BARELY said a word at breakfast the next day, or at lunch. He
barely ate. I heard him and Julien through my wall that night, talking in muffled voices . . . I guess about his parents again. Unless it
was about Rosa. I lay on my bed and imagined living on my own.
So far from my parents they didn't need to know a single thing I
didn't choose to tell them. So much weight lifted off my heart at
the thought I wanted to jump up and shout. But no: knowing they
were sick, in trouble, in danger. Knowing I might never see them
again.

Never.

I thought about the people in the camps. Paquerette said families were split up there, the men in one block and the women and
children in another. And there were kids who didn't know where
their parents were at all. Hanne and Lise's father had been arrested
back in Germany. No one knew where he was now. He probably
didn't know where they were either. Where was the father of that
girl who'd broken down sobbing on the road to les Chênes? What
had happened to her to make her do that? What made people
capable of things like this, of putting ten-year-old girls behind
barbed wire?

*I want to do more than this. Than washing diapers, putting babies
to bed. I want to go to those places with wire cutters. Get them all out.
I want to do something, I want to do.*

But I washed diapers. Put Grigory to bed, while Rosa rocked

Lilli. Lilli cried, weakly and constantly, her little face screwed up
as if she was in pain. Rosa bent over her, whispering *sh, sh,* and
little words in Spanish, things about *mama.* I wondered what she
was saying. If she was saying, *Your mama's coming, it's all right.* I
wondered if it was wrong to lie to babies.

I wondered if the world would ever make sense again.

Paquerette came back.

It was a windy, raw-cold day, with the dirty melting snow all
frozen again overnight; jagged ice in the streets, the wind whipping *la Galoche's* steam into ragged clouds. But Paquerette, when
she stepped out of the passenger car, was smiling, with color in her
cheeks.

"Magali!" she said, giving me the *bise.* "Just the person I wanted
to see." My heart warmed like a bonfire. "But for now," she added,
"do you suppose you could run to the Café du Centre and get
Rosa? I've got some Spaniards here who don't speak any French."

She'd brought a baby, a little boy, and a teenage girl named
Sonia, dark-eyed and dark-haired and thin. We took them to
l'Espoir first. When Madame Sabatier got out a bottle of formula
to feed baby Marta, her sister Sonia started to cry. She said some
things to Rosa in Spanish, and Rosa told us Marta had been born
in the camp, and you couldn't get anything for babies there. Rosa
was pretty close to crying herself.

Rosa and Sonia left to take little Julio down to les Chênes.
Paquerette made tea for us all while Madame Sabatier took care
of Marta. When we were by the fire drinking our tea, hearing
the soft sounds of Madame Sabatier crooning from the nursery,
Paquerette turned to me.

"Magali," she said, "I have something to ask you."

I gave her a swift glance and my heart started beating hard. "Yes
Paquerette?"

"I've been thinking about Rivesaltes, and about how it's been

for me, these past two months or so. It's been . . . difficult." She
looked into the fire. "That last trip from Gurs truly made me
think. I likely either need to give up my resolution to leave no one
waiting, or I need help." She turned to me. "Especially if Marylise
can get as many releases at Rivesaltes as she hopes."

My blood was pounding in my ears.

"You seem to care about these children a lot, Magali, and I've
seen you deal rather well with them. What would you think," she
said slowly, "about traveling with me?"

It was all I could do not to jump up and shout. "Yes!" My voice
cracked. "Yes, yes, I'll do it, Paquerette, I—"

"Magali. Just a moment. Take a deep breath now." Paquerette
looked at me, the firelight dancing in her gray eyes. "Has it occurred
to you that you're going to have to ask your parents?"

I RAN up the stone stairs three steps at a time and threw open the
door. Mama stood up fast from her seat by the fire, staring at me.

"Mama? Can I ask you and Papa something?"

There was absolutely no way I could wait. I wouldn't sleep all
night. Mama looked at me for a long moment and then said, "Your
father's in his study. We can join him there."

We sat down in Papa's study, in the high-backed chairs around
his desk. I took a deep breath.

A trial run, she'd said, over Easter vacation. *Emphasize to them
that it's legal, the children have papers, and we have the full consent of
the authorities. It'll be hard, Magali. We'll sleep on train station floors.
And keeping the kids together, keeping them fed, keeping them safe,
you can't relax for a moment. It's not glorious, Magali. I want you to
know that. It's just very difficult babysitting.* I had listened to her, my
heart beating. Picturing it.

"Would it be okay—if—" They were both looking at me. "Um."
The words came out in a rush. "Paquerette asked me to travel with
her. To the camps."

Total silence.

My mother was chalk white.

I should have known.

I tried to gather the words, tried to force them past the pain that was growing in my throat. They were gone, scattered like birds. "It's . . . it's legal. She needs help. So she can bring more. She wants to do a . . . a trial run with me, during Easter vacation—"

"And what made her think she could ask you without saying a word to your parents?"

"She wanted me to ask you!" My voice was high. My throat hurt, my eyes hurt, I could feel the awful, awful welling of tears. They were the only ones who could do this to me. Make me break down and stammer, make me *cry*. My voice broke. "It's not even *dangerous!*"

"Is *that* all you know?" Papa's voice was like steel.

"It's legal! The kids are released, they've got permission from the authorities, they've got papers, they've got *everything!*" I blinked hard and fast. The tears stayed back. Mama was looking at me, her eyes huge and very black in her drained face.

"And how long does Paquerette expect this situation to continue?" He gave me a long pause to answer that. Since he knew I couldn't. "Do you have any idea what she and the CIMADE are up against, Magali? Does *she?*"

I shut up. I looked at him and did not move.

"They are up against the Vichy government. Which is bending over backward to give the Nazis every concession they can. Many of the people in those camps are Jews, Magali. How long do you think the Nazis are going to condone the official release of Jewish children? Yes, the CIMADE's work is legal. *For now.*" He gave the last two words a weight like a boulder. "But do not tell me it isn't dangerous. When you walk unarmed into a lion's den to take his prey, do not tell me that it is not dangerous, permission or no permission."

Into a lion's den. A sudden image flashed through my mind—
Paquerette, tall and straight, walking slowly into a high dark cave.
*To take his prey.* "That's why we have to get them out, Papa. They're
in danger. Don't you see?"

"Magali, you are fifteen years old. Yes, those children desperately
need help, but you are not the only person in the world capable of
helping—"

"She asked me," I said with my head down. I was raised to respect
my elders. But right now I was dangerously close to the edge.

"Yes, well, we may need to speak to her about that." He glanced
at Mama. "Quite honestly, my first instinct is that this is work for
adults and adults only."

So that was it? They'd go tell her off for even asking me? And
that would be the end, the end—

"*You* need to focus on your studies. Your exams . . ."

I cracked. "My exams are more important than kids' *lives?*"

Papa's voice was steel again. "Do not make assumptions, young
lady." The anger in his eyes was like a physical force, pushing me back
against my chair. My eyes flew up to the books behind him: Greece,
Rome, Charlemagne, all dead and dried between pages—this he
thought was important. Living children, on the other hand—

It came out of my mouth. The thing I'd held back for so long. "I
don't even *want* to go to *lycée.*"

I tore my eyes from the books and looked at my parents. Papa
wasn't looking at me anymore. He was looking at Mama, whose
face streamed with tears.

I stood. "I'm sorry," I whispered. "Forget I said anything. Forget
I asked."

I turned, and fled up the stairs.

*I* DON'T *want to be like my mother.*

I sat cross-legged on my bed, trying to stop crying. *Never. Never.
I'll never be her.*

She let life *break* her. I don't even know what it was. She never told me and she probably never will. But something in her, it's like Nina's twisted leg.

When we thought the Germans were coming here, during the invasion, Mama hid the silver and the radio in the attic and ordered me to stay inside. Then she took *me* up into the attic and made me hide in the space between the insulation boards and the roof to see if I fit. It was hot and itchy and made me sneeze, and she told me not to sneeze, as angry as if she was telling me not to curse. When I told her I wasn't afraid of the Germans she called me a fool and grabbed my arm so hard it left a bruise. I didn't let anyone see the bruise. It made me ashamed.

I hate that white face. Those tears. The way she hasn't even got the guts to tell her own daughter what happened to make her like this, the way she doesn't fight. She isn't even *angry*. It's like you have to lie down and let life walk all over you. Or hide. Those are the options. Fighting back, forget about it. That's for men. "You know, Magali, women just have to accept certain limitations." She said that to me, those exact words. Women stay home and cook and clean and wipe babies' bottoms, that's what women are for. Saving lives, fighting Vichy, well, no. You have to accept certain limitations.

*Her and Nina.* I rocked back and forth, trying to control my sobbing breath. *Her and Nina both.*

Nina—afraid, after more than a year, to face Monsieur Bernard. Overjoyed at the chance to do homework and dishes. Nina, grateful and scared, Mama's ideal girl. And Rosa too, shy and sweet the way the boys like, burping babies and helping her parents and never thinking of more till I made her.

*There are two kinds of people in the world*, I thought. *People like them. And people like me.*

There are people who do things, and people who have things done to them. People who say, "What can I do?" and people who say, "Oh no, who will save me?" It never occurred to my mother to wonder if I might be the first kind—if I might actually save someone. Because for her, the definition of a girl is someone who gets rescued. Or not.

I calmed my breath. I looked out the window, up at the moon in the cold sky, and thought, *no.*

No, Mama, I'm not doing that. I'm not hiding in the attic where I'm protected, while other people die. Let Rosa burp the babies, she's good at it. Paquerette asked *me* to save them. I thought of her face, that quick calculation—*can I rely on this person?*—and the answer *yes*, the confidence in me that I'd seen in her clear gray eyes. A tightness was growing in my throat. Mama and Papa had never looked at me that way.

*You're just a girl. A stupid little girl from a conquered country. What do you think you can do against the men who sit in Vichy and plan, against the men who stand in guard towers with their guns? Who do you think you are?* I heard that voice. The voice of the things I hated, the voice of the silence and the night.

Well, *down* with the night.

Limitations? *Forget* limitations. You couldn't put a *man* on a train with four kids and a baby and expect them to get where they were going in one piece. Paquerette was a woman, a real one, and she knew exactly what kind of lion's den she was walking into, and she kept walking. Because there were kids who needed to be saved, and there was nobody else to do it. Except me.

And I couldn't go.

So much for being Joan of Arc's assistant, I thought as I sat in the dark. So much for being anything at all. Besides safe. That's what Mama wants me to be. Safe.

Even if I'm never anything else.

I COULD hardly look at my parents the next morning. Mama's eyes were red. When I came home from school she'd cleaned my room as if I was a little kid. She called me in to help her with supper. I helped. Didn't talk, didn't look at her. I knew whose fault all this was, even if she let Papa do her talking for her.

I lay awake in bed while the moon traveled down the sky. Finally I slept. I woke up in my cold room, in a cold house, in a cold world where Paquerette was alone in some train station, waking up on a cold hard floor, where kids in camps were opening their eyes in the stinking dark wondering why, where Benjamin's mother was hidden in somebody's basement somewhere, struggling to breathe. And there was nothing I could do.

There *had* to be something I could do.

"Don't look at me like that. I'm on your side, you know."

I looked at Julien where he stood leaning on my doorframe and wondered what had possessed me to ask for *his* help. "Oh yeah?"

"Yeah. But you're shooting yourself in the foot. What you want to do is act cool and mature, like you kinda agree with them about what a serious thing it is—"

"But that's—"

"Magali, if you want advice then *listen* to it. I'm serious. You want to know what they're talking about? 'Is she mature enough?' That's it. So if you stop—*sulking...*"

*I am not sulking!* I swallowed. "What do you mean, 'talking about'? I thought it was over."

Julien shook his head. "Definitely talking about it. Last night while you were out."

I jumped up and grabbed my brother around the neck and hugged him. He stared at me.

"I have an idea," I said.

I tried Papa, alone in his study. He seemed like a better bet. I sat down, cleared my throat a couple of times, and reminded myself to act mature. And then I asked him if he'd be willing to talk with Paquerette.

He gave me an odd little smile and said he expected that was a good idea. But when I went down to l'Espoir after school to ask her, she was gone.

I had to wait almost a week.

She finally came in on Saturday, with three kids from Gurs. Nina and I took them over from her. We didn't get a chance to talk. I saw her the next morning in church. In the afternoon my parents walked down to l'Espoir.

They came back and sat me down in the study and told me I could go to Rivesaltes at Easter.

Then, while my heart hammered, they took turns explaining to me just how much of a trial run this was, and that as far as they were concerned they were giving permission for one trip only, and . . . and . . . My blood was beating in my ears, my whole body was alive with it. They expected maturity from me, they were saying. I was to take my cues from Paquerette and do everything exactly as she said, especially in the camp itself. I was to be as cautious and circumspect as she was. If she reported that I was not, I could expect never to travel with her again.

I wasn't sure what circumspect meant. But I was going with Paquerette.

I had to wait two more weeks. Then Paquerette came and spent Easter with us, and the next morning we boarded a train to Rivesaltes.

## Chapter 4

# The Place That Should Not Exist

As WE were waiting for the train, I heard my mother behind me say in a low voice to Paquerette, "You'll take care of my daughter?"

And Paquerette answered in the same low voice, "Madame, protecting children is my life."

I didn't turn around.

I'd only ridden *la Galoche* a handful of times. My heart beat fast as I climbed into the passenger car behind Paquerette and settled myself on one of the long wooden benches. There's a reason Tanieux people talk about *la Galoche* as if she were a person, and it's not just because she brings us supplies. That train is a daredevil.

For the first half-hour, from Tanieux southeast to Saint-Agrève, she just steams between the same rolling hills that are all around Tanieux—nice, friendly, walkable hills with snow-patched pastures and scrubby *genêts* and pine woods. Then at Saint-Agrève she takes a sharp right turn to follow the Eyrieux River, and starts coming down off the plateau.

Down, down. I twisted around on my bench to stare out the window at the depths that opened up below us. The river was dropping fast into a gorge between steep slopes of pine and rock, deeper and deeper as I watched; through the window across from me you could see nothing but bare, dark pine-tree trunks whipping past. The track is set right into the mountainside. And *it* goes down too.

She was starting to pick up speed. The whistle sounded once, sharply, and then we all felt the scrape as the driver put on the brake. It hardly slowed us down at all. I felt the rattle of the train beneath me and I looked at all that air down there, all the way down to the white flowing water, and I wanted to whoop.

"You like mountains?" murmured Paquerette. There was a light in her gray eyes. "So do I."

We stayed glued to the windows as *la Galoche* ran down the gorge with the brake on, all the way to le Cheylard, twisting and turning, going through tunnels, over high stone bridges, sometimes high above the water, sometimes near enough to hear it foaming. Sometimes you could see the whole valley in front of you for half a kilometer, the air blue and hazy with distance—tall pines and snow on the slopes, pale winter pastures and a huddle of slate roofs beside the swift river. But always down, down, and the scrape of the brake, and the speed.

You forget, living up on the plateau, sometimes. You forget you're in the mountains at all.

WE CAME out of the mountains at la Voulte-sur-Rhône. I caught one glimpse of the wide, flat Rhône Valley stretched out beside its big river, and then we were among houses, and the train was braking to a halt. End of *la Galoche*'s line.

In la Voulte we had to wait three hours for a train to Montpel-

lier. It's a little station and not all the trains stop there. We sat on
a bench in the pale April sunlight and Paquerette unwrapped the
lunch Mama had packed—a couple of baked potatoes and some
hard cheese. We ate with our fingers, quickly. Paquerette wiped
hers carefully on a handkerchief, and looked around.

"It's warmer here."

"Yeah." I breathed in. "And the . . . the air's different, somehow."
She nodded. "Thicker. I always notice it. I love how clear the air
is, up in Tanieux." She turned to me. "So, Magali. I hear you used
to live in Paris. Do you miss it?"

*Oh. I get to talk to you.* A smile spread across my face.

I suppose I talked her ear off. I told her about Paris, about moving,
about how we didn't hear from Uncle Giovanni and Aunt Nadine
for months after the invasion. I told her about Benjamin and his
parents. On the train she asked me something about my parents,
and I ended up telling her, as we watched freshly plowed fields roll
by on either side, about Mama during the invasion. How she broke
down, or whatever you might call it. Paquerette listened with serious eyes, and nodded a few times, and then asked me where Mama
grew up.

I told her what I knew. It doesn't add up to much. Then she
asked me if I thought my father really felt the same way as my
mother, about my traveling with her.

"Oh," I said. "I . . . I don't know. You mean what would he say if
it was just him?"

She nodded. I tried to remember.

"Well, he asked if you knew what you were up against."

She let out a short laugh. "Ah, yes." She looked out at the broad
brown landscape, then turned back to me. "You know, we take a
lot of precautions in the CIMADE. The false names for some of
us. The way we keep records." She lowered her voice, even though
we were alone in our car. "Some of my coworkers think it's foolish,

a spy game, and too much trouble, but our office manager makes them do it anyway. I think she's right, and so is your father. You should listen to your parents, Magali. They've seen a lot of life."

I blinked. Right? *Both* my parents?

"Even my father knows a thing or two," she continued, her voice growing dry. "And *he* says we're children playing in the trenches."

I looked at her. "Your parents didn't want you to go?"

She gave me a glance out of those inscrutable gray eyes. "No," she said. "As a matter of fact they didn't."

I asked her some questions about her family. There were things she wouldn't tell me, like where they lived, even. She showed me a drawing of her house instead, a pen-and-ink drawing she kept in her purse. She drew, sometimes, when she was alone on the trains, she said. She'd drawn the house from far away, in a deep valley; the mountains filled the picture, rising steep on either side. There was a little stream at the bottom, going past the house and barn. There were even some living figures, tiny but so precisely drawn that you could see it was an older woman beside the barn holding a pail, you could see the eagerness of the goats running toward her. It was all just black-and-white lines but I could almost see the sunlight and smell the clear cold air. "It's beautiful," I said. She thanked me, and put it carefully away, and looked out the window at the brown tilled fields lined with tiny shoots of green.

It was late and dark when the train pulled into Montpellier. Paquerette knew people there who would have put us up, but she said it was too late, and we'd better sleep in the station.

We found ourselves a spot by the wall. The benches were already taken. A family camped beside us, their clothes looking like they hadn't washed them for weeks, their luggage tied together with string. I remembered how Gustav and Nina had been camped in a train station when Samuel found them. Paquerette put up her suitcase like a wall between us and them, spread out a blanket from her bag, and settled on it, lying on her side, pillowing her head in the crook of her arm. She stretched once, like a cat, looked at me and patted the space beside her. I lay down too.

The station floor was rock-hard through the thin blanket. The dim electric light above me buzzed. I turned over on my other side, but it was just as hard. A baby started to cry somewhere in our camp of huddled families. Paquerette did this all the time. This was what I was asking for, to do it with her. I looked over at her.

She was asleep.

I'd heard some people could do that. Soldiers, mostly, or hunters out in the woods. Go to sleep instantly. Wake at the slightest sound. I wondered if I'd ever be able to.

I turned and turned, as the quiet deepened with the night. I think it must have been hours before I slept.

PAQUERETTE WAS shaking me. My eyelids were stuck together and my head was full of gravel. "Magali, wake up. We've got a train to catch."

Horror shot through me. She had to *wake* me. I was just another burden, another child. I sat bolt upright, jumped to my feet and started folding up the blanket. She smiled. "Ready?"

"Ready."

We washed our faces in the women's bathroom and went to the platform. We ate breakfast, a chewy hunk of yesterday's bread, while we waited. The train came, and as soon as we were settled in I fell asleep.

She woke me for lunch—bread and more cheese. There was green outside the windows now, green living grass, and orchards, row on row of short graceful trees reaching their limbs out wide like dancers, covered with pink blossom. We were in the *real* south now. The houses were pale stucco, with red tile roofs. Passing out of a town we saw a huge, old cherry tree in bloom, dazzling white against the blue southern sky.

I turned to Paquerette, and stopped. There were tears in her eyes. My heart beat hard, but I dared. "Paquerette? Are you all right?"

She gave me a moment's smile that didn't reach her eyes. She wiped them with her sleeve, and shrugged. "It's so beautiful," she whispered. "And it's the same world."

I opened my mouth, slowly. She turned and looked at me. Drew herself up a little, Joan of Arc again. "Magali," she said quietly, "you're going to see some very bad things today. I have a phrase that goes through my head sometimes—'the knowledge that is poison.' It . . . it gets into your soul, when you see these things every week." She looked out the window, and the tears welled up again. She wiped them, and shook her head. She turned to me. "Listen. I want this clear now. I won't be able to talk about these things with you. The times when I'm free of them, I need to leave them behind. So you and me, we don't talk about evil. You may need to speak to someone about it, but I'm sorry—I'm not able."

"Of course," I whispered. "I won't."

She gave me a sad smile. "Thank you for coming with me, Magali," she said.

RIVESALTES IS the name of a town, a lovely little town of sandstone houses and red-tile roofs, flowers in the window boxes, vineyards all around the town. Camp Joffre is the real name of the camp. It was early afternoon by the time we pulled into Rivesaltes village and got off the train. I followed Paquerette through the town, and we set out down the road to the camp.

It took us an hour and a half. We walked between vineyards, rows and rows of gnarled brown vines covered in shiny, pale-green new leaves. There were low humped hills on the horizon, but where we walked it was flat. The wind gusted and kicked up road dust in our faces. We walked, and the land got poorer as we went. First the poorer vineyards—more brown and less green. Then the scrub—bunchy grass, thirsty bushes, brambles and stones. The wind got much worse across the open dusty ground; grit got in my eyes and nose and mouth. Paquerette stopped, and we took a drink from her water bottle. She took out a handkerchief and tied it over her nose and mouth, and handed me one too. Her eyes were watering and so were mine.

"It's the *tramontane*," she said, raising her voice above the sound of the wind. "I hoped it wouldn't be blowing today."

The *tramontane*. I'd heard of it. *They've got a name for the wind. Watch out.*

We walked, and the dust whipped around us; dust and sand on my skin, my eyes stinging and watering. We walked, and in the distance I started to see it.

The camp.

A wide low shape between the hills, gray and red and tangled lines. A few taller shapes rising up from it here and there like trees. We walked, and I saw the trees were watchtowers. We walked, and the long low tangle became a camp, a huge, sprawling grid of long gray, red-roofed barracks, row on row on row; blocks of them, with dusty roads between, each block fenced in with matted barbed wire. And around it all an outer fence, tall, barbed, impassable. A high gate. Behind it, two or three buildings that weren't barracks. And people moving, there in front of them. Guards.

After another minute I started to see the other people.

Small dark shapes against the gray barrack walls, against the pale dust and gravel on the ground. People standing, walking, sitting on the ground. Standing in line. Hundreds of small figures, moving here and there. Like an anthill. I can't help it, that's what it looked like. What the camp made them look like. I stopped for a moment, swallowing. Paquerette gave me a searching look. I started walking again.

I saw something move in one of the towers. I saw the small silhouette of a man up there, and the shape of his rifle against the sky. A chill went down my spine.

I looked at the people moving between their barracks. At the tangled fence that kept them in. I looked up at the man looking down on them with a gun. I felt a pulling deep in my guts, a sick feeling I'd never felt in my life.

The flatness of those long buildings filled the horizon as we got closer; they were all there was, they were the world. I could see the people in the nearest blocks clearly now, their clothes and skin pale with dust. Straight ahead, I could see the buildings at the entrance, and guards standing behind the gate, men in khaki uniforms with rifles. I swallowed again. Paquerette stopped and pulled her handkerchief off her mouth, so I took mine off too; then she turned to me quickly and took my wrist in her hand.

"You do exactly as I say while we're in here, you hear? Don't speak to a guard except to answer a question. Be very polite. And quiet. Understand?" Her eyes were steel again now.

I tried to speak, but no words came out. I nodded. Paquerette gave me one nod, and began to walk again.

We were very close to the gate now. Paquerette's back grew straighter with every step, her black skirt swishing around her calves as her walk turned to a stride, her head held high.

One guard stood right behind the gate, his rifle held against his chest. He looked at us. His eyes were red and watering. "Authorization papers," he snapped.

Paquerette handed them to him without a word. He looked through them, and gave a sharp nod, stepped back, and swung the high gate open just wide enough for us to pass. I looked up at the nearest guard tower. The guard up there was looking at me. A cold whisper ran down my spine. Paquerette was striding in already, through that narrow opening, into that place ringed with barbed wire. That place that should not exist.

I followed her, and tried to keep my knees from trembling.

THE GUARD shut the gate behind us.

Square gray buildings; gravel underfoot. A sign on the building we were headed for: *poste de commande*. A guard walking past; a woman in a dusty nurse's uniform; a young woman in a faded dress with ragged cuffs, staring at us with wide, dust-reddened eyes, a green card held before her in one hand like a shield. Paquerette motioned her to go in the door before us, but she shook her head.

Inside, a clerk at a metal desk checked our *cartes d'identité*, issued us green cards like the one the woman had. Passes. Ours said *Entire camp*; others on his desk said, *Block F, Block J*. As we walked out the door we heard the young woman speak to the clerk, her voice uncertain, a note of pleading.

I followed Paquerette down the dusty road between the blocks of barracks. An automobile came the other way, kicking up dust in our faces. Between barracks in the block to my left I caught a glimpse of a black-haired woman stirring a small cookfire, two small children by her side; she lifted her head and I caught alert, suspicious eyes, Gypsy features. In the block to my right they were standing in line, women and children and teenagers—no men— all with tin cups or bowls gripped tightly in their hands. Most of the kids had no shoes; their clothes were stiff with grime, the color of dust. At the head of the line was a building with what looked like a serving window.

I heard a yell. Two skinny boys shot out from between the barracks, the first one coming so fast he ran up against the barbed wire. I saw a barb sink right into him and he didn't make a sound. He took a big bite of the chunk of bread he was clutching, and then the other boy was on him, silent as well; a flurry of movement, and then the first boy's face was bleeding, and the other had the bread. He stuffed it all in his mouth, gave us a glance with wide angry eyes, and was gone between the barracks.

The first boy stood up, wiped the blood off his face with his sleeve, and walked away.

They both looked about nine years old.

I realized I was trembling.

Paquerette kept walking.

WE PRESENTED our passes at the guardhouse of Block J. Almost before we were through the gate an ash-blonde woman in a blue dress came out of the next building over, her eyes growing eager when she saw us.

"Marylise!" And then she and Paquerette were embracing, giving each other the *bise* on both cheeks, hard, four times. "Marylise. How *are* you?" Paquerette gave her a long, searching look, as if she really wanted to know.

"I'm holding up," said Marylise. "Some stories to tell you, certainly." What looked like a flash of anger in her eyes. "But the children first."

"Yes," said Paquerette. We followed Marylise into her building: a bare concrete floor, a wooden table in the center, benches around the table and around the walls. A doorway with a curtain in it hid what might be her bedroom. She stepped into a tiny kitchen and brought us glasses of water. I drank mine in two long gulps, sweet and cool against my dusty throat.

"How's Zvi?" Paquerette said.

"Worse. But he's released. Can you take him?"

"Of course." Paquerette spread her hand out toward me, as if I was proof. Marylise glanced at me. I sat up straighter. Paquerette hesitated. "Just him?"

Marylise nodded. "The doctor wouldn't sign off on her. I don't know what these people are thinking, Paquerette." She shook her head, the anger growing in her blue eyes again. "The doctors, the nurses, they act as if they're not treating *people*. I put diapers on the babies in the infirmary and within two days they were all naked again and no one knew why. The nurses *stole* them. There's no other explanation."

Paquerette looked at her for a moment. "You're braver than me, staying here," she said quietly. "So who do you have for us today?"

I SAT and watched quietly while Marylise and Paquerette worked over several sheaves of forms, signing some, exchanging others, consulting. Paquerette asked about someone named Léon and Marylise sighed and shook her head. "All that's left is the *commandant's* signature, and he's got the form but his secretary made it very clear that if I ask one more time I won't get anything at all. I hoped you could take him today, but . . ." She shrugged helplessly.

They went back to their forms for a minute and then Marylise stood up and went outside. "Back in five minutes." I heard her calling to someone out there, saying to go get Kurt and Hania Steinhaus and Eva Grosch. Paquerette turned to me. "Feeling all right?"

I nodded.

"Think you can handle a baby? He's very sick. He'll likely be rather passive, but he'll need to be handled gently."

I nodded. It didn't sound too hard.

Marylise came back with a tall, thin woman who wore a skirt made of patches—faded red, faded green, faded pink—and had red, watering eyes. She held a baby with skinny arms and a swollen belly like Grigory used to have, and eyes half-lidded like a cat's, looking at nothing. He was eerily still in her arms; it made my skin crawl in a way I didn't understand. She coughed, the rough, useless cough of someone whose chest is blocked up but who can't get anything out. Her eyes fastened on Paquerette. "Mademoiselle," she said, her accent so thick I could barely understand her. "You will take my Zvi?"

"Yes, Madame," said Paquerette, looking into her eyes. "My helper and I. He will be very well cared for where we're taking him. I can promise you that."

The woman coughed again. "I thank you," she said in a hoarse whisper. She turned to me. "I thank you also, Mademoiselle."

My throat tightened at being called *Mademoiselle* by this woman. I could hardly look into her red grateful eyes. "You're . . . welcome. Madame. We'll take good care of him."

Marylise gestured to the bench by the table. "So, Madame, there is the form to sign . . ."

I sat on a bench against the wall, watching. A thin girl my age with limp, tangled brown hair came in and stood in the doorway, looking around, her eyes wide. Paquerette and Marylise had their heads together. The girl looked at me, kind of desperately.

"Are you . . ." I groped. "Are you Eva?"

She brightened. "Yes, Mademoiselle."

The pit of my stomach dropped out.

I'd called her *tu*. I mean she was *my age*. And she'd called me . . . called me . . .

When one person's called *vous* and the other's called *tu*, it's because they're an adult and a kid. Always. Because if not, it means one person matters and the other one doesn't. And it never happens. Never. We don't have lords and serfs anymore. We don't have *slaves*.

Until now, apparently.

"Don't *call* me that!"

She pulled back, her eyes afraid. "I . . . I am sorry . . . Ma—"

"*Magali*." My voice sounded strange. "I'm Magali. I'm not a *Mademoiselle*. I'm not anything *special!*" My voice was raw. I was shaking again.

Eva stood looking at me, motionless for a second. Her watering eyes made tear-tracks down her dusty cheeks. The sleeves of her dust-colored blouse were rolled up around her thin wrists; the collar was ragged.

"I'm sorry," I whispered. "I mean . . . I mean please call me Magali."

She looked at me, her face very serious. I felt horribly self-conscious. My year-old blue blouse looked new compared to hers, there was flesh on my bones. *You're not special?* her eyes said. *I couldn't tell.*

She finally opened her mouth. "It's okay," she said very quietly. And then, "You help Mademoiselle Paquerette?" Calling me *tu*. I relaxed.

"Yes." I offered her my cheek for the *bise*. She only hesitated a moment before putting her dusty cheek against mine.

KURT AND Hania came—a skinny guy my age and his sister, who was pale and sweating and walked slowly. Kurt said she was sick but the block nurse had told him she wasn't contagious. There was a quick debate. They had decided they agreed, and Paquerette had gone back to talking about some kind of food distribution Marylise was doing for the kids, when a woman walked in—thin like a refugee but breathless and not at all hesitant.

"Marylise," she said, "he signed it. Just now."

"Léon?"

"Yes." She took a breath. "And there's a transport coming in. If you want a ride, I'd say—"

Paquerette and Marylise looked at each other for about one second and sprang into motion.

"Magali, change of plans. I'll take Zvi, you'll have another baby. If his mother chooses to send him on such short notice. Marylise? The parental release?"

Marylise, wildly scribbling on some form, paused to hand Paquerette a paper. Paquerette turned back to me. "They're in this block—I'll take you there and leave you with her and she will have five minutes to decide. This paper here is what she's got to sign if so. Do *not* lose it. I'll need to go to another block and get our other kids. You'll meet me at the main gate—show the block gate guard your pass and this form. *Do not* lose it." Her eyes bored into mine and I nodded jerkily. I could feel my heart speeding up.

"All right." She beckoned me to follow and strode out the door. The sunlight was blinding, and the dust hit my face again. I blinked. She led me through the block, past the dark doors of barracks, past red-eyed women standing and talking in the narrow shade of a building, children sitting in the dust. I could feel people's eyes on me.

Paquerette stepped into a barrack, and I followed her.

It was dark, and it stank. Sweat and urine and things I couldn't recognize and didn't want to. The windows were slits—wooden shutters just barely opened, no glass—making little islands of light among the shadows, among the bedrolls and piles of ragged belongings, the people sitting or lying on the ground. Here the corner of a dirty blanket was lit up, and there a little girl's feet in broken sandals. A child was crying, and it echoed harshly against the bare walls. Paquerette picked her way between the people. Heads turned.

"Suzanne," I heard someone whisper. "Suzanne. Must be for you."

A young woman stood up from her bedroll, a sleeping baby in her arms. A long brown braid lay like a rope over her shoulder. "Madame Blocher," said Paquerette, and gave her the *bise*. "We've just learned the release forms for your son are complete. If you will sign for him now, we can take him to Tanieux today. Only, our transport leaves within ten minutes. This is my assistant Magali; if you choose to send him today, she will take charge of him during the trip, under my supervision. You can give his papers to her. I am sorry to hurry such a thing, but I must go." She looked at me. "You have five minutes. Meet me at the gate. It's Madame Blocher's choice whether you bring the baby with you or not."

And then she turned and walked out of the barrack.

I stood there, feeling all the eyes on me, trying not to shake, trying to see the expression of the woman's face, in the gloom. She hadn't moved.

"The . . . the paper?" she said, and reached out a hand.

I held it out to her. She took it and crouched down to sign it on the floor, while I stood awkwardly above her. When she stood my eyes had adjusted a little more; she was looking me over.

"You will care for him on the journey?" *Vous* again.

"Yes, Madame."

"And have you seen this place? This place where they take care of babies?"

"Oh yes. Yes. I help them feed the babies and so does my friend. It's . . . they're very good people, Madame, they treat them as if they were their own, they'll take good care of—of—"

"His name is Léon," she whispered. I looked at him. Her arms were tight around him. He nuzzled against her in his sleep. I felt a pricking behind my eyes and a tightening in my throat. Her baby. She was about to give me her baby.

If she could.

She lifted her head. "Mademoiselle?"

"Yes?" I whispered. *Mademoiselle.* They kept calling me *Mademoiselle* . . .

"You will take good care of my Léon?"

"I promise you." I meant it from the bottom of me, from that place in my guts where the pulling feeling was beginning again.

She bent her face down and kissed him on the forehead, and whispered to him. I didn't hear what she said. When she lifted her face it was streaming with tears.

Then she handed him to me.

For a moment we looked at each other, me clutching her baby, and neither of us spoke. Then in a flash she was crouching on her bedroll, stuffing things into a ragged pillowcase. Rags, a bottle, a little box of something. She hesitated, then reached into her pocket, and slipped a small flat thing into the bag. It looked like a folded photograph. My guts turned over inside me. A photograph. *To remember her by.*

She stood up and gave me the bundle. There was an urgent light now in her eyes. "You must go, now. You must not miss your ride. Here are his papers. I am glad you can take him. I am so glad. Babies . . . babies don't live, here." She looked at him in my arms and I saw a faint shimmer of tears beginning again. "Go," she whispered. "Go."

I went.

Chapter 5

# Not Glorious

I STEPPED out of the barrack and blinked in the blinding sun and the dust, and the baby in my arms screwed up his little face and began to cry. I turned my body to shade him—too late. My heart was beating hard. I'd made him cry already—she could hear me— *I'm sorry*—I had five minutes to get to the gate. Paquerette was waiting. I walked away fast and jerkily, trying not to see the women staring at me, trying not to look like I was stealing someone's child. The pillowcase bag banged against my legs. Sudden panic stabbed through me, and I checked through my own bag for the papers— the two releases and my pass—*yes*. I gasped with relief.

I was alone here. No one knew me. No one to say, *Oh, Magali, you're so forgetful, bring it next time.*

I approached the block guard, my heart hammering. I handed him the releases and my pass, trying to stand straight like Paquerette, feeling the weakness in my knees. He opened the gate. Out, out to the wide, straight road between the blocks, to the far glimpse of freedom beyond the barbed wire—freedom, that wide, scrubby wasteland with its long low hills. I walked fast along the dusty road, crooning under my breath to Léon, then just trying to catch my breath. There was some kind of crowd ahead at the entrance. The gate was open, and people were streaming in. Armed guards were herding them.

Beyond the fence, a small group of kids stood apart, in a little huddle around a tall woman. Paquerette standing at the mouth of the lion's den, waiting for me.

I almost broke into a run. But there were guard towers behind me, and men in them with guns.

The guard was closing the gate. Someone was shouting.

"Stand still where you are until your name is called!"

The new internees had been herded to the right of the *poste de commande*; they stood holding their bundles, looking around with scared, tired, wary eyes. *Welcome to . . .* Oh, I didn't want to think about it. *What makes people do this? What?* Beyond the gate stood two trucks with high wooden sides. *A transport.* That was what she'd meant.

The guard stood by the gate with his back to me when I reached him. The internees were looking at me. "Uh . . . *excusez-moi, Monsieur?*" My voice came out high, and when he turned around I could see the disbelief in his red eyes. Shame and anger flooded me, and suddenly I wished I had a gun too. Wished I didn't have to stand there and play along with this poisonous game. I swallowed. "Excuse me, Monsieur," I said, and my voice hardly even shook. "I'm with that lady—from the CIMADE. I have a release for this baby. Could, um . . ."

He held out a hand. I gave him the papers, and he leafed through them with one hand while the other held his rifle, keeping one eye on the people in line. He glanced up at me. "They've got kids doing this stuff now?"

I felt my face flush hot. "I'm a lot older than some of the kids you've got in here."

When it was out of my mouth I could not believe I had said it. Standing there with the gate of the camp still closed in front of me. To a man with a gun. I could see the danger growing in his eyes, and it froze my feet to the ground.

He thrust the papers back at me, his eyes hard and cold. "You shouldn't be *touching* them. Now take your Jewish baby and get out."

For a moment I just stood there blinking. *Léon's Jewish?* Then the guard jerked the gate open and gestured at me with his rifle, and I moved. I got out that gate before I could swallow against the anger rising in my throat. Paquerette stood a few feet away, wary eyes on the guard.

"*Merci, Monsieur,*" she said. I stared at her. *Thank you. Yes, thank you for letting* one child *leave your unbelievable pigsty and go to a decent home.* She gave me a sharp frown.

"Get in the truck," she said.

We sat in the truckbed, leaning against the high wooden sides that blocked out everything but the white dust that boiled up over them and the choking black fumes of the *gazogène* engine—one of those charcoal-burning engines that someone came up with when gasoline became worth its weight in blood. I could hardly hear Léon crying above the roar of the motor and the jolting and creaking of the truck. I tried to shield him with my body from the dust. Zvi lay in Paquerette's arms, motionless, his eyes half open. Two black-haired girls and a little boy huddled in the back corner, looking at me with dark eyes. I could see the calluses on the undersides of their dirty bare feet. A boy of maybe ten with matted blond hair sat in the other corner, not looking at anybody. In the front were Hania, Kurt, and Eva. Hania sat slumped and sweating, her head back against the wood with her brown braids hanging down; Kurt and Eva crouched down beside her.

Then Eva stood, holding on to the side of the truck, and let the wind blow in her face and stream her tangled hair back. Kurt stood up too. I caught a glimpse of his face as he did it, and the smile on it made a sudden little joy jump up in me, in spite of everything, and I saw that dusty, wasted plain for a moment the way he must be seeing it: *freedom, freedom, freedom.*

Through the seams between the boards I could see the camp away behind us, the people small as ants again, the barbed wire just a scribble across the low gray blocks of barracks. Rivesaltes. I had been inside it. It was almost hard to believe. I looked and looked at it, that stain on the face of the earth, that rabbit hutch for human beings. But Kurt and Eva didn't look back. Not even once.

WE GOT down out of that banging, roaring truck in the middle of Perpignan, and the silence was loud in my ears. There we were on a street corner among red-roofed, stuccoed houses: a clot of scared, filthy children and teenagers with their eyes on the ground. People were staring. I stared back.

"We have a half-hour's walk to the guesthouse," Paquerette said. "Vladek—you follow me. Magali, you're in charge of the Spanish kids. That's Carmela, this is Manola, and the little one's Adrián. They don't speak French. Watch them closely now." I nodded.

We walked. People stared. Others looked the other way. Hania limped. Eva walked with her eyes on the ground, her tangled hair hanging around her face. The three Spanish kids cast huge, scared eyes around, ready to bolt. I watched them, walking scared. If they ran I didn't know what I'd do. When Paquerette finally stopped at a townhouse door and rang the bell, I was already blinking with weariness.

A black-haired woman in an apron let us in, gave Paquerette the *bise* as if they knew each other, as if ragged, feral children were all in a day's work. Paquerette called her Madame Alençon. She announced that there was hot water, and that we could go straight back to our rooms. Paquerette gripped her hand for a moment, her eyes bright with gratitude; then led us in. We tracked in quite a lot of dirt.

Then, baths.

Paquerette took Léon. I ended up shut in a bathroom with the Spanish kids. Because when I took Adrián the others screamed and wouldn't let him out of their sight. He struggled as I stripped off his filthy shirt. Crusted dirt dropped on the bathmat. I went on ruthlessly. He screamed and struggled again as I picked him up to put him in the tub under the warm shower.

"Can't you help me?" I shouted at his sisters, and they stared back at me with their black eyes. Spoke in Spanish. The boy flailed, flinging dirty water on my face and blouse. "STOP!" I screamed, and he cringed away from me and whimpered. I set him down in the bathtub, my heart banging stupidly in my chest. "I'm just trying to *bathe* you," I whispered, feeling weakness wash over me.

He sat with tears trickling down his face as I worked up a lather in a washcloth and started to soap him down. "It's all right," I murmured, "it's all right." Old sweat and grime was crusted into his skin; it felt like scrubbing a floor. He gave a high scream when I reached his feet. I pulled back; the suds were pink. There were deep cracks in his heels, that had been hidden under the dirt; they'd opened up red and bleeding. I bit my lips, trying to control my breathing, and my wish to hit someone.

It was like three kinds of nightmare all at once. Their poor feet. The sores and scabs on the girls' bodies when they finally stripped down. The way they cried when the water got too hot, and I didn't know what they were crying about. The way they flung dirt around like they didn't see it, and I had to wash their brother's feet again. The way they looked at me like I was the enemy and fought me every step of the way. Pressure built up in my head like steam. When Paquerette finally knocked on the door and passed in the clean donated clothes for them, and they ripped them out of my hands like they thought there wasn't enough for everyone, and the oldest girl ended up with the smallest shirt, and wouldn't let go of it, I was within a heartbeat of slapping her face. I grabbed both her poor, bony wrists in one hand and held them hard, and I got up in her face and said, "Let. Go." And the fear in that child's eyes; I still remember it.

Finally they were dressed, and I was leaning against the gritty, filthy tub with a vague, awful feeling that I was supposed to wash it now; then a knock, and Paquerette's voice.

"Magali? Do you feel up to feeding Léon?"

I FED Léon. There was no way, on my first day, that I was going to let Paquerette see me fold.

I couldn't focus. My mind drifted like a person half asleep, stumbling in the road. When Madame Alençon called us all to supper I stayed where I was, mechanically jiggling Léon awake to drink a little more.

"Magali?" said Paquerette. I looked up, and suddenly realized I'd never eaten lunch.

I wolfed down Madame Alençon's thick, spicy bean soup, but the Rivesaltes kids ate like refugees: even faster. They drank their soup in long, hard gulps; didn't touch their silverware, didn't put anything down on their plates. The little ones took two pieces each from the bread basket, one for each hand. Then two more.

After supper I tucked the Spanish kids in bed, wet matted hair on their pillows. Adrián cried for Mama; the others started to cry too. *Sh, sh, it's all right, your Mama is coming soon.* I couldn't say it. I can't lie to kids, even in a language they don't speak. *Sh, sh, I* whispered. *You're safe now.*

The next thing I remember is jerking awake. I'd nodded off over the crying kids. I'm sorry; I really had. Manola was dry-sobbing now, quietly, and Adrián was asleep. With the last of my strength I stood, and slipped into my own bed, by Léon. I don't even remember my head touching the pillow.

I WOKE up with a jerk. Léon was crying. It was dead dark. He wailed and whimpered. No one else woke. I had to stumble around in the dark for the baby-bottle bag. Then creep down and find the kitchen, and boil the bottle and mix the formula, which I'd never done, and then he kept on sniveling and wouldn't suck. I banged the bottle down on the counter and started to cry. He wailed. I got a whiff from his stinky diaper and pinched my own arm, savagely, for being so stupid.

So it was back up to find the diapers, and then changing him on a bathroom floor, with a headache starting up like an ice-pick through my temples. And then he still wouldn't sleep, so I gave him the bottle, and then time to burp him, and he didn't know how, just like Grigory, and after a while I started crying again, a little. When he finally calmed down I went back to bed and took him with me, but I couldn't sleep. I lay awake with my head pounding and in less than an hour I saw the sky outside the window begin to pale with dawn. A few minutes after that, I heard a whisper from Paquerette's bed.

"Ready to face the day?"

I swallowed. "Ready," I breathed.

KIDS NEEDING this, kids needing that. Kids sneaking bread into their pockets from the breakfast table, while I barely had time to take a bite. Kids needing the bathroom in a language I didn't speak, halfway to the train station. Léon starting to cry again while I was in charge of the group and Paquerette was off buying train tickets. Zvi never crying at all.

You'd think sitting on a train would be the easy part of the trip, but there's this about kids, ex-internees or not: they don't *sit*. So it was Paquerette running down the train aisle after Carmela, or me finding Adrián hiding under his seat; it was one thing and another, for hours, and Léon crying, needing to be fed, needing to be changed in the cramped, smelly train bathroom where if

you lifted the toilet lid you could see the tracks racing by underneath. I'd do everything I could think of for him and still he'd cry,
his little face screwed-up and red, like a living, breathing proof of
my incompetence. When Paquerette got out bread and cheese for
lunch, I was walking the aisle with him, over and over. So I ate
mine Rivesaltes-style like the others: grip it tight in one hand and
gnaw.

When Léon finally fell asleep, Adrián and Manola were asleep,
too, and finally the train car was quiet. I rested my head against
my seat and let my exhausted mind drift.

"Magali?" A whisper. I opened my eyes. It was Eva, her hair
washed and combed now, her eyes still red. "I wanted to ask you.
You live in Tanieux?"

I nodded.

"Where did you come from, before that?"

"Paris."

"Oh." She hesitated. "And . . . before that?"

"Nowhere. I was born in Paris."

"Oh! I'm sorry." She looked down. "I'm sorry," she repeated,
kind of intensely, her face expressionless. "I thought . . . you look
Italian."

"Well I am. Half. My mother came from there after the war. You
don't have to be sorry."

She looked up at me, looking like she didn't believe what I'd
said. "Really you are not angry?" she asked kind of flatly. "That I
thought you were a refugee?"

"No. Why would I be?"

She shrugged, and her eyes turned down again. "I probably
would be," she said.

I stared at her. In my arms Léon woke, and started bawling.

LÉON FUSSING, Léon crying, Carmela and Manola screaming at
each other and needing to be separated; people turning their

heads and muttering about us; us ragtag refugees, disturbing the peace. Paquerette trying to feed Zvi, who sucked weakly and didn't open his eyes; the lines in her face growing worried and strained. Paquerette looking at her watch every time we pulled into a station. Finally she leaned over to me.

"Magali, our connection in Avignon is going to be very, very tight." She'd explained this to me: we had to switch from the express to a train that made local stops, to be able to get off at la Voulte. If we couldn't get the local in time to catch *la Galoche*, it meant an extra night and more travel: continuing north to Valence where there were people who'd put us up, and doubling back down to la Voulte on the next day's local. "If we miss this one, we're spending the night in Valence. I'll need your best efforts."

I nodded. The motion brought back a twinge of yesterday's headache. "Yes, Paquerette."

I organized. I put Eva in charge of Carmela and Adrián. I was ready. We had to walk down along the train we'd gotten off and cross the tracks behind it to get to the platform we needed. Everyone was together, we were speed-walking. A train whistle sounded. We broke into a jog. Kurt caught his leg on his suitcase and stumbled. I saw it all happen as if in slow motion.

Kurt stumbled. Hania, leaning on him, lurched, her white face scared, her hand opening to break her fall. Eva let go of the kids and caught her.

And Adrián took to his heels, off across the platform, his little legs pumping like pistons.

There's this thing that happens to me. That's the moment I found out about it for sure.

It's like a different mind inside me, a new person who takes over. She has all this energy. She knows what to do. I felt fear flash through my body; and suddenly she was there.

"Take her!" I yelled to Paquerette, shoving Manola's hand into hers. Because that was what it said to do, the instinct; then I had

Léon pressed against my shoulder with one hand and I was running faster than I thought I could run. Adrián was half a meter from the edge when I caught him by the wrist and lifted him clean off the ground, swinging him back behind the painted danger line to safety. He screamed. I stood gripping his wrist and panting, my heart hammering. The wheels on the train began to churn.

I caught up the screaming Adrián onto my hip and walked back to the group, light-headed, as the train we'd come in on whistled and began to pull past us. We could see the other platform now, and the local train to la Voulte, pulling out too.

Paquerette's face was pale. "Good work, Magali," she said in a strangled voice. "Let's all sit down."

WE TOOK the next express north, and got off at Valence, and walked our desperate little band to a place Paquerette knew, an office where two ladies ran an agency to help war widows. They laid out thin mattresses for us on their office floor and made us tea in their tiny kitchen for us to drink with the loaf of bread Paquerette had bought on the way. We sat cross-legged on our mattresses and ate and drank Rivesaltes-style. I changed and fed Léon. I don't remember anything else, really, but clean sheets, and sinking like a stone into sleep.

In the dead of night, someone crawled into my bed, jolting me awake. It was Adrián, and he was crying. I rubbed his back, and after a long time he fell asleep. After a much longer time, I did too. Léon woke me at dawn, and I changed and fed him. When we set out for the station, my head felt heavy, and my eyes burned. Strange, bad feelings washed through my body, deeper than a muscle ache, as if my bones were groaning: *you need to stop.*

Someone lost the bag of baby bottles. We never found out who. Léon cried his lungs out from le Cheylard all the way up the Eyrieux gorge, as the train puffed and labored her slow, slow way up the incline, and nice farmers' wives leaned over to give me free advice on babies, and I tried not to scream. Then, finally, Saint-Agrève—*la Galoche* picking up to a decent speed—every minute like an hour as we drew closer. And then the familiar curves of the hills around Tanieux—that ridge you go past before the town appears—the houses!—our house, I could see our house, my bed, my own bed without any crying kids who needed me, oh please . . . and the station and Monsieur Bernard in his kepi and I'd never have believed I'd be so glad to see his face—and Mama, Mama!—her face lit up with joy, looking at me from the platform, and Rosa and Nina with her.

And getting the children out—one last headcount, all of them off the train—all three Spanish kids were there, thank God . . .

"Rosa!" I'd never been so glad to see her in my life. "Rosa, these kids, will you take them, they're from Spain, just *don't let them out of your sight!*" and I heard her voice speaking Spanish and felt the weight lift off my shoulders, turned blindly, and shoved the baby at Eva. She took him.

And then I flung myself into Mama's arms and cried.

*Chapter 6*

# No Promises

I *REALLY* shouldn't have done that.

For one thing I had turned into a huge sobbing mess and my work wasn't even done. I still had a baby to hand over. But worse than that, Mama started to cry on *me* too.

She didn't sob or anything. She just held me tight and did that weepy, silent crying, murmuring my name. She swayed us both back and forth. I couldn't move my arms. My head was pinned against her shoulder. I finally got my hands against her and wrenched myself loose.

My head hurt and my throat hurt and my heart hurt, and it wasn't quitting time. Mama's eyes were red and had dark circles under them, and her cheeks were shiny with tears. Everyone was staring at us, everyone, even Monsieur Bernard. Léon was still crying. I turned back to Eva, and I took him.

"I promised his mother I'd get him to Madame Sabatier," I said.

Mama smiled at me through her tears.

NINA TOOK Kurt and Eva and Hania. Rosa took the Spanish kids. Paquerette and I carried Léon and Zvi to l'Espoir, and Mama walked beside us until the Rue Chambert, and then stopped and said, "I'm sorry, Magali—I need to meet you at home. You'll come home?"

"Sure."

She hugged me again, long, till I couldn't breathe. Then she left us. Paquerette and I walked in silence. She looked as wasted as I felt, and I felt *terrible*. Like a headache through my whole body. Like I'd never feel okay again.

We gave the babies to Madame Sabatier. She fussed much more over Zvi than Léon, and asked Paquerette questions about his eating and his stools. I gave Léon to Madeleine and sank down on the couch, looking blurrily into the fire. *I kept my promise, Madame . . . Suzanne . . . whoever you are . . .*

"Magali. Will you come over and see me tomorrow?" said Paquerette. "Afternoon," she added, rubbing her face. "It was a hard one."

I looked at her. "Yeah," I said.

I WALKED home slowly, breathing the clear Tanieux air deep into my lungs. Alone. No one hungry, no one crying, no one running into the path of a train. Just me, with the dust of Rivesaltes still on my skin. I was going to go home and take a shower. But lunch first. I could eat a horse. And then I'd go to bed, my own bed. And then at supper I'd tell them all about it. I imagined the pride in Papa's eyes.

I walked up the stone stairs, imagining all that, but my bed most of all. I opened the door and walked in.

The house was quiet. There was a sickly burnt smell to the place, like charred flesh. The floor was gritty with dust and the fireplace was full of ashes. On the table there were two dirty plates, and a clean one with two pieces of bread on it, and a piece of cheese.

The smell came from the kitchen. The gray food spills on the counter looked like nothing anyone would eat even in Rivesaltes. Our biggest stewpot sat in the sink with black crusty things floating in it. Also beans. I reached into the cold, slimy, ashy water and felt one. It was rock-hard.

"What *happened* here?" I said out loud. I stepped out into the dining room. "Mama?" No answer. Muffled voices from the bedroom. I stood there, the past springing up vivid in my mind: Mama and Papa shut up in the bedroom at mealtime, and me left alone. The day Hitler invaded Poland.

Papa came out, and shut the door carefully. He beamed at me. "Magali," he said. "I'm so glad you're home." He glanced back at the bedroom door and quit beaming. "Your mother has a headache."

I blinked. "So do I."

He frowned. "She's had it since you left."

I stood there for a moment in the filthy kitchen, looking at my father. "Well. I'm back."

"I was wondering, Magali, if, uh . . . if you might be willing . . ." He made this little gesture, with his hand. Sort of gesturing around. At the kitchen.

There was a hollow echoing feeling in my head. No. *No.* He must have seen it on my face—he started to frown again—and I shattered like a hand-grenade.

*"Do you have any idea where I've been?"* I screamed it. It might have woken the dead.

"Magali! *Quiet!*"

"*No! No!*" I started to sob. I hate it. I *hate* crying when I'm angry. "I just got home from *Rivesaltes* and you want me to clean up your mess? No!"

He grabbed my arm. "Magali, be quiet and listen to me! Your mother is in—"

I yanked my arm back from him. I was sobbing so hard now I couldn't have yelled again if I'd tried. My chest hurt so bad

and my head was killing me. "You . . . you . . ." I couldn't finish my sentence. I turned and ran out the stairwell door and
slammed it shut behind me. I flew up the steps and down the
upstairs hallway; Benjamin jumped back as I almost ran into
him. I slammed my own door behind me and threw myself on
the bed and cried.

I DON'T know how long I cried. At some point I must have fallen
asleep. The next thing I remember is waking up in the dark,
hearing a soft voice by my ear. "Magali?" It was Papa. My eyes
felt crusty and my body felt even worse than before. Aching and
heavy. "Mmm," I mumbled.

"Are you hungry?"

I didn't feel like I had the strength to sit up, but I *was* hungry.
Always. "Mm." I didn't think I could get down the stairs.

"Is it all right if I turn the light on?"

"Mm." I managed to pull myself up to a sitting position. A white
flood of light stabbed my eyes and I closed them. I blinked, and
blinked, and finally looked around.

There was a tray on the desk. The same bread and cheese and a
glass of goat milk. My *father* had brought me food. In *bed.*

"Wha—where—"

"Your mother's still in bed. She has a migraine headache,
Magali. It's very, very bad. She's in a lot of pain. She's spent most
of her time in bed for several days."

She'd seemed all right. Except for the whole crying thing. I took
a big bite of bread so I wouldn't have to say anything. It was good.

"I wasn't going to ask you to clean the kitchen, Magali." He took
a breath. "I was going to ask you to make supper. You should not
have shouted at me, Magali, especially after I had told you your
mother had a headache. But"—he held up a hand—"I also wish
that I had not asked you to do work right as soon as you got home
from Rivesaltes. I imagine it was a, ah—difficult journey?"

I nodded. I could still hear Léon's crying in my head. I could hear my own scream, too. I could see the barbed wire and the face of the guard with the gun when I'd sassed him. I felt the tears starting to come back.

He turned away. "So I'm sorry I asked you to do that," he said, looking at my desk. "I'll admit to you, I was desperate. But you deserved some rest. I hope you slept well. I wasn't sure about waking you, but I thought you might need to eat."

I nodded. The tears were calming back down. "You, uh . . . did you have bread for lunch too?"

He nodded.

"What did you eat while I was gone?"

He got the funniest look on his face. "Magali . . . I think you saw what we ate. Wasn't the pot still in the sink . . . ?"

"You ate that stuff?"

"We couldn't waste food."

"What was it, anyway?"

"Stew. We boiled some water and put in potatoes and carrots. And then, uh, beans."

"You mean dry beans? *After* the potatoes and carrots?"

"Well, yes, as a matter of fact."

"Did you soak them or anything?"

"Well, no."

I gaped at him. *Men.* "Wow," I said slowly. "Is Mama . . . d'you think she'll get better?"

"I don't know, Magali. She . . . she used to get headaches when I met her, but she hasn't had them in years and I've never seen it this bad. I was counting on her feeling better when you came back. And then . . ." He shrugged sort of helplessly. He looked different, somehow, from usual. Like he didn't know everything after all. I couldn't really remember him ever apologizing to me before.

"I'm sorry I yelled, Papa. I didn't know."

"It's all right, Magali." He put his hand on mine and squeezed a little. Then he picked up the tray with the empty plate on it. "How do you feel? Think you'll be able to go back to sleep?"

"Yeah. I guess."

He shut the door carefully as he went out, almost as carefully as he had with Mama.

It was nice, Papa apologizing. It was especially nice given that Mama was still not out of bed at six o'clock, and he came up to knock softly on my door and ask if I had any ideas for supper. I'd taken a bath by then, and I felt a little better, but not much. I opened the door and just stood there and looked at him, and he added that just telling him what to do would work. I told him how to stew lentils, which have the advantage of not needing to soak for twenty-four hours. He thanked me.

Nothing in my body or my head felt all right until I woke, slowly, the next morning, with light pouring in my window. No one had woken me. That *was* nice.

When I came down there was bread and lukewarm mint tea waiting for me at the table and Dr. Reynaud was in the bedroom with Mama and Papa. Apparently the verdict was that yes, it was a severe migraine headache, and had any new source of stress come into Mama's life lately?

In other words: it was my fault.

Nobody said that. Not *exactly*. Papa just told Dr. Reynaud yes and then started asking him all these questions, and went around looking down in the mouth for an hour afterward.

It didn't make sense. She hadn't gotten migraines when we thought the Germans were going to show up on our doorstep with tanks. Obviously she was scared, she measured me for a hole in the attic and all, but she never quit *cooking*. She scrubbed under the stove for Pete's sake, she acted like work was the only thing that could save her.

But I go on a legal, supervised visit to an internment camp and *pow*. She's in bed pale as a sheet with pain lines and her eyes shut tight like the light burns them . . . I just couldn't understand it.

So Papa asked me to make lunch, and I made it. Theoretically, I guess, it was the least I could do. And if you think cooking is hard, try cooking with this: Beans. Lentils. Potatoes. A handful of onions and garlic. And a few canned tomatoes from last summer, and wrinkly turnips and carrots, and dried thyme and rosemary. That's it. Goat milk and butter? Those are for Sunday dinner.

Well, I made lentil and tomato soup. You should have *seen* the looks on those guys' faces when I served it up. They all said I was amazing, and how grateful they were that I was back. I noticed that, actually. They thanked me for being back. Not for cooking.

Men are so funny. I think they think we're magic. We make good food appear on the table and—poof—make the house all clean, in some mysterious way, just by being women. I know it sounds dumb, but that's really how they act. It's just work! That's all it is! And of course they talk like they could never learn how to do it in a million years, and then, in the same breath, like their work is *way* more important. Well. At least they weren't talking like *that* today.

Mama came out of her room to eat lunch. She smiled at me a lot, but the pain lines didn't go away. She asked me about the trip. I made sure to tell her I'd just cried because I was so tired. I told her about Léon's mother giving him to me, and her eyes filled with tears. Within another minute she closed them like it just hurt too much, and Papa helped her back to the bedroom.

After lunch I went down to see Paquerette.

There was a fire in the fireplace at l'Espoir, and the babies were sleeping. Paquerette sat on the sofa with a cup of tea in her hands, and smiled at me as I came over to give her the *bise*. "Sit down," she said, patting the sofa. "And tell me how your first trip was." My heart skipped a beat on the word *first*.

"Oh," I said, not even thinking about whether it was truth or lie, "all right."

Paquerette's eyebrows rose. "*Really.*"

I sat. We talked, or maybe I talked. We said all the things we hadn't had time to say to each other. About the camp, about Marylise, and Léon's mother. About Madame Alençon, and bathing the Spanish kids, and how hard it was when the kids didn't speak French. I told her how Adrián had gotten in bed with me. She sobered.

"You showed quick thinking, Magali, there on the platform at la Voulte. That was *very* well done."

Something warmed in me. Deeper than praise. The eyes of Joan of Arc, saying *I choose you, you're just what I need.*

"Thanks," I whispered.

She nodded, and looked into the fire for a moment. "What did you say to the guard at the gate?" she asked abruptly.

"Um. I . . ." I swallowed. You don't pretend to Joan of Arc that you don't know what she means. When you do. "He called me a kid, and I said I was older than a lot of the kids in the camp."

"Is that exactly what you said, Magali?"

"Uh, I . . . I think I said 'the kids you've got in this camp.'"

"Mmm." Paquerette's lips thinned. "And you said this why?"

"I'm sorry."

She looked into the fire and drew a breath. "Magali, that was a very dangerous thing you did." She shook her head. "God in heaven knows we have reasons to be angry. But we are not in the business of satisfying our anger. We are getting children to safety and that is the *only* priority." She turned and looked me in the eye. "Magali, I need you to learn this: you never try to have the last word with a man holding a gun."

"Yes, Paquerette."

"If you're ever going to travel with me again, I need you to promise me that you will never show defiance to anyone in power. No matter how contemptible they are, you will follow my lead, act polite, act submissive if you have to and then you get out of there with the children we came to save. Promise me this."

I looked up at her eyes—firelight on steel. "I promise," I whispered.

She gave me a firm nod. "As long as you can do that," she said quietly, "you'll do well. Now, there was one more thing I wanted to ask you about. How did your parents respond, when you came home?"

I swallowed and opened my mouth to answer. My stomach tied up in a knot.

"MAGALI?" SAID Papa. "Can I talk to you for a minute?"

Mama was down again. She'd had two good days and I'd thought it was over, I'd prayed it was over. And now it was back. Papa was beckoning me into his study for, I supposed, a Talk.

"Your mother's having a difficult time, Magali," he informed me as I sat down on one of his straight-backed chairs. *You think so?* "We may need to do some thinking about this."

I just nodded. You don't interrupt Papa when he's starting a speech, even if he says *we*.

"I know how important it feels to you to do important work in the outside world. And Paquerette has informed me that you've proven yourself very competent at it." My heart started beating faster. I didn't quite dare look at him.

Then he said "but."

"But there's an order to the maturing process, Magali. An adult is someone who does what needs to be done, even when they don't want to, and doing what needs to be done for your family is where that starts. It's how you prove that you are ready to do greater things. And"—he glanced away and sighed—"it looks as though you may have a real chance to mature here."

"Yeah?"

"Yes, Magali. Dr. Reynaud says migraines are very unpredictable, but even on his first visit he didn't think it likely that this would just go away. We may need to make some, ah, adjustments to our life. Magali, I want you to know I don't blame you for any of this. You couldn't have known."

I sat back and stared at him, my stomach churning. He didn't *blame* me? He was about to ask *me* to make "adjustments," not himself. But at least he was generous enough not to *blame* me.

"But I do think I have the right to ask for your help."

I started to read the titles of the books behind his head. *Watch it, Magali. Do not try to have the last word.* I breathed slowly, carefully.

"So I am asking, Magali, from now until you take your *troisième-*year exams, that you be an adult. I know it's a lot to ask. But you need to pass your exams, and your mother needs your help very much, and together those add up to adult-sized responsibilities." From now until the exams. Until school let out. I stared at those books, seeing it all with a hard, hot clarity: this was a test. If I passed . . . when school let out . . .

"So I'm asking that as well as studying as hard as you can, you also take responsibility for the essentials of your mother's work when she's not able to. I will make sure you have help, but you will be the one with the responsibility and that is always difficult. It's a difficult time for all of us. But I believe you can do it. I believe you have the makings of a very mature young woman." *And if you prove me right, I'll know that you are ready for "greater things."* He didn't say it. But I heard it.

Loud and clear.

Promises to parents can be cheap. As a kid I used to make them by the dozen. Yes, I'd do the dishes right away, I'd get my homework done, yes, I'd come home from Julie's house as soon as the church bells rang six. It doesn't matter how hard or how often you promise. What matters is what you *do*.

I was making no promises today. But I was going to travel with

Paquerette. And to that end, from now until the exams, I was going to be an adult.

"I'll do my best," I said quietly, looking my father in the eye. And my new life began.

I HAD never worked so hard in my life, or for so little reward.

Papa gave me his alarm clock. He said he didn't need it, that he woke at six out of habit, and maybe I'd learn too. I tried not to think about that as I wound the clock. Then I saw Paquerette's face as she shook me awake in the train station. *Paquerette can do that.*

Maybe I'd learn.

I learned to flip out of bed the moment it rang, run downstairs, and check on Mama. I learned how cold it is in our house before someone lays a fire in the fireplace. I learned to lay a supply of wood and kindling on the hearth every night; two trips down the icy stairs in my fraying slippers at dawn were enough.

I learned harder things. How to go back up to my room—if it turned out Mama was down there putting water on the kitchen stove and singing—and wrap my blanket around myself and get out my trigonometry and spend the hour between six and seven trying to understand what a cosine was. I'd never have done it for anything less. I'd never have thought that I *could* do it. But I did.

I learned to light the kitchen stove fire and have fake coffee and tea ready when Papa came home with the bread. I learned to think ahead and lay out my lunch ingredients ready for when I came home from school. I learned to put beans in to soak every evening. I learned to make big pots of soup that I could reheat at noon on a roaring fire and not have to wait for coals. I learned to throw down my school bag and build a fire, light-headed with hunger—quick, stoke the fire, put the soup pot on, set the table. Snap at Julien when he asks what time lunch is and set him to slicing bread. Get the stuff dished up and bring it out to where the guys are waiting,

and Mama with her pale face, saying in a weak voice that this is
the best soup she ever tasted. Which is ridiculous, really. Nothing
can be the best soup you ever tasted if it doesn't contain bacon.

I learned what it means to be tied down.

I'd never understood it before. The difference between being
someone who stands in the kitchen and peels what they're told
to peel and doesn't have to think about it, and being the person
who has to think about it all day. Who flubs questions in history
class because she just realized she forgot to put the beans in to
soak. The one who has to run straight home after school to get
supper on the stove. Making crazy jokes with Lucy, or sitting on
the café stools with Rosa kicking our feet against the bar and talking about nothing—those were as long gone now as the free hot
chocolate Madame Santoro used to give us before the war. I saw
Rosa at l'Espoir. I saw Lucy at school. She said I was taking this a
little far. "I cook for Auntie every day and that doesn't mean I can't
ever see my friends!"

I shoved my hands into my pockets. "If you'd come to l'Espoir
you'd see me."

"Magali, you do not want to see me try to hold a baby. It's a terrifying sight. I plan to do the world a favor and not have any kids."

I laughed. Then I sighed. I turned to her, and opened my mouth.
I almost said, *Let's go study at your place tonight.* In my mind I saw
the two of us sitting cross-legged on her lumpy eiderdown with her
cheerful clutter of books and clothes around us, laughing our heads
off. I thought of Rivesaltes, and Paquerette's eyes when she'd said
*very well done.* I said nothing.

There were worse things. I couldn't meet the train, either.

I'd walk out of the kitchen where I was boiling beans for supper,
and I'd stand at the south window and look down over the town,
and see the white steam rising in the air where *la Galoche* was pulling into the station. I'd close my eyes, take a deep breath, and walk
back to the kitchen. And buckle down hard on my homework at

the kitchen table, so after supper I'd have time to go to l'Espoir and find out whether Paquerette came in.

I didn't see the kids she brought. Only the babies. Léon was gaining weight. Zvi too, but he still had a sleepy look about him, and they worried. I sat on the couch by Rosa—her feeding Zvi, me feeding Léon, smelling the top of his little head. Babies weren't so bad. I held him against my chest and remembered his mother, the tears streaming down her face, and my promise. *I'll take care of your baby.* I had. I'd gotten him safe home. I wanted to do it again, I wanted it so bad I could feel it in my body, in that place in my guts I hadn't known existed before this year. I wanted to save as many as I could.

When they were all asleep I would walk home across the *place du centre* and up my dark street and push open the heavy door of my house, thinking of my bed and my pillow, thinking of Paquerette bedding down on the stone floor of a train station somewhere, ready to wake at dawn, like a hunter, like a soldier; wanting nothing more than to do that with her, to become like her. Knowing this was the way there. Like a hunter, like a soldier; a person who does what she has to do.

And then I went up the cold stone stairs to my bed, so I could wake the next morning at dawn, and do it all again.

MAMA WAS better. She sang Verdi in the kitchen while she did the dishes. Then Mama was worse again, only strong enough to give me a pale smile and chop onions while I cooked. The days blurred together. They seemed less and less different from each other, her good days and her bad days. I came down in the morning and she'd be sitting at the table, reading her Bible. She'd look up and smile, and say, "I'm so glad you're up, would you mind starting the stove fire?"

Lucy came to school one day and didn't smile, didn't talk. At break she took me off to the riverbank and told me she was moving to America.

"*What?*"

"My father wants me to live with him now. He already paid for my visa. Without asking me."

"*America.*" I blinked. "Lots of people would kill for a visa to America."

"Well they're welcome to it." She turned to me and I saw her eyes were red. "He bought me passage on a boat. In August. He didn't even ask me!" Her voice cracked and tears welled up in her eyes.

*August.* Somewhere deep in my stomach I felt like I was falling. I was losing it all, leaving it all behind. Lucy, and laughter, and feeling free. "I'm sorry," I whispered. "I'll miss you."

She looked down, and kicked at the frosted grass.

I was leaving it all behind. Becoming a person who shut up, who'd learned to do what I had to do and not think about what I wanted.

Who worried about money.

The first time Papa put our family's money and ration cards in my hands, I was terrified. I couldn't believe he was doing it. I mean it's one thing for your parents to send you to buy something they don't know the price of in peacetime. This was something else.

"You sure, Papa?"

"I think you can do it, Magali. You're doing very well." There was pride in his eyes. Good sign.

I learned *real* math. I stood in the grocery store and calculated over and over till I was sure I was right: how much did we have for the month, what weight of beans did we need, would we be able to afford milk from Monsieur Rostin this week. If we could just make it till spring really got going, Grandpa would have eggs for us again. There'd be greens, and then summer would come on and there'd be tomatoes and cucumbers and carrots and fresh potatoes, I'd make spaghetti sauce—

No. No. *Mama* would make spaghetti sauce.

Because Mama would be better by then. She'd make spaghetti sauce and she'd garden and cook while I traveled with Paquerette and saved children. Maybe I'd still have to help her a little. I'd quit Scouts so I'd have enough time. Yes. That was how it would be. There was a high whine in my head like a radio tuned wrong. Wrong, wrong.

I couldn't picture it. I couldn't.

The buds came out on the trees. I worked; I studied. I put my winter boots away and got out my summer shoes and a week later they started to break, the leather cracking around my big toes on both sides. Papa didn't say anything and I didn't either. I knew how much shoes cost now.

Mama got better and got worse again. The new green grass began to show beside the roads. At the end of May I turned sixteen. Mama bought some goat meat from Monsieur Rostin, but I had to cook it myself. I boiled it tender and saved the broth carefully for soup. My present was a pair of shoes Grandpa had made, with canvas uppers and wooden soles. They gave me blisters.

At home no one mentioned Paquerette, ever. I fed Léon, and Rosa fed Zvi, and I looked at his half-closed eyes and remembered how hungry we were during the invasion, that tired-blood feeling, and thought I knew how he felt. I saw Paquerette, when she happened to be there. I asked about her trips. I could almost smell the dust of Rivesaltes on her skin. That high gate, that wind. I wanted to walk in that gate again and save whoever I could save. I wanted it so much it hurt.

She asked me, a couple of times, whether my parents had said anything about the summer. I said no.

"But do you think they're still thinking about it? That they're still open?"

The words stuck in my throat. I couldn't lie to Paquerette. "I don't know."

There was acceptance in her eyes. Quiet, practical acceptance. They slid off me; I could read her thought: *I wonder if there's anyone else I could ask.*

It hurt so bad.

*Chapter 7*

# Everyone Has Her Child

THAT WAS the year I figured out why people write poetry about spring.

Two words: warmth and food.

A wind that doesn't try to knife you. The sun on your skin, like the world becoming kind again. You could almost forget we were at war.

The first mess of dandelion greens Julien brought me. I would've turned up my nose, back in Paris. Now I tossed them with vinaigrette. New grass came up in the pastures. The price of goat milk went down. Julien set snares in the hills, and promised me a rabbit. I hugged him.

The last of the ice melted off the banks of the Tanne, and the river rose. The birds all twittered madly in the trees. The apple blossoms opened. My feet didn't hurt anymore in my wooden-soled shoes. Mama had a whole week with no headaches. I met Paquerette at the train.

It had just rained, and the sun was shining, and Nina's crutches clicked on the wet pavement; Rosa squeezed my hand, and Sonia, who'd started meeting the train with them, smiled shyly at us as we walked together. Tall white clouds raced through the blue sky just as fast as my heart wanted to go, and I watched them, and remembered the cold nights walking home from l'Espoir, and without even thinking about it I prayed. *Oh let this be my life.*

Every morning I got up and came down, and there was Mama, sitting in the slanted morning sunlight reading her Bible. Every time I saw her there, something loosened deep inside me, like the crusts of ice at the edges of the river, melting in the sun.

It was hard to believe. I had to work at it. I kept bracing for the bad day—and it came. One here, two there. But then it was gone again. As if she'd relaxed, now. As if I had done whatever it was she needed. I didn't feel a fist gripping the center of my chest anymore when I woke in the morning wondering what I'd find downstairs. Day after day, what I found was her, sitting with her Bible in the morning sunlight, looking up, when I opened the door, with a peaceful face. Those dark cold mornings laying the fire by myself were gone. Now the sun came up early, now the chill was off the air. The young leaves were all unfolding, and the grass was green right down to the riverbank when I came out the barn door of my classroom on break and stood there with Lucy in the soft warm air, talking and laughing. Like normal people. It was the most amazing feeling.

Hope.

My grades were good. I raised my hand in history class and gave Papa the right answer, just to see his eyebrows go up like that again. I stood in the kitchen and chopped green onions and washed young lettuce for my mother while she cooked—my mother who had put the beans in to soak yesterday and done everybody's laundry and who was singing *Rigoletto* and whom I'd honestly never appreciated enough. I went down to l'Espoir and told Paquerette maybe I'd been wrong. Just to see her eyes light up.

At the end of June the Germans invaded the USSR. My father stared at the radio like he literally believed he might have gone crazy. They used to have a treaty, see, swearing not to attack each other. Hitler seems to be the backstabbing type.

And then Papa started to laugh like it was the best joke ever.

"Papa?"

He took out his handkerchief and wiped his face. Took a couple of breaths and then shook his head, sobering up. "I'm sorry. I really should not laugh about the invasion of a country—I'm sorry. Apparently I'm a little far gone." But his lips twisted upward a little. "Still," he said, "those who fail to learn from history are doomed to repeat it."

"Napoleon," said Julien.

"Yes indeed." He looked at me. "You know what he means, Magali?"

I managed not to sigh. *I'm a good student too now, remember?* "Napoleon invaded Russia too."

His odd smile widened. "He did indeed, *ma chère Lili*. It was a very serious mistake. In fact it's widely considered"—he was grinning now—"to be the mistake that brought him down."

See?

Hope. Everywhere.

I took my exams. All day answering word problems and essay questions in a big room, dead-quiet except for the scratching of pens. It was hard. But I'd done the work. I wasn't winning any prizes, but I walked out the door without a single reasonable doubt that I had passed.

It was one of those completely glorious June days, with high white clouds hanging in the baby-blue sky and the warm soft wind in your face and feeling like you could just spread your wings and fly up into it. It was almost five when they let us out, and the sunlight glittered blindingly on the river as I walked along it toward the Bellevue Hotel, where Papa taught seventh-hour history to the *sixièmes*. I could walk home with him. I could *tell* him. I was done, done, done, *I had done it.* There was no better feeling in the whole world. Except the feeling I was waiting for.

*Yes, Magali, you can do it. You can go save children.*

Papa came out, ran his hand through his hair and gave a huge sigh. "Well, Magali," he said. "You're done! Headed home?"

I nodded. We fell into step together, up the sloping street. I was trying to decide if I could wait till the grades came in, or if it was stupid to go for it now.

"So, Magali, how do you feel it went for you?"

I never was good at waiting. "I passed." I said it with the certainty I felt. "I didn't get top grades," I added so he knew I wasn't just being arrogant, "but I passed."

He smiled at me. "Well, that sounds like the assessment of a level-headed young lady."

I grinned. "So, Papa. Think I did it?"

"Did it?"

"You know. What you asked."

It took him a moment. Then his eyebrows went up. "Oh! When I asked you to take on responsibility at home? Yes, you *have* done it. You've done very well—better than I imagined, to be honest."

"So . . ." I wished he'd bring it up on his own. "So what have you decided?"

"Decided?"

"About . . . about my traveling with Paquerette?"

There was a pause and my heart began to quicken. I looked at him; his face was clouding. My fingers clenched, suddenly, like they held some hard-earned coin I couldn't afford to lose.

"We . . . we haven't discussed it, Magali. I . . . I . . . well . . . I . . ."

"You what?" My voice cracked.

We'd both stopped on the sidewalk by now. He stood there and swallowed. About three times. And didn't speak.

"We had a deal, Papa. Remember? We had a deal? I'd be an adult—prove I was ready for . . . greater things?"

He stared at me. His face had fallen completely; there was no expression on it. "That," he said very slowly, "was why you helped your mother? Because you thought I had made it a condition of . . . of . . ."

I could feel it slipping through my fingers. My hard-earned hope. Another second and it would go spinning down into the dark. I swallowed and blinked hard. "I did it. You said I did it." My voice was almost normal. The June sun hurt my eyes.

"And here I thought . . ." He ran a hand through his hair. He didn't speak for a few seconds. "Magali," he said finally, quietly, "I am very sorry and very surprised to find that I gave you the impression we were making a deal. It was not my intention. I don't even remember whatever I may have said about proving your readiness for greater things, but whatever it was, I meant it in a general sense, Magali. I thought you had taken it that way." He looked at me, his eyes wide, and after a moment ran his hand through his hair again. "It seems to have been rather careless of me. I suppose I ought to have known."

I took a breath. *Rather careless? You ruined my life and you think you were*— I shut my mouth. *Mature. I. Am. Mature.* I took another breath and stood straighter, and looked him in the eye. "Even if you meant it in a general sense, Papa, it's true. I did an adult's work and I know what that's like now. I'm ready."

Those eyebrows went up again. And down. He looked away, somewhere off behind me, as he spoke. "No doubt you are, Magali. But it was never my decision."

And that was it. I felt it drop from my numb fingers. What does hope look like? Some little blown-glass thing, all see-through, hardly even there. It shatters on the pavement, and no one but you hears the tiny sound.

I could barely get the word past my lips. "Mama?"

"I'm sorry, Magali."

I stood blinking in that horrible sunlight, exposed there on the wide-open street, blinking and blinking. I was not a child and I would not cry. Finally I thought I could trust my voice. "What can I do to convince her?"

"I have to be honest with you, Magali. I don't know. I'm not sure anything will."

I took it like a woman. I stood there looking him in the eye above the sharp little shards of my dream. I took it like Paquerette would have.

Well, except for the part where I lied to my father.

"I forgot to tell you," I said, forcing the words past the lump in my throat. "They asked me to help out at l'Espoir today. Right *now*. I don't know if I'll be home for supper. Is that okay?"

He nodded. I think he knew, really. I opened my empty hands and turned away.

I COULD barely see the street through my tears as I rounded the corner to l'Espoir. So far I had kept them from running down my cheeks and betraying me to the world, but I wasn't sure it was going to last. The brown door with the painted wooden sign over it looked like home. I knocked and pushed it open. We don't wait to hear an answer, at l'Espoir.

A wave of heat hit me. It was stifling in there. There was a fire in the fireplace and a bassinet on the coffee table and a hard, hot tension in the air. I froze. Madame Sabatier and Madeleine bent over the bassinet. Madame Sabatier's eyes flicked upward in her pale, strained face; she saw me, but made no sign. Dr. Reynaud knelt on the wood floor with his stethoscope on. For a moment no one moved.

Then Dr. Reynaud straightened suddenly and bent to his black bag, his fingers working fast, putting something together. "I'm going to give him an injection." I took a step closer. His face was very intent. "That way the medicine will take effect as quickly as possible. Will you hold him, Madame?"

I watched, not moving, as Madame Sabatier lifted him up. It was Zvi. Of course it was Zvi. In the silence that fell I suddenly heard the tiny rasp of his breathing, and dread grabbed my heart like a fist.

I heard him try to cry, as the needle slipped in. I heard him choke instead.

Madame Sabatier put him up against her shoulder. She patted his back while he choked and coughed. He writhed. Her face scared me. "Doctor," she said, "what should we do?"

Back in the nursery a baby started to cry. It sounded like Léon.

"You have been doing the right things, Madame. Keep him warm. Keep his nose clear. Try to help him cough up anything he can, as you are doing. Try to get him to drink, as I said yesterday, but for now, only a little. If he is able to sleep let him sleep. Rest will be more important for him now. I expect the crisis will come today."

Madame Sabatier's eyes were big and dark. "You mean—"

"I mean you will know whether he is going to recover."

"Do you think he will?"

The doctor bent to his black bag again and began to pack it up. Avoiding her eyes. Léon was screaming by now. Suddenly my feet came unstuck from the floor. No one seemed to even see me as I went to the nursery door.

I heard the doctor finally break his silence as I opened it. "Madame," he said, "I am very concerned."

I sat in the one big chair in the nursery holding Léon tight against my chest. Rocking backward and forward, rocking. "It's going to be okay, Léon. Sh. Sh. It's all going to be okay."

Léon believed me.

It was pneumonia. Zvi had taken cold earlier in the week.

Madeleine kept thinking of things that would have made it not happen: she should have put a hat on him, she should have made a fire, it had been so cold for June, she'd thought of making one, and then she'd thought it would be a waste.

"And now, Magali . . . if I'd just . . ."

I kept telling her it wasn't her fault.

I kept seeing his mother, his tall thin mother in her patched skirt. She'd called him "my Zvi." She'd coughed. Tuberculosis, they said it was.

Madame Sabatier was walking him up and down by the fireplace, up and down. His little eyes screwed up in his red face as he fought to cough and breathe. Madeleine and I had fed all the babies now, and she'd gone to get her mother something to eat, and then us. We could wait. I didn't feel hungry, I didn't feel anything but this deep, tight ache all through my chest that nothing could soothe. Except the warmth of Léon's little body pressed right against it. He was asleep. Breathing deeply. He was all right.

I gripped him tighter.

Madeleine brought bread, and we ate. She went back out to take a turn with Zvi. I hadn't taken a turn. I hadn't asked for a turn. I sat and rocked Léon. After a while he woke up and pooped his diaper and I changed it and rocked him some more. When Grigory woke up and started fussing I put Léon down. Grigory cried. I picked him up. He needed a diaper change too. I had just put him down and was pulling the first pin out of his diaper when I heard a cry from the living room.

Sudden. A high, scared, woman's cry.

I put Grigory back in his crib, fast, and ran out to the living room. Madame Sabatier stood in front of the fire with her hand over her mouth and tears running down her cheeks. I couldn't see Madeleine's face. She held Zvi in her arms; I could barely see him at this angle, a tiny bundled form.

Then I heard the sound. I've never forgotten it. I've tried.

A harsh, gurgling gasp. And then a pause. And then a gasp. Another pause; another gasp. And another.

The pause was longer every time.

And then one more gasp.

And then silence.

THERE WAS a numbness all through my body, and a sound in my ears like the sea. The world blurred. My limbs moved slowly, as if through deep water; I heard the high piercing sound of Madeleine's voice. I tried to breathe. *Come on. Come on, Magali.* I heard Madame Sabatier: *Listen to me! Vichy killed that child and no one else. You did everything you could and more. Listen to me!* I heard Grigory start to wail again from the nursery. I heard so many things and yet none of them covered that silence.

I turned away. The nursery. Grigory. I got in there and I shut the door behind me. I unpinned Grigory's diaper and wiped his bottom. I had to take his little feet in my hand to lift him up, his soft little warm feet. The feel of them made my hand shake.

The stupidest things were going through my head. Memories of killing chickens with Grandpa. Helping to pluck them. The feathers come out easier if you start right away, while the body's still warm. A little body like that doesn't take long to cool. It doesn't take long at all.

I could almost feel it in my fingers.

I pinned the clean diaper on, my hands still shaking. There'd be fewer diapers to wash now. Zvi's diapers had always smelled the worst. Something wrong. There'd always been something wrong. His mother had put him in Paquerette's arms and sent him away hoping. Hoping. I picked up Grigory and rocked his warm live weight against my chest and tried to shut my mind. I could see it coming: an image of Paquerette at the camp again, face to face with her, that tall Polish woman in the thin patched skirt. Saying—

My heart was beating like I was in the camp again. I wanted to run. I couldn't run. There was a baby in my arms. I rocked him. *Go to sleep, Grigory. Please go to sleep. I want to run. Oh please, oh please.* I sang the Italian lullaby Mama used to sing me. *Star, little star. The ewe has her lamb, the hen has her chick, everyone has her child.* My throat hurt so bad. I don't know how long it took before he started to grow heavier in my arms. Asleep. I put him in his crib so carefully. His little pointed face and his closed eyes made me want to cry, hit something, scream. I had to run. I looked out into the hallway and the living room. They'd ask me to do something. To stop by the parsonage and tell Pastor Alex to plan a—a funeral—

They weren't there. Neither of them. The bassinet was still on the coffee table. I didn't look into it.

I ran.

I took the stairwell three steps at a time. In my house you don't have to go through the living room to get to your room, not if you don't want to. I didn't want to. There wasn't a reason in the world why I should face Mama or Papa and tell them why I'd missed supper. No reason at all.

If Mama hadn't been in my room.

She was making my bed, tucking the sheet in, when I burst through the door and stopped dead staring at her. The blanket was in a heap by the pillow. She was down on her knees. Making hospital corners, like she tried to teach me to do, and I never learned.

She stood up slowly, not taking her eyes off me. I don't know what I looked like. But my whole body was shaking like a tree in a storm. "Magali," she said, "I'm so sorry."

I think part of my mind knew she couldn't be talking about Zvi. Part of my mind remembered that I couldn't work with Paquerette and that it was her fault. I don't think that was the part of my mind that was running me, anymore. Tears filled my eyes. I couldn't think, I couldn't see, I almost couldn't breathe. She held out her arms and I threw myself into them.

I was shaking, and I couldn't stop. I wasn't in charge of my body anymore. I was shaking, and she was holding me. That was all I knew. Somehow we were on my bed, and my face was buried in her shoulder, and my hands were clutching something tight—her skirt, the blanket, I don't know—as if I could make my fingers forget the coldness of dead flesh. Dead. *Dead.* I opened my mouth and let out a sound I had never heard anyone make before—a deep, rasping moan. My stomach clenched and for a moment I thought I was going to throw up. Then Mama had me by the shoulders and was pulling me up, shaking me a little, making me look into her face. She was pale. "Magali. What happened? What happened?"

I swallowed. I opened my mouth. I tried to bury my face against her shoulder again. But she wouldn't let go. "Magali." She sounded frightened. "What happened?"

The words were like stones, almost too heavy to lift. I forced my voice to come out of my throat. "Zvi . . . just . . . died."

"Magali. Magali." Her voice was tiny, and came from very far away. My head was back against her shoulder, and she was holding me hard. And she was shaking too. My mama and me, on my bed, holding each other as hard as our arms could hold, and shaking; locked together like one trembling person, shaking with what almost seemed like fear. Like fear that it was true. That this was the kind of world we lived in.

But we weren't one person.

I stopped trembling. Suddenly. I went stiff in her arms, I pushed myself up, away from her, till I could see her face. There was something in my body, like a kind of wild energy running through it. Fear, maybe. Or anger.

She knew this was the kind of world we lived in. Why else would she be like she was?

And she wouldn't let me go.

I looked at her. I couldn't speak.

She looked at me. She was pale, and her lips were trembling.

She looked almost exactly the way she had looked that night when I asked to travel with Paquerette. "Magali," she said slowly, as if she was forcing the words past her lips. "How was he when he left the camp?"

My mind was whirling so hard I almost didn't know what she meant. I swallowed again. My voice came out thin and dry. "There was something wrong with him. I could tell. He didn't— *move* enough. When I saw him with his—" *Mother,* the word was *mother,* and I couldn't say it. I could smell the dust of those barracks, the dust on her skin, and her patched skirt, I could see every line of her face. *My Zvi.* Her eyes on him—Léon's mother's eyes as she handed him to me—*Promise you'll take care of my baby. Promise. Promise.* I was sobbing so hard I couldn't catch my breath and Mama was holding the back of my head and dry sobs were ripping through me, sharp pain in my breastbone like I was going to split wide open. My body not even mine anymore—taken over. I fought for breath; breath to speak, to scream. "Mama," I gasped, "Mama." Somehow I couldn't stand the words inside, unsaid. I pushed myself up away from her again. "How—are we going—to tell—his mother?" I wailed.

I thought she was going to pull my head down against her shoulder again, but she didn't. She stared at me. Her face was white and her eyes were very big and dark. She couldn't take them off me. I couldn't either. My whole head and chest hurt, everything hurt more than I'd ever believed it could, and my mother and I looked at each other. She opened her mouth, and I watched it, as if I had never seen it before.

"Magali," she said very, very softly. "You may travel with Paquerette this summer."

My mouth opened. I started to cry again. She blurred, everything blurred. My head went back down against her shoulder, and I wept.

It was a long time, I think, before I stopped crying.

WHEN I came to myself it was very dim in my room, the lowering sun painting a last line of tawny red light across the wall. Mama was stroking my hair. The world had changed. Zvi was dead and that was something no one could undo. And I was going to travel with Paquerette. And I was going to save as many as I could.

"Magali," Mama whispered. "I'm so sorry. I wanted so much for you never to have to know."

"Know what?" I whispered.

"The things people do to each other." Her voice was hoarse. "To people who can't fight back."

"Like children." Like Zvi. Like Grigory and Léon and the Spanish kids. Carmela. Manola. Adrián. Their names bloomed up in my mind like little prayers: *Keep them safe, God. Keep them healthy.*

"Like children. Like women." I looked up at her. "Like the people you saw in that camp. I'm sorry I never asked you about it. I could picture it so vividly, Magali. I couldn't bear to picture you there."

"Mama. Mama, it's not because—" I couldn't bear for that to be why. "Is that why you didn't want me to go? So I wouldn't see it?"

Her face hardened for a moment. "Tell me this, Magali," she said. Her eyes were black and bright. "What kind of people are they, these men in Vichy? These men who thought that putting women and children behind barbed wire would be good for France?"

"They're evil."

"And do you think that's enough for them? Do you think that's good enough for their masters back in Berlin? Penning up Jews and Gypsies and immigrants and letting their children go? Where do you think things are going from here, Magali? Better? Or worse?"

Same way they'd gone every day for the past two years. "Worse." *She's right. It's not over. It's nowhere near over.*

"Worse. And it will continue. We have no idea where these people will stop. And now my daughter, my youngest child, is going into their world, beyond my reach. Setting herself against them. Magali." Her eyes on mine were dark and deathly serious. "It terrifies me."

She'd said I could go. She had.

"Do you understand that, Magali? Please. Look at me." I looked at her. "You remember Léon's mother, giving you her baby? You remember that?" I nodded. There were tears welling in Mama's dark eyes. She opened her mouth and shut it again. The tears ran down her cheeks, bright lines in the last light from the window. "That's what it's like," she whispered. "That's what it's like. Magali, promise me you will be careful out there."

I looked at her. The time for cheap promises was long, long past. I took a breath. "I promise, Mama."

She pulled me in again, a hug as tight and fierce as Madame Minkowski's. "My daughter," she said. "My grown-up daughter. This whole time I wanted to protect you and all you ever wanted was to protect them."

I felt something open inside me. Something I hadn't even known was closed. I felt warmth welling all through my chest and tears in my eyes again. "Mama?" I whispered. "Mama. I love you."

She held me even tighter. She held me like Madame Minkowski, like Léon's mother, like she wanted to keep me there pressed against her heart forever.

And then she let me go.

## Chapter 8

# The Kind of World We Live In

I SLEPT till about noon the next day. The day after that was Zvi's funeral. Madame Sabatier's brother-in-law had made up a little pine box for him. About half-a-meter long. It was closed. So I never did see him after he died.

Rosa and Nina were sitting together, in a pew with Rosa's mother. It was strange seeing them in our church. Nina sat stiffly, casting her eyes around as if she was afraid of something. Rosa was crying, tears sliding quietly down her cheeks. She grabbed my hand when I sat down. I sat and looked at that box and I remembered everything at once: the gasping, and the silence afterward. His mother's face. The warm weight of Léon against my chest, and the way I couldn't stop thinking about dead chickens getting cold. Pastor Alex was saying God would welcome Zvi the way Madame Sabatier had. I tried to imagine it, but how are you supposed to imagine that stuff? When I was a kid in Paris I thought heaven looked like the picture of it on the Sunday school room wall—a big green field under a sunrise and kids playing in it. But Zvi was just a baby. I tried to picture Jesus holding him. I even pretended I was Catholic like Rosa and tried the Virgin Mary instead. None of it stuck.

I don't know. I just can't do it sometimes. People tell me all this stuff about God, and of course I believe it. But—I don't know—it's not *there*. Sometimes I just have to touch something, you know? It's not that I don't believe, it's just . . . We go to church and talk about God all the time and yeah, I've never seen him and like Papa pointed out when I said that, I never saw Hitler either—but that's just it. I can see what Hitler does. I've seen it up close. But what God's doing, I don't know.

Because what's *there* is a dead baby in a box. Who has got to be put under the ground before he rots. And if his little soul flew up out of there when he took his last desperate breath, I didn't see it. And maybe there was an angel standing behind Madeleine just like in an old-fashioned painting, but he quit breathing all the same.

"We are dust," said Pastor Alex. His voice was rough all of a sudden. I looked up. "And to dust we shall return. We ask you, Lord, for mercy."

THEY PUT him in the ground. Thierry Sabatier and his son Emmanuel, carrying the box between them, like one of them couldn't have held it up with one hand. They shoveled the earth onto the lid, and they filled in the hole, and at the end there was this little mound of dirt left over beside the grave. I stood looking at it, and Rosa stood with me, as people started walking away by twos and threes. Then I turned and went over to the low stone wall and leaned on it, looking past the houses at where the land fell away and you could just see a little corner of the river reflecting the sun. The inside of my head felt like it was tied in knots. I kept seeing all these things. The barbed wire and the gate at Rivesaltes, and the guard's red watering eyes. My mother's face when she'd said *my grown-up daughter.* Zvi lying eerily still in his mother's arms. Eva and Kurt standing in the back of the truck with their hair streaming out in the wind. That little pile of dirt. *Zvi is dead, and I can travel with Paquerette. I can travel with Paquerette. And Zvi is dead.*

*We ask you, Lord, for mercy.*

My hands tightened into fists. *Mercy. This is your idea of mercy?* I wanted to scream. Someone touched my arm, and I jumped. It was Rosa. I looked up across the grave and saw Nina standing with my mother.

"Madeleine said you were there," Rosa whispered. "When . . . he died."

"Yeah."

"Why didn't you come get me? I could've helped."

I opened my mouth and shut it again. *Seriously?* "Rosa—it wasn't—you would've hated it."

She looked at me, her black eyes burning and full of tears. "I said I could have helped. At least you got to help! I didn't even get to say goodbye!"

"I didn't either."

"I tried so hard, Magali. I thought he was getting better. He started eating more . . ." Her voice was thickening. She'd started to cry again. I grabbed her round the shoulders and hugged her, trying to think of something to say. I remembered her sitting on the couch at l'Espoir bent over Zvi, trying to get him to drink one more swallow of formula. I remembered what Madame Sabatier had said.

"You did everything you could and more, Rosa."

She didn't say anything. She just cried. I held her and felt her body shaking, and thought of Mama holding me. *Magali, you may travel with Paquerette this summer.* The words came into my mind and a shudder went through my body, something like joy and terror at the same time. I clutched my friend hard and looked up into the sky, and it was so deep and blue and thousands of miles high. More words came into my head. *I don't know. I don't know.* Over and over. Those were the only words I could find.

WE WALKED down to the Catholic church afterward. Rosa wanted to light a candle. It was getting hot. We didn't say anything as we walked down through the streets, and there weren't a lot of people out. I could hear the doves cooing up on the rooftops. We went from the bright sun into the deep cool dark of the church, and I blinked as my eyes adjusted to the darkness. Rosa rummaged in the candle box and found one, and dropped a coin in to pay for it. It was tall and white, and it stood out in her hands against the dark as she set it up on the candle rack. She got the matches and struck one and put it to the wick, carefully, her face very intent. I almost felt embarrassed to watch. I saw her eyes light when the wick took the flame. It burned blue and gold same as every candle in the world; it lit up the crucifix behind the candle rack and reflected bright against the tears that were streaming down Rosa's face again. She knelt down and closed her eyes. Her lips moved silently and fast. I looked at the candle flame, how slowly it moved against the dark.

After a minute Rosa crossed herself, and stood up. She smiled shyly at me, and wiped her eyes on her sleeve. "Thanks for coming with me, Magali," she whispered.

We walked out of the church in silence, back into the bright light of the day. My feet took the road to the river, without my really thinking about it, and Rosa followed. I wanted something. I wanted the sound of the river, to look at the shifting water like I'd looked at the flame. I wanted something that would make the ache in my breastbone go away.

We walked down to the river, to a place where there's a little footpath along a low stone wall. We stood on the grass right by the water's edge, looking downstream where the water swirls around the rocks and leaves the town and goes out between the hills, round a bend where you can't see. We watched it swirling away, always away, toward those green fields.

"Rosa?" I said quietly. "What d'you pray for?"

She looked at me and then quickly back at the water. "Oh. You know."

I didn't really know, though. Papa had told me Catholics pray for the souls of the dead. But I didn't really want to ask her that. "Rosa . . . do you think babies go to heaven?"

She looked at me, surprised. "Of course. Don't you?"

I nodded, looking at the river. Neither of us spoke for a moment. "D'you think they get to . . . you know . . . grow up?"

She shrugged. I could see tears starting to gleam in her eyes again. I hadn't meant to do that. I trailed my fingers through the grass. There were tiny white flowers in it, little stars as small as grass seeds. I picked one and looked at it for a moment, so tiny I could crush it between two fingers. I leaned over and dropped it in the water.

One tiny flash of white in the current, and it was gone. So fast. I looked toward the riverbend, picturing it swept along in the current, out of sight.

I opened my mouth. "Rosa," I said slowly. "My mother changed her mind. I can travel with Paquerette this summer."

She looked down at me and her dark eyes widened. "Magali! When?"

I looked down at the grass again. "Day before yesterday."

"Oh."

"When I came home. From l'Espoir."

"Oh."

There was a long, long silence. I watched the swirl and speed of the water, and shivered. I thought of Rivesaltes. Thought, oddly, of Adrián's bleeding feet. *I should pack some rags this time.* I felt it rise up in me then, sudden but slow, like something out of the earth, a plant pushing its way through the soil: it was true. I was going. I stood up. "Rosa! I'm gonna go!"

She took my hand and squeezed it. "You're gonna go," she said.

THE FIRST night I went back to l'Espoir, I was almost afraid to open the door. Rosa was there on the couch feeding Lilli, and there was the coffee table and the exact spot where the bassinet had sat. The spot where Madeleine had stood, holding him— I swallowed and walked forward, and gave Rosa the *bise*.

That night after the babies had gone to sleep, Madame Sabatier and Madeleine made tea, and seemed to want us to stay. We sat around the coffee table in silence for a little while. I couldn't take my eyes off that spot. Madame Sabatier started talking about her late husband, who'd died four years ago, and Madeleine joined in. They talked about him for almost an hour. How he used to get up at three to start baking in his *boulangerie*, and how much he liked dogs, and how he'd spend hours and hours in the woods in the spring, hunting for mushrooms. They didn't even talk about how he died. They talked slowly. They looked at each other a lot, and at Rosa and me, like their eyes were saying what they really meant. I'm not sure what they meant. But it was good to be with them.

WHEN PAQUERETTE came in I took the kids from her—three toddlers from Gurs for a private home—and didn't see her till the next afternoon. I didn't want to be the one to tell her. I wanted to be the one bringing good news after the bad.

I looked up at the blue June sky as I walked down to l'Espoir, and I saw the swallows were back, swooping over the town in dizzying curves. I stopped and stood there following one with my eyes, feeling the dive and lift of it in my body as if it was me that was flying. *I'm going. I'm going to tell her I can go.*

Madame Sabatier hugged and kissed me. Paquerette gave me

the *bise* and stood looking at me, her gray eyes warm and sad. "I'm told you were a great help. I hope it wasn't too hard on you."

"I . . ."

"I was afraid it would happen from the beginning, Magali. It was always a possibility. We had to try."

A lump rose in my throat. *We had to try.* I took a fast breath, then another. "I can travel with you," I blurted.

Paquerette's eyebrows shot up. "Your mother said yes?"

I looked into her eyes. "*Yes.*" Hard, hot triumph warmed the center of my chest.

Paquerette stood for a moment with her mouth open. "Well now," she said finally. "I thought— Well now. Actually, that solves a problem I have."

*Well, yes . . .*

"Yes. Hm." Her eyes had an inward look now. "Magali, do you think your parents would let you travel to Perpignan without me if you were with Rosa?"

"Rosa?"

"Yes. She's agreed to travel with me. I've arranged it with her parents. And now both of you can come—that's going to be a tremendous asset. Now I think switching off may be the right method ordinarily, but you see, I leave tomorrow for my headquarters in Nîmes, and I'll continue on from there to Rivesaltes on Monday. I'd hoped to have Rosa meet me at Madame Alençon's, but her parents object to her traveling alone. With you along, on the other hand . . ."

I tried to swallow, but my throat was too dry. *Have Rosa meet me at Madame Alençon's,* she said, as if it was something she said every day. Had they already been on a trip together? Rosa, nice little *Rosa* walking into Rivesaltes? Rosa sprinting across a train platform, catching a toddler before he went off the edge? *Really?*

"Do you think your parents would let you?"

"Um. Um, yeah. I think so." A tremendous asset, she'd said. Not having me. Having *both of us.*

"Should I ask them myself? That seems to be the approach I ought to have taken last time."

"Um, yeah. Yeah. That's a good idea."

Paquerette smiled and put a hand on my shoulder. "I'm glad you're coming," she said kindly.

I gave her what I hoped was a smile.

I PRETENDED to Rosa that I hadn't noticed she'd been keeping secrets from me. I didn't say a thing, from then till the day we left on our trip.

It was raining hard the day we left. I stood under Papa's umbrella, Rosa under her mother's, as *la Galoche* pulled in, her white steam heavy in the rainy air. I boarded, and heard Rosa following me. I sat on the far end of the bench. She joined me. On the platform Papa waved goodbye. The whistle sounded, and I watched the houses begin to go by, and then the open country.

"Magali?"

"Mm."

"What . . . what's it like? Rivesaltes?"

I turned to her. "Pretty bad." I wondered how she'd take it, when we got there.

"What was it like? The first time you went?"

I turned away and looked out the window. The rain was letting up. Everything was blurred and watery; the grass in the pastures was so green it glowed. I shrugged. "There's barbed wire around the place," I said. "There're men with guns. Little kids fight each other over food. It's not nice."

She shut up, and looked out the window. The fields went past. Then the first houses of Saint-Agrève. "Magali?"

"Mm."

"Did Paquerette say anything about . . . if there'll be any babies on this trip?" she asked in a low voice.

I sat up a little straighter. "There might be," I said.

"I keep thinking about . . . Magali, do you suppose . . . we'll see . . ."

I drew in a sharp breath. *Oh.* "I guess . . . Paquerette needs to, you know. Tell her."

Tears filled Rosa's eyes. "I couldn't bear it, if I had to."

My throat was tightening. "Yeah," I said. "Yeah."

"Paquerette's so brave."

I glanced over at her. "Yeah," I said.

The train went round its sharp bend, then, and began to pick up speed as it plunged down into the gorge.

THE TRAINS ran on time. We made it all the way to Perpignan by nightfall. I led Rosa through the darkening streets to Madame Alençon's. Paquerette wasn't there.

Instead there was a telegram:

DELAYED STOP MEET ME AT THE CAMP
STOP PAQUERETTE

We lay awake a long time in our room at the guesthouse, hearing each other's breathing in the dark. I lay there wondering if Rosa would say anything. About Benjamin, maybe, or about Zvi. I lay there thinking about tomorrow's walk to the camp, about seeing Zvi's mother. I looked up at things I couldn't see and tried not to remember the harsh sound of Zvi's last breaths. And then I stopped trying not to and just remembered them. This is the kind of world we live in. I shivered and turned over, and thought of Rosa's face as she lit the candle, Rosa's face as she cradled Zvi, my mother holding me close, then letting me go. Paquerette's drawing of her valley. The green fields beneath the rain. The hateful gates of Rivesaltes and the men with guns. This is the kind of world we live in, I thought, and I could not make sense of it. I just couldn't. I went to sleep.

AFTER BREAKFAST we took the Rivesaltes train, and then I led
Rosa along the road to the camp.

The *tramontane* was bad that morning—hard and hot and wild.
The sky was dark and heavy. I pulled handkerchiefs out of my bag
to cover our mouths. The dust stung our eyes. We walked.

As the camp came in sight, I watched Rosa draw into herself.
She couldn't stop looking at it. That wide plain bounded with
barbed wire, those guard towers. She stopped suddenly, fumbled
in her bag.

I pulled my dusty handkerchief off my mouth. "You okay?"

"I'm thirsty." She got out a water bottle and took a long pull,
not taking her eyes off the camp. She held it out to me. "Want
some?"

I took it, and watched her as I drank. She was still looking
straight ahead. She was very still. "You sure you're okay?"

She put the bottle away. For a moment she didn't speak. Then,
"You know what the difference is," she said, "between Sonia and
me?"

I shook my head.

"My family left Spain a year earlier. That's the difference. I
could've been in there." She was still staring at it.

"Rosa." I grabbed her hand. "Rosa, look at me. You know what
you're here for?" She looked at me. "You're here to get people out.
You're a rescuer. That's who we are. Remember?"

She glanced again at the camp. She tore her eyes from it, looked
at me. Nodded slowly.

"Ready to go on?"

She nodded.

We went on.

When we walked up to the gate, Paquerette came out of the
*poste de commande*. The guard let us in and we began our walk
down the dusty road between the blocks. Three of us walking into
Rivesaltes, carrying bad news and hope, one in each hand.

BLOCK J looked deserted in the gusting, gritty wind. Still, I glanced between the barracks as we passed them, my eyes searching for a tall thin woman in a patched skirt. *I don't want to be there when she finds out. Please. Please.* The block guard let us in; we followed Paquerette into Marylise's quarters. Rosa stopped in the doorway, looking round the bare little room. Paquerette and Marylise embraced like they hadn't seen each other in months. Paquerette straightened, her face clouding.

"Marylise, how is Madame Novak? Is she still in the infirmary? I have a letter here for her. I . . . I have some news."

Marylise's smiling face fell. I swallowed, watching her. "I'm sorry, Paquerette," she said. "She's dead."

Paquerette stood motionless for a second. "Oh."

Relief washed through me. Followed instantly by shame.

"I saw her start to fail as soon as her son was gone," said Marylise. "I really think she was only hanging on until she could get him to safety."

A sick feeling went through me, a feeling of awful, awful waste. Paquerette stood with a face like stone. *She died believing he'd live.* Some people would say that made it better. Looking at Paquerette's face I saw the truth: it made it worse.

"Well," said Paquerette finally, hoarsely, "he's dead too."

They looked at each other for a long moment in silence. Marylise sighed. "Well," she said very quietly, "would you like to see the list for today?"

THEY SENT me and Rosa off to Block D, where a lot of the Spanish women and children were. I was moral support, I guess. Rosa did keep hold of my hand for the first two minutes, but by the time we'd found the family we were looking for, she was a part of their world, and I was not.

I sat beside Rosa on the end of Madame Villanueva's bedroll in the dark, stifling barrack, listening to Spanish, watching Rosa's expressive face move with every sentence she heard. She fed me bits and pieces in the pauses—"and then they had to climb the mountains," or "she says her nieces and nephew went to some town on the plateau, Magali, d'you suppose"—and then someone would say something, and she'd be gone again. When the bell for the lunch line sounded, we brought our group back to Marylise: Madame Villanueva and her three kids, a whole family released this time. There was a pot of turnip-and-rice soup on Marylise's stove; she and Paquerette sat at the table talking. They looked up as the group of us trooped in.

"Excellent. I have something to ask you, Magali."

"Yes, Paquerette."

"Do you think you can handle a really wild eight-year-old boy? If he's your sole responsibility?"

I stood up straight. That look in her eyes: *can I count on you?* I found myself breathing deeper than I had in months. "I—"

"I have to warn you," said Marylise. "Severe behavior problems. That's one reason we need to get him out—he's tried to escape his block several times, almost got himself shot. He did get himself hit with a gun butt. His aunt's very worried. She's his guardian here, his mother died of the typhoid that was going round earlier in the spring."

Paquerette nodded. "It's going to be tough. Don't undertake it lightly, Magali."

What was I going to say? *No?*

I took a deep breath. "I'll be in charge of him, Paquerette."

She turned to Marylise. "We'll take him."

His name was Marek. He had a dark bruise on his left cheekbone, and the eyes of a cornered animal.

He stopped in Marylise's doorway, his eyes darting round the room for danger. His tired-looking aunt prodded him to go on in. I had to rise from where I sat among our growing group and go out to him. His aunt said he spoke French. I went down on one knee but he wouldn't look me in the eye. He had this way of looking at your hands, as if you were going to hit him. I told him it was my job to take him to a place where he'd be safe, where there was food and no barbed wire, and it was his job to do as I said till we got there. You would've thought he hadn't understood a word. His aunt swore again that he spoke French.

When we walked out of the block—and later when we walked out of the camp—Marek looked at the open gate, looked at the guard, and then dashed. I caught a fold of his shirt and held him back to my own pace, wondering how a kid as scared as this had gotten himself hit with a gun butt.

For the next twenty-four hours Marek was my world. The rest of the group was a vague crowd whom I became aware of during head counts. The Villanueva family; two brothers who spoke only to each other, quietly, in Yiddish; a girl named Chloe, who spoke to no one, ever. A couple of other kids I don't even remember; and a thin, clingy toddler whom Rosa carried and sang to in Spanish. A ragged, dusty, exhausted group straggling into the train station in the center of town, finally, even Marek dragging his feet.

At Madame Alençon's that night everyone drank glass after glass of water. Marek tried to take his food from the table and go; I stood behind his chair and blocked him in. He wolfed it down, eyes darting round. They put me in the same room with him; he went to sleep in his clothes and broken shoes, on top of the covers.

By the next morning he'd decided I was just another jailer.

He tried to bolt, in Perpignan station. The crowd was pressing in around us and I saw his eyes go white and wild like a horse about to shy, and just in time I grabbed a fold of his shirt and hung on hard as he almost pulled me off my feet.

"Marek!" I shouted. "Calm down!"

I put my other hand on his shoulder and he jumped like I'd cut him. I yanked him along after the group. After about ten seconds of that—which is a pretty long time when you're dragging someone as hard as you can—he gave up and started following.

He tried to bolt again on the train. I caught him and brought him back to his seat, put him by the window, sat in the aisle seat and boxed him in. He kicked the seat in front of him, again and again, for hours. It's absolutely incredible what that can do to your nerves. Once in a while he stopped to turn and look at me, with hatred on his bruised face.

Our train was shunted into a siding just before Montélimar. Problems up ahead—no one would tell us what. Marek kicked and kicked, Rosa's little girl cried, Paquerette looked at her watch. Two hours in all.

We started moving again. Stopped in Montélimar. A boy got on and sat down in the seat in front of Marek. After about three kicks he'd swiveled back to look at us. "Hey, *quit!*" Marek glared at him, and kicked again. The boy jumped up, angry-faced, moving toward us. Marek jumped up and punched him in the mouth.

I stared. The boys were starting to grapple. I stood and grabbed Marek's collar and yanked back, hard. The father loomed up out of nowhere, and the French kid kicked into scene-making mode—"He hit me! He started it! He hit me!" Everyone stared. I pinned Marek's arms with all my strength while the man started to come down on me: public menace, blah blah blah, oughta be locked up. *What a great idea. Worked out well last time. They locked him up 'cause he was Jewish, and now he's completely insane.*

"Marek," I said, my voice heavy with command. "Come with me." I pulled him back toward our group, behind us.

He whirled and kicked me. I snapped, and slapped his face.

For a moment we stared at each other in shock. The voice inside me screamed, *No don't take it back you can't take it back* and I grabbed his collar again and pulled his face up to mine and said, "*You will obey me.*" He stared.

"Come." I took hold of his shirtsleeve and pulled.

He came.

WE MISSED *la Galoche* by hours. When we pulled into Valence it was full dark outside, raining, and very late. We bedded down in the train station, with endless mutterings and rearrangings, trips to the toilet, kids whimpering, crying, Marek sitting on the blanket watching us all with dull, angry, exhausted eyes. I didn't leave for the bathroom till he'd lain down and gone to sleep. Paquerette sat on a bench leaning her head back against the wall, eyes closed, face slack with weariness.

Rosa lay on the blanket stroking her little girl's hair. I sat down by her. She looked at me. "Wow." The way she said it summed up everything: Rivesaltes, the refugees, the kids, the chaos, Marek.

"Yeah," I whispered. There was silence for a moment. I stretched myself out by Marek, keeping him between the wall and me. I yawned. She yawned too. I reached for her hand, and squeezed it. Then I got a grip on a fold of Marek's shirt, and fell deep asleep on the hard station floor.

I think I dreamed. I don't remember it, except for a few images of running through Rivesaltes looking for someone. What I remember is the feel of my hand touching empty air. Touching the cold floor, feeling for a body that wasn't there. My eyes opening in the dimness, in the black and gray and the feeble light from the ceiling, and seeing the space where Marek had been.

Empty.

Chapter 9

# Gone to Ground

I sat up, my heart racing. He was gone. It was the dead of night, nothing moving, just a clutter of sleeping bodies in the light of a few dim, flickering bulbs. The tightness of fear in my chest was like nothing I'd ever felt. *I've lost him. Me. It's my fault.*

I searched. The men's bathrooms, then the women's. Then I went over every inch of that station, from north to south. I tried every door except the outer ones. Valence isn't a huge station. It took about fifteen minutes to make absolutely sure he wasn't there.

I stood by one of the doors that opened out on the streets of Valence, leaning my forehead against the cold glass of its little window, looking out. It was dark out there. No light in the sky. My heart sank like a stone.

I looked at Paquerette's slack, exhausted, sleeping face, and I almost turned away and walked out into the streets alone. But where would I start? *We'll never find him,* said a cold whisper in my mind, and my belly froze. I imagined it for a moment.

*We'd never know what had happened to him.*

I knelt down by Paquerette and put a hand on her shoulder.

She jolted awake the moment I touched her—jerked to a sitting position, drawing a sharp breath. She stared at me. Blinked. Groaned, rubbed her eyes, let out her breath, half-collapsing. "What's going on?" she whispered sharply.

I swallowed. "Marek's gone."

"He's what?"

"He's gone. I've looked everywhere. I kept him between me and the wall but he got past me some—"

She raised herself up on her elbows, glaring. "Unbelievable," she snapped. "I put you in charge of *one kid*, and you lose him?"

I couldn't speak. She might as well have pulled out a pistol and shot me. She stood up and strode into the women's bathroom.

I stayed where I was, on my knees.

I heard the bathroom door open. I saw her feet coming toward me but I didn't move. She knelt down to look me in the face. Her skin and hair shone wet in the dim light. She wasn't glaring anymore.

"Magali," she said, "I'm sorry."

I couldn't find my voice.

"That was a stupid and unkind thing to say and I hope you can forgive me. I was off-balance." Her voice sounded odd. For a moment in the flickering light I thought I caught the flash of tears in her eyes. "It's my worst nightmare, Magali. To lose a child . . . and never . . ."

The same feeling wrenched in my gut as before, but stronger. "*Yes*," I breathed.

She looked at me. Oh, she looked at me and her face said, *You understand*, and my guts wrenched again and I wanted to cry for joy and pain and fear and the need for Marek to be okay. "We'll find him," I whispered fiercely.

She didn't say anything for a moment. Then she sighed. "I need coffee," she said.

THERE WASN'T any coffee, of course.

We stood by the doors, watching the first pale streaks of dawn paint the sky, and Paquerette told me we had to wait till the group woke. It wasn't negotiable. It was her responsibility to get them on their train. I nodded vigorously.

"The group's your responsibility," I said. "Marek's mine. I'll go look for him. Now that you know—"

"Not alone," she said sharply.

I shut up, but I glanced outside. I couldn't help it.

"Not alone," she said. "I'm leaving Rosa with you."

Rosa listened seriously to everything Paquerette told her, glancing now and then at her little girl, still asleep on the blanket.

"I'll take care of Rivka myself," Paquerette promised.

Rosa nodded, not smiling, still looking at the girl.

She gave us money. She gave us instructions. We were to go first to the war-widow agency where we'd spent the night with Léon's group. We would speak to Madame Chalmette and Madame Moulin there, explain the situation, and ask for their help. Then we were to have one of them take us to the police station to file a missing child report. On no account were we to skip either of these steps. Then we could begin searching. She suggested we begin with the large park we'd find due west of the station. She gave me all of Marek's papers and his CIMADE release form. She wrote and signed a statement saying he should be entrusted to our care. She told us not to let anyone push us around. She looked at each of us in turn, with her deep Paquerette eyes, all the sorrow in the world in back of them and courage in the front. And said she was counting on us. And asked us if we felt ready.

I nodded, my throat tight.

Rosa bent over and kissed little Rivka on the forehead, and whispered goodbye. She was silent as we stepped out alone into the chilly morning air, as the pale streaks of dawn began to widen over Valence, and walked north. Far off on our left we could see the mountains west of the city, across the Rhône, lit by the first rays of sunlight, and on one crag the ruined walls of some old fort. I was quiet too. I was picturing the park—green trees and thickets of bushes for Marek to hide in, a fox gone to ground. Every step was carrying me away from it. *Paquerette's orders, Magali. Keep walking.*

The city was waking by the time we knocked on the agency door. I did the talking. Within a couple of minutes we were upstairs in their little office, with Madame Chalmette heating water in the tiny kitchen. There was light streaming in the east window, the sharp smell of fake coffee in the air. They asked questions. I sipped scalding-hot coffee and answered them. Madame Chalmette listened intently; Madame Moulin looked out the window, her face thoughtful. She turned to Madame Chalmette. "If you can cover the morning here, Marie, I can cover the afternoon."

Madame Chalmette nodded.

"So, first the police station."

She walked us there. Asked to file a report. The officer on duty pulled out a form and started filling it out. He asked for a description, and Madame Moulin turned to me. The policeman frowned at her.

"He's not your son?"

I stood up straight. "He's an orphan, Monsieur. He was in my care, temporarily, on a trip to his new home."

The man's eyes settled on me and his eyebrows rose in amusement. I felt my face start to burn.

"How'd he end up with *you?*"

"I'm working for the CIMADE. It's an organization that helps refugees. It's our job to bring kids to the homes they've been placed in."

He frowned at me, deeply, for a moment. "Does he speak French?"

It was my personal belief that his aunt, who said he did, was delusional. "Not very much," I said, just to hedge my bet. I tried to look him in the eye, like Paquerette had done to Monsieur Bernard, but he wouldn't look.

He frowned at his form, pushed his hat back a little on his head, and sighed. "All right, give me the description."

He wrote everything down. He said he would initiate a search. He said it like it was just to get us off his back. But what could I say to him? "No, do it, make sure you really do it." None of us had the power to command the police.

We looked at each other, walking out of there. "They don't care," said Madame Moulin. "We must find him ourselves."

WE FINALLY made it to that park. On the near side was a square plaza of blindingly pale gravel, with trees in ranks and a monument in the middle; I didn't like it. I thought it would scare any kid from Rivesaltes. Past it I could see the real park, green and thickety. Well, maybe.

We searched, calling, getting twigs in our hair. Oh, I was thorough. The dawn light strengthened into day. Madame Moulin asked everyone she saw if they'd seen a boy with a bruise on his cheek. We worked our way west until we stood at the edge of the park, where the trees ended and we could see the broad Rhône River between us and the mountains.

Then we went back east, and searched the streets.

HAVE YOU ever thought about what it would be like to actually look for a needle in a haystack? Pulling out a handful of hay and picking through it, oh so carefully, feeling for it, never glancing away, watching for that tiny sharp slip of metal that could so easily slide through your fingers to the ground—gone. You search that handful thoroughly, strand by strand. You wipe the hay dust on your skirt and sneeze a couple of times, then reach for another handful. And as you do, your mind takes in the size of that haystack. Tries to calculate how many more handfuls to go.

And suddenly you want to scream.

"Excuse me, Monsieur? We are looking for a child. He should be easy to recognize. He has a—" "Excuse me, Madame? . . ."

We searched the streets around the train station. Looking in alleys, peering over walls. *If I were an insane child, where would I be?* Streets blurred into each other in my mind. I was starting to hate this flat city, flat like a maze; only the mountains rising above the rooftops in the west kept me oriented. Kept me sane. The sun climbed the sky. We walked. My legs ached. "Excuse me, Monsieur?" Valence spread out around us in every direction. In my mind was a cold whisper. *You'll never find him.*

*Yes I will. I will.*

"Magali?"

"Mm." My legs hurt and my head hurt and we'd drunk our water bottle empty and I was thirsty. I leaned back against a wall and groaned.

Rosa leaned beside me, and turned to me. "Magali, I . . . I'm really tired."

I just looked at her.

"There's got to be a better way."

My head hurt so bad. Her eyes were accusing. "You can go to the agency and lie down, if you're not having a nice time." Now her eyes were hurt *and* accusing. "Or do you have a better idea?

She shrugged, looking down. "My father," she said, sticking her hands in her pockets and looking at her shoes, "says no official will ever help you out unless you make him tired of living. He says the only reason our family made it to France is that he learned how to be very annoying and always there."

I looked at her. "Hmm."

Madame Moulin came out of the alley she'd been combing. "Are you girls thirsty?"

"You have water?"

She handed me a bottle. I took a long, cold, sweet pull on it and handed it to Rosa. "Madame, what do you think if we went back to the police station this afternoon? Maybe I could make them look for him, if I stay there and don't go away till they do."

Madame Moulin's brows went up. "It's an idea," she said. She pursed her lips. "Yes. Hm. It's a very *good* idea. But do you think you're able not to back down?"

*Very annoying and always there. That's me, lady.* "Yes," I said.

We went back to the agency and ate. Madame Chalmette and Rosa went back out into the city. Madame Moulin walked me down to the police station again. I was light-headed by then from the lack of sleep, the heat, the fear. I had to stop at the door and take a few breaths before going in.

There was a different policeman in charge. Younger, thinner, a little less certain. I took a last deep breath, cleared my head, and told him about the missing boy with the bruised face. He frowned.

"Didn't someone already come in for that? This morning? Yes, here it is. Don't worry, Mademoiselle, we've got it under control. We'll let you know if we find him."

Madame Moulin and I looked at each other. Then I turned back to the officer. "Thank you, Monsieur. It will be easy to let me know. I'll be here."

His eyebrows shot up. "Here? But . . . there's absolutely no need to do that, it's not . . . it's—"

I sat down on a wooden bench along the wall. "I'll just be right here. Till you find him."

I think it took less than ten minutes for me to fall asleep.

WHEN I woke I was lying on my side on hard wood, my knees drawn up a little. There was a pillow under my head. I had no idea where I was. A police station. What was this pillow doing in a police station? Someone was shaking my shoulder. Gently.

"Are you all right?"

"Mmm."

"I need you to come with me and identify someone."

I blinked. Looked up at him. He was *smiling* at me.

"Mmm," I said, and stood up, trying not to fall. I followed him into the next room.

Loud voices. People. I shook my head and tried to focus. Two policemen, big guys, holding a kid between them who writhed and tried to kick; a kid with a bruise on his face, dust in his black wiry hair, and murder in his eyes. I cried out—almost went down on my knees and hugged him. Then I froze.

His hands were behind his back. He was in handcuffs.

Heat rushed through my body. "You take those handcuffs *off* that child!" I shouted. "He is *eight years old!*" I was shaking. *Don't yell at men with guns, Magali!* I was afraid in another moment I was going to cry.

Beside me the young officer cleared his throat. "Indeed. I confess I am somewhat surprised."

"You wouldn't be if you'd been there, Monsieur," growled one of the men. "He bit me."

"*Bit* you?" My voice came out high.

The man flipped his wrist outward, and I saw the deep marks. No blood. I blinked.

"He's never done that before, Monsieur. I'm sorry. He's been very frightened—"

The room erupted. Everyone started talking at once. "Frightened? The kid's vicious—" "He's insane!" A big man in civvies with a black frown on his face stepped up to loom over me. "That child is a menace to society. I am pressing charges so don't think you can walk out that—"

"*Order!*" the officer shouted. "*Messieurs,* have some dignity! This is a police station, not a bar." He cleared his throat again. "Now. Do you, Mademoiselle Losier, declare that this is the same boy you described as lost in a statement dated"—the officer checked a paper—"eight o'clock this morning?"

"Yes, *Monsieur l'officier.* It's him." I took a breath. *Be polite.*

"Thank you," I said to the two policemen. "Thank you for finding him. Is there anything I need to—"

"There certainly is." It was the civilian again, and he got up in my face. "You are going to pay damages, girl. Your little kike here broke a window this big and stole—"

I guess he told me what Marek had stolen, but I didn't hear him. I was staring wide-eyed into the red distorted face of a man who would use a word like that. About a child. I could feel my blood heating up. *No. Calm. No, what'd he say? Pay damages? Not good . . .*

The calm, dry voice of the officer cut through suddenly. "I'm quite surprised, Monsieur, to learn how, ah, *large* your storeroom window was. We'll need to look into that. Now, I understand you're interested in pressing charges, but I want to warn you that that might become quite complicated."

The store owner stared at him.

"After all, he's eight years old and it seems unclear who his legal guardian is. I doubt you'd be awarded damages against an aid organization," the officer said crisply. I stared at him. "Not to mention—"

"Seems to me there's some part of 'He broke my window and stole from me' that you don't understand! It is my legal right to sue—"

The officer shrugged. "Not to mention," he finished, "that civil lawsuits are definitely outside my jurisdiction." He dusted off his hands. "I certainly can't press criminal charges against an eight-year-old. Will that be all?" He made a motion toward the door.

The red-faced jerk turned to me. "You'd better pay for my window, young lady. I have connections."

I looked at him. I had no way of knowing. But maybe he did. I reached into my bag and found the money Paquerette had given me for the trip home. I counted out enough for our train tickets and handed him the rest.

"This! This is peanuts! This'll barely pay for—"

The officer leaned over and looked at the amount. "You're right, Monsieur, it will certainly not go very far toward your legal fees if you choose to sue. Although, as I said . . ."

"That boy is a danger to the public!"

"Monsieur," I said. "All I want is to get him out of Valence. I want for you never to have to see him again," *you racist pig*, "I want to take him to the country where he'll live on a farm and he won't be a danger to anybody." *Except himself. That seems to be a given.*

"On a farm? Where'll he live, the pigpen? That oughta be about right, for his kind."

I felt my face grow hot. But my mind grew icy cold. I was going to stand there and say nothing, because that was what I had to do, for Marek's sake. I was going to stand there and say nothing, and imagine this man with a gun shoved in his face, trembling and blubbering and soiling himself.

"Well," said the officer, my friend. "It seems to me that our business here is done. The young lady has paid you what she could and agreed to remove the child from our jurisdiction. So"—he gestured commandingly toward the door—"I wish you a good day."

*Oh yeah? I wish him a miserable death.* I stood and watched as the guy stomped out. I took a deep, deep breath. And then I took another. The officer turned to me. "Will the boy behave for you? If they release him?"

I nodded. What else could I do? Marek stood between the men, not trying to kick anymore; almost calm. Worn out. I went down on one knee. "Marek," I said. He looked at me.

He actually looked at me.

"Will you come with me, and not fight anyone? I want to take you away from here. To a good place, where there's . . . grass, and three good meals a day. I promise, Marek. Will you come with me?"

It was a tiny movement, but I saw it. It was a nod.

"You can let him go now, *Messieurs*," I said to the policemen. The officer nodded. One of them pulled out a key, and took the cuffs off him. He pulled away from them, rubbing his wrists, watching their hands. He came and stood by me. Of his own free will.

"Thank you," said the officer. "Although I must say I'd prefer it if in the future you can bring in missing children without the use of handcuffs."

One of the men reddened. I managed not to laugh.

THE OFFICER had me sign a couple of papers, then said he was getting off duty and would walk me home. We headed up the street toward the agency in the slanted light of the lowering sun, each holding one of Marek's hands. Marek walked quietly, his eyes on the ground. I don't think he had anything left in him. I didn't feel so great myself.

"So," said the officer. "I keep wondering."

I blinked and looked at him, wariness coming back to me.

"How did a young lady like yourself end up with a child like this on your hands?"

"Well, sir, it wasn't just me. There was a group of us, with a woman—I'm just her assistant—taking a group of children to the country for their health. Marek got lost, so I stayed here to find him."

"For their health, you say? The officer who handed the case over to me said he was from a camp."

"Yes," I said quietly. "It's, uh . . . not very healthy in those places."

The young officer's smile twisted a little in appreciation of that, and I was glad I'd managed to restrain myself. *I'm learning. See, Paquerette? I am.*

"Um . . . not to be indiscreet, Mademoiselle, but I couldn't help wondering . . ." He glanced away, looking a little embarrassed. "Are you yourself Jewish?"

"No!" I turned and looked at him. "Why?"

"You don't work for that Jewish aid organization? The O.S.E?"

"No. I work for the CIMADE, it's a Protestant organization."

His eyebrows went up. "But you help Jews?"

*Of course we help*— "Well . . . yes . . . why wouldn't we?"

"A lot of people seem to have reasons."

*Yeah, I noticed that.* "Monsieur . . . the store owner . . . how did he know Marek was Jewish?"

"I believe he might have had the men, er . . . check."

"Check? But I had his identity papers," I said. I said it with a quiet edge to my voice, because I knew he wasn't talking about identity papers at all. It made me want to hit someone. No wonder the poor kid'd been fighting like that. I hadn't been hard enough on that storekeeper. I should've finished my little fantasy by having him shot.

The policeman looked away.

"If you really want to know," I added. "We don't ask if they're Jews. When kids need help, we help them. I don't always look at their papers in detail, myself. I don't really know why I should care."

"Hm," said the officer.

We walked in silence for half a minute or so.

"And you do this all the time?" he said suddenly.

"No, Monsieur. My parents wouldn't let me. I travel with this woman for about a week every month. I wanted to help her, she wears herself out doing it. She travels almost all the time."

"Hm," he said again.

Silence fell. The slanting sunlight was gold everywhere now. I hoped Madame Chalmette and Rosa were back at the agency now. I wanted to see the joy on Rosa's face. Marek walked quietly beside me. Once I saw him take a sidelong glance in my direction. I pretended I didn't see. *You, kid, you're something else.* Something wild. Like a fox, in the woods, who goes his own way, trusts no one. Who'd gnaw his own leg off rather than stay in a trap. Taming him would be a challenge for real.

I was almost starting to like him for it.

We got to the apartment building and paused. "Monsieur, I want to say thank you. You—" *You ended up on my side and I don't even know how.* "You really helped us. I don't know if I could've—"

"Please think nothing of it, Mademoiselle. I'm the one who's indebted to you. I've found this afternoon . . . inspiring." I looked at him. He cleared his throat. "In my job, you see, you get to watch a lot of people curry favor with those in power. You . . . you can tend to forget there's any other kind of person."

"Oh." I glanced up into his eyes and then down. It was a very intense look that I'd seen in them, just for that second. He meant it. I felt odd, and a little embarrassed, but I also felt warmth spreading through my chest.

He waited with me while Madame Chalmette came down to answer her doorbell, and together we watched her face light up. He tipped his hat to us as he said goodbye. "And good luck. I think you may need some of that."

I grinned at him. "Really?"

Rosa cried when she saw him. I washed his face. Madame Moulin brought us dinner from her house—soup with real meat broth; Marek drank it down Rivesaltes-style, holding the bowl in both hands. We took down three mattresses from the pile and spread them out on the office floor. I asked Madame Moulin to lock us in. She smiled a little, and said yes.

Marek was asleep on top of the covers, in his shoes, before the key even turned in the lock. I lay down on my mattress, feeling the heaviness of my body, feeling my head spin. I turned my head and looked over at Rosa in the fading light from the window.

"We did it," I whispered. She nodded. Her eyes didn't quite look at me. "You had a great idea." Her eyes lifted and met mine, brightening.

"We did it," she whispered.

Marek lay on his left side, his dark bruise hidden, his hard little face open now and relaxed. He looked strangely sweet like that; he looked just like somebody's little boy. I saw Rosa looking at me. She smiled.

"He's all right, I guess," I murmured.

She smiled even wider.

I DOZED. I woke, and dozed, and woke again. It was dark outside. I got up—I couldn't help it—and checked the door. It wouldn't open. Then I checked every single window, all the way around the room. None of them opened either.

I crawled back under the covers, on my thin mattress on the floor. I don't think I'd ever slept so deeply in my life.

Chapter 10

# How to Tame a Fox

THE NEXT morning was golden. The young sun was up in a cloudless sky and the birds were singing in the wet trees and everything was all right. That lasted till we got on the train.

There were two Nazi soldiers in uniform in our car.

Marek froze like a hunted deer. I raised my eyes then, and saw them—two men in *that* uniform, at the back of the car, talking in loud German and laughing.

I snapped straight into that other awareness. My emergency mind. "Do you feel all right?" I said aloud to Marek. "Let's find a window where you can get some air." I herded him gently away from the soldiers. He went. I put him in a windowseat with a balled-up sweater for a pillow, and murmured to him that he should pretend to sleep. I rubbed his back, tried to breathe, to slow my heart down. *It's all right now, don't be scared. There's nothing to be afraid of.*

*Besides, they can smell fear.*

It worked. By the time we were well underway Marek's breathing was deep and even, his face relaxing again.

I watched the Germans. One of them spoke louder than the other, laughed out loud. The other shushed him. I craned my neck for a moment and saw something leaning against the seat beside the quieter one: crutches.

Wounded. *Wounded* German soldiers.

We made it to la Voulte. I woke Marek. Rosa went down the aisle in front of him and me behind—just in case. At the last minute I went back to get my balled-up sweater, and an old lady who was getting off blocked me in. Of course that's when I saw the German soldier standing up on his crutches.

Getting ready to get off.

I was helpless. I heard it all. A shout from Rosa as the German stepped out of the train. Then the sound of running feet. I followed, trapped behind the old lady, agonizingly slow. I wanted to scream. I heard Rosa's voice shouting from *la Galoche*'s platform over to the left. I stepped down out of the train; she had Marek by the collar. It was the most beautiful sight I'd ever seen.

The Germans were staring.

I laughed out loud. It was pure instinct. The Germans turned to look at me instead.

"You just never know what that boy's going to do," I said lightly.

"Your brother, Mademoiselle?" said the one on crutches. His accent wasn't bad, and he was smiling. I smiled back, swept forward on the crazy tide of what I'd started.

"No, Monsieur. He's"—*lying is dangerous*—"an orphan. This girl is taking him to a charity children's home in the country."

"Ah. There he may run away and meet only cows, eh?"

I laughed again.

"And to where are you going, Mademoiselle?"

I swallowed, smiled. "Oh, only a little village on the plateau. I need to go wait for my train—" I gestured to *la Galoche*'s platform. The only other platform in the tiny la Voulte station. *Wait . . .*

"Oh, is that the location for the plateau train? Excellent. We are going to the plateau also. A village called Tanieux."

Unbelievable. *Unbelievable.*

"Ah. Yeah." I forced the words through my dry throat. "That's, um, I'm going there too."

He made an "after you" gesture toward *la Galoche*'s platform. Polite, these *boches*. Rosa and Marek were at the far end. I led them over slowly, smiling and chatting, and stopped as far away from Marek as possible. They stopped with me. I kept them talking. I found out they were convalescents, billeted for free at the Bellevue Hotel, courtesy of Vichy. I found out the one on crutches had broken his leg when an automobile turned over and the other one, who didn't speak French, was getting over internal injuries from a bullet wound. I wondered who'd given it to him, and hoped they were okay. They finally started talking to each other in German, and I had a moment to breathe. My heart rate began to slow down. I looked at them, standing there smiling, courteous, scaring Marek out of his mind, and suddenly I wanted to punch them.

We waited for the Nazis to come, the year they invaded. We waited in fear and trembling for them to come with their tanks and their guns and occupy us and shove us down, and then Pétain signed the surrender deal and made us the unoccupied zone and they didn't come. And now here they were smiling, on *vacation*, acting like they were our friends. I hope somebody shoots them in the back, I thought, and then I couldn't believe myself—me, the daughter of a pacifist. Not that I'd never thought about shooting people before. But never anyone I'd looked in the face. A weird shudder went down my spine.

When I heard *la Galoche*'s whistle I turned to them again and smiled. "Excuse me, Mademoiselle," said the one on crutches, "but since you are from Tanieux, might you know where the Bellevue Hotel is located?"

"It's not far from the station," I said. "I'll walk you there."

I kept them away from Marek. In a different car, in the closest seat to the entrance, ready to get out fast and clear the station of Germans before Rosa had to disembark. God willing. I prayed as the train steamed her slow way up the gorge. It wasn't till we pulled into Tanieux that a sudden panic grabbed my guts as I remembered who was going to be on the platform waiting.

My mother.

I couldn't stop. Not to scream at my own foolishness or even think what to do. I walked down the steps of that train and looked around, my heart pounding, and I saw Sonia and then—my heart leapt like a startled cat—I saw Julien. Not Mama. Julien.

And then I was free to turn and witness the arrival of the first German soldiers in Tanieux.

Oh, the people staring. Monsieur Bernard with murder in his eye, not bothering to hide it; Bernard has guts, I'll give him that. Monsieur Thibaud and Monsieur Raissac and half-a-dozen other farmers in shades of suspicion and wary contempt. And Julien looking just like one of them.

And Sonia staring, her black Spanish eyes very dark in her white face.

And then there was me. Me, with the German on crutches turning to me with a broad smile, me nodding courteously and saying, "The hotel is this way." Me with my eyes not meeting anyone else's, especially Julien's, and the voice in my head screaming *Collabo!*

It's short for *collaborator*. With the Germans, that is. It is the worst insult possible.

But these people knew me. They knew my family and they knew what I did. They would see Rosa get off trailing a boy with a bruised face, and they would know. I swept past Sonia and Julien without even looking at them, playing my part. Julien frowned after me as I led the Germans past the stationhouse into the street.

Well, what can I say? The day the first two Nazi soldiers arrived in Tanieux, I walked down the Rue de la Gare with them, one

of them clicking down the cobblestones on his crutches and telling me how France needed to realize what a service Germany
was doing for her by keeping the menace of Communism away.
While I made polite noises and pretended I couldn't see the people
stare. Step by slow step down the street, a crazy joy rising up in
me as I went. *I am walking with two Nazis who do not know I am
their enemy. I am leading them away from a Jewish boy. A boy I rescued from a camp and then from the Vichy police.* Let them stare, I
decided. They'll know, they'll all know. Likely most of them knew
already. The first Nazis in Tanieux and the first act of resistance to
them. *It starts now.*

We were at the hotel doors, and the German was telling me
his name. Erich Müller. He asked for mine, so I gave it to him. He
said France was much more hospitable than he'd expected, and
thanked me. I smiled, pictured myself spitting on his shoes, and
wished him a good stay in Tanieux.

"So," said a voice behind me. I jumped. "Want to tell me what
that was about?"

Julien. Of course.

"You were *following* me?"

He gave me the *"You idiot"* look.

"You have no idea what was going on. I *had* to do that."

"Go on." He folded his arms.

"Rosa was in the other car with Marek. That kid we were looking for in Valence? He was terrified of those guys. If I hadn't drawn
them off he'd have run off again or given himself away or both."

"Hm."

"Julien?"

"Yeah?"

"How's Mama?"

He gave me an ironic look. "You mean, do you have to clean
the house now?"

I bared my teeth at him. That was *so* unfair. "What did I ever do to you? I washed your muddy pants all spring after your stupid soccer games and you didn't ever say a word of thanks and now when I'm out saving children's lives—"

"Yeah, you're a big hero, Magali. Believe it or not we got that, after all this time. And if you really want to talk about my muddy pants, I got mud on them doing spring planting with Grandpa to put food on the table for our family. So don't act like you're suddenly the only grown-up in this family just because you finally learned how to work. Mama's in bed. She met the train yesterday and Paquerette was on it without you. Not your brightest idea."

My stomach was getting cold. "I had to. And Rosa was with me. We were fine." I glanced down the street toward the hotel. "Um—"

"*I'll* tell her about the *boches*. You just let me handle it."

"B—"

"You don't think you can keep her in the dark about that in this town, do you? Don't worry, I don't want her upset either, I care how she feels." There was just the slightest emphasis on the *I*. My fingers clenched. "You just let me handle it, okay?"

I bit my tongue, and nodded.

He kept his word, at least.

There was soup on the stove, scorching on a too-hot fire built by Papa. I scattered the fire and stirred. Mama came out of the bedroom and beamed at me through her pain lines. Everything was normal. We sat down and ate.

It was a sight to learn from, really, the way Julien handled her. Smiling, explaining that the *boches* had asked for my help, that I'd felt it was safer to be polite—his voice even and confident. I could see the nervousness grow and then die back in Mama's eyes.

"It looks like we've got to live with them, after all," he said calmly. "We don't want to get them angry."

Papa nodded. "I think that's probably true."

Mama turned to me, her face very solemn. "Magali—you'll be careful, won't you? Promise you'll be careful, with men like that."

"I was very careful, Mama."

"I'm not sure you know how dangerous they are." Her eyes were intense, staring into mine. "Some men, Magali . . . when they think they can get away with things . . ." *No.* I could see it all coming again—see her huge eyes, in the attic during the invasion—disgust rose in me. Men, it was always men. Sure I hated Erich Müller's guts and I had a right to, but he hadn't looked at me *that* way, nor his friend, not even once. She didn't even know what she was talking about.

I lowered my head. *Control yourself, Magali.* I took a deep breath and raised my face to her, very serious. "Yes, Mama," I said in a low voice. "You're right. I need to be very careful."

Mama nodded. Convinced.

After lunch I went down to les Chênes.

The les Chênes kitchen was full of kids and noise and sunshine. I stopped in the doorway and watched Carmela, whose bleeding feet I had washed months ago, hand a plate from the sink to a boy with a dishtowel and laugh at something he said. Her long black hair was combed and soft. Her arms weren't stick-skinny anymore, and there was color in her face. The boy turned toward me. I saw a scar on his right cheek.

"Oh hi, Magali!" called out Claudine. "You bringing us another?"

"No, I, uh—"

"Magali!" Manola came running to me and hugged me round the waist. I stared down at her in my arms. After a moment she looked up shyly. "Hi."

"You speak French now . . ."

"This fall I'll go to school!"

"You remember Carmela and Manola I guess. D'you remember Stepan and Chanah? You brought them yourself too, I think."

The boy with the scar turned to me again and I remembered seeing a bandage there, months ago on a cold winter day. A girl who was wiping the long, scarred pine table looked up at me under brown bangs. She had collapsed in the snow in hysterics that day because some kid on skis surprised her. She smiled shyly at me.

I swallowed through the tightness in my throat. "Yeah. I remember them." I remembered praying for them. Turning back and looking at the two huge oaks, and hoping they'd be happy here. I turned to Claudine. "Do you all here need any . . . you know . . . *help*?"

Her eyebrows went straight up and her mouth twitched like she was trying to keep from laughing. "Well, if you have any idea what to do with that boy you all sent us this morning, that might help. Seeing he's locked himself in his room." Julie, the other les Chênes counselor, nodded vigorously. "You go on up. Tell Papa Thiély we sent you."

Monsieur Thiély glanced up at me from where he knelt by Marek's door, screwdriver in hand, his friendly young face looking weary and intent. "Stand back."

The door startled to topple, and I darted forward and helped him catch it. He gave me a raised eyebrow. We looked inside.

The bed was pushed up against the window. On it stood Marek, trying to crank the window open, his bruised face red.

"Marek!"

He looked up at me. His eyes changed. It did my heart good to see it. He looked at Monsieur Thiély and pulled back. Monsieur Thiély looked at him for a long moment, and at me, and stepped behind the doorframe.

I swallowed. "Marek," I said, in my most cheerful, confident voice. "Come with me. There's something I want to show you."

I added, with a glance at Monsieur Thiély, "Outside." Monsieur Thiély nodded: *okay.*

He followed me. I didn't try to take his hand this time, or even touch him. I beckoned and he followed me down the hall and down the stairs, through the living room where an older girl was playing on the piano, and out the back door. He followed me along the edge of the sprawling vegetable garden, where a group of kids were on their knees weeding a long line of cabbages. "Hey, it's the new kid!" "Hi, new kid!" "D'you remember his name, Aurélie?"

Marek glanced at them quickly, then away. I led him through the back gate into a goat pasture, where a trace of a footpath in the grass led to a winding line of pine trees. Sure sign of a stream. I took him there.

It felt sheltered under the pines, quiet. No sound but the soft happy chatter of running water. Marek's eyes were as wild and unreadable as those of a fox in the woods. "C'mon, Marek," I said, taking my shoes off. "Get in."

We stayed out there for an hour and a half. I talked to him, told him about les Chênes. I sat on the bank and watched while he tried to catch minnows. I splashed him once, but he flinched, and didn't splash me back.

There was this about Marek: yes, he was like a fox in the woods, with his fierceness and his wanting to be free. A creature who'd chew his own leg off if it was caught in a trap; you could see it in his eyes, and I think that's what I loved about him. But there was this too: he wasn't just someone who would chew his own leg off. He was someone who already had.

That night I went down to l'Espoir and talked to Madame Sabatier. She listened and nodded, and Paquerette nodded too. Madame Sabatier told me Sonia was coming every day now that school was over, and so was Madeleine's cousin. She could spare me this week, and she could go on sparing me if necessary. Paquerette gave a half smile, and said Monsieur Thiély was a smart man. I stroked Léon's downy hair, and in my mind I said, *I'm sorry. I'm sorry. But you'll be all right—you won't even remember me—and there's something I have to do.* And it would take a long time, I knew that too. Grandpa's told me before how you tame a wild fox, or a deer, or any wild thing really. It takes day after day after day.

But I had to. I had to make Marek stop chewing.

THERE WERE four teams, at les Chênes. They switched off each week on their chores: dishes, cooking, cleaning, gardening. The Squirrels were on kitchen duty that week. It was Wolves, Hawks, Owls, and Squirrels; don't ask me how *that* happened. Carmela and Manola and Stepan and Chanah were the Squirrels, and by the next day, Marek was one too. I was there to help him "integrate."

I handed him a broom and he held it as if he thought it was a weapon but wasn't quite sure how it worked. He started knocking it against the counters. I took it from him and showed him how to sweep, but he wasn't looking, and he just started knocking it against the counters again. I told him he better sweep. He didn't look like he'd heard me. I could see Stepan, who was waiting to mop, heating up. Then he lost it.

"Sweep, stupid! I don't have all day!"

I could see his point. Marek, on the other hand . . .

Well, Marek hit him with the broom.

Claudine grabbed him by the collar. I was glad she was there. "Marek, you're not allowed to hit. Because you hit Stepan you can't come to singing time tonight."

I saw Marek's face fall. He tried to control it but I saw it. Interesting.

I had to see this singing time.

"HE'S A *Squirrel?*" Lucy laughed out loud.

It was so great to be with Lucy. I hated to think of her leaving. Only three weeks. I wanted to sit cross-legged on her bed forever, with her slanted attic-bedroom ceiling over us, laughing. She took just the right attitude to the Erich Müller story, of course.

"And you totally fooled them?"

"They said France was 'more hospitable than they thought.'" I imitated Erich Müller's overly polite tones, and Lucy rewarded me with a snort.

"Man, I wish I could've done that. Magali . . . can you keep a secret?"

My heart beat a little faster. "Yeah."

"I . . . I know what I could do, now. Who I could help, for the, you know . . . the Resistance. Auntie knows someone who—oh, I really shouldn't tell."

"Oh, c'mon! You got me all curious and then you chicken out?"

She leaned in very close and breathed one word. "Forgery."

"You mean—?"

She laid a finger on her lips, her eyes bright. Then they clouded. Then she took that finger and made it part of a fist, and hit her bedroom wall. Hard.

"Three weeks," she said. "Three. Stupid. Weeks."

"Man. Lucy. I'm sorry." What else could you say?

"Yeah," she said. "Me too."


IT WAS its own world, les Chênes. The Squirrels sitting in the kitchen singing *"Savez-Vous Planter Les Choux"* while they peeled potatoes. Game time, everyone in one big circle on the grass, their eyes shut tight while the "fox" went round. Singing time after supper with Papa Thiély at the piano, all those child voices rising together in a round: *fresh morning wind, lifting the tops of the tall pines, joy of the passing wind,* they sang, and I saw the joy on their faces, in their flushed cheeks and bright eyes. Joy of the singing circle. That was les Chênes—a little happy world of working and playing and singing, all together in one circle; and outside it, Marek. They didn't want him to be; he just was.

He didn't talk. He didn't sing. He peeled potatoes like a convict sentenced to hard labor. At meals they put him at the end of the table, because he hit kids who got their hands too close to his food. He stood on the edge of circle games with sad wariness in his eyes, and I took him away again to the stream. I took off my shoes and we walked downstream in the shallow water together, all the way to the river. He climbed a tree barefoot and jumped from it into the river, with all his clothes on, without even warning me. I saw his face as he came up. He was grinning.

On Friday night he was allowed to come to singing time; he'd gone a whole day without hitting anyone. He sat at the edge of the living room, silent while I sang and clapped along with the kids, his dark eyes taking everything in. I thought I saw less fear in them now. More longing. Wondering if maybe he did want to be a part of this little world of work and play and music.

Or maybe I just thought that's what I saw, because I was wondering that myself.

"YOU'RE SERIOUS about this, Magali?"

"Yes, sir. I thought I should ask now. So you have time to think about it."

"And what do you think could convince us that this is a wise course?"

I lowered my eyes, and raised them to Papa's. If I could keep my cool through this whole conversation . . .

"Well, Papa, the work I'm doing at the children's home is useful. They want me to stay. And the work I do with Paquerette as well. It's, it's worth doing. And I've passed my *troisième*-year exams now, and I can still go to *lycée*—I can start a year from now. When I'm more ready and mature." I took a breath. "And it'll save the family money."

Papa's eyebrows went up at that last one. But Mama sat silent in her chair. She wasn't turning pale this time. Her eyes were on the ground.

"Well," said Papa.

"We can't make you care, can we?" said Mama. "We can send you to school but . . . in the end . . ."

*Can't you see how much I care? But yeah. Not about that. Why did she care?* She didn't even have an education herself. She didn't even *know* what it was like.

She didn't know what it was like.

I saw her, for a moment. My age. Working in a field because she didn't have any other choices. A farm girl. Poor. *Mama, this is different.* Someone called you stupid, didn't they, I thought. A stupid little girl from a conquered country. *Mama, I'm sorry they did that. I wish you hadn't believed.*

"Mama . . ." I lifted my head, my breath coming ragged, and looked into her dark eyes. "Mama . . . aren't you glad I'm helping kids?"

Tears welled in her eyes. They almost came to mine too. "Yes," she whispered.

I waited.

Mama sat silent. Papa put a hand on hers. "We will consider your request, Magali," he said.

I bent my head.

PAQUERETTE CAME in on Monday. I missed her. Sonia came in to les Chênes by herself, trailing one Spanish ten-year-old named Tonio, with a fiery look in his eye. I met them on my way home.

I had to do the dishes that night, and it was late by the time I was free to go to l'Espoir. If it'd been a bad trip, Paquerette might be in bed by now, I realized as I walked down.

I'd just check.

I pushed the heavy door open—we don't knock at l'Espoir—and stood listening. There was a faint sound of voices from upstairs. I could at least go up and greet her.

I started up the stairs, then stopped. The voices were from her room. I listened.

"But you know, Rosa did think she had reason. It didn't seem like such a large risk," Paquerette said. "She does know how to handle herself, you know."

"You did not see her, Mademoiselle. She did not understand what she was doing. I—she was flirting with them."

I froze.

The voice was Nina's. Unmistakable. *Flirting with them?* What did she mean?

What else could she mean?

"Nina, I don't think Magali would flirt with Germans. Really."

"Not because she likes them, Mademoiselle. Ah, how can I say? Perhaps not flirting. She was . . . enjoying. She thought that she had . . . what is the word . . . control. You must believe me. I see this." She was getting agitated, louder. "I know. Once, I was like this. I trust, I think I will not fail. She is not wise, Mademoiselle. I am afraid she will be hurt. This work, it is for adults."

I couldn't move.

"I know she's not fully mature, Nina, but she's growing up very fast, and I can't tell you what a help she's been to me. Besides, do you mean to say Rosa is unsuitable too?"

There was a silence.

"That is different, Mademoiselle."

Another silence. And the awful sound of Paquerette, not contradicting.

Then a loud scrape of wood, of a chair on the bedroom floor. *She's getting up, she's coming down, she'll know*—I moved. I have never been so swift and silent in my life. The huge door swung shut without a whisper. The only sound was my mind. Screaming.

I don't even know which way I ran.

Chapter 11

# The Voices

It's NOT the kind of secret you can tell somebody, not this.

It's the kind of secret you keep in your heart, shifting it around from one spot to another because it burns. Because if it burns through something might begin to leak in. *You're just a girl. A girl from a conquered country. Who do you think you are?* The voices will leak in, the voices you hate.

So you shift, and you shift, because you can't get it out. And because they can't be right about you. They can't.

I lay on my bed facedown on the pillow, for hours, shaking, my whole body wanting to hit her, to hit Nina the poor crippled girl and knock her off her crutches onto the ground— No. Wanting her to be strong, so I could *fight* her. Grapple hand to hand and do *something* with all the wild helpless angry strength that ran through me. Nina, the crippled girl, the one you're supposed to feel sorry for, *Nina* going behind my back like that, going to *Paquerette* and saying I wasn't fit—

Paquerette wouldn't listen, would she? She knew me. I knew her. The look in her eyes, the confidence in me, she knew!

*I know she's not fully mature.*

*Do you mean to say Rosa is unsuitable too?*

*That is different, Mademoiselle.*

And that silence. That silence.

The words stabbed through me again and again; but the silence, that burned. The back of my throat filled with the taste of betrayal. *Nina*—Nina had never worked with her, not the *real* work. Nina had never exchanged that glance with her that said *I've got your back*, and then made good on the promise. *I* had.

And yet she could sit there listening to Nina say *Rosa* was fit for the work and I wasn't—and not say a word to contradict? Nina who was so scared of Monsieur Bernard after almost two whole years that she still stayed behind the stationhouse when we met the train—what did she know? Nina had never saved a child's life. *I* had. I'd saved Marek. If I hadn't been there Paquerette couldn't have taken him—not him. If I hadn't stood up to those policemen and gotten him back, he'd have gone back to Rivesaltes, or worse. And I knew now how a kid as scared as him had gotten himself hit with a gun butt—he was *too* scared. Too scared to do as he was told. To do anything but run or fight.

He wouldn't have lasted much longer in that camp.

And *I* had gotten him out, and kept him safe, and this was what I got. Paquerette listening to a scared girl whispering that I took *risks*. As if Paquerette didn't walk into a lion's den every week to take his prey.

There were two kinds of people in the world. And *I* knew which kind Paquerette needed, if Nina didn't.

She would see.

PAQUERETTE LEFT again the next day. I didn't even get to see her. I didn't go to les Chênes. I couldn't. I went to the farm with

Julien and Benjamin, and hoed turnips. Chopping at the earth again and again numbed my mind, a little. Nina's voice played in my head in an endless loop. I felt sick to my stomach. I lay down beside my hoe, between the rows of turnip greens, with my arms around myself and my face practically in the dirt. I didn't know what to do to make it stop. *Make it stop!* I kept swallowing. I felt strange.

"Magali?" I sat up fast. Grandpa was peering over the plants at me. "Are you all right?"

"Yeah. Yeah."

He looked at me. "Are you sure?"

But this wasn't the kind of secret you can tell someone, not this. *Someone I don't even respect thinks I'm a little fool who flirts with German soldiers, Grandpa, and it's killing me. She said so to Paquerette, and it's killing me.*

*Why is it so terrible, Magali? You don't think Paquerette would listen? You don't think she's right?*

*Do you?*

"I'm fine."

Grandpa nodded slowly, and turned away.

THE NEXT day I pulled myself together and went to les Chênes. They asked me where I'd been. Marek had a black eye, and Tonio had a split lip and fresh scratches on his face. They'd both been sent to bed with only bread for supper, the night before. Apparently Tonio really *had* tried to steal food from Marek's plate. I was secretly impressed with Marek; Tonio was pretty big.

We took them to the river during afternoon free time. I walked behind the others with Marek, trying not to think about Nina. I watched him run on the grass, his legs already sturdier, that terrible Rivesaltes dryness gone, now, from his skin. I felt a twinge deep inside me. *Isn't that worth something? Isn't it?* But when he turned his face toward me—the faded, yellowing bruise on his left cheek and the fresh black eye on his right—I felt guilt. I hadn't been there to stop it. Keep them apart, calm him down. There they were, getting too close to each other again. I tensed as Tonio swaggered toward Marek. I stood poised and staring, as Marek *got out of his way.*

"Well." Papa Thiély stood behind me, smiling a little ruefully. "Now we have two of them, eh?"

*They're not alike. Tonio's just mean*— I shut my teeth on that. Tonio'd been in Rivesaltes too. *Yeah. One of those kids in Rivesaltes who steal from the younger ones—*

"I wanted you to know, Magali, that I'm putting Tonio with the Squirrels."

I stared at him. "You are?"

"I'm afraid it's time for extreme measures. Marek has gotten into ten fights this week. In an ordinary situation I would consider sending him home at this point. Of course this is an extraordinary situation . . ." He raised his eyebrows and looked out at the kids. The girls had gotten some kind of dancing game going. I heard them clapping and singing, "*Allons passe, passe, passe, allons passe donc . . .*"

Papa Thiély turned to me and said, "I hope you understand how important it is, that he learn to trust us and obey. We don't know what is coming."

A little chill went down my back. I nodded.

The next day we put Marek on sweeping the floor and Tonio on mopping.

Marek swept.

I TURNED over and over in bed at night, trying not to think of Nina and Paquerette. Trying. I couldn't stand it.

Finally I got my courage up and told Lucy.

Lucy told me not to worry, Paquerette wasn't going to fire me for that—she'd probably just tell me to be careful or something. I imagined Paquerette telling me to be careful. On Nina's say-so. I shuddered. I looked at Lucy.

She was looking out the window, west, toward the sea.

On Saturday I met the train. I wasn't going to skip *that*.

I had to walk down there with Nina, and listen to her and Rosa talking about the summer tutoring Nina was doing with Mademoiselle Pinatel. Learning dead languages while the live world around her burned.

"Magali," Rosa said suddenly, "when is Lucy leaving?"

"Next Thursday."

"Is it true," said Nina, "that she does not wish to go to America?"

I turned round. "That's right." *Want her visa?* "She wants to stay and help."

"She was helping?" Rosa asked.

"She never got the chance but she knew something she could do. Only it's a secret."

Nina's brows drew down. "What did she tell to you?"

"Well I can't tell you."

"And she?" Her long over-serious face looked like an old lady's. "Was she permitted, to tell you?"

"She barely told me anything. And she's leaving. And I'm not telling anyone either. Not even you."

"You promise this?"

"What's it got to do with you?"

She was frowning deeply now, her eyes smoldering. A very un-Nina look, really. I remembered when she'd been scared to ever displease anyone. "I know how it is to almost die. This is not a game. There are men who will kill us."

"I know," I snapped. I turned and kept walking. I didn't look back.

We walked the rest of the way in silence. I stood and watched Nina hide in her alley, wondering how even she could expect me to listen to someone who acted like that. She didn't meet my eyes.

PAQUERETTE BROUGHT a group of teens from Gurs. They were all bound for les Aigles and Nina's dorm, so Nina took them. They walked off speaking German to each other, and Paquerette turned an utterly weary face to us and said she'd better get to l'Espoir. I carried her suitcase.

She said nothing about what Nina had told her that night, nor the next day. I didn't ask about our next trip. She talked about Gurs, and I talked about les Chênes, and the singing and the skits they put on every Saturday night. She smiled, and said not every man could do with children what Monsieur Thiély could.

She left for Rivesaltes the next day. She took Rosa. Because she was scheduled to take her, it was her turn. I told myself it would be all right. I worked long hours at les Chênes that week, came home and helped Mama with the dishes. That made me tired enough to go to sleep, and not lie there thinking in the dark. Most nights.

LUCY LEFT. On Thursday, a hot, still day with a thin layer of damp cloud over the sky like a lid. We all sweated, walking her to the train. I carried one of her suitcases. I wished I were leaving too. Not for America, God forbid. Just Rivesaltes. Just Rivesaltes, where the barracks would be like ovens right now, dark and stinking with sweat. A little knot of fear lay still and heavy in my belly, fear that I would never see that terrible place again. Life is too strange. Sometimes you can't even try to understand it.

I hugged Lucy, Irish-style, and when I let her go I caught her wiping her eyes. I told her I'd write her letters. I could see in her eyes that she remembered the censors at the same moment I did. Her face twisted up into the oddest grin and laugh I'd ever seen on her.

"Just make sure you write *Vive la résistance* on every one, okay?"

"Oh yeah. I promise."

Her grin straightened a little. Better. My last Lucy grin, to remember her by.

The long high whistle of the train as it pulled out was like a far-off scream.

PAQUERETTE CAME back. She asked if she could take me on the next trip. I almost died of relief.

Then Mama got a migraine. Her first since I'd come home with Marek. I had to miss a couple of days at les Chênes, filling in for her. Nina and Gustav were invited one of those nights. I made potatoes and cabbage. It wasn't very good, but what do you expect? With me chopping cabbage and onions and stoking the fire, hearing Mama and Nina's muffled voices from the bedroom, while Gustav leaned on the counter and cracked jokes at me. I put a knife in his hand and told him to peel potatoes or get out. His black eyebrows shot up into his hairline. He peeled. And kept the jokes coming. Eventually I even started to laugh.

Marek only hit Stepan once while I was gone, but he did disappear for an afternoon. They found him wading in the creek, almost down to the river. Apparently Stepan had told him he wasn't a Squirrel and he wished he'd go away, and Marek hit him. Papa Thiély gave them each a Serious Talk, after. Maybe it helped.

Manola and Chanah ran up and hugged me when I got there. The Squirrels were on weeding duty. Carmela was showing Marek that you could eat the chickweed, but Marek was too busy yanking up the big pigweeds—just ripping them out of the ground. I caught Tonio watching him. Then Tonio started doing it too, trying to go even faster. I almost laughed.

In the afternoons we took them swimming. I only went with the girls of course. I taught Manola how to dog-paddle. Complimented Hanne on how far she could swim underwater. They splashed me and I splashed them back. It was amazing, really, in the middle of everything that was happening; to be in the middle of a group of laughing girls, in the water, in the sun.

LUCY WAS right. On the way to Rivesaltes, Paquerette told me to be careful.

She asked me questions. First about the police in Valence, then the soldiers. I wasn't supposed to notice I was being interrogated, I guess. Then she took a deep breath, and I braced.

"Magali," she asked, looking in my eyes, "were you afraid of these men?"

I blinked. I had absolutely no idea what to say.

"I . . . I guess so. At first. I don't know, I mostly thought about what to do. Like keeping Marek away from them. He was drawing way too much attention to himself. He's got to learn not to be so scared, it puts him in more danger."

"Mm." Paquerette looked out the train window. We were deep in the south by then, riding past lavender fields, line after line of deep purple. It was hot. "Fear isn't a bad thing, though, Magali. In right measure."

My heart sank. I'd given her the wrong answer.

"Marek, for instance. I would guess he has excellent reasons to be afraid of German soldiers. Our convalescents here may have no intention in the world of doing us harm, but that doesn't mean we can afford to treat them as safe. I'd say Marek is just as afraid of them as he needs to be. But he does need to learn to hide rather than run."

I nodded. "Yes, I see."

She turned to me. "You know, people are always saying, 'Don't be afraid.' That may have been good advice once, but not now. When there's really something to fear it's foolish not to. I don't stifle my fear, Magali. It makes me think of all the possibilities, before I make a decision."

I turned and looked at her. Her eyes were dark.

"I'm afraid all the time, Magali," she said in a lower voice. "I'm afraid every time I walk into a camp, and more when I walk out with the children. I am afraid of being arrested. I am afraid of being shot. I am horribly, deathly afraid of one of the children under my care being arrested and taken back. Or deported. Or worse."

Neither of us spoke. The train went *clack-clack* over its rails. *Clack-clack, clack-clack.* The fields ran by outside the window: purple, green, green, purple, gold. The gold was colza in bloom; they grow it for oil. I thought of the oil bottle at home, of pouring a little into the frying pan and chopping up an onion—one more weary day, one more meal for my family, in the exhausted days before the spring had come. I thought of what people don't know about each other. How easy it is to think someone's a child, when you haven't seen their real life. I thought about how I was sitting on a train listening to Paquerette praise fear. After standing at the foot of the l'Espoir stairs listening to Nina do the exact same thing.

So they were going to make me prove myself a second time. Fine. I gritted my teeth, and looked out at the fields, and vowed to be a quiet, gray little mouse. Like Nina.

I hated Nina.

When I walked in the gates of Rivesaltes for the third time, I bent my head submissively to the armed guard, and murmured, "*Merci, Monsieur*" as he clanged the gate behind us. I did what I was told. I walked into dark, hot, stinking barracks and walked out of them with children who should never have had to see them, and at the block gate I was polite to the man with the gun.

We got a ride into the village behind a tractor. We had to share the wagon with another group—a woman taking five kids to some children's home run by a Jewish organization. We scrambled up into the dusty wagon bed littered with cabbage leaves, and the kids didn't miss a beat. When the engine roared into life and we jolted away from Rivesaltes, they were all chewing.

We sat huddled together, our sweaty clothes sticking to the

wagon sides and to each other. I had two little girls in my care, and a boy who limped from a cut foot. Paquerette had two more kids plus three Polish fifteen-year-olds. Just barely making it out. They won't release boys older than that—no matter where they're from—in case they go join the German army. I have to wonder what goes through those people's heads.

Halfway there the engine coughed and thumped and died. We heard clanging and a few unprintable words from up front, and then a hand banging on the high wooden sides of our wagon. "Can I get some help out here?" We all looked at each other, then at the boys. The boys looked at each other. Paquerette looked at me. I sighed, and got out.

The farmer frowned at me, then shrugged. "Hold up the hood," he said. "Here, use this rag, the metal's hot." It was heavy. He rummaged inside the engine, then in a toolbox, muttering to himself "I should know better" and "Don't know how long I can keep running this thing." He had a thick Provençal accent. Finally he glanced at me. "Young lady, I don't suppose . . ." Then he froze, his eyes on the road. A cloud of dust was approaching. An open-topped automobile, with two uniformed men in it.

The farmer spat on the ground. "*Les boches,*" he said.

"Here?" My voice came out too high.

"They inspect that camp. That camp was for foreigners and Communists and enemy sympathizers, that's what they told us. Now we got the *boches* themselves inspecting it. It smells."

I glanced at his tractor. He followed my gaze. "They have to eat, don't they?" he snapped.

The German automobile slowed. My heart sped up. It stopped, and the man in the passenger seat snapped out, "*Was ist los?*"

Yeah. We were supposed to know *German* now.

"Well, Monsieur, I just made a delivery to Camp Joffre there, and my tractor's broken down. I don't suppose you might have—"

The man lifted a hand. "Stop. Repeat. Slower."

I saw his eyes flash a little, but he tried. Provençal people aren't really good at talking slow, I've noticed. The German frowned. I looked at the long, hot, dusty road ahead and I thought of Joseph with the cut foot and—

"Excuse me, Monsieur." *Shut up, stupid!* screamed my mind. "Maybe I can explain?"

The German gave me a little smile. "And from where have you come, *mein schönes Mädchen?*"

*I'm not your pretty girl. I'm an idiot. There are ten Jewish kids in that wagon. They're legal. Legal.* I didn't look at the wagon. I waved my hand toward a dusty side road. "I live that way. My mother has sent me into town. This man asked for help, and so I am helping him."

"Ah, and so perhaps he will give you a ride? Yes? You will give this young lady a ride?"

"Sure, Monsieur."

"So now." The man smiled at me again. He was tall and blond and he looked at me like I was put on earth for him to look at. I didn't like him. "What does he need?"

He needed a rope or a strip of canvas. To replace the fan belt. I told them that in slow, simple French. They found a piece of tough cord in the back of his automobile that lit the farmer's eyes right up. "*Merci, Messieurs*, now that'll do."

"No need to thank me, it is only for *la jolie fille* here." He looked at me expectantly.

I made myself look him in the eye, and smile. "Thank you very much, Monsieur."

He winked at me.

I held the hood up for the farmer while he fixed the engine. Then I walked back to the wagon to meet my fate.

It DIDN'T come till the next day. It was a tough evening. Almost all the kids were sick. One of the girls threw up her supper. Joseph's foot was infected, which honestly we had expected; I washed it and helped Madame Alençon press out and disinfect the cut and put on a clean bandage. One of the girls had an infection that made her yell with pain whenever she used the bathroom. Another kid wet the bed. I pulled the wet sheets off and balled them up in the corner to sit till morning, and went groggily back to my bed. The next day was basically more of the same. I can still see that tiny train bathroom; I saw it so many times.

It wasn't till Montélimar, when we'd settled the group down on a couple of benches for two hours' wait for the local train to la Voulte, that Paquerette had time for the Talk.

"Magali, why did you speak to those soldiers?"

I swallowed. "I was already out there. I just thought it . . . it would help." I motioned toward Joseph. *He would've had to* walk. *Oh Paquerette, you won't fire me for helping, will you?* "I shouldn't have. I'm sorry."

She blinked. "You're sorry?"

I nodded. "Yeah. It was stupid. I won't do it again."

"Not stupid, but rather incautious. I'm concerned about the pattern I'm seeing here." A chill went down my spine. "Don't trust your cleverness with these men, Magali. They are the masters of this country, and they are very dangerous. With them you are never in control."

I turned away so she wouldn't see the word *control* go through me like a knife.

Joan of Arc was speaking to me, and all I could hear was Nina. Nina's words. It was a terrible feeling, like a void opening up beneath my feet; a cold voice whispering, *You will lose everything.* I swallowed. The words came to me instantly, without thought.

"It's true, Paquerette. I know. I was really scared."

I watched her face; it opened. Her eyebrows slightly rising, her serious gray eyes growing just a shade wider. *You do understand. I've misjudged you,* said the look on Paquerette's face, as I watched her believe my lie.

THE LOCAL train never showed up; we had to take the late express to Valence. Madame Moulin and Madame Chalmette gave us supper, and two of the kids threw up again. The whole milk was too rich for their starved stomachs. Joseph woke up crying in the night when someone rolled over onto his bad foot. We waited all morning in the train station with our sick kids. The local got there at noon. Problems with the track, they said.

At least there were no Germans on *la Galoche*, on the last leg home.

Mama met us. She hugged me, and took the littlest girl—still sick and subdued—from my arms and kissed her. "What's her name?"

"Sarah," I whispered. My legs felt shaky.

"Go home and lie down, Magali," my mother said. "Rosa and I will take them."

I went home and lay down.

WHEN I woke I had no idea what time it was. Bright slices of light came in through the chinks in my closed shutters. I got up and went downstairs. Mama was doing the breakfast dishes. I stood blinking in the morning light.

"I didn't wake you for supper. You looked so tired. You slept fifteen hours."

She sat me down and practically hand-fed me. She spread real butter on my bread, and real, precious raspberry jam. She watched me drink my glass of milk, her forehead furrowed with worry. It was very good milk. She poured me another. "Mama—"

"Drink it," she said.

"Mama, did you have any headaches? While I was gone?"

"Of course I had a headache," she said almost roughly. "How do you feel? Are you still hungry? There's more milk."

"Mama, I can't just drink three—"

"You can and you will." She grabbed the half-full glass from me and went to the icebox to fill it up. Her hands shook. She put the glass in front of me and then suddenly she had me in her arms, my head against her belly, shaking. "My daughter," she whispered. "My daughter."

I didn't fight her. She was holding me so hard. I remembered clutching Léon to my chest in the l'Espoir nursery, just that hard, as I heard a cry from the next room. I remembered Zvi's gasping breaths. My heart turned over inside me. "Mama," I whispered. I didn't know how to say what I felt. *Mama, I know.*

"My daughter," my mother said softly. "I am so proud of you."

I SPENT the morning lying on the sofa and reading. I was that tired. When I walked down to l'Espoir in the afternoon, Paquerette was barely awake. She said she wanted to talk to me. She said she needed to get out of the house. She drank a last gulp of her tea, rubbed her face, and took me outside, down toward the path by the river. We didn't speak for a while. Then she turned to me.

"Would your parents let you travel to Marseille? If you went with Eva and Pastor Alex?"

"Marseille?"

She nodded. "There's news. Léon's mother is free, and she wants him. She and her husband have visas to Brazil."

I stopped and stared at her. "Free?" I couldn't help myself; I grabbed her and hugged her. "Brazil? Really? Free?"

She hugged me back and then put me at arm's length, laughing. Her eyes were bright. "You're good for my heart, Magali," she said. She blinked. I realized the brightness was tears. A strange lump rose in my throat.

We were at the footpath by the river now. Paquerette sat down on a bench, rubbed her hands hard against her face. "I'm going home," she said.

"Home?"

"My director's making me. For two weeks." Her voice lowered. "I haven't seen my parents in almost a year."

I stared at her. "A year?"

She made a jerky, half-finished gesture. "We . . . I don't know if we're on good terms."

"Why?"

She shrugged. "The last time I saw them, my father made a last attempt to . . . dissuade me. From my work. He told me we were fools and children playing in the trenches. Oh yes, and that Pétain was an honorable man. And then I raised my voice to him for the first time in my life and my mother started to cry. And then I walked out, and went to the barn to cry, myself, and talk to the cow." She gave me a sideways glance. "Paquerette. I named myself after her."

I pictured her—Paquerette, Joan of Arc—leaning against a barn wall in the dark, crying.

"That wasn't the very last time I saw them. But close." She took a long, deep breath, and let it out slowly. "My father's a retired officer. He served under Marshal Pétain in the last war. It gives him a certain point of view on things, you see. But they're good people, for all of that. They've always given me the best they had."

I looked at her.

"I'm afraid, Magali." She said it very low. "I'm afraid to go."

The sun came out, and glanced blindingly off the water. I had no idea what to say.

"I'm at the end of my strength," said Paquerette. "It's been so long since I've felt . . . all right. They'll see that. They'll see how much I need them. They'll say, 'Stay.' Because they want to give me the best they have. And I. Can't. Stay." She turned her eyes on me fierce as a hawk's.

I would have done anything for her. My Joan of Arc.

But I had no idea what to do.

I wanted to say, *You are strong.* She was everything I knew about strength, this woman with the deep, quick gray eyes and the spine of steel. She was always ready, always. From the day I met her, she was always ready, no matter how weary she was, to stand up straight and do what had to be done.

But I looked at her, at the dark circles around her fierce eyes and I thought, *Everybody breaks sometime.* I thought. *She's not God.* I looked down at my empty hands.

She sat looking out at the running water. There were tears in her eyes.

A breeze rose, sending us cool air from over the water. Strands of hair blew around Paquerette's face. She breathed it in, deep, deep, and slowly she straightened. She sat perfectly still for a moment. Then she turned to me with her gray Paquerette eyes: kindness and irony and sorrow and strength. Just like always. I don't know how she did it.

"Well," she said. "Let's go see if your parents will let you start Léon on his journey to Brazil."

It was all arranged. I'd leave for Marseille in a week. I'd travel down with Pastor Alex and with Eva, who was going to see her French aunt in Aix-en-Provence. She'd actually sent Eva her French cousin's papers to travel on so she'd be safe. They had a family for me stay with, too—the same American that Lucy was still staying with. *Lucy.*

I would also see Benjamin's parents. This American we'd be staying with worked for the American Friends Service Committee, getting people visas to leave the country. Trying to get hundreds of people out. Benjamin's parents were on the list.

Benjamin got jumpier than ever when he heard we were going to see them. My parents suggested I could take them a letter from him, and he nodded and then he just shut down. Looking at nothing. Every now and then for the rest of the day he would look at me—stare at me—then turn suddenly away.

"What?"

"Nothing."

The night before I left we got terrible news. Papa heard it from
Pastor Alex. There'd been a round-up in Paris—police going
round the city specifically to arrest Jewish men. Foreign Jewish
men, Papa said. "That seems to be the line they are drawing. As
if they believe the French people won't resist as long as their own
aren't threatened." He ran his hand through his hair. It shook. "I
hope to God they're wrong."

Benjamin just turned and walked out.

It was past eleven that same night—I was still packing—when
I heard a quiet knock on my door. It was him. Benjamin. His face
was pale and his eyes were red and he had that intense look of
his—I almost couldn't look. "Magali," he said. He was breathing
hard. "I need you to do something for me. I need you to promise."

I swallowed. "What?"

"When you see my parents—well, give them this letter." He
pulled out a sealed envelope. "But that's not the favor. I . . . you
know my mother's sick."

I nodded.

"I—" He was forcing his words out, visibly straining. They came
in a rush. "I think they're lying to me. About how bad she is. When
you see my mother, Magali, find out. Find out how badly she's sick
and then come home and tell me the truth. Please. Please promise
me, Magali." Tears were streaming down his face.

I swallowed. Nodded. My heart was beating fast. "Yeah. Yeah,
Benjamin—I promise."

He opened his mouth. Closed it. He turned around and walked
out, closing my door quietly. I heard his footsteps, unsteady, as he
walked down the hall.

I put the letter in my bag.

*Chapter 12*

# Control

Eva looked so different now. Clean, calm, her skin and eyes healthy, her hair in a neat braid. I'd barely seen her since Rivesaltes, where her eyes had been red and running. On the train she took turns holding Léon, while Pastor Alex read. It wasn't till Avignon, where we spent the night, that we got a chance to talk.

Pastor Alex took us on a walk around the city after supper. Through the medieval part of town, the streets winding and narrow with the last light of sunset above them. Léon lay asleep in my arms. We walked through a turreted gate in the old city walls, to the edge of the wide Rhône River, flowing like a dark, smooth ribbon in the dusk. The most amazing ancient stone bridge stood over half of it, with a tiny chapel perched on one of its pilings near one end, the rest of the bridge sweeping its long stone arches across the river until the half-way point where it suddenly cut off short. A flood, Pastor Alex said. No one had crossed that bridge in three hundred years. He shoved his hands deep into his pockets, like a boy, and wandered off down the bank.

"Gives me the creeps," said Eva after a moment.

"What does?"

She gestured at the broken bridge. "You ever think about how things can just break like that? The world can just . . . *break*."

"It must not have been built right."

"Neither's the world."

"Eva?"

"Mm?"

"Where are you from, anyway?"

"Mannheim."

"Why'd you leave?"

"We didn't. They shipped us out. Arrested us and shoved us into a train, fifty to a car. I was with my grandmother. We were locked in there four days, no one told us anything. Then they open it up, and there's Gurs."

"You were on one of *those* trains?"

She shrugged and nodded, looking at the water.

"They told us—Vichy tried to send them back—they just left them sitting there for days . . ."

"At least my grandmother got out of Gurs. In a coffin."

I looked at her. "You mean—"

Her mouth twitched a little. "My aunt bribed the guards who were carrying out the coffins. My grandmother's fine. She's in Aix with my aunt now. I was lucky," she said evenly, looking at the ruined bridge. "A lot of the old people on that train died."

I shivered in the warm night wind.

THE NEXT morning Lucy met us in Marseille, with a tall American who shook my hand as if I were a boy. Lucy! The same old Lucy with her grin and her sudden laugh. We sat in the back of Monsieur Lawrence's automobile and laughed and shouted over the roar of the *gazogène* engine. "Lucy!" I yelled. "You want to come with me to look for Madame Blocher?"

"Sure!" she shouted back, but I had to read her lips because the engine roared up even louder than before and Léon finally cracked and started screaming at the top of his lungs. We both started giggling helplessly, looking at each other, wiping tears out of our eyes, each of us not even hearing the other laugh.

MARSEILLE HAD even twistier streets than Avignon, some of them, and near the old port they smelled like fish, fish, fish. Tanned men swabbing the decks of fishing boats or mending nets; seagulls crying and diving, people calling in twanging *Marseillais* accents. Lucy and I walked for two hours trying to find the address Paquerette had given us. Lucy was jittery. Said she wanted to show me something later, then clammed up. Léon was whiny, squirming in my arms. *Brazil, kid. You're going to Brazil.* I'd never see him take his first step now. He'd take it on another continent.

A woman was running toward us along the quay, shouting and crying. Suzanne Blocher, her braid flying behind her and her face lit with joy. I held out Léon, and she grabbed him to her breast.

Léon started to cry.

Madame Blocher's face fell. Léon held out his arms to me. I started talking fast.

"It's only that he didn't have his nap, Madame, he's been fussy this whole afternoon—every time one of us picked him up he wanted the other." Lucy, who hadn't carried him even once, gave me a look.

Madame Blocher straightened, and looked at me. "It's been five months," she said quietly. "He doesn't remember me. I should have known." She stroked the silky top of her son's head as his crying died down to a whimper, her eyes bleak. All her joy gone. "Sh, sh, *mon bébé*. Thank you," she said to me. "I don't remember your name."

"Magali."

"Thank you, Magali. Will you thank the people who cared for him?"

I nodded.

"He's beautiful," she whispered. "He's gained so much weight."

I pulled a folded photograph out of my pocket and held it out to her. "I thought you'd want this back," I said. She took it, swallowed, and nodded.

Lucy held out the bag she'd been carrying. "There's a bottle in here, and a few diapers and stuff. You should take it," she added. "It's donated, and I'm not carrying it for another minute, so if you don't want it I'm giving it to a sailor."

Suzanne Blocher laughed, and took it. Léon started to cry again. She kissed him on the forehead. She said goodbye, and we watched her walk away down the quay, carrying her crying son.

AFTER SUPPER at the Lawrences' Lucy showed me up to her little guestroom under the eaves. She lay down on her bed and I flopped down on the sleeping pallet they'd made me on the floor with blankets and pillows, and she said, "Magali, I don't want to go to America."

"Um, wow. Earth-shattering new revelation."

She picked up a piece of paper and sailed it at me. "No. For real. Did you ever think of just . . . doing what you want to do? No matter what they say?"

"You mean like my trips? I couldn't." I glanced at the paper. "Lucy . . . This is in English!"

"Oh," she huffed, and took it back. "Okay: 'Dear Lucy, I decided to drag you to America to live with me, but it turns out you can't, because they just kicked me up to front-line war correspondent and I'm leaving for Egypt a couple of weeks after you arrive. But hey, I already got you a visa and anyway adults hate to ever back down so I found an American family you never met in your life for you to live with instead. Too bad, so sad, your dad.'"

"It doesn't say that!"

"Yeah it does. A lot more nicely. But pretty much that."

"*Egypt?*"

"Yeah. He's wanted this since forever. So that's great. Except for the whole living with strangers thing. And Magali—look at this."

*VISA*, I read. "What am I looking at?" Name Lucy Irene Fitzgerald, nationality Irish, date of birth 1901—

"Hey, Lucy."

"Yeah."

"How come it says you're forty?"

"That's what *I'd* like to know."

"Can you even use this?"

"Well, do I look like I'm forty?" After just the slightest pause she added, "Don't answer that," and my laughter came out in a loud snort and for the next half minute or so we were rolling around on our blankets laughing. It was so darned good to be with Lucy.

"So what're you gonna do?" I finally asked.

"I have the craziest idea."

"*Yeah?*"

"I'll—I'll tell you tomorrow."

I rolled my eyes.

THE NEXT day Benjamin's parents came to visit. The Kellers. I'd only met them once. All I really remembered was that they were short and plump.

Well, they were still short.

Madame Keller looked . . . *withered*. Pale, with dark circles around her sunken eyes. She spoke in a near-whisper, and went into spasms of coughing, so hard she lost her voice for a while. Bad, helpless coughing, like there was stuff in her chest she couldn't get out.

Benjamin was right. It came out gradually: their apartment was drafty and cold and the winter had been awful for her, and Monsieur Keller was worried sick. They couldn't get a better place—no money, no job—it was too dangerous. They couldn't come back to Tanieux with us, that was too dangerous too, their papers could get checked on the train. They'd had a close call last time they'd dared to go to a hospital. They were scared. If she got worse, they'd have to decide again which thing to risk: dying in an internment camp or dying at home.

Seriously.

Just because they weren't citizens. Like Suzanne Blocher. Just because what Vichy wanted from anyone who wasn't a citizen and had the gall to be Jewish on top of that was to clear out of the country or else come with us, Monsieur, Madame, don't mind the barbed wire.

And they were *trying* to clear out of the country. They were trying real hard.

But all this came out gradually. What they really wanted to talk about was Benjamin. I gave them his letter. Told them he was top of his class and stuff. I said he was worried about Madame Keller, which I shouldn't have, because it made her cry.

And then we ended up talking about visas. Visas, visas, what everyone in Marseille wanted. Monsieur Keller's shoulders sagged just talking about it. Monsieur Lawrence sighed a lot. I asked if they had tried Brazil, and they said yes. And then Lucy started asking questions.

She asked Monsieur Lawrence what papers you needed to show with your visa when you traveled. He said your passport. She asked what would happen if your *carte d'identité* didn't match your passport. He raised his eyebrows and explained carefully that all of a person's papers needed to match. Any other way was much too risky.

I looked at her, and she had this look. This look like a taut bowstring. Ready to fly.

"What on earth was that about?"

Lucy sat at the desk in our little attic room, chewing on the end of a pen as if she was planning to swallow. She made a note instead of answering me. A fierce light was in her eyes. "What do you think, Magali? Think she can pass for forty?"

The light dawned. The crazy, crazy light. "You're insane."

"Toldja you'd laugh."

But I wasn't laughing. "D'you think she could?" *Oh, Benjamin.* "How old is she for real?"

"I don't know. She has a seventeen-year-old kid."

"So maybe forty. She looks old. But who doesn't these days? I think she'll pass. But she needs the full set. Birth certificate, ration card, *carte d'identité*, passport—can you think of anything else?"

"Where're you gonna get those?"

She turned and looked at me with that light in her eye. "I don't know, Magali. But I'll bet you fifty American dollars that Monsieur Lawrence does."

MONSIEUR LAWRENCE looked at Lucy, then at me. "Well," he said.

We sat in his office on lumpy chairs, between file cabinets, among piles and piles of forms. Monsieur Lawrence had been a refugee from the north a year ago, on the roads being shot at with everyone else. Now he was the head of the Society of Friends' aid office in Marseille, and getting refugees out of the country was what he did.

"And you're sure, young lady, that Madame Keller wants to go to a foreign country alone?"

Lucy sat back. "*I* would," she said. "But if not you can find someone who wants it, right?"

Monsieur Lawrence gave her a wry smile. "Yes. I could."

"So then—"

"So then, here is your answer. I do not feel authorized to make this decision on behalf of your father. You will write out your father's address—his most current one, where he can immediately be reached. And you will write out a telegram, asking his permission, and *not* hinting at illegal activities."

"And the—the papers—you know someone who—"

"The less said about the papers, young lady, the better. You remember that."

*PLEASE MAY I STAY IN TANIEUX STOP*
*REASON VERY IMPORTANT URGENT STOP*
*LETTER FOLLOWS STOP LUCY*

Oh, I can't tell you how it felt. I was drunk on excitement, floating ten centimeters off the ground, I could leap tall buildings. We were doing it! For real! I was sent down to the Swiss Red Cross to deliver Lucy's letter; the next time they sent someone to Geneva they could mail it from there, away from the censors. The worker I gave the letter to just smiled at the name Lawrence, took the letter and the money, and said nothing. That smile floated me even higher. *You know, I know, but we don't say a word.* I couldn't begin to imagine all that was going on beneath the surface in that place, all the secret ways. It was beautiful.

Meanwhile Monsieur Lawrence was contacting . . . a contact. Someone who knew the secrets of Marseille, the people who closed their shutters in the evening and sat down at their desks to do work that could get them shot. Oh, it was like a spy story. Lucy couldn't stop pacing, couldn't stop talking. Every now and then she'd shut up and grab me and hug me and then jump up and down a couple of times.

"Oh Magali, we're doing it, we're doing it! Oh Magali, what if he says no, what if—"

What if *she* says no. I saw Madame Keller's face after she'd been closeted with Monsieur Lawrence for half an hour talking about it. Talk about stressed.

"It's really dangerous," Lucy fretted to me. "I didn't know. He says if they caught on she'd be locked up for sure. And she doesn't speak English. What if she got deported? It'd be my fault!"

"She's an adult, Lucy. She can make her own decision. Monsieur Lawrence still thinks it's a good idea."

He did. And he knew a lot. He knew the secret ways out of the country, what they cost, what they risked. He knew so many people. He had refugees sleeping on his floor, coming to dinner. Other people too. I don't think they all went by their real names. Monsieur Lawrence knew how to get Monsieur Keller out after Madame was gone, the hard roads he couldn't have taken a sick wife on. A *passeur* to guide him across the Pyrenees, or a secret night ride on a fishing boat down to Morocco.

It made sense. It all made sense. I couldn't believe my luck to be a part of it all.

The answer came within two days:

*YOU AND YOUR AUNT DECIDE STOP*
*PLEASE EXPLAIN STOP YOUR FATHER*

Then some German bigwig got assassinated in the Paris metro, and the *boches* rounded up a hundred hostages and threatened to shoot them. Monsieur Keller was there when the news came through. He just whispered, "I have to get her out of here." I never realized how much he looked like Benjamin till that moment. That night Madame Keller let us know she'd decided to go. For Benjamin.

They made us promise not to tell him till she was safe in America.

Then Lucy had to telephone her aunt, which involved a lot of English and sweating. She couldn't tell the truth on the telephone, see. She said her aunt got pretty mad.

But she said yes.

And then the papers. Monsieur Lawrence's connections were amazing. By the end of my week's visit Madame Keller had the papers in her hand. One visa and one full set of identity papers for Lucy Fitzgerald, forty years old.

Then it was time to go. Healthier for the two Lucy Fitzgeralds to be far, far apart.

PASTOR ALEX had already left, so it was only us girls on the northbound train. Lots of us. Me, Eva, some people Monsieur Lawrence was sending—Gabriella and Klara from Hungary, and a stunningly beautiful girl going by the name of Juliette—and, of course, Lucy, headed back to Tanieux.

It was festive when we started out. It was *fun*. We got our own compartment because of our incredible amount of luggage, and Lucy and I fell all over each other telling the others what a great time they would have in Tanieux. Since we couldn't talk about why we were *really* so crazy excited. We kept catching each other's eye—*it worked, it worked!*

Gabriella and Klara told us about their parents, who'd been arrested for vangrancy, also known as running out of *money*, and about how they'd had to leave Hungary because of the leftist pamphlets their father wrote. Gabriella wanted to know what people in Tanieux thought about Communists, and I couldn't come up with anything, except I'd heard Monsieur Barre and Monsieur Moriot had a fight about it one time. We finally caught on she was asking if they'd *shun* her, and we laughed out loud. She brightened right up.

WHEN WE switched trains in Montélimar it was raining, hard. You could hear it beating on the roof of the platform. We had two hours to wait. It was warm inside the station, all the voices and footsteps echoing in there. We found ourselves a bench and set our boxes and bags all around us. I got up to find the bathrooms.

It was on my way back that I saw them.

Again. Two German soldiers, smiling, striding through the station like it belonged to them.

They were young. Bright-eyed. The taller, blond one shot a

devastating smile toward a young woman in an elegant coat; she pulled away, her face tight with distrust. The soldiers kept walking, glancing casually around.

That's when I realized I was between them and my friends.

It all flashed through my head in a about a second. *They just want to pick up girls. That's all.*

*That's not good.*

I thought of Juliette, with her black curls and big dark eyes and her flawless skin. And she *looked* Jewish. And then Eva, traveling on her cousin's papers—and Lucy—

Yeah. The only one out of our group with nothing to hide was *me.*

I had about three seconds to get between the soldiers and my friends. My heart beat like a drum. *No. No. You swore—never again—*

*So what then? Do nothing?*

A watery gleam of sunlight broke through from a skylight above. I stepped into it, looked at the Germans, and smiled. "*Bonjour, Messieurs.* Are you looking for something?"

"Ah, Mademoiselle," said the blond one, brightening. His French was perfect. "I was told there was a bar in this train station?"

"Um . . . not in the station. There's one across the street . . ."

"Ah." He glanced out the window. "Terrible weather. Are you waiting for a train?"

"Uh, yeah. A couple of hours . . ."

The German smiled, and bent closer to me. He had soft blond hair and deep brown eyes and strong shoulders and I won't lie, he was gorgeous. "What wonderful timing. I need a drink to warm me up. Perhaps I could escort you with my umbrella, and get you something too?" He was calling me *vous,* in this deep, courteous voice, his face inches from mine, his deep brown eyes searching me. I felt strange. A little unbalanced. Like when you're climbing and your boot starts to slip in the mud. That moment where you haven't fallen yet but nothing's holding you up. Where there's only air.

"I . . ."

"And where are you going? You are perhaps returning to university?" His smile was warm. Admiring. How old did he think I *was*? *Old enough for him. Stupid.*

"Oh no," I said. "I was only, uh . . ." *THINK OF SOMETHING!* My mind had gone blank. My brilliant emergency mind, lost in the mists, sliding slowly away from me through empty air . . .

"Please, do come. I would so enjoy your company."

At the bar. Yes. Across the street. Away from the others . . . The vision rose up before me of *me*, sitting down at the bar, allowing this gorgeous German to buy me a drink. Drinking the drink. Then another. Having him walk me to my train. Where the others would see me and—

And then he had his hand on my back.

Oh, so gently, elegantly, so perfectly in control. A firm, warm hand on my back, near my waist, a gentle pressure, turning me slowly round. "Please, *ma chère*, do me the pleasure," he said softly, and his smile was warm, and the touch of his hand on my back, well so help me God I try not to lie anymore, so I'll tell you the truth.

It felt good. Really good.

And *that* threw me so completely that it might as well have been a gun.

I didn't know what was happening to me. I didn't have time to think this stuff out. I just knew I was falling, falling through soft, warm air, my heart flapping like a trapped bird. The smooth pressure of his hand, the light in his smile, warmed me and scared me. I was being taken over. He had no grip on me—I could have turned and walked away.

I followed.

He didn't need me to tell him where the bar was. He knew. It

was me he'd wanted. And I was following . . . *This isn't happening*
. . . *This isn't* . . . My stomach clenched. We were passing the
bathrooms. With a swoop like a bird diving off a rooftop, my mind
dived for escape.

My hand went to my stomach, and I stopped. His hand kept up
the gentle pressure, with smooth authority. "I feel sick," I blurted.
"My stomach." His eyes on me weren't quite so warm now.

"I am so sorry, Mademoiselle. Perhaps you need a place where
you can lie down."

"The bathroom—"

His eyes were deep and brown and hard. He didn't take his hand
off me. He knew.

I swallowed, working my throat. "I'm going to vomit," I said,
fast and hard. I felt a flutter of his hand, a hesitation. The next
moment I was gone. I saw the other German, the one I'd barely
noticed—black hair and a thin face—looking at me with very
sharp eyes as the bathroom door swung shut.

And then I was safe. Safe in the world of women, the place
where they let you alone, safe to dive into a stall and lock it, and sit
down on the toilet lid and lean against the wall, my cheek against
the wood, shaking.

I THINK I was in that bathroom for an hour.

I didn't dare go out there. He knew. They both knew. And those
eyes, and that hand, what was it about him that had made me feel
so trapped? *They are the masters of this country, and they are very
dangerous.* It was horrible, horrible. *I'm a strong person. I am. What
was that?*

I stood over the toilet bowl for a minute, looking down into it,
swallowing.

After a minute I sat down on the lid. It was bad. I didn't dare go
back out there. I couldn't lie well enough, not to him. What could
he do, if he suspected? I didn't even know. *I didn't know!* The long

list of secrets I knew blazed through my mind, and I shuddered. I'd thought I had *nothing to hide . . .*

The worst was knowing I would lead him to the others. One way or another. Because he was—*oh please don't make me say it*—he was smarter than me. He wasn't as young as I'd thought. And I wasn't as old. My emergency mind hadn't saved me. Hadn't been there. Maybe it had never been there. Maybe it was Paquerette who'd made me smart somehow, and without her I was stupid and helpless. Sixteen years old and alone.

And I had made a Nazi suspicious, and left him out there with my friends.

I sat on the toilet lid and prayed. I don't think I did it very well. I didn't have that much practice. *God, help. That was stupid. I'm sorry. Please don't let this hurt my friends. It was my fault, punish* me.

I sat praying, trying to count the minutes going by; straining to hear what was happening outside. Should I go? What if they were watching for me? What if I missed my train? What if I missed my train and *he was still there?*

*This is what a mouse feels like, listening for sounds outside its hole.*

I could hear Nina's voice. *She thought she had, what is the word—control.*

"Magali?" It was Lucy's voice. My heart nearly burst with relief. I threw open my stall.

"Are you all right? We looked for you *everywhere.* Don't you want any lunch?"

"I'm all right, I'm all right. Did the Germans see you?"

"What Germans?"

I leaned on her, weak now. "There were Germans. I was trying to get them away from you all. They were picking up girls. They tried to take me for a drink, they . . . I don't know, Lucy, I got scared."

"You mean you—"

"I talked to them," I snapped. "It's not a crime."

Her eyebrows flew up. "Hey, sure, um, sure it's not."

"I'm sorry," I said. I was shaking a little. "I . . . it was too strange, it . . . he got suspicious, I . . . Lucy, will you promise not to tell Paquerette? Please? Please?"

She looked at me. "I wouldn't."

I swallowed. The others. There were too many to keep a secret. "Tell the others I felt sick. I do."

Her face shut down. "You want me to lie to them?"

My cheeks started to burn. "What's the big deal? We lie to people all the time! You just got *papers* f—"

"*Shut up,*" Lucy hissed. She glanced swiftly at the closed bathroom door. Her face was hard. "We're in a *train station.*" *You idiot* hung in the air, unsaid. I shut up.

"All right," she said. "What're we gonna do?"

"We can't be together. Tell the others to pretend we don't know each other. Then I'll go wait alone on the platform. What time is it?"

"A quarter to one. What about your luggage?"

"Can you bring it in here?"

Five minutes later she brought me my suitcase and a packet of bread and cheese, and left. I couldn't tell if she was still mad at me.

I went out to the platform and waited for the train. It was still pouring, and the wind was whipping the rain around under the platform roof. I stood there shivering, chewing my bread and cheese and slowly becoming soaked to the skin, remembering how the German had offered me his umbrella.

I had thought the hardest thing about getting home would be keeping the secret about Lucy. Because of all the excitement. But that wasn't hard at all.

Chapter 13

# Secrets

THE NEXT few days were strange. It was like being two people. One happy and proud and moving forward; one sitting in the shadows, trying to figure out what on earth has happened to her.

First there was supper, the night I got home. I was cold and shaken and exhausted, but my parents didn't notice, they were in such a glow. I answered Papa's questions about Lucy, and Benjamin's questions about his parents, and then Benjamin's questions about Lucy's visa—horror in his eyes, as if he suspected her of blithely throwing away someone's still-beating heart—well, you can imagine. I finally said she'd given the visa to Monsieur Lawrence, and everyone unbent. Of *course*, said Papa.

And then. Then the Family Announcement. My proud parents, beaming at me. "We've been doing some thinking and praying," Papa said. I swallowed, and it hurt all down my throat.

"We think that in light of what we've heard from Monsieur Thiély, your taking one—and I do mean *one*—year out of school to work at les Chênes would be an acceptable option."

I stared. He'd said what? Was I dreaming already?

And then they started to shower me. With praise.

Papa said I'd matured so much. My dedication to my work was impressive—Monsieur Thiély wanted me back as soon as possible—Mama said she felt so proud, always, seeing me get off the train with the children. Tears came to her eyes, and she added, "Even though I'm still afraid."

Papa nodded, and put a gentle hand on her shoulder. "She's not quite herself when you're gone."

"But you see, Magali, I don't regret my decision. I don't. When I see you with those children, I don't see a child anymore. I see a young woman who has found her calling." She gave me a brave smile, stretched tight over tears. "It's a beautiful sight."

*Mama, Mama, I walked up to a German soldier today and smiled at him, and he put his hand on my back and invited me for a drink and I didn't know what to do. Mama. What do I do?*

She thought I was crying because she was crying. Because I was moved. She didn't know I was crying because there was no more truth in the world, anywhere.

I was dreaming. He was there. Walking me around Montélimar, through the old town, a maze of high, narrow streets, his hand on my back pushing faster and faster. He held an umbrella over us, but it wasn't raining. Hitler was there. Hitler tried to kiss me and I yelled, *No, No,* and I climbed the façade of the house beside me, up wrought-iron grillwork, and perched on the bracket of an ancient streetlamp hung from the wall. The German's umbrella was in my hand. The wind whistled down the street as if we were in a canyon. Hitler was gone. Someone was shouting at me to come down. A gust blew the umbrella inside out. I was falling, slowly, the air was pushing against me and my whole body hurt.

I was in my room, in bed, light coming in the window. My whole body hurt. I tried to move, and groaned.

A little later Mama came in, felt my forehead, and told me to stay there, she'd get me bread and tea. I'd feel better soon, she said. It didn't help much, now that I knew just how wrong she could be.

I was sick for three days. Flu. Aching and shivering. Mama bringing me tea. Turning in bed, my thoughts tangled in my head like brambles, thick and spiked. Looking at my ceiling remembering how lost I'd felt, how stupid. *A young woman who has found her calling, yeah.* The German's beautiful brown eyes, looking at me, that hand on my back and the flutter I'd felt deep inside. To have looked at him like *that*—at a man in *that* uniform. *There are decent men in the German Army,* Papa had told us once, but something deep, deep inside my mind answered, *Not that one.* Blond and stunning and used to being obeyed. And *Nazi.* I felt like I had flirted with the Devil.

I lay there in the dark watching the awful truth revolve slowly in my mind: *Nina was right.*

*She did not understand what she was doing. She was . . . enjoying. She is not wise, Mademoiselle. I know because once, I am like this. I trust, I think I will not fail.*

That was the worst thing. Nina. Nina was like me?

That broken girl. That nothing girl. Scared of her shadow, scared of the stationmaster. That girl who didn't believe she could *do,* that girl whom other people protected, whose idea of helping someone was opening the door for them as someone else brought them in out of danger, and telling them they were safe. And she said she saw what I was because she used to be *like me?*

I jammed my face into the pillow. I punched the wall. A muffled voice came through from Julien's room: "You okay?"

"Fine!" I yelled.

So women *changed?* Was that it? From strong into weak, from me into Mama? Why? Because of *men? Down* with men, then. In the dark my hands locked around the blond German's throat, I saw him flailing, turning red. *Die, scum.* Yeah. Down with *him*. Not Papa or Grandpa or Monsieur Lawrence, sure, but down with *him*, down with Erich Müller and Pétain and Hitler and that Rivesaltes guard who'd as good as threatened me, and all the Rivesaltes guards, *scum*, and that German in the automobile who'd come to see if they were doing a *good job*. I had a knife in my hand, in my mind, I was stabbing, stabbing. There was blood. *I will never be like that. I will kill them. I will fight.*

The next thing I remember I was lying on the bed again, my mind drifting in and out, sleepy. But awake and sane enough to understand I would never stab Hitler with a knife. To say to myself, *so I got worked up. It's still true I'll never be like that. I'll be like Paquerette.* There was still Paquerette. Thank God, thank God. There was always Paquerette.

I woke up healthy the next morning. It wasn't as much of an improvement as you'd think.

I lay and looked at the sun coming in my window, and for the first time in that whole confusing year I seriously considered going to someone and telling them absolutely everything. Someone older this time. Someone who could help it all make sense.

The problem was who.

Not Mama. Not Papa either, because of Mama, and because I could just see his face when I told him I'd had a German soldier's hand on my waist, and I did not want to see it in real life.

Then there was Grandpa. I used to go down to Grandpa's winter apartment and drink tea by his fire and tell him about Rosa and Lucy. How it wasn't fair having my friends fight over me like kids who thought I hadn't given them equal pieces of pie. He listened really well. Then he said life wasn't fair.

If I started asking him questions about men and women, and are women weak or strong . . .

Honestly, I was afraid of what he'd say. *Well, yes, Magali. Life isn't fair. Women have to accept certain limitations.* I shuddered.

I wished I had a grandmother.

And then, of course, there was God. I pictured myself lying on my bed and talking to the ceiling. And then what?

Besides, the walls weren't that thick.

That left Paquerette. I couldn't tell *her.* I was already terrified someone else would—Eva, maybe. The thought chilled me to the bone. Paquerette finding out how right Nina was, how when you dug through the layers of determination and *yes I'll do it* and so-called heroism in Magali Losier you'd find an inner core of stupid. So stupid that in trying to save my friends from some maybe-possible danger I'd put them in *more* danger, all by myself.

*Yes I'll do it, I'm a hero, I will save everybody. Stupidly.*

Finally I couldn't lie there anymore. I got up and went down to tell Mama I felt better, and ask if she needed any help.

I didn't tell anybody what was in my head.

Late that evening Benjamin came to my room. He stood leaning on the chair by my desk, looking at me.

"So," I said finally.

"How is she?" His voice was low.

*She's going to America.* "Well. I saw her." I had to think for a moment. "She was a lot thinner than I remember her. She had dark circles under her eyes. She coughed sometimes and it sounded like she couldn't cough anything up."

"How long did she cough?" he said quickly. "How often?"

"I don't know . . . maybe half a minute? Every . . . five minutes or so."

"Was she weak?"

"Kind of. Not . . . terribly."

"When's the last time she saw a doctor? Did they say?"

I nodded slowly. "A couple of months ago they took her to the hospital. They had a close call. They got asked for their papers and had to slip out the back."

He clenched his fist, then dropped it abruptly. "They didn't tell me. I knew they were— They should've bought false papers *months* ago." He turned on me. "The *hospital*? She was bad enough to go to the hospital? Even—" He was pale, and his eyes were very dark.

I looked at him. I wanted to tell him so bad.

He looked back at me, and the expression slowly faded from his face. "Thank you for telling me," he said in a flat voice. He turned around and walked out, shutting the door behind him.

The next morning I told Papa the truth about the visa. He sat behind his desk, his eyebrows climbing higher as I spoke. "She really . . . Yes, that makes sense of everything." He sat back. "Magali, that is . . . that is *remarkable*."

"They asked us not to tell him. Till we get word she got there safe."

He nodded soberly. "I'll pray."

I went down to les Chênes. I could still do that. That was worth something.

I took Marek to the stream. He'd started having episodes while I was gone, waking up screaming bloody murder. He sat and stared at the water, and ripped up long grasses by the handful, a look of deep concentration in his black eyes.

Oh, Marek.

August was ending. There was a coolness in the air that spoke of fall. It comes quickly, when it comes, on the plateau. I threw myself into les Chênes. I dug carrots with the Squirrels, I went with the girls to swim in the river one last time. We dug the potatoes, all of us together, Papa Thiély and the oldest boys turning them up with shovels while the rest of us gathered them into sacks, lumpy and brown and smelling of the earth that clung to them. The kids handled them almost reverently. They would feed us through the winter. They were beautiful.

We were at the river with the kids a few days before school started; I was crouching on the bank with Marek, teaching him how to skip a stone. They were going to try sending him to school, though he still hadn't spoken a word. The sky was deep blue and the first few leaves had turned yellow, blazing against it. I heard one of the counselors—Julie—say to Stepan, "What's your name?" and I listened sharp.

"Etienne Michaud," he said.

"Very good, Etienne. What's your sister's name?"

"Anne Michaud."

"*Very* good. Now what's *your* name?" she asked Tikva, the new girl whose father had just brought her up from Marseille.

"I don't remember, Mademoiselle."

"It's Marie. Marie Lenoir. Say it for me, please."

"Marie Lenoir."

"Do I get a new name?" It was Tonio, bursting in from a game, his chin thrust out.

"No, Tonio."

"Why not? I want one!"

"Some of the children need new names, and some don't. You're safe with your old name, but some of the others need new names to be safe, so that bad people can't find them. You'll have to learn to keep secrets, because you mustn't ever tell anyone their old names."

Tonio huffed. "I'd never tell a cop anything. But I want a new name."

Julie sighed. "How about Antonio?"

Tonio considered for a moment. "Naw," he said. "Tonio's better." Marek's eyes trailed him as he walked away. Then Marek did something incredible. He spoke.

"I don't want a new name," he said very softly.

I stared at him. *A whole sentence?* He looked away.

A whole sentence.

The exact wrong one.

PAQUERETTE CAME in with kids from Gurs. She hadn't heard. She wouldn't hear. I would never do it again, I would be the person she needed now, and the past would not exist. That was the thought that made me able to lift my head and look into her warm eyes as she asked if I could travel with her the last week of September. That was the thought that kept my voice steady as I said yes.

She looked so much better. Calm and energy in her face. She showed me sketches she'd made. Steep mountains and streams; a straight-backed man holding a horse's reins. That was her father. It turned out they were on good terms. Mostly. He'd given her some helpful insights on politics, in the end, she said, and on Pétain. "He's gotten quite a bit more cynical about him lately. He's no fool."

"They're giving the Jewish kids at les Chênes new names."

Paquerette nodded. "That's very wise. Very timely. Do they have false papers for them?"

"Claudine says they're coming soon. I don't know from where."

"Of course not."

"Marek says he doesn't want a new name."

"Marek spoke?"

"Just that once."

She looked at me without speaking for a moment. Then she shook her head.

"I'll pray for him," she said.

I WALKED Lucy to school, on her first day. Then I walked down to les Chênes, and my new life.

Marek went to school with the others. He fidgeted, picked at the wood of his desk, we heard; he only copied half of what was on the board. We were overjoyed to hear he copied anything. He didn't hit anyone the whole first week.

And me? I helped Claudine and Julie plan the meals and keep the budget. I took the wagon home and brought in bread from town in the mornings, brought in milk from the farms on the way. I helped the Squirrels with their homework, I helped the Hawks peel potatoes. I got roped into pranks Hanne and Aurélie and Carmela were planning—short-sheeting Claudine and Julie's beds or hiding the Wolves' clean underwear on laundry day. I stayed for supper on Saturdays to be there for skit night, I helped Erik practice his Papa Thiély impression, I found Carmela an old red sheet to be Red Riding Hood in. I made up little songs to help them practice their new names.

I loved it, the round of our days, the working and the playing and the songs. Little kids rode on my back, big girls whispered secrets to me. I knew Joseph liked Lise and Carmela liked Stepan. I knew how Tikva—Marie—worried about whether the food was kosher even though her parents had said it was all right to eat anything at les Chênes because God understood people had to stay alive. I thought at first I could fix it for her, but when I found out there were rules about not using the same *dishes* for milk and meat, I told her that her parents were right. She was still too thin to go passing up milk or meat. I knew Aurélie hadn't had a single letter from her parents since they'd brought her here. I told her maybe they wanted to write her but couldn't. I knew Stepan and Chana's father had been murdered in an anti-Jewish riot in Poland before the war even started, and they'd seen their mother shot by soldiers while they fled the invasion, but she'd made it. And ended up in Gurs. That's the reward of courageous survival these days. Gurs.

Oh, I wanted to take those kids in my arms and never let them go, I wanted to remake the world for them. I'd never felt like this before. I'd kill anyone who laid a finger on them. I could feel it in my body, how bad I wanted to keep them safe.

The only one I didn't know any secrets about was Marek.

He didn't speak again. If you tried to make him talk he'd pull away, stop looking you in the eye. His new name was Jean-Marc Meunier. He didn't even turn his head at the sound of it.

Paquerette took Rosa on a trip. They brought back six kids and went through a *contrôle* on the train, the police asking for everyone's papers. Rosa told me it had scared her. I bet it did, I thought.

I went on working at les Chênes.

THERE WAS another shooting up north. Someone killed a high-up German officer, the guy in charge of the city of Nantes. The Germans rounded up hostages again. Forty-eight of them.

This time they shot them all.

I saw a look in my father's eyes that day that I'd never seen before. As if he felt just like me, as if he wanted to kill someone. My brother was red-eyed and shaking with anger. Benjamin sat watching them, his face very still.

Two nights later Lucy came and told me her aunt had gotten a telephone call. Madame Keller was in America.

I asked her if she wanted to tell him herself. She shrugged and looked down and shook her head. I grabbed her hand and squeezed. "We did it," I whispered. Lucy grinned.

I could hardly stand it. Papa was out at a meeting. Mama was in bed early, trying to stave off a headache. It had to be one of them who told him. I had to wait till tomorrow. I walked up the dark stairwell to the third floor, my heart hammering. *Your mother is safe, Benjamin. Your mother is free.*

He was in the hallway, coming toward me. His eyes were red. He looked away. I wanted to blurt it out, shout it. He turned and glared at me. "What are you looking at like that?"

"Benjamin," I said. I swallowed. "Your mother is in America."

"What?" he breathed. He'd turned white as a sheet. "What?"

"She's in America." The words tumbled over each other. "Lucy gave her her visa. Monsieur Lawrence got her false papers. She went to America. We just got word she's there safe."

He was starting to breathe fast. "Is this—some kind—of joke?" His breath caught strangely, out of control. "You—you—"

"I'm sorry!"

"You're lying to me! You're *lying!*"

"No, it's true!"

Julien's door banged open and Julien stopped dead in his doorway as Benjamin screamed with tears running down his face, *"Everyone lies to me! Everyone!"*

"Benjamin!"

"Magali, what on earth is going on here?" Julien's eyes were very wide.

"I . . . I . . ."

*"When do I believe you?* You lied to me when you came back from Marseille! I could see it in your eyes, *I thought she was dying!"*

"I'm sorry, Benjamin." Tears sprang to my eyes. "I'm so sorry—I didn't mean to—"

"I can't stand you people! *I can't stand you!"*

"Magali?" said Julien.

My mouth was dry. "Lucy gave her visa to his mother. She's safe in America now."

Julien's jaw dropped.

Benjamin was gasping, wiping the tears that still streamed down his face. "Magali," he whispered, "is it true?"

"Yes," I said. "Yes."

Julien closed his mouth. "We—"

Benjamin turned to him. "You *all* do it. You have no idea what it's like being—kept in the dark—like that . . . And you all do it. Magali here—*Magali* keeping secrets . . ."

I flushed hot. *What do you mean, Magali keeping secrets?*

"Your parents told me to." I was shaking. "They made me promise!"

He rounded on me. "Next time my parents tell you to lie to me, tell them *I* said no. Tell your father. I've had *enough*." His voice cut hard, like a meat cleaver. I flinched.

Julien whispered, "I'm sorry, Benjamin. I really am." He had tears in his eyes. We all did.

Benjamin blinked hard, looked at him, nodded. He breathed in sharply. "I'm sorry too. I'm sorry. Magali"—the tears spilled out of his eyes again—"Magali, do you swear? Swear it's true?"

Papa says it's superstition. But I had to, that's all. I crossed my heart and said *Croix de bois*. "Cross of wood, cross of iron, if I lie I go to hell. It's true, Benjamin. It's true."

He started sobbing. Julien put an arm around his shoulders. I did too, and we stood holding him up while he cried and shook and smiled through his tears. "Magali," he whispered, "thank her for me, will you? Thank her."

"Of course I will," I said.

THE NEXT day, Paquerette came in. Two days later I was to go with her. The world was going mad, the Nazis were shooting hostages, but me, I was packing sweaters and diapers and rags for Rivesaltes, I was going to rescue children. Benjamin was starting to smile again. Paquerette still wanted me. I was glad this was my life.

At les Chênes, they invited me to stay for supper. They were glad I was going, they said. It would be a test of Marek's adjustment. They had good hopes. I walked home happy in the dark, and went to bed, and woke early, and lay there feeling my heart beat. *I'm going.* I couldn't lie still. I padded down the stairs, heard Papa shuffling papers in his study, tore a piece off the fresh baguette he'd left on the kitchen table, and went on out into the fresh morning air.

I hesitated at the door of l'Espoir—it sounded so quiet in there—and glanced across at the café. They were open. I'd just drop in and say goodbye to Rosa. Maybe she'd give me something hot to drink. There was a real chill in the morning air.

The café bell dinged as I went in. Madame Santoro was behind the bar with her apron on, pouring something coffee-colored into a cup. She looked up. "Ah Magali! You have heard, yes?"

"Heard?"

"Yes yes, about Rosa."

I looked blankly at her. *About Rosa . . . ?* "No."

"Oh, she has gone. With Paquerette."

My stomach plunged deep, deep down. "She, she what?"

"Paquerette came here, in such a hurry. She says, the train is leaving now, where is Magali?"

"But . . . but the train . . . but she was leaving today!" Could I have gotten the wrong day? No. No. Unimaginable.

"No, you see. No train today. No train for four days at least. A problem with the rails, they are fixing it, the train is stopped. Yesterday is the last train."

"And I was—I was—"

"She says, where is Magali? Rosa says, she is at les Chênes. Paquerette says, too far, I will miss the train. She asks me, please, can Rosa come? I say yes. I am proud of my Rosa, helping children. I can manage, for a little while, with the café."

I couldn't say anything. Waves were washing over me. I was at the bottom of the sea. I could feel the blood draining from my face, from all of me. *It's happening after all. Rosa. She wants Rosa. That's the truth.* I was standing there with my mouth open. I am absolutely sure that no one has ever looked stupider than I did at that moment.

"You are not angry, Magali, are you? Rosa, she was worried. I said, no, no, she is your friend. You are not angry?"

"No," I said white-lipped. "I'm not angry. Thank you for letting me know, Madame Santoro. I . . . I should go now."

The café door dinged as I walked back out into the cold.

*Chapter 14*

# The Other Voice

I stood looking at Rosa, trying to look like I was over it.

I'd tried to get over it. I'd tried. I wasn't over it. I'd stayed away from the children's home for two days, too humiliated to go tell them the truth. Then I'd gone. I had to go. My explanations were lame. Marek's "adjustment" was awful. He'd had an episode in class and hit a teacher, and they'd sent him home. When I came to get him he kicked me. I hated him. I hated everyone.

I hated Rosa.

It didn't help that she looked scared of me. Didn't at all.

"So how was it?" I said. I couldn't keep the flatness out of my voice. I could see her watching me. I could see her flinch.

"It was all right . . . We had five kids and a baby . . ." She was looking everywhere except in my eyes. "It went all right. Kind of tiring. I took the baby." She hesitated. "You didn't meet us at the train."

"No, I didn't meet you at the train." And don't you have the sense to leave well enough alone, you idiot? If you ask me to tell you I'm not angry *you will die*.

Her dark eyes got darker. She finally looked me in the eye. "I don't know what else I could have done, Magali," she said quietly.

"Well, of course not." I turned away.

"Magali . . ."

I turned on her. "*What?*"

"Please, Magali—I—"

"What do you want from me? You want me to tell you it's all fine? You want me to tell you it was fun packing for Rivesaltes after waiting for a month and then going down to meet her and hearing you'd gone? You want me to tell you I'm just so thrilled? If that's what you want, *dream on!*"

Her big, dark eyes. Like a wounded doe. They made me so angry I wanted to hit her. We stood staring at each other for a moment. I knew what my own eyes looked like. Like a snake's. Yeah, I was the bad one. I'd tried not to be. But she wouldn't *let* me.

We stood staring at each other. And then she lowered her eyes. Took a breath.

When she raised them again they were like hot black coals.

"I found something out this summer, Magali," she said very quietly. "I wasn't going to tell you. But on second thought maybe I will."

I couldn't look away. I couldn't move.

"I'm good at this," she said. "You didn't think I would be, did you?"

I flinched.

"You didn't think I was good for very much." She stood very straight and spoke very evenly, her eyes burning. It hurt to look at her. "I even believed you, some of the time. Why not? I'm just a refugee. I'm just a girl who dropped out of school to work in her parents' café."

Nothing. I had nothing.

"Well, I'm worth something too. I can save kids' lives too."

"Of course you can . . ."

"And you never thought any different?" Her voice was hard.

"I—"

"And you never thought Lucy was better than me?"

"*You* didn't like her, I—"

"Don't you start, Magali Losier. You think I didn't *want* another friend? Whenever she was there you shut me down. Acted like I was stupid. Well I'm not stupid. And I'll tell you something else, neither is Nina, and neither is Sonia even if she can't speak French. You think you're so much better than other people. You think people can't even see. You're a rotten friend, Magali Losier."

I saw someone get beaten up once. He just curled up on the ground, didn't even try to hit back.

"And I'll tell you something else. Someone who cared about the kids would've been glad I went. Just plain glad. And you know it."

Of course I knew it.

She turned on her heel and walked away.

I lay on the ground, curled around myself, bleeding.

I guess that's not true. But since when is what a person sees walking down the street the truth?

I WALKED away. Not toward anywhere. Away. By the time I came to myself I was on the riverbank, walking downstream, already so far north of town that a hill hid most of the houses when I turned to look back. I walked over short green grass and through tall dry weeds. I slipped under barbed-wire fences into pastures. I followed the river. I just kept going.

I think I thought that if I stopped it would all be true.

I knew it was all true. But knowing and walking was different from knowing and standing still. The sound of the river drowned it out. The bite of the cold wind numbed it. The memory of Rosa's blazing eyes and the message they carried—*some people might say things like that and not mean them, some people might have made them up just to hurt you, but not Rosa, not Rosa*—those things lived in the back of my mind, but they were pushed backward by my motion, pinned in place. It was there, but quiet. I could see it, but only as a shadow lying over the sunlit pastures and the wet brown leaves plastered to the riverbank by the current, and the tall dead grasses waving in the wind.

But there comes a moment when you have to stop.

It came when I realized I was shivering, and my teeth were chattering, and I couldn't make them quit. I sat down in the middle of the tall dead grass, feeling the stalks prick my legs, and brought my knees up to my chest and put my arms around them. My teeth went on chattering. I laid my head on my knees, sideways, and closed my eyes. I started rocking. It felt like something inside me was burning. It felt like I was going to die. Rosa. Rosa had said I was a rotten friend, and it was true.

Rosa had said I never thought she was good for much, and it was true.

I mean, I knew it was true. It was *what I thought.* I just hadn't known she knew it.

And it sounded so much uglier in her mouth.

You see yourself through your own eyes and you look beautiful. You look strong and smart and funny; you look determined and self-sacrificial; you have just the right blend of compassion and courage. You look almost like Paquerette.

And then you see yourself through someone else's eyes and you just see a self-centered jerk. A person in love with her own importance. Who wants to rescue children but *doesn't want anyone else to rescue them.*

That—that was the worst thing.

I lay down on my side in the prickly grasses, still half curled up. Somewhere inside me I knew what was supposed to come next. I was supposed to talk to God. I was supposed to tell him this stuff as if he didn't know it yet.

But it was so humiliating.

I just lay there, and silence filled my mind. The grasses pressed into my cheek. Near my left eye a feeble old cricket, one leg torn off, dragged himself through the grass. The river ran, down the bank to my right, singing its liquid song. I thought of Marek. I thought of Lise, Carmela, Chanah. I thought of Zvi. I started to cry, tears slipping sideways down my face into the grass, into the earth.

*But I do*, I said to God. *I do love them.*

The river ran. The wind rustled in the grass, in the few brown leaves still clinging to the oak above me. Out of my right eye I saw small white clouds blowing fast across the blue, blue sky. That blue so deep it was almost dark.

And, I don't know how to explain it. I don't know at all. But somehow in all these things there was a voice. That was how it was. It wasn't in my head. It was around me.

The river said yes. The deep dark sky said yes. The wind said yes, and the leaves and grasses all agreed, bending down their heads. There was a voice in them, and that voice said, *Yes. I know. You are not lying.*

That's when I really started to cry.

I lay there in the tall grass, sobbing, shaking, the salt of my tears getting in my mouth, soaking into the cold earth beneath my cheek. I lay there and cried, for Zvi, for Marek, for Paquerette, for Rosa. For Nina. For me. I lay there and cried for the things people do here on the cold earth to the people they despise. I cried because people shut women with babies behind barbed wire and let them die as if they were nothing. I cried because I had made Rosa think she was nothing. I cried because the world looked like a world without a God in it and yet there was a voice in the river and the wind. I cried because, of all the things for that voice to speak here and now on the cold earth where people kill each other, it had spoken kindness to me. I cried hard, wrenchingly, until I didn't have any tears left at all.

Then I lay there silent, my eyes closed, listening to the river and the wind. Hearing the grasses whisper together. I didn't tell God everything. I didn't tell God much at all. I don't know, it's hard to explain, but somehow it seems to me like there are words you use to say something, and then there are words you use to do something. Like *I'm sorry*. That's definitely one of those.

I said that.

*I don't want to be like them.* I remember saying that too. And *help*.

After a while my teeth started to chatter again.

I got to my feet. There was damp earth on my cheek, and tears. I wiped it with one sleeve and then the other. I had that empty, clean space inside me that you have after crying. I was also very cold.

The sun was slanting down in the west, making black silhouettes of the oaks and the pines. The grass was flattened in the place where I had lain. I brushed at the right side of my skirt and my sweater. There was grass seed on them, and dirt. I shivered. Above my head the oak leaves rustled in the wind.

I turned south, and began to walk home.

I MADE it home in time for supper. Mama asked me how Marek was. I shrugged. Then I felt wrong trying to fool her.

"He was pretty bad yesterday. But I didn't see him today."

"You didn't go? Where have you been?"

"I took a walk beside the Tanne."

"For hours?"

I shrugged.

"Magali! Aren't you cold? Your hands, they're frozen. Here now, there's hot water. Go and take a hot shower, you have just enough time before supper."

I took a hot shower. It was bliss, the steam rising around me, the warmth seeping back into my chilled white hands. I put on clean, warm clothes and sat on the bath mat, holding my knees to my chest the way I'd done by the river, and drifted. I came to myself when I heard Mama call me to supper.

It was lentil soup, with tomato in it, and steaming mashed pumpkin on the side. It was warm, solid and warm in my belly, it was better than anything. I could barely keep my eyes open.

I went upstairs, and crawled into bed. After a minute I got up and got the extra winter blanket from the closet. I remember the warmth growing in me there, in and around me in that little space of air under the blanket, warmed by me, warming me. I heard the wind singing in the eaves outside. Thought of wind in the withered oak leaves, and a warm voice. I went to sleep.

I WOKE, and thought, *Rosa. I will have to face Rosa.* I shrank from waking.

I pulled back into that floating place for a moment, under the surface of sleep. There was something I'd forgotten, something I'd just now been thinking about, something so good.

*God spoke. God actually spoke to me.*

*For real?*

*What's real?*

*Rosa,* my brain reminded me. *Rosa.*

I pictured myself walking up to her. Pictured her face. It kept shifting, it said a million different things. There was a Rosa who still hated me and always would and a Rosa who couldn't believe she'd said that stuff and was scared I was going to kill her and a Rosa who felt bad and said she hadn't meant any of it. I had no idea which of them was real. And there were so many voices in my head.

*Go down and see her this morning, right away, say you want to talk. Take the bull by the horns.*

*Are you insane?*

*Don't go see her. Wait till she comes to see you. When she's ready.*

*What if she never comes?*

*Then* good! *What part of "I hate you" didn't you understand?*

I rolled over and put my pillow over my face. *God? Help?*

I didn't want to face her and I had to face her. Oh, I wanted to run away from the whole thing—if I'd had a choice of never seeing her again I think I would have taken it, but I didn't have that choice. If I'd had a choice of shoving it off on someone else I would have taken it, but I didn't have that choice. It was either face Rosa now or face Rosa later. It was either treat Rosa right or treat Rosa wrong. Sometimes it just comes down to it.

And the thing was, now I understood just how bad treating Rosa wrong could backfire.

Yeah, it sounds crass. But that's how it works sometimes. You have to stick up for yourself or people run over you. People like me. I'd wanted to tell Rosa that a hundred times. And now she'd finally done it.

I respected her for it, to tell the truth.

But boy, I did not want to get out of bed.

I stayed there with my covers over my head till Julien knocked on my door and called, "Hey! Don't you want any breakfast?" And then I got up and did the only thing I'd been able to think of.

Well, first I got dressed and went down and ate breakfast.

Then I wrote Rosa a letter:

> Dear Rosa,
>
> I'm sorry. I <u>have</u> been a rotten friend. I can't believe I made you think less of yourself, and I'm really, really sorry. You didn't do anything wrong and it was completely unfair of me to be mad. I hope you can forgive me.
>
> Your friend,
> Magali

So YEAH. I guess it was more of a note.

Made it look easy, didn't I? I guess I just won't mention how my hand seized up when I started to write "rotten friend." Or about the twenty minutes I spent after each sentence, chewing on my pen and thinking of things to add after it, all of which added up to, *But it wasn't all my fault you know, my life is tough too!* But I couldn't do it. Because it was Rosa. Because I'd heard of righteous anger but I'd had no idea what it looks like when it's directed at *you*.

And because God said I did love the kids.

So I wrote that letter. It took me an hour and a half.

I folded it up. Twice. Wondered how to seal it. Wished I'd written it in code. Went downstairs and asked my father for an envelope.

"An envelope, Magali? I don't have very many of those. Are you mailing a letter?"

"No. Just giving it to someone." I felt stupid. "I just . . . really don't want anyone to open it."

He handed me a piece of string. I rolled my letter up and tied it.

"Are you going into town?"

"Yeah."

"If you would . . ." He rummaged in his desk. "Please give this"—an envelope—"to Mademoiselle Pinatel?"

"Sure, Papa."

"Thank you."

I walked down into town. It was cold, cloudy, with rain on the wind. I was scared. What if I saw her, what if I didn't see her, who should I leave the letter with, all that. I peeked in through the café window. She wasn't there. I went in, my heart thumping in my chest. It was warm and crowded. Madame Santoro was working the tables. Monsieur Santoro was behind the bar. He saw me.

"Rosa isn't here."

I held out the letter. "Please Monsieur . . . would you please . . . give her this?"

He frowned at it. "All right."

*Oh and please don't open it, please, please.*

I turned and fled.

I crossed the *place du centre* with Papa's envelope in my hand and went into the bookstore. It was open, but no one was inside. I started to lay the envelope on the desk, and stopped. It might be important. Or secret.

I went to the stairwell door at the back of the shop and knocked. Then I opened it and called up.

"Mademoiselle Pinatel? Mademoiselle?"

No answer.

I hesitated, started to lay the envelope on the steps. Then I thought it would be better to just open her apartment door and slip it inside. I started to climb.

Her apartment's tiny. A little landing with a couple of bedrooms off it, a little living room with a desk, the walls covered with books. To my right was the room Nina'd almost died in, the year before. I'd seen it once. A narrow white room like a coffin, barely room for a chair between the bed and the desk, everything white. I glanced in. It was still the same, except for a half-burned candle and a litter of papers on the desk.

Odd-looking papers.

Sometimes I just can't help it. That was one of the things I almost put in the letter to Rosa. Lame, I know. I took a few steps closer.

They were identity cards.

Mademoiselle Pinatel's card lay apart from the others. The others were piled haphazardly except for the one in the center of the desk. Georges Tallier, it said. He looked vaguely familiar. His card was complete except for the fingerprints and the seals, and beside it lay a strip of some kind of gummy cloth, with a perfect backward copy of an official seal traced on it.

Like some kind of stencil.

I picked a card out of the pile with shaky hands. Nicole Saillens, it said. I looked at the picture. The picture was Nina.

The one underneath it said Etienne Michaud. The picture was Stepan.

That's when I heard them. Feet on the stairs.

I fumbled frantically with the cards. Which one had been on top? I gave up, dashed out of the room. I'd left my envelope in there. I ran back in, grabbed it, ran out. It was around then I noticed what was odd about the footsteps.

Clicking.

There was a click of crutches, after each step. They were very close now.

I bent down by the door, trying to look like I was just delivering the envelope like I planned to. It was hopeless. The door opened.

It was Nina.

It was Nina and her eyes were wide with shock and anger. It was Nina staring at the guilt in my eyes and throwing back rage so hard it hit me like a fist. She swept me aside with her crutch and lunged past me to the door of the white room. She knew already. From my eyes.

She turned back to me in the doorway of the white room on her crutches, her green eyes blazing. "*You*," she hissed. "You little *sneak*."

I felt dizzy.

"If you tell anyone," said Nina very quietly, "I will find a way to hurt you. This is a promise."

I swallowed. Took a shallow breath. Not enough. Another. "You don't need to promise that," I said. I heard pleading in my voice. "I won't tell. I'd never tell."

Her eyes were cold on me. "You will say to yourself 'I must never tell.' Then one day you will want to look good to your friend. You will say, 'I have a secret.' She will say, 'Oh, oh, please tell.'"

*Forgery*, Lucy had whispered in my ear.

"I . . . I'm so sorry, Nina."

"Sorry does not save me."

Her. It really was her. Dizzily for a moment my days in Marseille came back to me, the excitement and the sense of secrecy, the brave and secret people doing, at night behind locked doors, work that could get them shot. *Nina*. The world shifted around me. *You really just don't get it, do you, Magali?* said a scornful voice inside me. It was the voice I hated.

It was right.

I swallowed. "You're right. It doesn't. But I am sorry. I came to give this to Mademoiselle Pinatel." I held out the envelope, and the suspicion in her eyes was so unbearable I snapped. "I haven't read it!" I took a breath. "I shouldn't have looked. I don't want to put you in danger. I'll forget everything I saw. I promise. I . . . I swear. If I ever tell anyone, I . . . I hope God gets me arrested and *shot*."

She was still staring at me. That anger and suspicion, that coldness, in her eyes. That un-Nina look, I would have called it months ago. But I didn't know *anything* about Nina. I understood that now.

After a moment she said coolly, "Did you know about this before?"

"Before?"

"This summer. You said that your friend Lucy had told you a secret. Was it this?"

I swallowed. "Lucy told me someone was doing forgery. She didn't say who."

"Mademoiselle Fitzgerald," Nina said bitterly. "Even her. You people, you think it is a game! You tell your friends, you tell your families! Magali, my brother does not know what I do. Do you understand? *No one* should know. *No one.* Now instead we have—" She started to count on her fingers and broke off with an angry gesture, as if flinging something away from her. She sagged on her crutch and looked at me wide-eyed. "Do you people not understand that we could die? That these children could die? You think they are safe because they are *here?*" She flung a hand at the window. "Do you see *French tanks* out there to defend us?"

I just looked at her. *No. I don't.*

"That is why I cannot take back my promise," she said quietly. "I am sorry. I cannot."

I nodded. My stomach and chest felt tight, tight. My throat burned. "Threat," I said.

"What?"

"It's called a threat. When you promise to hurt someone."

She looked at me, and didn't say anything. She held out her hand, finally, for the envelope. I gave it to her.

"Well," I said. "Goodbye."

"Goodbye."

I turned and walked down the stairs. Above me I heard the door shut and lock.

I WENT home. What else could I do? I helped Mama make lunch, and I ate, and went to my room.

I wanted to hide. I wanted to go down to les Chênes and make sure Marek was okay. I wanted to go find that place by the river where God had talked to me in the wind and the grass. It seemed so far away already. It was too much. In the space of just two days. She'd threatened me. Nina. I couldn't take it in. *It's not fair, God. This, now. I just started trying to be a better person. Yesterday. This morning. I just started.* I lay sprawled on my bed, crying silently, tears slipping down onto the pillow. Words came into my head: *I want to go home.* It didn't make any sense. I didn't mean Paris. Not really.

I wanted to go home to the Time Before. The time when I couldn't remember who was Chancellor of Germany and didn't care. The time when you could trust the police, when secrets didn't kill, when doing your best was good enough. When there were French tanks defending us . . .

I was like a child. I didn't care. I wanted to be a child. Let someone else take the blame.

*You think they're safe because they're here? Do you see French tanks
out there defending us?* No. I didn't. No. No, I hadn't saved those
children's lives. My work, our work, wasn't done. *Oh, Marek, Marek.
Tell me you want a new name.* I needed Nina. We all needed each
other. If we didn't do our work right, I hadn't saved those children's
lives. I had only delayed their deaths.

I felt so tired.

Voices downstairs. Footsteps on the stairs up to the third floor,
light feet down the hallway. A knock on my door.

I sat up cross-legged on the bed. Wiped my eyes as thoroughly
as I could. "Come in."

Rosa opened the door and stood in it, hesitating, her dark eyes
meeting mine. She held a baby pressed against her chest. It was
tiny, an infant, I'd never seen it before.

"Hi, Magali," she whispered.

"Hi." I looked at her, at the child. My stomach squeezed tight. It
was like seeing her holding Zvi.

"You're not a rotten friend," Rosa whispered, and started crying.
Tears running down her face, one hand behind the baby's head,
shaking a little. *No. No. Rosa, stop crying. Don't apologize to me,
Rosa. Don't . . . knuckle under.* I didn't know how to tell her. That
no matter how much it hurt, what she'd done had made me respect
her. That taking it back would be even worse.

After a moment I cleared my throat. "Um, *yeah* I am."

Rosa laughed through her tears, hard. She wiped her face with
her sleeve. I could see her smile flash out from behind it. *Yeah.
Yeah, like that.*

"Is that the baby you brought home?"

"Yeah," she whispered. "Yeah. I brought her to meet you."

I put out a hand and stroked the fine, downy black hair. Her head was warm and soft under my fingers. She was deep asleep. "What's her name?"

"Rosa."

"Really?" I lifted my eyes. She looked happy. So happy.

"It's spelled with a 'z'."

"Roza. Wow. She's . . . beautiful."

"Yeah."

"Here, sit down. You . . . you want to go downstairs and have, you know, tea or anything?"

She shook her head. We sat on my bedspread, side by side. She rocked Roza. The child stirred, and her little lips made a sucking motion. So tiny. *Live, child.*

"Hey Rosa . . ." *If you promised someone you'd never ever do something, and they didn't trust you to never do it . . .*

"Yeah?"

*Then you never do it. That's all. And she keeps believing every day that you'll do it tomorrow. Quit kidding yourself, Magali.*

"Nothing. I mean . . . I mean thanks for coming over."

"Of course."

*Quit kidding yourself. Maybe that's the way to be a better person. Oh man. That doesn't sound fun.*

"Are you all right, Magali?"

"Yeah," I said. "Yeah."

*Chapter 15*

# The Thing That Had to Be Done

THEN CAME the winter. The winter of 1941.

It was worse than the winter of 1940. Which had been the worst in living memory. I don't even know how to talk about it. Life changed. I thought it had changed before. And it had. But you don't know, you just don't know until it happens to you.

There was one thing, though. I knew what I was living for.

It was work and more work. Life becomes simple: *keep everyone alive*. Warmth and food. They were scarce now. It was our job to make them last till spring.

Hauling firewood, hauling milk. Digging the last turnips and carrots. Grandpa let me eat the small misshapen ones—oh, the sweet cold crunch of them between my teeth, the sharp pain in my thawing fingers by the fire. Gutting chickens, pulling out the raw livers and feeling only hunger. Stoking fires, cooking bean soup with chicken bones in it, teaching Hanne and Aurélie how to mend their clothes, how to layer for warmth. Warmth and food.

Bringing children back from Rivesaltes.

There was a new desperation at the camp. Winter was coming. There was no heat in those awful barracks, no insulation. The rain poured in, ice-cold water pooled in and between the barracks, people walked in it in broken shoes or bare feet blue with cold. Hopeful eyes followed us; and desperate. Mothers put their thin children into my arms with nothing in their faces but relief. They felt heavy. Heavy with the weight of the unknown, of what Nina had said. *We'll try, Madame. I promise we'll try.*

Up on the plateau the cold bit deep, and deeper. The snow came up to my knees. My boot started to break, right where Madame Minkowski had mended it. Mending only goes so far, I guess.

Mending was all we had.

Mama lined the broken part of my boots with canvas. There wasn't anything else. We sat by the radio all evening, me unraveling old sweaters and her knitting them into hats and scarves. Listening to censored war news, every night pulling our chairs closer to our little fire as the cold grew fiercer. Papa'd tell us the real news when Mama was in bed.

Grandpa gave me a sled, to get to les Chênes faster. I worked all day there—they gave me lunch for my pay. And good pay too; they had milk, and eggs. Sometimes even chocolate. Those Swiss were doing all right. The kids had energy, they ran and laughed, they threw snowballs. Even Marek, his black eyes intent on his aim. He was better, he was worse. He hadn't spoken again. If you pushed him to, he'd withdraw, a fox disappearing into the thicket of himself; the spark would go out of those beautiful fierce black eyes of his, and he'd start kicking the furniture. My Marek. He still woke up screaming sometimes. Once he disappeared and I found him behind the toolshed crying in the snow. Just crying. I watched, out of sight, till he went back in.

I helped him with homework. He could write simple French now. I wrote him questions in the margins of his papers. Easy ones. *Which do you like better, jam or chocolate? What's your favorite game? Do you want to be the lion, in our skit this week?*

*Chocolate. Soccer. Yes.*

THE DAYS got shorter. The cold deepened. It got worse, worse. The kids we brought out of Rivesaltes were thinner than ever, swollen bellies, dry skin, bleeding lips and sores. They took weeks to recover. Most of them went to the new homes that were opening up one by one—le Terrier, or Sous les Pins. At les Chênes we were full.

Paquerette came home to l'Espoir with her eyes burning, and said the police had come to CIMADE headquarters. Asking for addresses.

"Whose?"

"The addresses we've taken the children to." Paquerette put a hand up at Madame Sabatier's sharp intake of breath. "They didn't get them. They went through the files for hours. My colleague foresaw it and worked out a secret record-keeping system. Thank God for her. Those men . . ." She swallowed. "They called our children 'germs.' Polluting the French countryside. I pretended not to understand, I said we give them baths." She put her head in her hands. "I wanted to say some very unchristian things."

"It's not unchristian to be angry at this," said Madame Sabatier quietly.

"No. But I can't afford anger. It distracts."

It was always the work, for Paquerette. Just get the kids home safe. Just do it.

Again and again and again.

Madeleine said slowly, "What do you think they wanted the addresses for?"

"I don't know," said Paquerette. "Nothing good."

Rosa was my friend again. Nina wasn't. Nina came for supper like before, and we pretended. Rosa came to see me when she could, and we sat by the fire and talked. No one sat on anyone's bed anymore. No one sat any further from a fire than they could help. I finally asked her about Benjamin. She said she thought maybe he liked her, but she wasn't sure she liked him back enough. She said she'd wished so bad that she could help him, and that she was glad about Lucy and the visa. I looked quickly at her, and she looked down.

"It took me a little while," she whispered.

I squeezed her hand.

There was war news in December, news that made Papa run down from the attic where he hid his short-wave radio and call out to us. It was 36 degrees below zero in Moscow, he told us, his eyes bright as coals, and the Russians were true to form. They'd been burning their crops as the Germans advanced, they'd led them into a trap. Tough people, the Russians. The Germans were pinned down in front of Moscow, learning the hard way that history repeats itself. "I suppose they thought Napoleon failed because he was *French*," said my father with a fierce grin.

Maybe there was hope.

I was tired all the time. Everyone was. The cold wears you out. At night I sat with my feet almost in the fire, till they were warm enough to crawl into my cold bed with. It took me longer and longer to get warm enough to fall asleep. I wore a wool hat to bed, made out of old sweaters. The same hat I wore everywhere else. There was a time I'd have thought that was embarrassing. That it made me look poor. I'd seen Rivesaltes five times since then.

Besides, we were all poor now.

More news. Papa pounded down the stairs while we were making supper, shouting that the Japanese had bombed America. I put down my knife and stared at him. *America?*

"Their biggest naval base. On the island of Hawaii. No warning—a massive attack—"

"*Why?*" said Julien.

"Well, it looks like they *might* want to start a war with them," Papa said dryly.

I almost laughed.

"Isn't Japan allied with Germany?" Julien said slowly.

"Yes," said Papa quietly, but with such intensity my heart sped up.

"America'll fight," I breathed.

"Yeah." It was Benjamin, his voice so bitter I jumped. "They'll fight *Japan*. A world away. Someone just bombed the other side of the world, Magali. When it's midnight there it's noon here. That's not hope. That's nothing to do with us. The Americans won't help us, they'll defend themselves. Like everybody does."

"You think the Russians defending themselves doesn't help us?" said Julien.

"Lucy says the American president wants to help us," I put in. "But most Americans didn't want to get involved. They're involved *now.*"

Papa gestured for quiet. "I think you're right," he said, "Julien, Magali. That's why I came down to tell you. The Russians are draining Germany's resources. The British have held out against them. And now the Americans, as you say, are involved. Remember this, Benjamin: this war is not over yet."

"The Russians and the Brits and the Americans," said Julien. "What're *we* doing?"

There was a time I would've told Julien what *I* was doing. But I was trying to be a better person. I shut up.

THE AMERICANS declared war on Japan the next day. A few days later Germany declared war on the U.S.

The day after that, we heard Benjamin's father was in Spain. In jail. Benjamin took it pretty well. He said better Spain than the Nazis any day.

Us? We went on trying to survive.

THE TRAIN was always crowded now. Ragged people, rich people, all those scared, hopeful eyes. It wasn't strange, anymore, to hear Polish or German in the street. They came by ones and twos, or by families; they knew where they were going, or they were met; or they asked the way to the pastor's house. Lucy was with us often at the station; she and Rosa stood beside each other, almost like friends. Lucy was there to report to Madame Alex on who was coming to her door, and to be sent round town to look for rooms for them. She liked knocking on doors, she said, she liked talking to new people. She never said a word about forgery. Neither did I.

It got colder, and colder. It never stopped. Our December trip to Rivesaltes was like a trip into Hell.

Yes, it was south of us. But those barracks, people might as well have been sleeping outside. Oh, I can't even talk about it. It makes me want to curse. The parents and kids huddling together under old blankets, making little fires in the barracks with roots and scraps of wood. The *tramontane* howling through the camp so hard people could hardly walk. Children out in it with bare legs and rags tied round their feet with string.

A woman sat in Marylise's office and told me two kids in her barrack had died that week, and thanked me for taking her daughter and called me Mademoiselle, while I sat there feeling sick to my stomach. We took ten kids on that trip. I didn't complain about my feet after that, or the hunger, or the beans and the bad bread day after day. I'd met people who'd kill for a plateful of beans and barley bread. Maybe literally. I'm not sure I would have blamed them.

We went on. We washed children and fed them and carried them and bandaged the places where they bled. I watched Paquerette's gray eyes grow blank and weary and full of pain. I watched them snap open when a child cried or wandered, I watched her give what she didn't have left to give. I did what I could. Sometimes when I got home I cried; I was so tired and my feet hurt so bad with the cold.

One day in church a strange thing happened. I was nodding off; it's warm there, with so many bodies close together, and I get sleepy. We were doing communion. We don't do it often, in the Reformed church. I'd never taken it since my confirmation; Papa told me not to unless I knew what it meant. So I didn't. I closed my eyes and listened to Pastor Alex's deep voice. I was so tired.

And then Pastor Alex said, "This is my body, broken for you," and I started to cry.

I didn't understand why. But it made me think of Paquerette. It made me think of the time I saw her cry. Of sleeping on a train station floor. Of her weary, weary eyes. It made me think of going on, and beans for lunch and beans for supper, and broken boots and the pain in your feet when you warm them by the fire, and the brightness in Marek's dark eyes. I wiped my cheeks and looked straight ahead of me, hoping no one noticed. Words came into my mind: *Is it really? Is it?* I almost went up with the others. But it was too late. They had gone.

Lucy came over with red eyes one bitter-cold evening, stripped off her socks and put her feet up to the fire, and told me why her father had wanted her to go to America.

"He was gonna get *married*. That's who he wanted me to live with. His new wife and her parents."

"He wha— Wait. *Was?*"

She nodded gloomily. "I fouled it up. He put off the wedding and went off to Egypt."

"Is he mad at you?"

"Bit hard to tell, in a letter."

"But . . . but you got Benj—"

"Yeah, and now his father's in jail. If it weren't for me he'd be still in Marseille."

I stared at her. "You don't know that! They could both be in *Rivesaltes!*"

She bit her lip. "You don't know either. Oh, man, it's cold in here." She put her feet almost into the flames. "I don't know, Magali. It just feels strange. I feel like I did something wrong."

I looked at her. "She's in America, Lucy."

"I did it so I wouldn't have to go. *That's* the truth."

"She's still in America."

"What do you think about . . . doing the right thing for the wrong reason?"

I looked into the flames for a moment and didn't speak. *It's what happens in the world that counts. We don't have time to waste trying to figure out if our souls are all lined up right.* "The right thing is the right thing."

"But what if it isn't? What if you do it for the wrong reason and it makes you . . . do it wrong?" She sighed. "I don't know. It made me think that's all. I mean, you go around thinking you're . . ." She shrugged, and looked down. "I'd never regret helping her out, Magali, in a million years. I just can't feel like a hero about it. That's all."

"Oh." *I see.* "Well," I said slowly, "you could pray about it. Maybe."

She looked at me. "I never heard you suggest *that* before, Magali Losier."

"Um—"

She let out a ringing laugh, and clapped me on the shoulder. And then smiled sheepishly. "Well," she said. "Maybe I will."

CHRISTMAS CAME. Grandpa killed two chickens for us, and I helped pluck them. We had the Thibauds over. You can't stop having people over because there's barely enough food. We told stories and laughed round the table over our chicken and potatoes and our precious wild blueberry preserves, just the same as we would've done in the old days over turkey and chestnuts and chocolate and oranges. It's hard to explain, really, how good that feels in your soul. It's like in the old days we used to think it was the food that made us happy. And now we knew the truth.

Lucy's aunt had written a Christmas song, to an Irish tune about a boy named Danny—a high, haunting tune. Mama sang it, in the dark church with all the candles lit. It was a sad Christmas song, about war and how hard things were when Jesus was born, and Mama's voice made me want to cry. I shut my eyes and saw the inside of a Rivesaltes barrack, the beams of the roof, the shadows, as sharp as if Paquerette had drawn it, and I saw a baby lying in a pile of rags. Mama sang the last lines high, high: "An outcast child, in darkness and in danger . . . A hidden light, rejected light, the gift of love."

After the moments of silence, as everyone shifted in their seats and stood up, I wiped my eyes with my sleeve, and wondered if maybe Mama would let me take an extra trip.

Over the next three months I made five trips. They blur together in my mind, to tell the truth. Twice we went to Gurs, where the people thanked God for the cold that froze the clay mud so it was safe to walk to the toilets. I heard awful stories. An old lady had gotten trapped in that mud, in the rain, and died. It was poison, that place, worse than Rivesaltes. We did the only thing we could do; we got a few children out and to Tanieux.

They're what I remember.

I remember Christof and Anya and Rebeka, three blond-haired kids—half Jewish. They'd left Germany with their aunt when their parents got arrested. She'd disappeared in Lyon. Two months later when they got sent to Rivesaltes, they found out from Marylise their aunt was in Gurs. I remember Ilana and Miriam, twins, whose mother was dead and whose sixteen-year-old brother had been trying to get them released since the day they arrived at the camp. He walked them to the camp gate in the bitter January wind, with his scarf over his face so you could hardly see he was crying. I remember

Georges, a five-year-old whose mother told me they were French, naturalized as soon as they'd moved from Italy, and much good it had done them since Vichy had stripped the whole family of their citizenship in that purge a year ago. Georges fought me as I led him away, and his mother had to turn her back on him to make him go.

I remember too many of them to tell.

I remember seeing the other workers—CIMADE workers, O.S.E. workers, Swiss Aid. Taking other groups of children, to other places. Our allies. Just to see their faces gave me strength. I remember nights in stations, sleeping lightly like a soldier, listening for whatever might come. I remember head counts, that awful moment before you're sure. I remember so many trains. So many kids, some clinging to me and crying, some wild, some very, very quiet. I remember the moment of handing them over to someone, the relief. Walking to l'Espoir with Paquerette, sitting down by the fire, exhausted. Not saying anything, not needing to. There's a gladness that you feel, and it passes between you, and you both know it's there. Those were hard times. They were the hardest times in my life, in a way. I wouldn't trade them for anything.

Rosa traveled too. She met me after my trips, every time, and I met her after hers. We didn't promise each other that, but it was as if we had. As if we'd sworn on our lives. We both knew how it felt, stepping off the train half dead and seeing that trusted face on the platform, that friend you could hand it all over to. I loved Rosa. There wasn't a shred of me, anymore, that felt anything but glad she was part of this.

It was hard, though. Day after grinding day. I could feel my energy leaving me, not coming back. The kind of tiredness I'd seen in Paquerette that summer. It was harder to think, to be patient with the kids, to laugh with them instead of wanting them to shut up. It was harder with Marek. I smacked him again, once, when after two weeks of no trouble he tried to kill somebody. I'm serious. This new kid kicked him, and Marek went absolutely insane—had him down on the floor in seconds, trying to smash his face in. Oh, and crying. Crying so hard.

When I hit him he stopped crying. Some. "Come with me," I snapped, hauling him to his feet. He came.

It was so cold it hurt, but the creek was where we had to be. I stood on the frozen bank under snow-laden pines, and listened to the cold, cold water gurgling under the ice, and to the labored sound of Marek's breathing, the sobs that still hadn't let go of his chest.

"Marek," I said when he was quiet. "What's wrong?"

Nothing.

"I know you can talk."

A split-second glance.

"I don't know what to do with you. You run, you fight. That's gonna get you killed, Marek. Hiding is the only way to be safe now and you *stink* at hiding. I'm doing all this work just so you can get killed the first time a Nazi shows up because you'll either bolt or *hit* him"—*shut up, Magali*—"and it's not fair. Why should we wear ourselves out for you when you don't even *try*—"

"My papa's dead," said Marek suddenly.

I froze. The world shifted, swiftly and silently, to that moment when the wild fox takes a step out of the woods toward your out-stretched hand. You don't look him in the eye. You don't make any sudden movements.

After a long time, I decided I dared.

"How did he die?" I whispered.

"The soldiers kicked him."

Ice went down my spine. *You don't mean . . .*

"His head was all bleeding."

My stomach turned over.

"When did it happen?"

Out of the corner of my eye I saw him shrug a little. "In Gda'sk."

I tried not to. But somehow naming a place to it made me see it: the circle of men surrounding a man on the ground . . .

I don't really think I understand life, but I know this is true: we live in a horrible world. These things happen. To children, even. I don't know why. I wish it wasn't like that. But this is the only world we've got.

"I'm so sorry, Marek," I said. There was nothing else to say.

"My papa was good at fighting," he said.

A gun added itself to my mental picture, lying useless on the cobblestones outside the circle. It didn't help. *Is that why, Marek? You want to be like him? Well I want you to live longer than him . . .*

Silence. My cheeks were starting to sting.

"I'm cold," said Marek.

"Yeah. Me too. You want to go home?"

"Yeah."

We went home.

AFTER THAT he talked. Now and then. Only when you gave him his space, when you didn't push him. A yes or no, maybe a sentence. It was a little miracle, every time. Except for his name.

That was a disaster.

I told him and told him why he had to be Jean-Marc. It made him go away inside himself, but I had to do it. Even worse, though, was when he was in a *good* mood and someone called him Jean-Marc.

"My name's Marek."

Every time. Just like that. It made me want to hit him. It made me afraid for him.

"My name's Marek Adamczyk."

I couldn't even *say* his last name. But he could say it fine, and any cop who believed he was French after *that* was deaf in both ears. Papa Thiély pulled him out of school for a while. For his own protection.

My Marek. I couldn't think of him as Jean-Marc Meunier either, if you want to know the truth.

WORD CAME to us about arrests in the occupied zone. Not the usual kind—refugees or poor immigrants from Eastern Europe or suspected Communists—but French Jews. Families who'd been in the country for generations, Papa said, doctors and lawyers; well-known names. Benjamin knew some of them. He used to be pretty high-class himself. He skipped school the day after we heard, and stayed in his room, and Papa pretended he didn't notice.

It seemed to hit Paquerette almost as hard. She got in to Tanieux, and then turned around and went back to Rivesaltes without even a day in between. I had to scramble to pack in time. On the train she said something about "when the work is done."

"Done?"

"Yes, done. When they stop releasing the kids we're done."

"You think they'll stop? Soon?"

She shrugged. "What do I know? Yes, that's what I think. Look at them changing tactics like that. Do you see?"

"They only arrested foreigners before. But this was in the occupied zone—"

"And we're in the free zone?"

She had me there. Calling it *the free zone* was against the law.

"They didn't even try to pretend it made sense," she said quietly. "They didn't even try to pretend there was a reason. *That*—"

"They're not trying to look humane anymore," I said suddenly, remembering what she said long ago about Vichy.

She nodded.

It was like a jolt of electricity through me. "You think they'll do it here? Arrest people just for being Jewish? *French* people?"

She looked at me oddly. "What did you think I was saying?"

"But Benjamin!"

"Yes."

But. But they couldn't arrest Benjamin. He was *French*.

I couldn't say anything for a while. I looked out the train window. When I looked at Paquerette again, she had paper and pencil out, drawing. A barrack under snow; a child in front of it, rags tied around her feet, looking off to the left at something you couldn't see; and in front of her, barbed wire.

WE WORKED, and we worked. We forgot about spring and we forgot about freedom and we put one foot in front of the other. We brought home kids from Gurs who, when we unwrapped their feet to wash them, had toes missing from frostbite. It made me ashamed, to put our donated socks and shoes on those poor wounded feet. It made me want to say, *I'm sorry we came too late.*

It gets worse, worse, and you stop believing it will ever get better. There's no time like the second week of February, for not believing anymore in spring. Paquerette and I didn't say a word to each other, going down to the camp on the train. We slept. We could feel it, both of us, pulling at us like the sucking of the tide. No one lasts forever. I might like to think of Paquerette's spine as steel, but it was bone like everybody else's, and we were bone weary. I saw her in those moments when a child started to cry, or walk away from the group; I saw her fight to summon up the strength. I tried to spare her, do it for her. I saw her, walking away at the end of the trip, how she stumbled in the snow from nothing but weariness. I wondered how much longer she could last.

I didn't hope for the work to be done. No. Not the way Paquerette had said. And not hoping for that, I didn't know what to hope for.

There wasn't anything to hope for, really, except that we could save a few.

I'll never forget that time, ever. If I live to be a hundred. The feel of it, hard as Tanieux ice, Paquerette's eyes gray as the winter sky, just going on, and yet knowing. Knowing the end was coming; and knowing that the thing we were doing, out of all the things in the cold and terrible world then, was the thing that had to be done.

We went on. We went on. I wish to God that was the end of the story.

*Chapter 16*

# Fight Them

IN MARCH we had a short, glittering thaw that refroze into icicles and hard ice on the streets. In March I saw Erich Müller again. The first German soldier I had ever seen. Or met. Or showed to his hotel. He was limping. I think I jumped visibly when I recognized him.

"Mademoiselle Losier . . . are you well?"

"Yes. I'm fine."

"And how have you been this winter?"

"Fine." What was he doing here? He'd left. All those convalescents had left. No one spent the winter in Tanieux who didn't have to. "And, um, how are . . . you?"

"Not entirely well, or you wouldn't see me here. I was shot in the same leg that I broke last year. By a Communist, actually."

I didn't ask him how he knew. I could imagine. The guy was probably dead by now. I tried not to let my voice falter. "Where were you stationed?"

"Paris."

I put my hands in my coat pockets so he wouldn't see them shaking. I was afraid of him, I realized. Not like the first time, the

226

shock at seeing my first German soldier, that had worn off before the train pulled in. No, I was afraid of *him*, not his uniform. Why was he here? "It's probably warmer in Paris right now," I said, smiling, or trying to.

He smiled ruefully. "It's true. I requested to be billeted here. I had fond memories. No one told me."

"It's starting to get warmer."

His eyebrows went up. "This is warmer?"

"Yes."

"You seem to be a very tough people here." He sounded approving.

I took a breath. *Get out of it, Magali. Go.* "Well. I, uh, wish you a good recovery."

"Thank you, Mademoiselle. It was a pleasure to see you again."

I watched him move off carefully down the icy sidewalk, and told myself it would be all right. One more thing to be afraid of. I was so tired. I glanced up at the *mairie* as I walked across the *place du centre* and remembered standing in that line with Lucy, the day I broke my boots. The day before I met Paquerette. Wanting so much to *do* something.

Well, I didn't regret what I was doing. Not for a moment. But I couldn't remember what it was like to be that girl.

I TOLD Papa about Erich Müller, and about the Communist. He nodded. "There's rumors they've been organizing. Starting to fight them." I asked him, because I couldn't quite help wondering, if he thought Müller was telling the truth about why he was here. Papa's eyebrows went way up.

"And this is the man you blithely walked to his hotel last summer?"

It's a bit hard when your own father mocks your stupidity. "Yes," I said, looking away.

"Magali," he said, more gently. "We're nobody, here. And if we weren't, they'd send someone French to spy on us, not German. No. Why send a German when you can buy someone French?"

His voice turned bitter as he said that, and I looked up and saw on his face the same disgust I felt. I wanted to say something about that kind of French people, but I couldn't find any words that wouldn't make him angry, coming from his daughter's mouth.

It was a time for anger. It was a bad time, and getting worse. Benjamin hardly spoke these days, nor Julien either. Julien paced. Looked fiercely at things the rest of us couldn't see. One day he knocked on my door, said he wanted to show me something. "Not here. In my room."

He shut the door carefully. "Just had to show it to someone," he muttered, and pulled a newspaper out from under his mattress. I stared at it for a moment, and he sat down on the bed with his elbows on his knees.

The paper's name was *Combat*. The headline read "Resist: The Time Is Now." A shiver ran through me. I scanned the first few lines—*Vichy has betrayed us, it's time to fight them*, basically. "Who gave it to you?" I was whispering, without even meaning to. It finally occurred to me to glance at the date. October 1941. It was months old.

"Pierre," Julien whispered. "He got it from Philippe Sarlac—you know him?"

I nodded. A guy in his twenties stands out around here. These days.

"His cousin in Lyon sent it to him. He wants it back—he loaned it to Pierre—"

"Who . . . who printed it?"

"The Resistance," he whispered.

"*Here?* In the . . . the free zone?"

He nodded.

"Thanks." My hand tightened on it. "Thanks for telling me."

He nodded. He ran a hand through his hair, just like Papa does when he's stressed. "Pierre wants to join them," he said.

"How?"

"I don't know. He won't tell me . . . everything. He's been talking about it to our scout troop, on the quiet. He seems to think . . ." His eyes got distant. "If I was organizing anything, it'd be up in the Tanières. All those caves . . ."

*Hang on now.* "So what do *you* think? About . . . all this."

He looked at me for a long moment. "I think I'm a pacifist," he said.

"You *think* you are?"

"I guess you *know* what *you* are."

I kind of wanted to tell him I did. If it had made sense for me to fight, I would've fought. It didn't, so I transported kids. That was what I did, that was what I was. But I could see he was going through something heavy. I shrugged.

"Look, it's complicated, but anyway—we've got people hiding here. If we fight we'll bring them right down on us—"

My belly clenched at the thought. "And we couldn't keep them away," I said.

"Well, no. Can you imagine? Maybe if we lived in *real* mountains, like the Swiss, but here . . ."

"You think someone'll try it? Around here?"

"I don't know. Pierre seems to think that might be the idea. I've tried to tell him, but you can't talk to that guy." He jammed his hands in his pockets and looked away. "He thinks I'm a coward."

"I don't think you're a coward," I told him. "I'm not a pacifist, but I think you're right."

"Thanks."

"You going to show it to Papa?"

He shook his head. "Pierre made me promise."

"Well—thanks. Thanks a ton."

"Sure. I had to show it to somebody."

I felt so many things, walking out of his room. The hope, the danger. The fact that my brother had wanted me to know. That was a warm feeling, that part. In spite of everything it made me feel like something was still right.

THEN PAQUERETTE came in from her next trip, with her face even grayer than usual. Rosa didn't look much better.

"It was a hard one. Really . . . hard. We got news, Magali."

"What?"

She hushed me, gesturing to the children.

I found out the news that night, from Papa. He'd been at a meeting with Pastor Alex. When he came in the door Julien took one look at him and switched off the radio.

He stood in the doorway and looked at us. Looked at Benjamin, unhappily.

"You promised, Monsieur Losier," said Benjamin quietly.

Papa nodded, and rubbed a hand over his face. It shook a little. "Yes," he said. "You have a right to know." He sat down, and looked into the fire, and said, "Paquerette got some disturbing news on her trip. Apparently a friend of the CIMADE sometimes gets inside information from Vichy, and . . . they've learned of a policy change. A very recent change. Regarding the internment camps in the north."

"What?"

"They're"—he cleared his throat—"they're going to start deporting the Jewish internees from the northern camps to Germany."

We stared at him.

"Why?" Julien asked.

"Didn't Germany deport them here?" Some of them anyway. Like Eva, in those nightmare train cars—that was why Vichy had left them sealed like that, because they were trying to send them back to Germany, and Germany wouldn't take them back . . .

"Will Germany even accept them?"

"Germany has *asked* for them."

There was a short silence as we looked at each other. It made no sense. But it felt wrong. Wrong. *The camps in the north,* I reminded myself. *Not ours.* It didn't help.

"I wish I understood it," Papa said.

"I understand it," said a grating voice. We turned and stared at Benjamin, at his eyes so dark in his chalk-white face, at his shaking hands. "Getting rid of us wasn't good enough," he said. His voice lowered. "Now they want to kill us."

"Benjamin," Papa breathed. I don't think I'd ever seen him so shocked. "Benjamin," he said again, his voice picking up volume, "think. They can't do that. They—the German people aren't so lost to humanity—such a thing couldn't be kept secret—and—what *good* would it do them?" He was talking too fast, stumbling over his words, he didn't sound like himself. "What advantage? They're planning some type of forced labor—of course they are—"

Benjamin cut through it. "*Not so lost to humanity,* Monsieur Losier?" His voice was terrible. "Were you *there*? Have you *seen*?"

Papa said nothing. I almost thought he looked scared.

"My parents *know.* They were *there.* My parents left everything to get away from those people. Everything. Now my mother's alone in a foreign country and my father's in a Spanish jail and they think they're better off, they *know* they're better off than the ones who stayed." He was trembling. Papa had risen, his eyes wide, looking at him. "They knew. They saw it coming. They tried . . . tried to convince—" Something shook his chest, like a sob, but without sound. I couldn't move.

Papa laid a hand on his shoulder. "Benjamin." Benjamin gasped for breath, shaking. "We won't let anything happen to you. I promise."

"We promise," whispered Julien.

I stared at my father and brother. Making promises like they were God. *And what do you people think Paquerette should have promised Zvi's mother?* I said nothing.

Benjamin went on shaking.

PAQUERETTE AND I left on our next trip two days later. On the train I told her what Benjamin had said. She turned away from me for a moment. "Do you remember what I said to you, a long time ago? That you and I, we don't talk about evil?"

Oh, so long ago. *The knowledge that is poison,* she had said, and I hadn't known what she meant. Not really, not then. "Yes, Paquerette." I looked down at my hands. "But—the kids—"

"They mustn't be deported," she said flatly. "Do you have any doubts about that?"

"No."

"That's what we need to know, then."

IT WAS warmer, at Rivesaltes. It was five days before Easter. In Rivesaltes village there were dabs of green on the trees, the grass was coming alive. In Rivesaltes camp there was nothing green nor ever had been. The only sign of spring was a slight easing of the misery on the people's faces. It did my heart good, though not enough. I looked around the camp with a feeling of dislocation, of dread. What would happen to these people?

We had a brother and sister, about thirteen and fourteen: Jakob and Sarah, whose father was dead and whose mother was missing. We had four siblings whose mother said a prayer over each of them when she said goodbye. The youngest was a frighteningly thin, silent baby girl, one year old. Trina. I carried her. Jakob carried the four-year-old, who was very weak too. Their mother hugged each of them at the block gate, whispering things in their ears. I looked back, after the guard had shut it behind us; I looked back at her standing there behind the barbed wire and my stomach clenched. *She'll never see them again.* That was what went through my mind.

I threw it out. *You don't know that,* I yelled at myself, *how do you know what'll happen?* But I sounded like Papa the other night, talking fast, panicked. There was ice-cold dread in my belly.

I couldn't get rid of it. Back at Marylise's barrack, as we got ready to go, I pulled Paquerette aside and told her we could handle more kids. Trina wasn't going to be any trouble, she clung to me like she was drowning—

Paquerette put up a hand. "This is all there is right now."

"Just six?"

"They haven't given as many releases this month."

I looked at her. *This is it. Oh God, help us, this really is it . . .*

By ten the next evening we'd gotten them to Valence. The local train to la Voulte was doing only one run per day now, we were going to have to start sleeping in Valence every trip. Trina still clung to me, silent, as we bedded down in a corner. I let her sleep on my stomach, feeling the tiny rise and fall of her chest. Looking up into the dark and trying to forget Benjamin's shaking, the fear in Papa's voice. They'd stopped giving out releases. They were going to give the Nazis what they wanted, just like they always, always did . . .

How had our lives become this nightmare?

*This can't be real. It can't be real. Oh God, please tell me—*

But I stopped. Please tell me it's not real? You can't say that. It's cowards' talk.

PAQUERETTE SENT me out into the dark before dawn to buy bread for breakfast. I took Trina, because she wouldn't let go. When I came back the others had found a bench, and we all sat on it tearing pieces off the baguette with our hands. Trina sucked her bottle, weakly. It was eight o'clock, the station filling with people and voices, footsteps echoing on the hard floor. We had an hour till our train.

Trina's diaper started smelling, and I got up to find somewhere to change it. I was headed into the hallway to the bathrooms when it happened.

It happened so fast.

Shouting. I turned round. People scattering—two security guards, running—I saw the man just as they caught him. Just beyond the bench where Paquerette and the children sat. One of them grabbed him by the shoulder and wrenched him round, while the other kicked his legs out from under him. He was screaming: "It wasn't me, it WASN'T ME!" He was young, barely older than Julien. His clothes were torn. He was on his knees. He had black curly hair like Benjamin's, he looked Jewish. Everyone was staring. Someone pointed—back the way he had come from. There was a hand-lettered sign pasted to the station wall. It read "Death to the Nazis."

"It WASN'T ME!" the young man shouted. That's when the police reached him.

Three Vichy police in uniform. Two of them grabbed him while the third opened a pair of handcuffs. The young man struggled, got one of his feet back under him, pushing the men who were holding him off balance. The one with the handcuffs didn't hesitate. He pulled back and kicked him, right where you should never kick a man.

The young man screamed.

He doubled over on the hard tile floor of the station. The cop kicked him again. All of us, the whole hall of people, stared. Nobody moved.

None of us lifted a finger.

He kicked him again. For a moment I saw the young man's face turned toward me, and his black eyes were full of pain and terror. Pleading.

There was a roaring in my ears; my world spun out of control. For a moment I saw a circle of soldiers kicking a man, I heard a child's scream. For a moment I saw Benjamin there on the ground,

Benjamin screaming. *He's Jewish, I know he is. They'll take him too. They'll take him to—*

I pulled back into the mouth of the hallway, clutching Trina and trembling. *No one will stop them. No one will help him. We're all scared, we're all sheep, we give them whatever they—*

*We have to. We can't fight them. You can't fight them, Magali. Men with guns—*

Beside me, a few paces back, a cord hung from a lever set in the wall. A sign beneath it read "Fire Alarm." I drifted back toward it as my heart began to race. *I can't fight them. But I can do something. Something.* My heart beat a wild tattoo of fear in my chest. I was out of sight of the main hall now. I glanced round.

Then I pulled the cord, hard.

A loud, high, brassy bell began to scream above me. Above me. Nowhere else. Fear raced hot and cold through my body. I looked round, knowing that now I should run. Realized the only way out was forward.

Back through the main hall.

I stood frozen, my mouth and throat dry, Trina heavy in my arms. I was trapped. I didn't dare go out there. No. I had to. No—

"What's wrong with you, girl?" An old man in a cloth cap frowned at me. Suspiciously. But he hadn't seen. No one had seen.

Why wasn't he running?

*Because there isn't any smoke, you—*

"Which way, Monsieur? The exits?"

He pointed toward the main hall. No choice. I began to run.

"There's no fire!" someone in the main hall was screaming. "No fire! You! Check that hallway! There's no smoke, check that hallway and if you don't find a fire, you arrest everyone near it!" I came to the mouth of the hallway as he said those words. My spinning mind took a moment to take it in. One frozen moment before I had the sense to move.

The policeman was shouting to the station guard, "Go!"

The other two police were holding the young man, with his arms twisted up behind him.

The station guard lifted his head and started across the space between us. Toward the mouth of the hallway where I stood.

Every man, woman, and child between him and that hallway cringed. I saw the motion of it like a wave. I saw Paquerette and the kids in the middle of that wave. I saw Jakob's head snap up, saw his white face look at me standing there in the fatal doorway with a child in my arms. I saw Paquerette's head come up a moment later, saw her eyes blaze out at me. I turned and ran. I wasn't two steps down that hallway before I heard the sounds I hadn't even known enough to dread. I heard the policeman shout "Who did it?"

And I heard a low clear voice. "It was me."

It was Paquerette.

MY LEGS were shaking, my belly was trembling. I reached the bathroom and shut myself in a stall and clutched Trina to my chest so hard she whimpered. *What have I done? What have I done?*

*Oh God, please tell me it's not real.* I leaned my forehead against the stall door and within my mind I screamed. *She said she did it. She said it for me. She saw me there—in the entrance—she saw me and she—*

They were arresting her. Now. It flashed through my mind— Paquerette putting her hands out for the handcuffs—it hit me like a blow. Jakob and Sarah and the kids looking on with huge eyes at the woman who was supposed to protect them. And had protected me instead.

That was when I snapped out of it. Instantly, like being plunged into cold water, or woken by a scream. The mind of fear, the other-mind, it grabbed me by the throat and told me why she'd chosen to protect me and leave them here alone.

*Because I could get them home.*

And then my mind was racing with what I had to do. Platform 5—I had to get them there right away. Out of the main hall. Maybe split up and give Trina to one of them, in case the police came for me after all. Jakob and Sarah were probably terrified now, wondering what to do. But I had to wait. I had to.

Because the first thing I had to do was not get arrested.

The fire alarm cut off short. That told me one thing. They'd believed her.

I pictured what they would be doing. The police might leave right away; the security guards would stay. Mop up, go around and tell people there was no fire . . . I couldn't stay too long. We couldn't afford to miss that train.

I'd change Trina's diaper. Like I'd planned. I'd change it and then go.

I made myself come out of the stall. I took Trina's diaper off, pulled a fresh one out of the bag, my hands didn't shake as I pinned it on. A woman walked in and I didn't look up. I washed my hands, took Trina, and walked out. I walked with even steps to the end of that terrible hallway and looked out.

There were no police in the main hall. I scanned the place three times. No police and no kids. My heart stopped.

Their bench was empty. They were gone.

I held Trina hard against my chest and hurried through the hall, weaving between people, my heart pounding. Would they remember the platform number, could they be there? Could they be hiding? Where—in some bathroom, in—

In the far corner a group of kids sat huddled on the ground, in the spot where we'd slept. I ran for them. Halfway there I saw one of them lift her head, and it was Sarah. I nearly died from the relief. What I saw in her face was the same.

I dropped to my knees beside them. For a moment I couldn't speak. We looked at each other and for a moment again I trembled.

Then I said, "We need to get to Platform 5."

I DON'T remember much of that trip, to be honest. I was underwater, deep, deep down, and someone else was living my life for me. Someone competent, who fed children and carried children and counted children, who bought tickets and knew where to go. While I drifted, far down underneath, unconscious, my heart drowsy with horror, feeling nothing.

Jakob and Sarah had Paquerette's purse. She'd set it down on the bench beside Sarah before she'd stood up to be arrested. I could picture her calm gray eyes as she did it. The money was in it, the papers, the releases, everything. I split them up. I sent Pesha and Trina with Sarah, Aaron and Isaac with Jakob; I gave them their papers and releases and sent them to opposite ends of the platform. I waited in the middle, alone. I'd told Sarah exactly how many stops there were before la Voulte, everything, who to ask for in Tanieux. Just in case. I kept looking over my shoulder. Once I saw police. Back in the main hall. One of them came to the door of our platform, glanced up and down. I put my head down, hearing my pulse pound in my ears. He looked familiar. I didn't think he saw me. He went away again. I stood and waited in dull agony. The train pulled in. I stood and watched until I'd seen Sarah and her kids get into one car and Jakob and his kids into another. Then I got in too.

I sat rocking with the rhythm of the train, barely remembering my name. Where my mind used to be there was deep water. Sitting in my seat was someone who had to get six kids to Tanieux station. That much I could remember. I got up when we passed Livron-sur-Drôme, to find Sarah and Jakob and tell them la Voulte was next. We got off. I found lunch in Paquerette's bag, and divided it up. I didn't eat. I would have thrown up. I took kids to the tiny station bathroom, one by one. Finally *la Galoche* pulled in, and I got them all on.

And then I was almost done.

We came into Tanieux on the five-o'clock train, and the hills and the platform and the face of Monsieur Bernard looked strange, unfamiliar, like I'd seen them only in a dream. I came out of the train with Trina in my arms, blinking in the sunlight. Rosa was there, and Nina. At the sight of Nina's face it came back to me, and the person deep inside me, the swimmer in deep water, began to thrash. Their faces were still turned toward the train door. It closed, and no one got out.

"Magali? Where's Paquerette? Are you . . ."

I don't know what I looked like. They stared at me. The trembling was starting to come back. Rosa's eyes went to Paquerette's purse hanging from my shoulder, and returned to mine dark with bewilderment and fear. But I wasn't finished. I had to get them where they were going. I thrust the little kids' papers at Rosa. "They're going to le Terrier. All of them. Except the baby, I can take her to l'Espoir. Nina, I think the little ones need some help in Yiddish . . . and Isaac needs to be carried . . ."

Nina gave me a nod, and crouched down in front of the little ones, the way she does, with her bad leg stretched out. Started talking in Yiddish. Rosa stood there, holding the papers, looking at me. "Magali," she murmured. "Where's Paquerette?"

I opened my mouth and no sound came out. I forced the words through my thickening throat.

"She got arrested in Valence."

*Chapter 17*

# Into the Lion's Den

For a moment no one spoke. It hurt to look at Rosa's face.

"What happened?" she whispered.

"I—please, I'll tell you—later. It's been—it's been—"

Rosa squeezed my hand. "Oh, Magali, it must've been awful. You got them home by yourself?"

I nodded. The tears started to my eyes. I tried to speak and couldn't.

"I'll take her." Rosa held out her arms for the baby. Trina's big eyes looked at me as I passed her over, but she didn't open her mouth. I never saw a quieter child. "What's her name?" Rosa asked.

"Trina," I whispered. "Thank you." I couldn't meet her eyes.

"She'll be all right, Magali. She has to be. I'll . . . I'll light a candle for her . . ."

I nodded, my throat tight. I turned and walked away. I was going the wrong way. Something beat and beat inside me, feverishly, a tired, urgent voice deep in my mind: I wasn't done. There was one thing left to do.

My feet were taking me to the parsonage.

"PLEASE TELL me exactly what happened," said Pastor Alex.

He was silhouetted by the slanting sun in his yellow-curtained window. I fingered a scar in the wood of his old oak desk, feeling like I was about to take a knife and drive it through my hand. But lying, that would be betrayal. I ran my tongue round my dry lips.

"There were police in the Valence station," I said slowly. "They were arresting someone, a young man maybe twenty years old. I thought he looked Jewish. But . . . I think they were arresting him for posting a sign on the station wall against the Nazis. He kept saying it wasn't him."

I looked up at him suddenly. "I don't think it *was* him. If he was Jewish he wouldn't be stupid enough to do something like that—not with the way things are. And I . . . I'd heard the news, you know, *Monsieur le Pasteur*, the news that . . . that Paquerette told you. So I was afraid for him. I—" I stopped. Looked at the scar in the wood. "I did something stupid."

Pastor Alex waited, didn't move, as I took a breath.

"I pulled the fire alarm. To distract them." I glanced up. "Only the alarm was in a cul-de-sac. I didn't think about that. I couldn't slip away. And I had—" I stopped again. Took a breath against the sick and dizzy pain I felt, as if I was losing blood. "I had a baby in my arms."

I heard it. His intake of breath.

"The police didn't believe there was a fire. They suspected, they started looking for who did it. They—I was still in the cul-de-sac, and—" I was breathing fast, too fast. The words came out in a rush. "And Paquerette told them she did it."

I stared at the scar on the desk. I remember the exact shape of the ragged edge where the fibers of the wood were broken. I barely heard Pastor Alex's low voice. "And then what happened?"

"I hid. Till they were gone. I couldn't get arrested, I had to get the kids here . . ."

"And you did? They are safe?"

"Yes."

He nodded, very slowly. After a moment he said, "You've told me everything, Magali?"

"Yes, *Monsieur le Pasteur.*"

"Do I understand correctly that you did not see them arrest her?"

"No, Monsieur, I didn't. But Jakob—he's fourteen—he told me. They did arrest her."

"Was it the *gendarmerie* or the police?"

"Police, Monsieur."

"I see. Thank you, Magali." He looked into my eyes. "Thank you very much for being so honest with me."

"Yes, Monsieur." I looked down.

I COULD not face my parents. I could not. I slipped up both flights of stairs, my heart beating fast. No one was in the hallway on the third floor. I made it to my room, stripped off my coat and sweater, kicked off my shoes. If they came looking for me I'd pretend to be asleep. I was so, so tired.

I crawled under the covers. I don't remember anything after that.

I GUESS I slept through the night. Morning light poured through my window when I woke, and sick shock went through me as I remembered. I shut my eyes against the pictures in my mind, my body knotted itself hard as rock under the covers. I didn't move.

I stayed there until they came for me.

My mother knocked on the door. I swallowed, opened my mouth, didn't move. "Magali? Are you awake? Are you all right? Pastor Alex is here!"

Pastor Alex? They knew, then. They already knew.

I was still dressed. I hadn't even taken my hair down last night. I got up and opened the door. Mama took me in her arms, enfolded me. As hard as the night Zvi died. I wanted to push her away. But I didn't. I didn't deserve to have my own way, ever again. "Lili, my Lili," she whispered into my hair.

She knew, all right.

Pastor Alex was at the table, and Papa, with cups of fake coffee. What was Papa doing here on a schoolday? No, it wasn't a school-day, I remembered suddenly. It was Good Friday.

They offered me coffee. I sipped it. It tasted horrible. Papa said Pastor Alex had told them what happened. He praised me for get-ting the kids home. He said there was one part of the story he didn't understand. He cleared his throat and looked at me.

"Do you have any idea, Magali, why Paquerette thought the police suspected you of pulling the fire alarm? I mean, why she thought it so likely that she took such a drastic step."

I looked at Pastor Alex. He was looking at his coffee.

He hadn't told them. He had told them everything *except* that. It flashed through my mind that this was what people mean by *tact*. But I couldn't feel grateful. I had to answer my father now.

I breathed in. *They'll know anyway. Jakob saw. Everyone'll know.* I pushed the words out. "Because I did it."

I stared at my hands. I didn't want to see their faces. I wouldn't, I couldn't, I never looked up.

"Why, Magali?" came Papa's voice. It sounded calm. Almost.

I picked at a scab on my thumb. It came off, and a tiny spot of red blood began to grow. "I was trying to save the guy they were arresting. He looked Jewish. I thought he'd be deported." I glanced up for a moment. Papa and Pastor Alex were looking at each other. "I forgot I was carrying a baby. She was so quiet. She never cried." My voice sounded flat to me. I covered the bleeding place on my thumb with my finger.

There was a long, long moment of silence.

Pastor Alex broke it. "I've spoken with the CIMADE leaders on the telephone," he said quietly, "as well as with Mesdames Moulin and Chalmette in Valence. I spoke with Madeleine Barot, who heads up the CIMADE, at some length. She believes we must wait. The political climate is changing, very much for the worse, and she fears that for the CIMADE to try to interfere on behalf of Paquerette might do her harm instead. I'm sorry, Magali. I know you had hoped for help from me."

I looked at him. *You can't fight them. Oh God, please tell me it's not real.* "What . . . what do you think will happen to her?"

"It's very difficult to know. Things are changing . . . very rapidly. Earlier, I would have been confident of seeing her again after a few months. Now . . . I must be honest with you. Now I simply don't know."

I was falling, falling through the dark. "Is there nothing we can do at all, *Monsieur le Pasteur?*"

As I said those last words I knew they contained the answer. The answer he would give.

"Pray," he said.

I TRIED.

I paced and paced in my dark room with my shutters closed, and I saw it happen, again and again. I screamed at my past self as her hand reached for the cord. I heard Pastor Alex's voice saying *I don't know.* I heard Benjamin, I saw his white face: *they want to kill us all.*

It's not safe to walk into a lion's den, to take his prey.

I saw myself arrested, in handcuffs, I saw Trina taken from me, roughly, some policeman rifling through her papers—*send the kid back to the camp.* Back to the camp to die, to die like Zvi.

I saw the black-haired man. His eyes. I saw him held, helpless, the way I'd seen him in that moment when the lightning fell on my world, when the station guard started toward me.

I saw Paquerette.

I could see how she'd done it, precisely, in my mind's eye. Setting her purse down on the bench beside Jakob, a natural movement, unconcerned, looking at nothing. Not attracting the eye to anyone, not even herself—not till she'd stood and taken a few steps, distanced herself from everyone she had to protect. I could see her taking those steps, then standing there, her straight, tall figure, her head high, her gray eyes defiant. *It was me. It was me.*

I saw her walking straight-backed into the lion's den.

*I am afraid of being arrested*, she had told me. *I am afraid of being shot.*

I could still hear her voice. So clear. So sure. *It was me.* Paquerette, my Joan of Arc. You didn't sound afraid at all. Did that help them to believe you were a resistance fighter? A hero?

A hero.

*Oh God, what are they doing to her?*

Would she get sent to some camp herself? Paquerette sleeping in a barrack, getting thin and weak with sore, red eyes. Paquerette thin and powerless and desperate. Because of me.

Or would it be worse?

*If she dies, I'll—I'll—*

I crouched in the corner, shaking, contemplating what I would do if she died.

I didn't eat that day, except for what I forced down to get Mama, and then Grandpa, to go away. They gave me bitter herbal teas. To calm me, maybe. Make me sleep. I didn't sleep. Rosa came to see me. She sat on my bed and told me God would bring Paquerette back. I cried, and she hugged me. I didn't tell her why I was crying. Finally she went away. Grandpa came, and sat by my bed, quiet. He fed me broth that Mama brought. I think I slept for a little. Waking was terrible.

There was a Good Friday service that night. They didn't ask me to go. I couldn't have. I paced my room, seeing the cool stone darkness of the church, the cross at the front. Then the Catholic version, with Jesus carved on it, twisting in agony. *Oh God, keep her safe, oh God.* I thought: they don't know. They don't know what it's like, when a hero gives their life for you because you did something incredibly stupid and wrong. When it really happens, I mean when it happens right in front of you—they don't know how it feels. It feels *horrible.*

I prayed the same things, over and over, into the empty air. *Oh God, keep her safe. Oh God, bring her back. Please. Please. God, punish me instead. Punish me. Please.*

I've never really heard of that kind of prayer getting answered.

Deep in the night, turning and turning beneath the weight of it, I started to bite my arm. Just a flap of skin on my wrist, just hard enough, deep enough, to hurt. The pain felt good. When the thoughts came back I just had to bite a little harder. I could feel the marks I'd made, feeling with my fingers in the dark. I managed not to draw blood, that night.

Eventually I slept.

On Saturday Lucy came. She knocked and let herself right in, flicked the light on while I was lying on the floor behind my bed biting my wrist. I jumped up. "I didn't say you could come in!"

"Don't be ridiculous," Lucy snapped. "Look at you, what's wrong with you? Your mother says you haven't come out of here in—" She grabbed my wrist and pulled my sleeve back. There was a blue-black bruise now. Lucy gave me the most incredulous look, like I'd turned into a stranger in front of her eyes. I snatched my arm away.

"What do you *think* is wrong with me? *I got Paquerette arrested!*"

We stood staring at each other for a moment.

"You what?"

I swallowed. *Now look what you did.* Lucy looked afraid. "I . . ."

I whispered. I cleared my throat. My heart was thumping. "Paquerette was arrested for pulling a fire alarm when there wasn't any fire. To break up an arrest. But really it was me."

Her eyebrows went up all the way into her hair. "You did?" she whispered. "Did it work?"

I shook my head.

Lucy chewed on her thumbnail. "Why didn't they get you?" she asked finally.

"Paquerette told them she did it."

She looked at my wrist again. I pulled the sleeve up over it.

"We gotta get her back," she said.

"We can't, Lucy. There's nothing the CIMADE can do, even. Pastor Alex said . . ."

Lucy chewed on her lip. "Your mother would kill me . . . but . . . just wondering, y'know? If you . . . went and told them the truth . . ."

I drew in a sharp breath. In my mind Paquerette shouted *Magali, NO!* But . . . but . . . to convince them I was just a stupid kid who did a stupid thing . . . *since that's the truth* . . . tell them Paquerette was just protecting me, and . . .

And make sure not to bring up the kids.

The dream evaporated. I gave her a painful smile. "I can't, Lucy. Just think. There's too many . . . secrets."

She nodded, her eyes clouding. "You're right. I'm sorry. I guess I just . . ."

"Don't be sorry," I whispered. I went to the window and opened the shutters. Weak sunlight came in. Dark clouds massed in the east. "Thanks for trying," I said. "Really."

It RAINED all day on Easter Sunday. Hard, pouring rain, and thunder. Papa said I had to go to church. I said I couldn't. He said I had to. I was too tired to make a scene.

I don't remember much. I guess people greeted me. Pastor Alex prayed for Paquerette from the pulpit. We sang songs about graves and tombs and the stone being rolled away, and I started crying right there in front of everyone. Somehow I managed to stop before the end. It's all right to cry during music in church.

And then Pastor Alex started preaching.

He started in on the disciples, huddled in a house after Jesus' death, their hopes gone, afraid they'd be arrested too. Only three days before, they had walked in triumph into the city with Jesus. Had they wondered that night, mused Pastor Alex, what he meant by *This is my body, broken for you?*

A sharp shudder went through me.

Pastor Alex opened the Bible. "The Lord Jesus, on the night when he was betrayed—"

It was like being shot in the gut.

I know it's different. But it didn't *seem* different. Not to me.

I was Judas.

I sat very still for a moment. Then I did a thing I'd never done before, or even thought of doing. I stood up and walked quietly down the side aisle of the church and went out the back door. I didn't ask permission. I didn't sneak out. I just left.

I walked home in the rain, slowly.

MAMA HAD made chicken for Easter dinner, but I gagged when I tried to eat. They let me go up to my room.

The rain beat down all afternoon. I sat and watched it. Imagined a life, stretching far out in front of me, in which she never came back. The sky darkened slowly. My mind darkened slowly. Finally I fell asleep.

I slept really deeply. I was so drained.

When I woke my mind was strangely quiet. Almost clear. I had the sense of some dream I couldn't quite remember, lingering. A good dream. I couldn't imagine how I could have had a good dream. There had been something in it about sleeping.

Finding a little space under a tree by a stone wall, where no one could see me, and curling up and sleeping there. It had felt so good.

I sat up in bed with my back against the wall, and closed my eyes.

I don't know how long I stayed like that. It felt strangely good, there in the half-light that came through the shutters, my eyes almost closed, my body finally rested, and the terrible truth sitting quiet in my mind. Not thrashing anymore, not screaming. As if I'd been fleeing for my life, running through tall brush that cut my arms and face, and now I'd lain down exhausted. *Okay. Kill me.*

The truth was the police had Paquerette. Because of me. And I couldn't help her. This was reality. I had made something terrible happen to the best person I knew. It had happened because I'd tried to save somebody.

Because I'd thought I could save somebody.

I'd thought it would work. The rest had never occurred to me. I hadn't thought of pursuit, or Trina, or handcuffs, at all. I remembered Paquerette praising fear, saying it made her think. *I am afraid of being arrested,* said her voice in my mind. And then the same voice said: *It was me.*

*You knew. You knew exactly. What I didn't know.*

I fingered the bruise on my wrist. It was like when I hadn't wanted to face Rosa, but we lived in the same town.

The truth lived in the same town as me too.

*I am a girl from a conquered country. That's not an insult. It's a fact.*

*That's what she was trying to tell me. She tried so hard.*

*And I failed.*

I'd been more afraid of the truth than I'd been of evil. Afraid of being the weak woman, the victim. Only two kinds of people in the world. So afraid I couldn't even look into Paquerette's eyes and see Joan of Arc herself telling me what a soldier has to know:

*Ignorance isn't strength. Denial isn't courage. Know your weakness, take it into account.* So afraid she was talking about being a woman that I couldn't see she was talking about being a human being. From a conquered country. In my mind I saw the young man doubled up on the floor in pain. *This is our life. They have guns and we don't. We all have to accept certain limitations.*

Like not trying to rescue a guy from the police.

I put my hands up to my face and started shaking. It was a terrible, terrible thing to think. *I shouldn't have tried to save him. I should have stood and watched like everyone else.*

But it was true.

I sat there with the heels of my hands against my eyes and I thought: *You can't save everyone. I can't save everyone. Even Paquerette. She had to choose. She's always had to choose.*

*Is that the knowledge that is poison?*

*Is this what it took, to make me know what I didn't want to know? Is this what it took?*

After a while I stopped shaking. You have to stop sometime. I couldn't change this by crying, or biting myself. I couldn't change it at all. I opened my eyes and I looked at the little sunbeams that came through the cracks in my shutters. They were beautiful. Light was beautiful. I wondered if God could ever forgive me.

And even if he did, could I ever go on?

*I don't deserve it, God. But please. Please.*

*Please save Paquerette.*

After a while I realized I was hungry. Very hungry. I got up, got dressed. I opened my shutters, and then I went downstairs.

WHEN I opened the door I found two people sitting at the kitchen table over cups of tea, their heads bent together, silent; frozen, looking at me.

My mother and Nina.

I turned and walked back out.

I heard their voices behind me as I ran up the stairs. I got to my room and closed the door. After a minute, down the hall, I heard the clicking of crutches.

I'd asked God to punish me. Was this it?

I said she could come in. She didn't. She stood leaning on her crutches in the doorway, her wavy hair hanging down around her shoulders, looking at me. After a moment she spoke. "Magali, I am sorry that I made a threat to you. That day, when you saw my work."

I just looked at her.

"I was afraid. Also I did not know you. I had seen you only here—I had not seen, you know. Your work. Jakob and Sarah told me."

I opened my mouth, slowly. "Told you what?" I said, trying not to let my voice crack.

"How you helped them to get home. You divided them for safety. You did very well."

I was dizzy. I was standing on the edge of a deep pit, clinging blindly to some handhold in the dark. She didn't know. Jakob hadn't told her, he hadn't realized— That meant—

My heart leapt and for a moment I was tallying the people who knew—the pastor, my parents, Lucy—wondering if I could keep this secret. Keep this secret *too*. The taste of bile rose in my throat. "No," I rasped. "I didn't."

"Magali, you must accept. Paquerette did right, to save the baby. It was not your fault you were suspected."

"No," I said, forcing the word out. "No. It *was*, Nina. Sarah and Jakob didn't see."

It was awful, the truth dawning in her eyes.

I shut my eyes. "I pulled that fire alarm," I whispered.

When I opened my eyes her face was like stone. Motionless, all expression gone. Looking at me.

"I was trying to save him," I said, and tears ran down my face.

"The man they were arresting, *I thought I could save him!*" My voice was a cracked scream.

She stood still a moment longer. Then she shut the door behind her, went to my desk, and sat down. The slanted morning sun lay on the desk and the chair, on her shoulder and her motionless face. Looking at me. I tried to hide the trembling of my hands. I couldn't bear the silence.

"You were right," I whispered, and the tears started to flow again. "I'm too young for this, I'm stupid."

Nina said nothing. She turned and looked out the window, didn't move. Then she frowned, suddenly, and turned to me. "Why do you tell me this?"

I shook my head.

"You do not like me. No. Do not pretend. We both know."

"I heard you," I said, my voice coming out strange. "That time you told Paquerette I was immature. I came into l'Espoir and I heard you up the stairs."

"And you think now that this is true?"

I nodded.

"And so this is why you do not like me," she said slowly, watching her finger trace a pattern on her crutch handle. "This I can understand. Why you tell me today the truth, that I cannot understand."

Neither could I. Nor why she hadn't blasted me yet, like I'd deserved ever since the day I'd smiled at a gorgeous Nazi in Montélimar station. "I'm tired of lying," I blurted.

She turned to the window, and her face changed again. She blinked a couple of times, fast. She took a breath, and then she turned sharply to face me. "Listen," she said. "I will tell you something."

I listened.

"When I left my country I followed a plan my father made. He made me promise before he died, to dress as a boy and to do all he said. But the plan failed. We came to the border with Italy, and we found that the man who was to help us was arrested. We are alone, Gustav is afraid. I must decide. I decide to lie to Gustav. I say there is a second plan, I know what to do. We will cross alone. Then"—she took a breath—"a man offers to help us cross." She looked down, away from me, at her finger tracing patterns on her crutch. Her voice was low. "This man looked like my father. I thought that we would have help, that it would be all right. We went with him into the woods, alone. He carried me. Then when we were alone and far away from everyone, he tried to make it that I would be alone with him. I understood then that I had made a very bad mistake. Because I understood . . ." She swallowed. "I understood while he carried me that he did not believe I was a boy. He knew I was a girl. You see?"

She looked at me. Her eyes didn't waver from mine for a good three or four seconds. I thought I saw. I was afraid of what I saw.

"We ran from him. We escaped. He could not find us, in the dark, when we stopped moving and sat quiet. But—"

"You were all right? You made it?" My heart had leapt up like a bird. I'd thought for a minute I was listening to a very different kind of story.

"Yes. We made it. What do you think, Magali? Was I all right?"

I looked at her, and didn't speak.

"We left my bag with him. It had all our money. We walked into Italy with nothing, knowing that there were such people in the world."

I looked into her bitter green eyes, and saw, for a moment, that walk. *Ignorance isn't strength. But knowing you're powerless, that is terrible.*

Nina took a deep breath, and let it out slowly. She looked out the bright window again. "So. You see."

"Is that why you told Paquerette you used to be like me?"

"I said that?" After a moment she nodded. "Yes. I suppose that is why."

We sat a few seconds in silence. "What will you do now?" she said finally.

"I don't know."

She nodded.

"So," I said after a moment. "Do you still take your threat back?"

"Yes," she said. "You will not tell now."

WE WENT downstairs together, and Mama gave us food. Bread and tea. We sat at the table in the late morning sun, eating, not saying much. There was a strange peace. Exhaustion, and the bitter taste of knowledge, and a gladness that didn't sweeten it, and that didn't go away.

It was better than nothing.

Nina was beginning to get up when we heard the footsteps in the stairwell, someone taking the stone steps two at a time. I stood up so fast I almost knocked my chair over. My heart was racing wildly as Rosa burst in.

"Marek's missing," she gasped. "They need you, Magali."

HE'D BEEN gone since before breakfast. Hours. They'd found his coat still hanging up, or they wouldn't have thought anything. He wasn't anywhere in the house. The river was really high, and they were worried. "And they thought you might know where he'd go, Magali—can you come?"

"Of course I can come." I was already pulling on my coat. It was muddy and raw out there, the wet, naked time between winter and spring. It had rained all day yesterday. Nina was asking Rosa who else was searching. Saying she'd go for Gustav, that he was out at the Gaillards' farm west of town. I tied my bootlaces and stood up. Rosa was still catching her breath. "Magali . . . do you think he'd . . . do something, you know, stupid?"

"Yes," I said, and started down the stone steps two at a time.

In the hallway below, I heard men's voices. I slowed. At the end of the dark hallway my father stood holding the door open, talking. I heard my name and froze.

"Best not to tell her. She's in a state . . ." His voice faltered. "Alex, she's so young."

"Courage, Martin. I still believe God will deliver. Remember, it's only the police. I would rather Vichy do its worst to me than hand me over to the Germans."

My heart pounded, I felt the blood beat in my ears. I heard my father's voice, very low, saying "We have no guarantees." And then, "I can only imagine what they'll think when she refuses to talk."

I couldn't move. The door was closing. I heard Rosa's feet on the stairs above me. My father came toward me down the dark hallway, stopped, and peered.

"*Magali?*"

I forced my voice out of my throat. "Marek's missing. They want me to help search."

"I could . . ." His voice wavered again. "Magali, are you . . ."

"I have to hurry," I said in a voice that didn't even seem to belong to me. "Bye, Papa."

"Magali—"

But I was gone down the hall. I heard Rosa's voice as the door slammed shut, but I didn't care what they said to each other. I ran.

*Chapter 18*

# To Take His Prey

THE SKY was bright, and the wind was high, and there were mud puddles everywhere. I ran down through town, feeling my broken boots crack further under the strain. *Best not to tell her— rather Vichy do its worst—when she refuses to talk—* I stopped for a moment, and turned. I'd go back—make him tell me—

*No, Magali. Marek. Do what you have to do!*

I ran.

When I came to the bridge at the edge of town I stopped to catch my breath. What I saw didn't help me calm down any. The river ran so high and fast that brown-and-white water beat against the bridge less than three meters below where people were walking.

*The river—they're worried—*

I started running again.

I had a painful stitch in my side when I walked in to les Chênes. Claudine gave me a *bise* and asked me about the places where Marek went. The stream, of course, and behind the shed. Papa Thiély had checked the stream. Claudine wanted me to check it again, just in case he got the wrong place. Sure, I told her, my heart sinking. They'd called me here for that? They were that desperate?

256

*This isn't good.*

The stream was swollen. Muddy water swirled over the roots of the pines. There were no tracks. I called "MAREK! MAREK!" The rushing of the water half drowned my voice.

*All right. Upstream? Or downstream?*

Downstream.

I started walking.

The footing was bad. I slipped and felt the mud getting into my cracked boots, caking between the leather and the canvas lining and wetting my socks. I walked like someone in a bad dream: *I would rather Vichy do its worst . . . We have no guarantees . . .*

*Shut up and do what you have to do.*

*No. Do what you can do.*

I called Marek's name. I called it till it sounded stupid, two meaningless syllables. I reached the river, turned, and followed it downstream. *When she refuses to talk. When she refuses to talk.* I started to run again, clumsily, in my mud-caked boots. I called.

*They're interrogating her.*

The wind blew cold against my face, and on my right the river raged, mud-brown water piling up into high white billows over rocks and fallen logs. *They're interrogating her.* I reached up a hand and slapped my own face, hard. *Magali, focus. Marek could be in danger.*

The river was so high now, it would be over my head. And flowing with such force you'd get swept out of sight before you could scream, get your head cracked open against a rock somewhere . . .

I walked, and called Marek's name.

I came around a bend and found the place where God had spoken to me. Months ago. Bare oaks, and tall grass flattened by the snow, colorless. And Marek was lost, and Paquerette was—

A big log lay lengthwise in the river, water surging around it, snagged on to the bank by just one dead root, shaking in the current. Any moment it would be swept down the river with awful force. I shuddered. *If he's in there, Magali, he's dead.*

"MAREK!" I screamed. I slipped in the mud and fell on my knees. I wasn't going to find him, and Paquerette wouldn't come back, and I was alone on the cold earth. God might have spoken to me once, but the dead grass and the naked trees were as empty of him as Rivesaltes. I didn't deserve anything from him. *They're interrogating her. Oh God, please—*

I got up. I kept on going.

It was around the next bend that I heard it. Like a faraway scream.

I started to run.

Again and again I slipped and fell. Slick, heavy mud caked on my boots, my hands. My heart was pounding and my breath was short. I heard it again. Definitely a scream now. Not fear, but a human voice stretched to its loudest above the roaring river. I ran faster.

The third time, I heard the word *help*. The voice was clearer now. It wasn't Marek.

It kind of sounded like Nina.

There's a bridge where the west road crosses the river, an ancient stone bridge. Lower than the one on the edge of town, but built really solid: there's two-and-a-half meters of stone from the parapet down to the round arch the water flows under. The road bends sharply before and after, so you don't see it till you're almost on it, a stone bridge standing alone among the trees.

I came round the bend and there was Nina, standing on that bridge and screaming.

Directly beneath her, a tangle of trash was jammed against the opening of the stone arch—a small tree trunk, fouled branches and dead leaves and torn cloth. And clinging to it, white-faced, up to his armpits in the raging water, was a boy in a red sweater.

Marek.

It was one of those moments that are gone in a flash and that you remember forever—Marek below, pale face and red sweater, fighting the river; Nina above, standing on stone, her huge eyes taking in who'd answered her call. The disappointment in them. To be honest.

I didn't blame her for a second. You can't mess around when there's a kid about to drown. She'd been hoping for someone stronger. But what she'd got was me.

I stood looking at the bridge, the branches, Marek. *We need a rope.* We didn't have a rope.

Marek had one arm through the mess of branches and round the tree trunk—if you could even call it that, no thicker than my leg—and the other hand gripping a branch. He was tilted back as if his legs were being swept from under him, his body shaking with the violence of the current. My belly was tight with fear. *Think.* We couldn't pull him up from above. No rope. And we probably weren't strong enough anyway, and if we dropped him— I scrambled down the bank, grabbing at roots.

"We have to try from the side," I called. "Here."

The water swirled around my feet. Marek turned his pale face to me, his dark eyes staring. He was still two or three meters away, even from this angle. I wanted a rope *so much*.

"No," said Nina, scrambling down the bank, not taking her eyes off him. "No, you must run to find help. If we do it wrong—"

I looked at her. We were a long way from any farm. Fear bloomed up in my mind, slow and terrible. I was seeing that log, shaking in the current, barely clinging to the bank. "Nina, there's a log upstream going to get swept down here any minute. A big one. Barely hanging on." I was shaking now. *Oh please.*

I saw her throat move, swallowing. She looked at the river. Foaming brown water slamming against the bridge pilings with the force of a charging bull, as deadly as anything either of us had ever faced.

"My crutches," she said slowly. She turned sharply to me. "We will use my crutch like a rope. I will go in, you will stay here and hold the crutch for me."

One arm holding the crutch—the other reaching out for Marek—no. "You'll need both arms." I took off my belt and looped it through the top of her crutch. It was metal, bolted, solid. It would hold. "Put that around your waist."

She nodded. She took the belt from me. My heart stopped. I grabbed her hand. "No. I'll go in. I'll go."

She pulled her hand out of mine and fastened the buckle. "I could not hold you. You are stronger, you are heavier. Think." She tightened the belt a notch.

"Nina, are you sure you want to do this?"

"Yes." She looked at the river, then at me, her eyes gauging the distance.

I looked around. I needed something to anchor to or I might as well push Nina in the river and then jump in myself and get it over with. The stones of the ancient bridge were too smooth and well-fitted. I tried one of the tree roots. My hands were slick with mud. I crouched to wash them off. I could feel Marek's terrified eyes on me, *hurry!* But to hurry now, that would be like pulling the fire alarm. It looks like the right thing. *If* you're stupid enough to think you can't fail.

I used to be that stupid. But I wasn't, now.

I wedged the second crutch solidly behind two roots. I pulled on it as hard as I could and it held. I heard cloth ripping and then Nina knelt by me, lashing the crutch securely to the roots with strips from her skirt, making triple knots.

I washed my hands. She tied back her long hair. She beckoned to me and tied my hand and wrist to the crutch I'd braced. Then she tied my other hand to the lifeline crutch that she wore. She adjusted the belt. We looked at each other. At the water. I took a breath. "Ready?"

Nina nodded. I gripped the crutches hard, and got my footing on the steep bank facing the stones of the bridge—one foot up on a root, one down in the water. Nina waded in.

There was a jerk, and my right shoulder and the left side of my face were slammed up against the stones, my cheek scraping painfully—and Nina was pressed against the bridge by that awful current, grabbing for the roots of the tree Marek clung to and hanging on like grim death. Without those roots I couldn't have held her; she'd have been swept straight through. It was terrifying. I tried to brace against the stones with my head and left shoulder, to give her a little more force against the current, but it was far too strong for me. Like so many things I'd met that year. Dread rose in me like dark water.

*I should have waited I should have tried from the top I'm stupid I'm stupid they're both going to die because of . . .*

Something in me slammed the whining voice down. Flat.

She was pulling her way to him. Her right hand was within reach of him. He clung to his log, huge-eyed. *Oh no.* Neither of them could let go to grasp each other. They'd be swept away—

She was pulling herself up by a root, up out of the water. I couldn't believe she could do it. *She uses those arms to* walk, *stupid.* She had a knee up on the log, one hand buried in a handful of Marek's sodden sweater. Dragging him upward. He wouldn't let go. He looked like he was screaming. Oh God, please— Then she had him, he'd grabbed a higher branch and was pulling with her, he was only waist deep now, yes!—her good leg was over the log and my left cheekbone burned with pain, scraping against the stones, and my chest was being pulled apart.

And Marek was straddling the log.

I gasped with the pain and held on like death, and I felt the pull slacken as they inched nearer along the log. *Yes.* They were among the roots now. I braced. In a moment they'd be in the current again.

And I'd have to pull them in.

I'll never forget that moment, as long as I live. Like hearing Zvi begin to gasp; like Paquerette's voice saying, *It was me.* Those terrible, terrible moments. Cold sweat broke out all over my body. My stomach literally felt like I was plunging through the air. I was just barely strong enough to hold them. *But not to pull them in.*

A hard jerk on both my arms; my bloody cheek scraped across the stone and I screamed. They were in the current again. The pull slackened as they jammed against the tangle of roots. I pulled with all the strength I had. They did not move.

I tried desperately to bring my legs into play, against the bank, against the stones; I slipped and almost fell. Nina was shouting something. I pulled and pulled, uselessly. Tears were streaming down my face.

Then the change. The pull grew harder. I almost couldn't hold on. Marek seemed to be nearer now. Yes, he was hanging on to one of the bars of the crutch. Yes, he was *climbing the crutch like a ladder toward me.* Joy and terror rushed through my body. *Oh God, help him keep his grip!*

And then the second change. It's a miracle I didn't die of shock right there—or worse, lose my grip. *Someone was behind me.* I felt a body behind mine, a warm hand beside mine grasping the bracing crutch, another on the lifeline crutch, pulling strong and smooth. As if it were easy.

Pulling them in.

In another moment Marek was in the shallow water, gaining his footing, scrambling out; strong hands plucked him up and out of my sight. Nina was on her knees beside me, gasping, fumbling at her belt buckle. I couldn't untie myself, the knots were hard, the cloth had cut itself into my wrists, and then there were a man's hands, and a knife, cutting me free. Then he was gone with Nina, and I was scrambling up the bank, breathing hard, barely able to believe. There was grass at the top, and level ground. I fell on it face-first. I lay like a baby on its mother's chest, safe, unable to imagine any better place to be. It was a long time before my heart-beat slowed, and my breathing.

*I'm alive. I'm alive. They're alive.*

Finally I pushed myself up to see who this man was, who had perhaps saved our lives, who could pull so easily against that terrible current.

It was Erich Müller.

I LAY on the grass, trying to breathe. Telling my body everything was all right. So he's a German soldier. He just pulled Marek out of a river. There's no reason to be afraid.

But the earth did not feel like my mother anymore. I was wet, and the grass stuck to my bloody cheek, and I was shivering. I sat up and forced my spinning head to take in what I saw.

Nina knelt on the grass, half turned away, shivering. Paler than I'd ever seen her. Her legs were bare to the knee where she'd ripped the hem off her skirt. She kept her face turned away from Müller. She surely knew who he was.

Marek lay on the ground, his eyes closed, his face white, wrapped in the long coat Müller had been wearing. His clothes lay in a sodden pile on the grass, and Müller knelt beside him chafing his hands. Müller must have stripped him to get him dry, figuring he'd get warm faster with just the coat.

Just the coat.

For a long moment everything slowed down. *All* Marek's clothes were on the grass. I remembered the young police officer, the one who'd said his men might have *checked*.

Müller wouldn't have . . . *noticed*. Would he?

They had Marek's release papers, up at les Chênes. Being Jewish wasn't *completely* illegal. Yet.

"You girls," Müller said. Nina didn't look at him. "You should not have tried to do this. You could all have been killed."

My stomach turned over. For a moment there was the brassy shriek of a fire alarm in my mind, and the hot taste of shame in my mouth.

"We must go," he said. "We must get you all warm. Where is the nearest house?"

I shook my head. I couldn't remember. "I only know it's that way to the children's home. The one where—" I gestured to Marek. "Where he lives." My stomach turned over inside me again.

I'd almost said, "Where Marek lives."

Müller turned to Nina. "Can you walk?"

Nina nodded, quickly, not looking at him. She didn't speak. She *couldn't* speak, I realized—it was too risky. Her Austrian accent. Her long, dark, curly, *Jewish* hair. *No, no, he just pulled us out of the river. He's not hunting anyone. He's not—*

*I have to get us out of here. No matter* what *he's not doing.*

I stood up. "Your crutches." One lay in the grass. I scrambled down the bank for the other. It was still lashed to the tree roots with hard knots. "Monsieur? May I borrow your knife?"

He came down the bank with the knife in his hand and crouched to cut the first knot. He glanced behind him at the river, then bent to his work again, and spoke without looking at me.

"That children's home, are there many Jewish children there?"

His voice was perfectly casual. Ice slipped down my spine.

For a second I couldn't speak. *He knows.* The answer rose from somewhere deep inside. My voice was unfamiliar, like a miracle—light and even, as casual as Müller's. "Just him, Monsieur," I said.

Müller nodded.

He finished cutting. I took the crutch and brought it up to Nina. She kept her eyes on the ground as she took it. Müller gathered up Marek in both arms, and I rolled Marek's wet clothes into a bundle, and we started down the road toward les Chênes. I think we had gone about three steps when it happened.

A huge splintering CRACK sounded behind us. My muscles seized with terror; I spun half-round and fell to one knee on the ground. I caught a split-second glimpse of Müller's wide eyes, his hand groping on his hip for a gun that wasn't there.

It was the log.

The log I'd seen shaking in the current upstream—the reason Nina and I had gone in. It had rammed the bridge. The smaller log was shattered, its inner wood showing pale as bone on the fragments that danced and tangled with broken branches in the current. A long shudder went through my body. *Oh, Marek.*

It was only then that I saw there was someone on the bridge.

Someone in a limp, mud-flecked dress and an old brown coat, a wide-brimmed hat shading her face, staring down at the river and its tangle of destruction. Something about her made my heart stop. She lifted her head and looked at us. I almost cried out.

It was Paquerette.

MY BREATH caught in a gasp. A gasping sob. I was still on one knee. Another breath, and another, I couldn't stop them. I tried, oh I tried. I heard a voice—Müller—telling me it was all right, he was safe. He. *Marek.* I swallowed my sobs, hard. He is safe. She is not. *Keep her safe.*

"I saw—that log," I gasped out. "Before."

"You expected this?" The respect in his eyes brought me back to myself. "Then you did right."

I nodded. Took a deep breath. I had almost stopped shaking. *Paquerette . . . Paquerette . . .*

She stood on the bridge, looking at us. At me and Nina, soaking wet. At a German soldier with Marek in his arms. She didn't move.

Mademoiselle Combe, in French class, told us a Greek myth once. A man goes down to the land of the dead to bargain for the soul of his dead sweetheart and bring her back. He charms the lord of the dead with his music, and he gets her, but there's one rule: she'll walk behind him all the way back to the living world, but he can't look back or she'll vanish.

He can't do it. He looks back, and she's gone.

Slowly and deliberately I turned my back on Paquerette. It was a signal. *I'm all right. Don't come near.*

We started our long walk away from the place of death.

She was like a fire behind me. A thing you can feel without seeing. *Don't turn around.* My heart ached in my chest with joy and terror. What had they done to her? *Paquerette, stay back there. Don't come near.* If only we could get Marek to les Chênes, safe. Safe in a bed, and then Müller would go away. This strange man who put us all in danger by wanting to keep us safe. *Oh Paquerette . . .*

I walked. Forever. The wind stealing warmth from my wet body, my arm aching from carrying the dripping bundle of Marek's clothes. My mind in agony from the things I couldn't say. *Nina. Be careful. He knows Marek's Jewish. Paquerette, stay back, whatever you do stay back. He knows Marek's Jewish and he tried to trap me in a lie.*

I swung the bundle of Marek's clothes close to Nina. *Look, look at it. Read between the lines.* When I glanced at her, I couldn't tell what she saw. *Don't tell Müller his name's Jean-Marc. Whatever you do, don't tell him that. Because then if he decides to check his papers— if he decides to check—*

I heard Paquerette's footsteps on the road behind us. Keeping us in sight. I could feel my fear for her all through my body. My fear that she'd try to protect us.

That it would happen all over again.

When les Chênes came in sight around the bend of the road, Marek stirred in Müller's arms, and opened his eyes. "Ah," said Müller. "You are awake. What is your name, little man?"

And Marek looked at Müller with big, dark eyes and whispered, "Jean-Marc."

As WE walked up to the door my knees were as weak as the day I'd first walked into Rivesaltes. If Müller asked for Marek's papers, he would know. He'd know, if he had any brains at all, the silent answer to his question: *Are there many Jews there?*

Was that what he was after? Look at how he was carrying Marek. He wasn't going to throw the kid into the fire. Not when he'd just pulled him out of the water. He was a decent man. A decent man who knew his duty. Who might figure it was his duty to check up on—illegal activities.

And if he found them? Then it would be his duty to call in other decent men who knew their duty, which was to follow the orders of men who weren't decent at all.

The door opened, and there stood Julie, her eyes wide for a moment, then her fingers going straight to Marek's neck to find his pulse. Sheer joy broke out on her face. "Thank you, Monsieur, oh thank you! He's alive!"

Under cover of this I risked a glance back at the road. Paquerette had disappeared.

"He needs warmth," said Müller. "He has been too long in the river. I do not know, he may need a doctor. And these young ladies here, they were also in the river, trying to rescue him—they will need some care also, I think."

"Oh, come in, please come in—oh, girls, you're so wet—oh, Magali, you're bleeding!—here, Claudine! Claudine! Can you get some dry clothes for them? Some of ours I think—and the first aid kit!—here, Nicole, please come in."

"Come with me, Nicole," I said. "I'll show you where the bathroom is." I beckoned Nina, and she followed me in her torn skirt, into the living room and down the long hall. She was so pale. When we were in the bathroom I locked the door and turned to her and spoke fast and low.

"Nina, he knows Marek's Jewish. He undressed him and, and he knows. He asked me if there are many Jewish kids here, he was trying to catch me lying about it. I said only him. I'm afraid he's going to ask for papers. If they show him the Jean-Marc papers . . ."

You don't have to say something like that twice to Nina. She was chalk-white now. For a moment her lips moved. Then she said suddenly, "Magali, I feel very sick."

"Sick?"

"Yes. I am having strong pains." She laid a hand on her side. "I need someone to take me to the doctor. I do not think that I can walk."

The light was dawning. Brilliantly.

"Nina," I breathed, "you are amazing." I hesitated. *Think. Don't be foolish.* But it made sense. So much sense. *No, no, I should do it, I should be the one.* But that voice, that was the foolish one. I would be worthless at faking sick, compared to Nina. "Are you sure, Nina? You . . ."

She nodded. "Magali . . ." She touched her side again, suddenly, and winced. "It is true."

I stared at her.

"I was too afraid to ask him. And all the other men are gone."

"Magali? Nicole?" I opened the door, and Claudine handed in two dresses, and long underwear. "You girls are still in your wet things, what are you waiting for—"

"Claudine," I said urgently and low, "he knows Marek's Jewish. He undressed him. And Marek gave his name as Jean-Marc. Don't let them show him any papers, Claudine, for the love of God!"

Claudine had snapped into focus. "I won't. You girls get dressed." She shoved the dresses at me and was gone.

I changed faster than I ever had before. Then I helped Nina. She was shaking now, uncontrollably. I started to be afraid there was something seriously wrong. I wrapped a towel around her wet hair. "You stay here," I said. "I'll go get him."

I ran down the hall into the living room. For a moment I hesitated, and the scene engraved itself on my eyes: Julie kneeling by Marek near the fire. Erich Müller, kneeling too, saying in a low, kindly voice to Julie, "I hope that you will understand,

Mademoiselle, and not be offended—" My heart stuck in my throat with the fear—the fear that I would call out to them, now at the crucial moment, and he would know why.

A cry from the bathroom jolted me to life. Saved me.

"Monsieur Müller!" I shouted, and there was nothing fake about my voice. "It's Nicole—she's having pains and shaking, she looks bad, I think she needs a doctor, Monsieur—I'm very sorry—"

He was on his feet already. "There?" he asked, pointing. I nodded and he was off down the hallway. The bathroom door stood open; Nina sat slumped on the side of the bathtub, the towel fallen off her head, barely holding herself up.

I'll say this for Erich Müller: he was strong. And he *was* decent. He gathered Nina up without a word, took her in his arms almost as easily as he'd taken Marek. He carried her down the hallway. I asked him if he knew how to find the doctor.

He threw a brief smile back at me. "I have been a convalescent in your village twice, Mademoiselle. I know." As we came into the living room he said to Julie, "Mademoiselle, there is no automobile here? Or motorcycle?"

Julie shook her head. "No, I'm sorry, Monsieur. I would ask Monsieur Thiély to do it but he's not back—"

He waved that away. He set Nina gently on the couch. "Mademoiselle Nicole, can you understand me? I will need to take you on my back, to walk so far as the town. Do you think that you can hang on?"

Nina nodded. She looked terrible. Claudine got a coat around her and put a wool hat over her wet hair. She helped her up to a sitting position as Müller crouched to offer her his back. She clung to his shoulders and he stood, carefully, his hands linked in front of him, his arms under her knees. Julie opened the door for them.

I'll never forget the sight of them there on the threshold. Him tensed and ready, glancing back for a moment. Her pale face against the back of his jacket, her wide eyes looking at me, tears welling in them. I remembered who was the last man who'd carried her on his back. I stood looking at her, the crippled girl who'd gone into a raging river to save Marek, and who now was facing her worst fear for him. I wanted to speak. To tell her "You are the second bravest person I have ever met."

Instead, I said what I could. I looked at those two: a strong and decent man ready to help, and a woman of quiet, bone-deep courage, and I felt something move in my gut, in the depths of me. I wondered why I had ever thought there was only one way of being strong. And then I spoke to the one I was allowed to speak to.

"Thank you," I said. "Thank you, Monsieur Müller, for saving our lives."

He looked me in the eye, and nodded. I swear something in his face relaxed. Like that's what he had been waiting for.

Then he went.

It wasn't until he was out of sight, past a bend in the road, that I turned back to the house. I heard Claudine's voice from inside, from the kitchen door. "He's gone, you can come in now—please, please come in. He's taking Nina to the doctor. It's all right. Oh, are you all right?"

By the time she was done speaking I was beside her.

There in the doorway, her hat off and her face unutterably weary, stood Paquerette.

## Chapter 19

# What God Never Promised

HER EYES were hollow. She stepped up into the doorway slowly, moving as if she was in pain. My throat tightened. I wanted to throw myself at her feet. I took a step back.

Claudine fussed over her, got her to a seat at the table, rummaged in the pantry for food. I stood paralyzed. I only realized I was crying when the sting of salt on my raw left cheek made me gasp.

I opened my mouth. "Paquerette," I whispered. "I'm so sorry."

Her eyes were wide, without defense. Almost afraid. She shut them for a moment. Opened them again. "Is everyone safe?"

"As safe as we could make them."

Her eyes were not satisfied.

I took a breath. "Marek ran away. Nina and I found him in the river. That soldier, he found us trying to pull him out, and helped, but he figured out Marek was Jewish—"

Her chair scraped loud against the floor. She had half-risen. "He *what?*"

"Paquerette, please sit down! You're not well, you must calm yourself!" Claudine put a plate of bread and cheese in front of Paquerette and glared at her. Paquerette ignored her.

"I couldn't stop him! He undressed him—to warm him—but that's all he knows, Paquerette. We made sure—he hasn't seen the false papers, everything any of us have told him will check out—"

"You are *absolutely* sure of this?" She looked at me, at Claudine. Claudine nodded. Paquerette relaxed.

"Only thing is if he comes back," said Claudine, looking at me. "Seeing as he said his name was Jean-Marc . . . after all that . . ."

"Jean-Marc," Paquerette murmured. She looked up sharply. "They've got to make him new papers. They've got to do it *now*."

"Yes. I'm going straight up to tell . . . tell them. I just wanted . . . I wanted—"

"You know who they are?"

"Yes," I said. "Paquerette . . ." My throat was getting tight and clumsy. "Are you . . . all right?"

Her face changed, moved strangely. She closed her eyes again. "I will be," she whispered. Her eyes opened. "Magali, I'm very tired. I've got to eat. And sleep. I'll be all right. After . . . a while. But you, you've got to go. You don't have time for this now."

I bent my head. To hear her command me again, that was almost better than forgiveness. My *Joan of Arc*. I stood to go.

"Magali," she said suddenly. "God bless you." I felt tears come into my eyes.

She held out a hand, and I took it. There was a white bandage circling the wrist.

"Go," she said.

I went. When I'd shut the door behind me I began to run. I could barely see the road.

I would have run all the way, but I literally couldn't. I had so little strength left.

I walked slowly into town, ignoring the stares at my bleeding face and my wild, muddy hair; when I got to the *place du centre* I skirted round its edge, making sure I couldn't be seen from the doctor's office. There was a CLOSED sign in the window of the bookstore. If Mademoiselle Pinatel wasn't there . . . I laid a hand on the door beside the bookstore, the one that led up to Mademoiselle Pinatel's apartment, and to Lucy's above it. I stood for a moment, breathing hard—and the door opened.

Lucy stood in the doorway, her eyes almost popping out as she took in the sight of me.

"Magali? What *happened?*"

"Lucy. I . . . Listen . . . Here, I . . . I think I need to talk to you inside."

"Of course, come in, I'll get—" The door closed behind us. I stood in her dark front hallway, swaying, a sound in my ears like the sea. "Magali, are you all *right?*"

"Lucy. If I said . . . someone needed new papers . . . you'd know who to tell. Right?"

"Yes," she said slowly. "I would."

"Would you know . . . two people?"

"Yes. Magali, what *happened?*"

"Please. I need . . . Please go to, uh, the closest one, and say that Marek Adam—Marek—Marek from les Chênes needs new papers, fast. By tomorrow if it can possibly be done. They should have his new name on them but say he's Jewish."

"Say he's *Jewish?*"

"*Yes!* Do I have to explain it all, or are you gonna believe me? I just saved that kid's life and now I'm trying to save this whole town and I *know what I'm doing!*"

She frowned at me. "If this *whole town* is in danger, yeah, I think you *do* have to explain it all."

I sank down on the stone steps. My legs were done. "Okay,"

I whispered, and put my head in my hands. I noticed they were shaking harder now.

"You are *not* all right. Hang on."

I sat there, my head spinning. She came back with her aunt. I let them half-carry me up the steps. Mademoiselle Fitzgerald put me on a couch, laid a blanket over me, swabbed my cheek with something that stung, and put a bandage on it. Their table was set for supper, the bowls steaming. Lucy brought me some.

I don't even know what kind of soup it was. It made my belly warm. I stopped shaking. I lay there, feeling my head float through nothingness, through rushing, rushing water. After a minute I realized I was on Mademoiselle Fitzgerald's couch and she had no idea why I was there.

After another minute I was able to sit up and tell her.

Then it was finally over. Lucy left on the mission she'd always wanted. And me, I could rest.

I rolled over and wrapped the blanket around myself. What I remember after that is sweet, sweet sleep.

But you have to wake sometime. That's the worst of it. You always have to wake. And go on. And what's been done can't be undone, not ever.

When I woke it was dark. Dark and strange, till I remembered why I was there—still on that couch, in a room full of shadows and silence, alone. I'd never even gone home. Paquerette was back. And I'd never even told anybody.

I started to cry.

And I mean *cry*. Big, wrenching, gasping sobs, tearing through me one after the other with barely space for a breath in between. I didn't know why I was crying like that. It scared me stiff.

I couldn't stop. It was like someone had taken over my body. It hurt. My chest, my heart, was like a piece of cloth being ripped down the middle. I knelt on the couch, doubled over, gasping for breath. Praying Lucy and her aunt wouldn't wake, and come, and ask me . . .

*What's wrong, Magali?*

*I don't know. I don't know . . .*

It seemed like an hour. It can't have been. There was no time, nothing, just me in the dark, shaking and shaking. Until the gasping breaths finally slowed. I lay back on the couch, breathing slowly, spent. I pulled the blanket up over myself and shut my eyes.

I lay there, trying to stop wondering what on earth had just happened. Trying not to think.

After a long time I got up and put on my shoes, and slipped quietly out the door. The air was still and cold outside. I started through the dark streets for home.

It's not supposed to feel like that, the day after you save a life.

But sometimes it does. That's all. Things don't feel like they're supposed to feel. Things don't go like they're supposed to go.

I used to want so badly to do something. Do something real.

It was three days before Paquerette talked to me.

The papers got there in time. Lucy told me so herself. Mademoiselle Pinatel worked on them half the night, and Nina finished them in the morning.

"Nina's all right?"

"She didn't look too good if you ask me, but Dr. Reynaud says so. He says all she needs is rest and food."

"He didn't think anything was wrong with her? Lucy, you should've *seen* her—"

"Well, he said it might be stress."

I had to laugh.

Müller did go to les Chênes again though. I found that out when I went down in the evening. Paquerette was still there, somewhere upstairs, resting. Papa Thiély was up there with her, Claudine said.

"You should have seen his face when he got home, Magali. He and Monsieur Thibaud and his boys searched every meter of both riverbanks, you know, all the way down to la Combe. Only thing they can figure is Marek must have fallen in after they passed that bridge. He probably wasn't in the water for more than a half-hour, and a good thing too."

I glanced at the stairs, and swallowed. "Is she . . . I mean . . ."

A faint embarrassment crept over Claudine's face; the look of someone who's been given an unpleasant message for you, and is hoping you won't ask. She might as well have stuck a knife in me.

I didn't ask.

I asked what had happened to her. If Claudine knew. Claudine shook her head. "She's got a real bad shoulder, it hurts her to move it at all. And her wrists of course. I guess they handcuffed her." Her face hardened for a moment. "Those pigs. Unbelievable. Thought this was supposed to be a civilized country." She shook her head. "Magali, you did good yesterday."

"I did?"

"Sure! Tipping us all off like that? Getting the papers sent down? That *boche* showed back up at three o'clock today. Wanted to see Ma—Jean-Marc, how he was doing. Then he got all apologetic and asked for his papers. So I'd say you made a pretty good call."

I felt my face shift and tremble. "Thanks," I whispered. I swallowed, and got my voice under control. "Was he . . . satisfied?"

"He asked some questions. Was it our usual policy to accept Jewish kids, stuff like that. We said we're a charity home, we accept anybody. He asked if we understood our duty to our nation. That was pretty rich." Claudine chuckled. Then she grimaced. "He said some stuff about how it's unhealthy to mix races, and Jews need to be separate for their own good. Seems to think that's what the camps are for. Seemed to think he might convince us Marek would be better off there."

"No!"

"Yeah. So Papa Thiély explains nicely that French citizens don't get sent to those places. Yeah. That was the worst bit. You know what he said? 'For now.'"

"Oh."

"Yeah." Her face was bleak. Then she drew in a breath. "But he went. He said it was out of his hands and he encouraged us to think about it." Her mouth twisted. "Well, he's leaving next week, anyway. His leg's all healed. I mean, obviously."

"He saved him," I said. "He saved him and then he wanted him sent to . . ."

"Maybe he doesn't know."

"What the camps are like?"

"Yeah."

"Maybe," I said.

I was afraid to go down to l'Espoir, or to les Chênes, in case she was there. In case she was there and hoping I wouldn't come. *It hurts if she moves it at all—and of course, her wrists . . .*

*Unbelievable. Thought this was supposed to be a civilized country.*

*Paquerette, what have they done to you?*

*I. What have I done to you.*

Rosa came to see me. She'd seen her, at l'Espoir. She'd heard everything from Nina, and said we were both so brave. I couldn't look at her. She fussed over my bandaged cheek like Mama had, worried I'd have a scar. I hoped I would. I asked what had happened to Paquerette, and her face fell. She didn't know much. They'd interrogated her and her shoulder was real bad. I asked if she had asked for me.

Rosa's eyes widened. "No! I barely saw her, Magali. Madame Sabatier told me this stuff."

"Oh. Yeah." I swallowed. I had no right to be jealous. If Rosa had been with her that day . . . *if only.* I looked down, and shut my eyes.

"Magali. She . . . she loves you. I know she does."

I didn't look up. I couldn't imagine anything worse, just at that moment, than for her to see I was crying.

She hugged me. I turned my face away, and let her. It didn't matter what I'd done for Marek. It would never matter. I wanted to die.

NINA CAME to see me too. That was good. Strange and good. We sat on my bed together, like friends, and I didn't want to die. We talked over the details of that long, long day. I told her about the awful moment I'd realized I couldn't pull them in. She said she'd told Marek to pull himself in by the crutch. Screamed it. So afraid he wouldn't hear.

We shuddered, remembering. We fell silent. The silence of soldiers who have fought together, who know. I felt a stab of pain, knowing I would never have that with Paquerette again. And yet this was here now, and it was good.

I never knew what they meant before, by "bittersweet." I thought it was a stupid word.

"Hey Nina? I thought . . . you were really brave."

"We both—"

"No. I mean with Müller."

"Oh." She shrugged a little. "But I was wrong to be afraid, I think. He wanted only to help. He paid the doctor himself."

"He did?"

She nodded.

*And then the next day he came down and asked . . .* "I guess you just never know."

She gave me a strange, twisted smile. "You never know. Yes, that is very helpful."

I laughed. I couldn't help it. She laughed. On an impulse I threw my arm around her shoulder, and we leaned our heads together, and we laughed some more.

THEN THURSDAY night, Papa met with Paquerette and the pastor. She told them everything. They needed to know, I guess. I wasn't invited.

Then Papa came home and told me about it.

He didn't want to, but she'd asked him. She didn't want to tell it more than once.

This is what they did to her.

The day she was arrested was mostly waiting. Handcuffed to a ring in a holding cell, then locked in a windowless cell of her own. Nothing to eat. Just waiting, and hearing screams. Mostly the young man I'd tried to save. In the evening a short wiry man came to get her, said he was the night guard. He took her down the hall to a little kitchen, gave her soup and bread, and put ointment on her wrists where the cuffs had chafed. He gave her a bitter tea that made her sleep heavily through the night.

The next morning he gave her another bitter tea that cleared her head. No breakfast. He tied strips of soft cloth around her wrists and then tied them behind her with cord. He said he was trying to make things easier on her. He told her not to be so worried, just to tell the truth.

Then he took her to a big, bare room where two men sat behind a desk, and gave her a chair. They asked her questions. She told them parts of the truth, the safe parts. When they wanted names and addresses for the homes she was taking the kids to, she said no. They yelled at her and badgered her for a while, then took her chair and made her stand with her hands tied behind her back while they asked the same questions over and over. Midmorning they had coffee and pastries, and she had a half glass of water. By the end of the morning she was feeling really faint. They broke for lunch and a younger policeman was sent in to watch her. She lay down across three chairs with her hands still tied, and went to sleep. When she woke up, the young policeman had come in with a cup of soup and a piece of bread that he hand-fed her, quickly, glancing over his shoulder.

"I'm sorry," he whispered. "It's all I can do."

The two men came back. They went on asking her questions till she fainted on the floor. They woke her up and a woman guard took her back to the kitchen and grabbed her suddenly by the hair and forced her head into the sink under cold running water. She let her up and then left her there, coughing and shivering, for a while. Then the two interrogators came in and forced her head under the water again, face up. She couldn't stop coughing when they let her up. They bent her head back and poured something fiery down her throat from a flask. They took her back to the interrogation room and let her sit down on a chair. Two new men were behind the desk this time.

They were nice to her. They asked questions about her work; they made admiring comments. She was drowsy and confused. She barely caught herself before mentioning Tanieux. *That* woke her up. "I'm sorry," she told them. "I can't answer your questions. Maybe I should stand up now."

They told her she should cooperate, or things were going to change. She didn't say anything. They took away her chair.

She fainted twice more that afternoon. The second time they just let her lie. When she woke the room smelled of food—they were eating supper. They forced some more drink on her. They told her they wanted to go home, but they had a responsibility to their country. They told her they were going to get serious now.

They got a freestanding coat rack from the corner of the room. They took off her shoes. They cuffed her ankles tightly to the coat rack's base, so tight that she only stayed upright because one of them had his hands pushing against her shoulders, his face right up in her face.

"Convince me to tell my assistant to unlock your feet now," he said. "You have one chance."

Paquerette took a deep breath, and told him she was only trying to protect children who were being put into camps and had done nothing wrong. He asked her why she protected the young man. She said she'd thought he looked innocent. He let go, and she fell forward, and caught herself on the floor.

He came back with a broad leather belt. The assistant propped her up again. He took the belt and put it around her shoulders, and pulled the strap tighter, and tighter, till her shoulders curved backward around the pole. He did it slowly, pausing at every notch. Each time the pain was more intense. It never stopped. He asked if she was ready to talk. She shook her head. He pulled the belt a notch tighter. She screamed.

They left her like that for a long time. Strapped so tight around that pole she couldn't think for the agony.

So that's what was wrong with her shoulders when she came home.

They let her down once. Told her she'd better talk. Put her up again. She fainted.

The next thing she knew she was lying in her cell again, with her hands still tied behind her back.

So that's what happened. That's what they did. There's only one word for it really. Torture.

I got Paquerette tortured.

MY FATHER fell silent, looking fixedly at a spot on his desk.

"And then?" I whispered, afraid.

He lifted his eyes. "That's the end of the bad part. I think she might want to tell you the rest herself."

"Herself?"

"She wants to see you. She'll be here till Monday."

"And then . . ."

"She's going home."

*Home.* It was like the world slowed down around me. I was still shaking. A weight like a stone was in my stomach. "Is she quitting?" I whispered.

My father looked at me as if he wondered what on earth went through my head. "Of course she is," he said.

I didn't say anything. I couldn't.

"Now don't go bothering her tomorrow morning before eight o'clock, all right?"

"I won't," I said. I barely heard him. My stomach was already balling itself into a steel-hard knot.

I didn't go to sleep until three in the morning.

I woke before dawn. Wide awake. I dressed silently, got my coat, and slipped outside.

Everything was quiet. It was cold, the streets were muddy. I walked down to the edge of town, to the Tanne. It was lower now, still deep, but the water was clear in the faint starlight. I shivered. There's a little chapel there by the river, that Grandpa says is as old as this town: four hundred years. I pushed the door open and went in.

It was pitch dark inside. I groped and hit a stone bench. But I couldn't sit down. After a moment I lay down full-length on the stone floor. It was cold and hard against my face and body. I pressed my forehead into it as hard as I could. I wanted to scream. I wanted to die. I wanted to be someone else, someone who'd never held such power in her hands as I'd held in mine. I wanted to scream that they hadn't told me, they hadn't told me I could try to do so much good and do so much harm; but they had. I knew they had.

I put my hands behind me, wrists crossed as if they were tied. I lay with my face against the stone floor, the mass of cold rock seeping warmth from my body. It didn't hurt enough. I pressed my cheek against the stone till the raw scrape under the bandage pulsed with pain. I told God he could do what he wanted to me,

I didn't care. He didn't need to forgive me. I didn't deserve it. I wasn't even sure what good it would be if he did.

My arms started to ache. My teeth chattered from the cold, and I clenched my jaw. I felt numbness, and a strange drifting feeling.

Then I think I went to sleep.

When I woke, my arms were flat beside me on the floor, and there was light outside. Dawn light. I got up and went outside, and walked down the riverbank to get warm. The river was clear, throwing back the pale blue of the sky. Smooth now and pretty, hiding the depths underneath. But that river, I knew it now. Last fall it had spoken, joined in the voice of the whole world around, and said God didn't hate me. And this spring that same river had risen up and tried to kill.

*God never promised any of us would make it*, I thought. *I should've known that with Zvi.*

God never promised my mistakes would never hurt anyone I loved, either. God never promised any of that.

He hadn't promised Paquerette would come back. He hadn't even promised she would live.

But she was there, up that hill, probably in l'Espoir kitchen right now finishing breakfast. She was there up that hill, the person I admired most in the world, the person I owed a debt to that I could never repay. And not one of those nice debts. A debt in blood.

I stood looking out at the clear, lovely, treacherous river, watching the sunlight strengthen on it, watching the little ripples shine as if nothing was wrong. Life does that to you. It shines, like that, on a spring morning, it lets you *imagine* God's promised that stuff. Your parents do it to you too, sometimes, I think. Mama didn't want me to see the camps. Didn't want me to know that that existed, in the world.

I regret a lot of stuff. But I don't regret seeing those camps.

I stood there looking at the Tanne, and behind me I could feel a pull. Paquerette was there, up that hill. Alive. Healing.

Waiting for me.

I turned and started up the hill.

She was sitting in the Sabatiers' living room. My stomach was a tight hard ball. I was glad I hadn't eaten anything. She rose to greet me, gave me a *bise* with her hands holding my shoulders. I couldn't look at her. She offered me tea. I shook my head. I couldn't speak. A child's wail came from the nursery.

"Let's go upstairs," she said.

There's this way Rosa walks into a room if she's afraid she's not wanted there. It always drove me nuts. That's how I walked into Paquerette's room. I almost couldn't go in at all. She offered me a chair. I just stood there.

"Magali," she said. Just that, and she looked at me. I couldn't force my voice through my clogged throat. "Magali," she said again. "Are you all right?"

I shook my head. I swallowed hard, and then my head snapped up and the words came out. "I'm so sorry, Paquerette. I'm so, so sorry. I wish I'd never done it. I wish they'd arrested me instead."

"Do you really wish that?" Her voice was quiet and hard. I saw myself being handcuffed. I saw myself being strapped to a pole. I shuddered. I saw the still, longsuffering face of that quiet, quiet baby in my arms.

"Not with Trina," I whispered. "I know, I know I put her in danger and you were right to do it but you shouldn't have had to suffer for me. You shouldn't have had to get . . ." My eyes went down to her feet again. I forced the word through my throat in a whisper. "Tortured."

I felt her step close to me, put her hands on my shoulders. "Look at me," she said. I couldn't look at her eyes for more than a moment. Like the sun. "Magali," she said, "I forgive you."

I'd like to tell you I felt better then. I'd like to say I started crying tears of release. I didn't.

Paquerette was a good person. The best person I knew. Of course she forgave me. What I'd been afraid of was something else, something as inevitable as the sun.

It didn't change anything about what had happened. What I'd done.

"Magali, look at me." I couldn't. I couldn't bear it. "Magali, what's wrong?"

"It's over," I whispered. "Isn't it?"

Her grip on my shoulders grew stronger. I looked up. There were tears in her eyes.

"Yes," she said. "It is over."

I started crying too. Hopelessly. "I ruined everything," I whispered. "It's all my fault." A sob caught me in the chest and brought me up short. I couldn't treat her to the kind of craziness that had come over me at Lucy's house. It wouldn't be fair. I made myself breathe.

"Did your father tell you, then . . . ?"

"What?"

"That I'm wanted?"

Fear stabbed through me. "You are?"

"Oh, they don't want me very much." The briefest flash of an ironic smile. "But . . . officially . . ."

It was worse than I'd thought. "They didn't release you? Are you—in danger?"

"They're not looking for me. But I've been advised never to go back to Valence."

"What . . . are you going to do?"

"Do?" She let out a hard breath. "Magali, I'm not going to be able to do anything, for a while. I'm going home."

"Oh." I bent my head.

"I suppose I needed a rest," she said quietly. I could hear the undercurrent in her voice.

"I'm so sorry." My voice was raw. The tears started to flow again.

"Magali," she whispered. "Magali." She put an arm round my shoulder. Her having to comfort *me*, for what I had done to her. "Magali," she said again, "I forgive you."

I started to sob.

There was nothing, nothing that would ever make this all right. There were children waiting for her in Rivesaltes and she would never come. Babies losing weight like Zvi had. People might die for what I'd done.

And she held me, while I cried for that.

You can only cry for so long. Your body quits, after a while. This time was shorter than the time before. There wasn't any relief or anything. I just stopped.

Paquerette still had her arm around my shoulder. "Magali," she said softly. "Did your father tell you what happened to me in there?"

"He told me they . . . they . . ."

"I mean after that."

I shook my head.

And so she told me.

*Chapter 20*

# Hard Bread

THE DAY after the belts and the coat tree—Saturday—Paquerette woke when someone shook her by the shoulder. She screamed with the pain. A huge dark silhouette stood over her. She tried to crawl away from him with her hands still bound behind her. She fell, and started to cry with wild wrenching sobs. It was going to start all over again.

He turned on the light. It was the night guard. He'd brought breakfast.

It took her awhile to calm down. He soothed her. He swore under his breath when he saw she was still tied—the only thing he ever said against the other police. He cut her ropes and massaged her numb hands. He gave her hot, sweet tea and hot cereal, chatting pleasantly to her as if he were a nurse. He brought her a comb and a piece of mirror to fix her hair.

She cried, telling me that. She'd spent two days being treated like a piece of furniture to be pushed around, and he was treating her like a woman. Someone with feelings, who cared what she looked like. Who could decide for herself when she felt strong enough to stand.

He rubbed balm on her wrists and ankles. She asked questions. She'd kept two teams busy for an eight-hour shift each, he said. No, they wouldn't come to work on a Saturday. She had the day off. He couldn't believe she hadn't talked. She didn't seem like someone with secrets. But she must know her own business, he said.

The day off.

She slept. Someone brought her lunch, and then she slept some more. When she woke, she lay there just enjoying being free, able to move her body. Then she started to think about tomorrow.

She wasn't free. They would come again. And again. And again . . .

She was crying a little when the next policeman came in. He was very young. He stood there frozen and awkward, a tray in his hands. She wiped her eyes and took it from him. It was bread and hot milk. She asked if it was supper. No, he said, a snack. He stood and looked at the wall till she was done.

A *snack*? To a prisoner under interrogation? Were they building her up to break her down again? She thought of flies in spiders' webs, calves being fattened. She cried some more.

She was sitting with her head on her knees, thinking of nothing, when the voice came. It was dark by then, with only a line of light under her door.

The voice said: *Paquerette, what are you afraid of?*

It was a voice in her head, I guess. A voice like the one I heard that one time. Only in the dark.

She looked up. There was nothing. It asked again. What are you afraid of?

So she told it. Told God, I guess.

She was afraid of not being strong enough. Of putting me and the kids in danger.

She was afraid that was exactly what she would do. She would crack. Because they had her, and she was helpless. They could keep doing this forever if they chose.

The tears came to her eyes, telling me. I cried too.

After that she slept again. The night guard took her to the kitchen at supper time. He was worried about her; the other police-man had told him she'd been crying. He asked how much pain she was in. She shook her head.

"You've taken very good care of me. I feel much better."

"Then why do you cry?"

She looked at him. "In my position, would you be able to forget about tomorrow?"

"Tomorrow?" He sounded surprised. "Mademoiselle, tomorrow's Easter Sunday! They're not going to do anything they don't have to do on Easter Sunday!"

She had completely forgotten.

Back in her cell, she sat cross-legged against the wall, her head resting on it, thinking about that, in the darkness and the silence. Thinking of the darkness and the silence in that tomb, on Easter morning just before dawn. She closed her eyes. The feeling grew on her—somehow—that someone was in the cell with her. Physically.

She opened her eyes, and she saw. Like seeing something invis-ible, she said—seeing and not seeing. Like a thing in your mind's eye so vivid it takes its place among real things in the world.

A slab of stone in the dark corner. A body on it wrapped in cloth. Outlined in shadow, in the dim light from under the door.

She felt shy. Like she was trespassing. She had no right to be in his tomb, it was too personal, too private.

The silent voice spoke again. No, it said, you have a right. They shut you in here, you can't get out. You have a right.

She started to cry.

She thought of being strapped to that coatrack, how it felt. The pain, and the thing that was worse than pain: being helpless in the hands of people who don't care about you. Who aren't interested in your pain.

She cried, and she told him, *I know. I know.* The words echoed back to her in the tomb.

*I know.*

After a while she saw an odd change in the body. A subtle shifting of the cloth over the mouth. A slight, slow lift and fall.

She laughed, telling me this. Self-consciously. She wasn't that type of person, she said, seeing visions and all. Maybe she'd gone off her head from the stress. But it felt so strange. So real.

A light appeared over the body. Like a candle—then it grew. It lit up the cell. She threw an arm over her eyes as it grew blinding. Something was moving, there in the corner—someone—

The cell door opened. The image vanished in the pale glare from the naked bulb in the hall.

It was quite an anticlimax, she said.

A policeman stood in the doorway. The one who had broken the rules to feed her during the interrogation, with her hands still tied. "I'm sorry," he said. "I know it's late."

She almost laughed. "Come in," she said lightly. "Do sit down."

His mouth quirked in a sad smile. He took off his hat and sat down on the floor with her. He asked her if she knew what a stir she had caused in that police station.

She didn't know.

No one knew what to make of her, he said. No one believed, anymore, that she was a criminal or had any ties to the young man. "But they don't understand why you refused to talk about your work. They went pretty far with you—farther than they're used to going, to be honest, with a woman. They couldn't figure out who you were trying to protect. But I have an idea of my own. That girl—the one with the curly black hair . . . ?"

I gasped.

Paquerette looked at me and nodded, her face lined. "Yes," she said. "That's exactly what I did. I felt sick when I realized how easily he got me to give myself away. But he didn't tell."

If he'd intended to tell anything he knew, he said to Paquerette, he could have done it earlier and spared her some pain. He said he didn't know exactly what Paquerette and I did, but he knew it was good. He told Paquerette how he'd first met me. Me and Marek.

It was *him*. And he *had* seen me in the station.

He told her about the disputes the police were having over her. How the night guard thought she was innocent—intuition, he said—and he wasn't the only one. But—he sighed—the chief interrogator wanted one more try. On Monday. He'd come to ask her which she would prefer: that, or being a fugitive from the law.

She told him if he had to ask, he must never have been on the wrong side of a cell door. He said no, he hadn't.

He gave her a lock pick, and had her pick the lock herself while he waited in the hallway. For realism. It took her fifteen minutes. She gathered her things, stepped out of the cell and dropped the lock pick in the hall. The man said the night guard would swear to having given her breakfast at six. He recommended that she stay away from the police for a while, and not come back to Valence.

"Don't worry," she breathed.

He touched his hat to her. And then he was gone, away down the hall. She stood blinking for a moment. He meant her to find her own way out. She looked the way he hadn't gone.

There was a light breeze coming down the passageway.

She followed it. Found an empty office with an open window. She was on the ground floor; she climbed out, and walked through the dark streets, not bothering to feel afraid. She found the agency, and Madame Moulin working there late. Madame Moulin started crying at the sight of her. She knew, apparently. She was the one Pastor Alex had called to find out what was going on.

Madame Moulin gave her new clothes, and a wide hat to hide her face, and food and money and a rain cape and a coat. She woke a friend who had a motorcycle, and Paquerette walked with him through the dark streets to the edge of town; then he drove her across the Rhône and far into the hills west of the city. Where he left her, she walked a little while, until the stars grew pale; then she bedded down under a haystack, and slept.

She woke to rain. It was a wonderful day, she said, Easter Sunday; walking under her rain cape and drinking in God's free, wet air, smelling the earth and the trees, hearing church bells in the distance, watching rare patches of sunlight come and go on the hills ahead. Drinking from a stream by the roadside, finding a dry shack to rest in. Even the beating of the rain was beautiful, she said, that day.

She spent that night in a barn. The farmer came in at dawn to milk his cows. It was odd, she said, how little he reacted. He brought her in to his wife, who gave her breakfast. Fresh, creamy milk and oatcakes, the best meal she'd had in years. Neither of them asked any questions. Maybe it had happened before.

She kept walking. She knew she was near le Cheylard. She had enough money for the train. She got on, and let *la Galoche* take her up the steep gorge onto the plateau. She got off one stop before Tanieux, and doubled round to the south and then to the west, so she wouldn't come into town on the main road.

And when she came to the old bridge over the Tanne, there I was, and Nina, and a German soldier carrying Marek in his arms. And then I turned my back on her, and walked away.

"You were telling me not to come near, I could see that. It made me afraid for you."

My throat hurt, just thinking of her there on the bridge, so close, in fear. "I couldn't stand for you to be in danger again. I didn't want you to . . . to try . . ."

She took my hand and squeezed it. She said nothing. There were tears in her eyes too.

"Magali," she said after a moment. "What exactly did the soldier say to you?"

I told her. I told her what he'd done too, and then what we had done. I told her about the log, because I couldn't bear for her to think I'd been a fool again so soon. Her eyes watched mine, her face very serious. She made a noise deep in her throat. "You did save his life, then."

I looked down.

"You and Nina did well, Magali." She looked away from me, a troubled look. "Yes," she said more softly. "You did well."

"It doesn't matter, though," I said bitterly.

She turned a sharp glance on me. "It does matter, Magali. Everything true matters."

*But the bad matters more.*

"Magali, do you know what you did wrong, in the train station?"

I swallowed.

"I'm sorry to ask you this, but I think it's important that you understand what happened."

"I did something stupid. And I had a baby in my arms."

"You are choosing exactly the wrong word, Magali. You're not a *stupid* young woman. I think you know that."

I just looked at her.

"You are in fact very intelligent. Quick-thinking, calm in an emergency, resourceful, capable, decisive. Far, far more decisive than anyone ever should be at the age of sixteen. No, what you did wasn't stupid. It was clever. Who knows? It might have worked."

I stared.

"In the hands of an adult responsible only for herself, who had counted the cost and was willing to pay, it might have been heroic, Magali. But not in your hands. You got that right. You had something else in your hands."

I nodded. "Trina," I whispered.

"And that makes me suspect you also hadn't counted the cost."

I shook my head.

"You thought it would work?"

"Yes," I whispered hoarsely. "I never thought about . . ." I couldn't finish.

She nodded. "Listen, I think I need to tell you, because I think you don't understand. What you did was prideful."

No. I *didn't* understand.

"It was pride that made you think it would work, Magali. Made you act without thinking, as if you had no doubts. Those things I said about you, you know those things about yourself. You've been proud of those abilities. Ever since I've known you you've wanted to be a hero. I tried to tell you over and over that this is not a hero's business, that getting the children safely to Tanieux is the *only* priority. I thought you understood."

"I'm sorry, Paquerette," I whispered. I could feel the tears coming on again.

"Magali." Her voice was gentler now. "I've forgiven you. I'm not saying this to hurt you. I'm saying this to help you learn. Because— look at me." She turned my face gently upward. "I still respect you, Magali, and I believe that you *can* learn."

I started to cry for real.

"I saw the worst and the best of you in that train station. The worst, you know. But do you know why I could step forward and take the rap for you the way I did? Do you know why, with five kids in my charge, I was able to do that?"

I could hardly see her through my tears.

"Because I knew you'd get them home. I didn't have any doubts at all."

WHAT CAN I say? I went home. I cried some more. She'd forgiven me. She'd been wonderful. She was a saint.

Nothing could change what I'd done.

I went down to les Chênes to see Marek. He was in bed with bronchitis, but okay. He was sitting up in bed with a book, his hair all messy, his face scratched up by branches he'd hit in the river.

He brightened when he saw me. I remembered his hard, untrusting eyes when I'd met him in the camp. I remembered him writhing in the grip of two policemen. I remembered so many things.

He opened his mouth and coughed—long, rough coughs. He lay back for a moment, then whispered, "I told him my name was Jean-Marc. Like you said."

I swallowed. "Yeah. That was right."

There was silence for a moment.

"Ma'm'selle Magali?"

"Mm-hm?"

"Will I always live here?"

"I . . ." I looked at him, his bright black eyes. "I don't know, Marek." He had nowhere to go, his parents were dead. Who knew if even his aunt would live? I shivered. "I don't know." His eyes were getting larger, darker. I wanted to throw my arms around him. Instead I gripped a fold of his blanket, hard, and searched for words. *Don't ever lie to him, Magali.* "We want you to be safe," I said, looking at him. "We're going to try to keep you safe, wherever you live. We're going to do everything we can."

He looked back at me. "Okay," he said.

I HELPED the Squirrels wash sheets and make beds. I went home. I went with my parents to church the next morning. I sat not hearing the sermon, thinking about Rivesaltes—the dust, and the *tramontane* blowing, and the kids waiting, waiting for someone who would never come.

Mama asked me at lunch why I wasn't eating. I started eating.

After a while I asked her if I could walk out to the farm that afternoon. She said yes.

The new green was coming out in the pastures. I could see it from the hilltop, just the first hint of it, nudging itself between last year's brown grass. Half of Grandpa's land was plowed, the furrows dark and fresh. I could see the horses were in the barn, the ones he hires from Jean-Luc, and the plow stood clean and ready for tomorrow. Today he'd be resting.

He seemed to know what I'd come for. He put the kettle on, and we sat at his scarred kitchen table, and he didn't say anything. After a while I started to talk.

I told him everything. Almost.

I told him the things I'd thought and felt, back before everything happened. About women, and strength, and people like Nina. I told him what I'd overheard Nina say, how angry I'd been. I told him she was right—that I'd thought I was in control.

Then I gathered my courage and told him about the gorgeous Nazi. He listened soberly, and told me my fear of him was a wise instinct, and I should listen to such instincts. I couldn't believe he was so calm about it. He said he supposed I had never tried such a strategy since.

I said no.

I told him about Rosa going on a trip instead of me, how angry I'd been. How angry *she'd* been. I told him about hearing God by the river, although it didn't go into words very well. He nodded, though.

I didn't tell him about Nina, of course. Except that I was wrong about her.

The whole time I talked, it was like this: like untangling a snarl of twine, like the moment it starts to work. You've found the thread, you're not yanking knots tighter anymore, just following the tangle and easing it out, slow and smooth. None of it was confusing anymore. Now that I wasn't trying to twist it into some shape I liked. I was ashamed. But there was something clean about it, too. Looking the truth in the face.

And then I did it. I told him why Paquerette got arrested.

He listened very intently. His weathered face looked sadder and sadder as I spoke.

I came to the end of the string, and it hung in the air, tied to nothing. The unshakable, intolerable fact of what I'd done. I stopped talking, and sat looking at him. Hoping.

He sat silent too.

"Grandpa?" I said finally, my voice tight in my throat. "What do I do?"

"Do?" he said.

"I . . . I can't change it, I know. But I can't live with myself either. I know it's forgiven. But . . . but they talk like that makes it like it never happened, and it doesn't. It doesn't at all."

"You want it to have never happened?"

I looked at him.

"Child," he said, and the way he said it, it didn't sound like an insult. He said it almost in a groan. Like he felt sorrier for me than anyone he'd ever known. "It's so hard," he said. "It's so hard to be a human being. And to learn it now. At your age."

His eyes were dark with pain, looking into mine.

"Magali," he said, "I'm sorry. I don't have anything to say that will comfort you." He glanced away. "I feel like you came for supper and all I have to give you is hard bread."

I thought of Rivesaltes. "People eat hard bread," I said. "It's still bread."

Grandpa nodded, and sighed.

"There's only one thing you can do, Magali. And that's go on. No one turns back time. Not even God. You're not alone. You're only young. But I tell you true, when you get to my age, there's no one, not a one, who doesn't have one thing they'd cut off their hand not to have done. You lie awake at night and think about it. But it's done. The past doesn't change. You can pray that God makes good out of it. I believe he can. But even that . . . even that you may never know."

It was like a hollow space slowly opening up inside me. A space like a piece of ground covered, enclosed, that would never feel the rain again; bitter and dry.

"But it's true that God forgives us. Even if we can't undo. We go on, and God still loves us." He looked at me. "Paquerette still loves you, yes?"

I nodded. She did, and I knew it.

It hurt me, to be loved like that.

"We've got to live with what we are, Magali. The bad as well as the good. I'm sorry. That's all I can give you."

He gave me tea. We sat in silence a long time.

Then I walked home.

I WENT to Paquerette that night. Somehow I understood that I could. I went, and let her love me as I am. Sitting by the fire with Rosa, talking about the children's health. I went again the next night, after working at les Chênes. I told her I would miss her. She looked at me with her gray eyes—sorrow and regret and that awful, painful, generous love—and said she'd miss me too. I asked if I could walk her to the train the next day. She said yes.

We all walked her there together. Mama and Rosa and Sonia and Madeleine Sabatier, and Nina and me. She hugged every one of us. Most of us were crying. Before she hugged me she pulled a rolled-up paper out of her bag, and slipped it into my hand.

I stood with the others on the pavement while her train pulled out. That long high whistle pierced right through my heart.

I was almost afraid to unroll the paper. But when I got to my room I did.

It was a pen-and-ink drawing, the finest of hers I'd seen. It was me, with a child held close to my chest, glancing over my shoulder. I looked determined and alert. But happy. I looked happy. There was something about the way I was drawn, somehow, that said danger couldn't have him, I was watching. It said fierceness and it said love. The kid was Léon, and he was laughing.

I laid the picture down carefully on my desk. Then I lay down on my bed and cried a long time.

YOU DO go on. That's the thing. You think the sun's going to stop rising in the morning, just for you, but it never does. It comes up, it goes down, it comes up again. There's another day, and then another. You've got to do something with them. I worked at the children's home.

I cooked. I did laundry. I cleaned toilets. I helped kids with their homework. I even sang with them, when I could stand it without crying. I stayed with Marek when he needed it. Yelled at him when he needed it too. I walked the kids home from school, helped with their shopping chores. I tried to be gone before the train came. Hearing the whistle hurt too much.

Some evenings I helped Rosa and Sonia with the babies, at l'Espoir. Roza was learning to crawl. Trina was gaining weight. She moved more now. She even cried.

I did what I had to do. What I could. It was work, all of it, and worth doing, and needed. I lived with myself. I lay awake at night and thought of Paquerette, in her mountain valley—where?—and in my mind I saw her lying awake too, her mind too full. Of the knowledge that is poison. Of the people she couldn't save.

On the good nights, I was too tired to lie awake for long.

I was glad I'd be going back to school next year. With homework as well, I would always be tired enough to sleep. That was what I wanted.

That, and to help the kids. Always that. To see Chanah's grinning face as she rushed toward me, or Stepan's serious expression as he wiped the table as if the earth depended on it; Manola's laugh, Tonio's cocky grin, Marek's rare, bright smile. It was for them. If they were the only ones I could help now, then so help me God I would help them. My kids.

Them and Trina. They always let me feed her on the nights I could come to l'Espoir. Feed her, and put her to bed, and sing to her. Mama's lullaby. *Star, little star. The ewe has her lamb, the hen has her chick, everyone has her child.*

APRIL PASSED into May. The grass grew green in the pastures beside the road to les Chênes, and the river ran clear and shining in the sun. I looked at it as I crossed the bridge and tried to forget, sometimes, what I knew about it; but sometimes I tried to remember. Because it was true what Paquerette said: everything true matters. So you don't forget. Sometimes I want to. But really, I don't know why I act like I have a choice.

April passed into May. I went on. Nina came every week for supper. We went up to my room and talked. Lucy and Rosa came—sometimes even together. One day I told Rosa the truth, finally, about Paquerette's arrest. She cried, and hugged me. She never mentioned it again after that day. Nor did Lucy. My friends are some of the kindest people. Each in their own way.

But with Nina I actually talked about it. Sometimes.

I told her how I felt, seeing the train come in and no children on it. A Swiss Aid worker had come once, with three kids. But no one brought anyone from Rivesaltes. Were they going elsewhere? Or just waiting? Did the CIMADE have anyone to take Paquerette's place?

Nina listened. Then she said, "There are many able women, in Tanieux."

"But they already have so much to do! Like Madeleine, she could do it, but she has all those babies. Why's it like that, Nina? The people who can do it should. I know I was stupid, before . . . or . . . or prideful, about doing it, but I wasn't wrong about that. Not everyone can do it, so those who can, should. Like you—what you're doing—giving you a different job would be a waste!"

Nina looked at me so long and so intensely that I was afraid I'd offended her. That I shouldn't have even referred to what she did. But what she said, finally, was, "And the work you should be doing, it is lost to you."

Tears pricked behind my eyeballs. "We're not talking about me," I said angrily. "I can *never* do it again. You *know* that."

"No, Magali. In fact I do not know that. It was your work. I saw that. As my work is mine. You did it well and you would do it better now. When the terrible thing happens, that is when a person stops being foolish. For certain there is someone at the CIMADE who understands that."

"Nina. They never met me. They look at me, all they see is the girl who got their best worker arrested. And tortured, and sent home."

"But she knows you. If they ask her, she will tell the truth. Always she told the truth."

The tears pricked behind my eyes again. "Yes," I whispered. "She did." I looked up at her. "But Nina—what are you saying? Are you saying I should . . . ?"

I don't know what it's like for other people, the moment when you see what you want to do with your life for real. But for me it was almost fearful. *The CIMADE.* My heart started pounding. I swallowed, dry-mouthed. *Never. Never, never.* I had ruined my own chances before they started. "You don't really think . . ."

She looked me in the eye, and her eyes burned a little. "You must understand, Magali. I do not say this to make you happy, or because you are my friend. Do you understand how it is for me? They are arresting my people. I do not know what is coming, but it is very bad. I do not want for us to lose anyone who is ready and able to help. So. I have in fact spoken to Madeleine. And I am speaking to you. I do not want you to say *never.* It must not be so. Because—" She looked down, and spoke fast. "Because I am afraid that we will need you, that we will need everyone. Soon."

My throat was tight. "But are you sure you want . . . *me?*"
She nodded.

My heart felt full of something. I wasn't sure what. Hope. Fear. Terror. A desperate, desperate wish for another chance.

*If you'll let me, God. If you'll just let me have one chance. I won't play hero. I'll think only of them and what they need. I'll do what I have to do. I'll do what I can. Oh please. Please.*

Nina was looking intently at me. I think something must have shown on my face.

"So?" she said quietly.

"But, Nina . . ." I closed my eyes for a moment, seeing Paquerette's face. The fire alarm cord. The faces of children: Marek. Carmela. Stepan. Trina. Léon. Zvi. The living room of l'Espoir with the fire burning; voices upstairs; the scrape of a chair across the floor. I opened my eyes and looked straight at her. "I thought," I said slowly, "that you said this was work only for adults."

"Yes," said Nina. "It is."


I SAT up late, that night, at my desk, chewing on the end of my pen. Finally I put it to the paper.

*Dear Mlle. Barot,* I wrote.

*Epilogue*

# Everything True

THEY JUST got back day before yesterday from their first trip together. Madeleine and Rosa. Mama and I replaced Madeleine at l'Espoir.

It was a hard trip, apparently. Five days. We spent them changing diapers, feeding children, taking turns making meals. I slept in Madeleine's bed, and woke in the night to feed babies when they cried. I hung rows of diapers on the line. It's June now. The *genêts* are coming into yellow bloom. We took the babies to the river, and Trina splashed in the water and laughed. There's life now in her brown eyes. Mama loves her.

When we heard *la Galoche*'s whistle in the distance my mother smiled at me, that smile only a mother can do. And said, "Go."

I still don't think I want to be exactly like her. But more than I used to, I guess.

Nina was there at the station, leaning on her crutches, right in front of Monsieur Bernard. She gave me a wry smile when she saw me. When the children came she crouched down and spoke to them in German, right there. Six children with dry Rivesaltes skin, red running eyes full of fear and hope. Six more.

I took the child Rosa carried, a six-year-old with a splinted ankle. Rosa looked so weary. I told her to go home and rest. I asked the child her name. "Claire," she whispered. It was the name on the papers Madeleine handed to me, papers someone like Nina had made. I told Claire she was doing very well, and soon we would be home.

We gathered the others around us, and began to walk.

THE NEWS came through a few days ago that they're making all the Jews in the occupied zone wear yellow stars. So they can find them more easily, I guess. I wonder what I'd do, if I still lived in Paris. What Benjamin would do.

I can't help but wonder, given what Pastor Alex heard about the camps in the north—I can't help but wonder whether one day people will start disappearing from Rivesaltes on eastbound trains. Bound for what? I hope Benjamin's wrong. I really hope so.

But Nina is right. I know that. Things will get worse, and we will need everyone who can help.

Rosa says there aren't as many kids now at Rivesaltes. That it's noticeably quieter. She says Marylise's waiting list is very short now. Still. If I hadn't gotten Paquerette arrested there might be no waiting list at all. I pray for them, in bed at night. I don't know if we can do it. I have no idea how long we have.

Mama and Papa want me to stay in Tanieux for now, they say, even though they were glad to see the letter I got from the CIMADE. It was Grandpa who explained it to me in a way that made sense. He said if Paquerette needed months to recover from being tortured, so did I. I opened my mouth to tell him I hadn't been tortured and there was no comparison, realized there were tears streaming down my face, and shut up.

So I wait.

There's some talk, though. On the quiet. Papa Thiély took me

aside the other day and started telling me about Switzerland. They
have an arrangement. You send them a list of people, and if they
approve it, then if those people make it across the border somehow
they won't send them back. He says that for some of the kids it
may be the only way to be safe. He says it may be doable—we do
have some people who know mountains. He asked me questions
about my experience traveling with kids. What did I think was the
best way to keep them quiet, things like that. That wasn't hard. If
they're old enough to know what's going on, they'll be quiet; if not,
use food. I asked him which kids he had in mind. Whether Marek
was one of them. He nodded.

I agree with him. Marek should go.

But I'll sure miss him.

AND I miss Paquerette. Those are the worst times, when I can't
sleep and I lie in bed wondering how she is. Where she is. How
badly I really did hurt her.

Papa Thiély's going to go visit her in a couple of weeks. Claudine
told me. I'm going to ask him to take her a letter. I'm almost afraid
of writing it. There's so much you can't say, in a letter. And so
much you can.

When I finally got a letter back from Mademoiselle Barot saying I could still work with the CIMADE, there was a letter from
Paquerette in it. The letter she'd written about me. I don't know
if Mademoiselle Barot put it in the envelope on purpose. I don't
know, maybe she did; I pretty much put my heart and blood into
the letter I wrote her. I wanted her to know that I knew what I'd
done. But it was in there, anyway, and it's under my mattress now:

> *Dear Madeleine,*
> *Thank you for your letter of the twelfth. It's good*
> *to know that you all are thinking of me. I pray for*
> *you all regularly, and for the work.*

*To answer your question truthfully, I am not
entirely well. I think you were wise to advise me to
come home. I think it may be some time before I am
recovered. But I am in good hands.*

*As to your question about Magali, I've
considered it carefully. In truth, it would be foolish
for anyone to suppose that a person's character is
fixed at the age of sixteen or seventeen. I do not
think I would consider working with an adult who
had taken such actions as Magali's. But I saw the
effect her actions had on her, and I believe it to have
been permanent. Only three days later, she took
initiative in a prudent and courageous way that, by
all accounts, saved a child's life. She is as competent
and experienced in the work as a person her age can
be. If and when her parents feel she is ready to do
such work again—and certainly when she reaches
her majority—I feel that I can recommend her to the
CIMADE. Should the occasion arise, I personally
would work with her again.*

*Please accept my best regards,*
*Paquerette*

I STILL cry every time I read it. It's Paquerette all over. *I am not
entirely well.*

Oh, Paquerette.

Maybe I'll see her again someday. Maybe the occasion will arise.
I lie in bed in the dark and remember her, try to call up all the
things she said to me during the last days she was here. I remember
her gray and tired; I remember her with fire in her eyes; I remember
her laughing. But so seldom. I hope she laughs, sometimes, at home
in her valley. I hope she doesn't lie awake, like me, and remember
things she never wanted to know. Things that are poison.

*Everything true matters,* she told me. *Everything true.*
I've read and read that letter. I think I know it by heart. The good things and the bad.
I'll keep that letter until the day I die.

I WENT out to the river yesterday, to that place where the oak trees are. I found the spot where I lay down in the dry grass last fall. So long ago. Before the winter came.
The grass is green there now, and ankle deep. I lay down in it again. I was so tired it only took a minute before I went to sleep.
When I woke I had a strange feeling. The wind was blowing in the grass, in my hair, in the young red oak leaves overhead. I had a strange feeling like I didn't exist. No, not quite. Have you ever forgotten you exist? That's what it was like.
It was a lot like being free.
I held up a hand like there was something above me I could touch, and I wanted to. Like I could touch the wind. Like I could touch God. It seemed like someone was there. I think I'd been hoping he would be.
It was like everything inside me moving, rearranging itself. All at the same time.
I used to think there were only two kinds of people in the world. Can you imagine? I used to think I had that figured out. Who can figure out life? Zvi died. Marek lived. Léon made it to Brazil. Do you know why? I don't. Who can figure out life?
I got one of the bravest people in the world arrested and tortured. I saved a kid's life. Am I a good person or a bad person? Answer me that.
Everything true matters.
I felt an ache in my chest, because I couldn't touch, and I wanted to. But—I don't know how to say it. It was there even so. I had felt it before, and I knew what it felt like. It was true.

I didn't have to be a good person. I didn't have to be a hero. My fingers closed on nothing at all.

But I wasn't alone.

I took communion yesterday morning for the first time since I was confirmed. I ate the bread and drank the wine. If Papa asked me what it meant I'm not sure I could answer him really. I'm not good at stuff you can't see. What I know is, I wanted to. They say, "This is my body, broken for you." And that makes sense to me, that's real. That's what someone like that does, steps in between you and the evil. With their body. Someone like Paquerette. If God's someone like Paquerette, I want to eat that bread. That's all I know, really.

I do know one more thing. And that's this: I see people giving their bodies for each other every day now. Grandpa does it in his fields, Mama does it in her kitchen. We do it for the kids, over and over. Madeleine changing a stinking diaper, Rosa feeding Trina, coaxing her to eat. Nina in her little room where no one sees. Me and Claudine, sitting in the les Chênes living room, listening to the kids shouting over each other about whatever happened today, listening.

Rosa and Madeleine, walking one more time through the gates of Rivesaltes.

I used to think saving someone's life was something you did one time, and then you'd done it. It was over. You could chalk one up for yourself. But a fat lot of good it did saving Marek if he gets arrested next month. Next year. And there are no guarantees. I can't promise him safety any more than my own mother can protect me. I'm not God. It's starting to seem like saving lives is more like mopping the floor. Cooking a meal. You do it, and then the next day you have to do it again. You do it together or you do it alone. No one notices, for all you know. It's not a hero's business. It's really better if no one knows at all.

I do what I can, that's all. I do what I can for them. And there's nothing I'd rather be doing. Nothing at all.

# Historical Note
*by Heather Munn*

In Le Chambon-sur-Lignon, the real town Tanieux is based on, there was no Paquerette. Many young women like her, employed by different aid agencies, brought groups of children to Le Chambon at various times, but there was no single courier designated to go regularly between Le Chambon and the camps. In this novel, Paquerette represents the many heroic young women who rescued children.

There was also no l'Espoir in Le Chambon. Such homes existed elsewhere in France, however. They were run by aid agencies, and took in babies along with their mothers when aid workers managed to get them released together.

There were convalescent German soldiers billeted in Le Chambon, but none ever denounced anyone nore threatened to—even though some lived so close to children's homes full of Jewish children that it seems impossible that none of them knew.

The rest of the book's background—the camps, the aid agencies, the children's homes—is real.

The names of the children's homes and their personnel in the novel are fictional, but we did base the descriptions of life at les Chênes very closely on stories from the real children's homes in Le Chambon. Like les Chênes, many of these were sponsored and run by aid agencies from France, Switzerland, or the United States.

Most of the children who spent time there during the war left with
very fond memories; the workers seem to have done an amazing job
of creating an atmosphere where kids with terribly uncertain lives
could find a sense of warmth, belonging, and joy.

The Camp Joffre internment camp at Rivesaltes was and is a real
place; you can still visit its ruins today. The same is true of the Gurs
internment camp. These two were the largest of the many internment camps run by the Vichy government.

These two camps were originally used to house refugees from
the Spanish Civil War, before World War II began. After the fall of
France the new Vichy government began to treat them less as refugee
camps and more as prison camps, using them to detain people they
considered undesirable: Gypsies, illegal immigrants, and especially
foreign Jews—men, women, and children.

These were internment camps; they were not death camps and no
one was deliberately murdered there. But people died all the same.
The internees were people whose lives the Vichy government did
not value, and there were already supply shortages. So they slept in
unheated barracks, often with no blankets but what they brought
themselves, were fed pathetic rations, and got just enough water to
drink—not to stay clean. Disease was rampant, and people weakened
by malnutrition died easily, especially children and the elderly.

Our descriptions of conditions at Rivesaltes are drawn closely
from firsthand accounts, especially the journal of a young woman
working there for Swiss Aid, Friedel Reiter.

The rescuers we've described were real as well: young women—
mostly in their twenties—who worked for aid agencies. Some lived
and worked in the camps like Marylise; others, like Paquerette, fer-
ried newly released children to their new homes. Many of the children went to children's homes like the ones in Le Chambon; many
others were placed as boarders with families who were paid to take
them in—and who often did not even know they were Jewish.

If it seems surprising that aid workers were allowed into these
camps, and that children were released, it's important to remember
that this happened in 1941 and early 1942—the "softer" period of
the war, which we hear about less often, especially in the United

States. In France, the authorities were still trying to appear (and sometimes to be) humane; and in Germany, Hitler's "Final Solution" was only just taking shape—the Nazis did not begin their mass murder in the gas chambers until mid-1942. German occupation (in Western Europe at least) was less harsh than it later became, and so was Vichy. Paquerette's treatment at the hands of the police reflects the times. In 1943 or 1944 it could have been much, much worse.

The internees in the camps were the first for whom things got much worse. In mid-1942 Hitler began to demand that France deport a specific quota of Jews to the East each month. In response, Vichy emptied the camps, sending thousands of Jewish internees to Auschwitz and the other death camps, most of them never to return. From Vichy's point of view, they were a sacrifice; by filling the quotas with foreign Jews they hoped that French Jews (whose lives they valued more) would be spared. Their betrayal was useless; as the war went on and Hitler demanded more and more, Rivesaltes and the other camps became transit stations through which France's Jews, as well, passed on their way to the death camps.

In 1941, none of these young women knew that they were saving children from the Holocaust; they were simply saving them from malnutrition, filth, disease, and despair. As the times grew worse and the stakes grew higher, their work became more dangerous; they moved from the legal, if risky, work portrayed in this book to underground, plainly illegal activities, in which they were risking their lives. Underground networks were set up into which children could "disappear"—their identities changed without leaving a trail. Elaborate safety rules made aid workers anonymous from one other, to minimize the danger if one was arrested. For they were sometimes arrested, and sometimes tortured as well. Some, near the end of the war, were even killed.

These young women devoted their lives, in secrecy and weariness and terrible danger, to their one overwhelming passion: to save as many children as they could, by any means necessary. They quietly did what they had to do; they were not in the business of being heroes. Perhaps that is why they are.

**Heather Munn** was born in Northern Ireland of American parents and grew up in the south of France. She decided to be a writer at the age of five when her mother read Laura Ingalls Wilder's books aloud, but worried that she couldn't write about her childhood since she didn't remember it. When she was young, her favorite time of day was after supper when the family would gather and her father would read a chapter from a novel. Heather went to French school until her teens, and grew up hearing the story of Le Chambon-sur-Lignon, only an hour's drive away. She now lives in rural Illinois with her husband, Paul, where they offer free spiritual retreats to people coming out of homelessness and addiction. She enjoys wandering in the woods, gardening, writing, and splitting wood.

**Lydia Munn** was homeschooled for five years because there was no school where her family served as missionaries in the savannahs of northern Brazil. There was no public library either, but Lydia read every book she could get her hands on. This led naturally to her choice of an English major at Wheaton College. Her original plan to teach high school English gradually transitioned into a lifelong love of teaching the Bible to both adults and young people as a missionary in France. She and her husband, Jim, have two children: their son, Robin, and their daughter, Heather.